I0653104

ACCESS
UNLIMITED

ACCESS
UNLIMITED

BOOK 3 OF THE ACCESS SERIES

ALICE SEVERIN

OWN ROOM PUBLISHING
NEW YORK

ISBN: 978-0-9882520-2-8

To those who remember the future
And to J, who teaches me.

ACCESS
UNLIMITED

chapter one

London

Airplanes flying over the Atlantic at 36,000 feet are great places to reflect on life. Or you can hit the champagne, and try not to think too much about what was waiting a very long way down. I was meditating on the rock musician whose path had so memorably crossed mine, not once, but twice. Tristan Hunter. Tristan was famous for having started Devised, and guiding them to success, before a very public split with his wife and the band he had formed. Some said it had been brought on by his own love of excess, of extremes. Others claimed it was his trusting nature that led him to be swallowed up in the nest of vipers that defined the music business and L.A. in particular. Now he was starting over. A solo album doing well, getting some buzz. And he had reunited for the tour with his fellow Devised member and guitarist, AC Clark.

Then there was me. Lily Taylor. The diehard music fan who became a music journalist. The woman who once literally fell at Tristan's feet trying to get an interview. The one who had the opportunity to meet him again, five years later. An interview, another chance encounter—and now I found myself covering the tour.

One small catch—Tristan and I were also lovers. In love, maybe. Love. Whatever that meant for two slightly damaged, very wary people. He risked showing me his scars. I was willing to fight for him. Both of us definitely unwilling to be apart. And ironically, we were better together because I had been willing to walk away at one point. I didn't like being told what to do. And neither did Tristan.

Then there was Trevor Sears, the man who discovered Devised, who apparently approved of me as well. And seeing as he had been responsible for keeping Tristan alive, his opinion meant a great deal. Especially to Tristan. Trevor had been there during the darkest times of the breakdown, when the people Tristan had trusted most betrayed him, when his body was struggling with the ravages of the drugs he had turned to hoping for help. There was no doubt in my mind that Tristan wouldn't be here right now if not for Trevor.

Trevor was also one of the groundbreakers in the music industry. He had set up his independent label in London, and spent his time and money trying to find what real artists were still out there in the auto-tuned world of shock tactics and skimpy clothing the music business had become. He followed his passion, but played the game with finesse. His forbidding stare had unraveled a lot of plans constructed by people who thought they knew better.

At this moment, a week before the tour, Tristan was rehearsing with the band. So with his blessing, and that of my boss, Dave Fanning of *The Core* magazine, I'd flown out to confer with Trevor, and do a couple of last minute interviews with other individuals linked to Devised for a possible documentary. I mostly wanted to see Trevor, though. I knew he was going to be in the States soon enough, but with Tristan otherwise occupied, I wanted to take the opportunity to find out what I should really be focusing on. As opposed to what they were expecting me to write about. I figured he would know, if anyone would, where the minefields were located and how to avoid them, if I could. And Trevor was the coordinator on the European side, and was now in charge of sales, touring, and anything else that might come up. In the States, it all went through the subsidiary of the larger record company. But I knew that interesting ideas in Europe frequently were shot down altogether in the chase after the American dollar.

Unfortunately, the stateside execs were not always right, though they'd never admit it. A path of poorly chosen singles, publicity images, release dates, and television appearances could be found in their wake. Good at business, bad at art. It was a bit of an American problem. The execs in the States thought Trevor was a loose cannon, which he could be, but where Tristan's future was concerned, there was no one who would fight harder. If Trevor knew something was a good idea, he didn't listen to no. He simply found another way to get what he wanted.

This tendency worried the suits, who wanted the American leg of the tour to run very, very smoothly. Weighing up the odds, they did have a reason to be concerned, considering Tristan's lurid tabloid past of drugs, sex, and eventual nervous breakdown. Their risky investment was going to be under very public scrutiny. If any of these problems were going to surface, they wanted advance notice. A lot of advance notice.

They were bankrolling it all, of course. They could pull the plug at any moment, blame it on illness, or vocal problems, or any of the other excuses that were put out in the press to explain a variety of real reasons that were kept hidden. I was sure that was some of the logic behind letting me tag along on tour and write up articles and the regular blog. But according to Trevor, now they wanted a business rep for their interests inside his office. One of their own. In Trevor's domain. I wished I could have seen his face when they presented the idea to him.

He told me all about it when he took me out to dinner the evening I arrived. As he was recounting the story, I realized that his curt manner had been replaced by a somewhat distant but basically trusting stance. I'd obviously moved up in his estimation. It made me feel a little closer to Tristan too, like we were all on the same side. Trevor began describing what we were up against. Apparently, the record company had chosen who they wanted in the London office and had flown him out to meet Trevor. Trevor had agreed to the whole plan, but insisted on reserving the right to interview and approve the final candidate. On the surface, it was all very reasonable.

Trevor laughed when he described it to me. "Lily, they thought I'd just neatly stepped into line, cowed by their money, and lured in by temptation. Can you imagine, they offered me a job in L.A.? A job? Working for them, writing up reports, endless meetings? And in L.A.? One of those all by itself would be a deal breaker, but both? Imagine." He poured me another glass of Retsina. We were sitting at a small table in a private corner at one of my favorite restaurants in London, Lemonia. Tristan must have told him I liked it, and it thrilled me a little, not just to be there, but that both of them had conspired to do something to please me. I took a sip of wine and listened as Trevor continued with his story.

"I'm not one of those individuals who has always wanted to live in America. It has its fascinations, certainly. Like most places. But some of these company people seem to think all they have to do is dangle a big city on the coast in front of you, and you're hooked, like a starving fish in winter." He laughed, and stabbed one of the stuffed grape leaves with his fork. "Hook, line, and sinker. At any rate, their man is coming tomorrow to discuss his place in the organization, and his brilliant marketing ideas." He placed the entire morsel in his mouth and chewed slowly. Finally he spoke. "You should be there too. We don't have to reveal your identity. We'll make you a PR person over here. Wear a bright color, that's it. Lipstick. Smile incessantly. Might as well assist with the deception." He washed down his words with a sip of wine. "Retsina. It's pleasant. Will always remind me of holidays. Not a bad thing."

"I've always liked it. A strange taste. Something different." I smiled at him. "Reminds me of happier times as well."

Trevor raised an eyebrow. "Yes. Indeed. Well." He looked directly at me. "I think you'll find tomorrow useful. One never knows what Tristan is planning, but knowing what they expect should help you navigate the waters when he starts to push back." I started to speak, but Trevor raised a large hand to stop me, and I did. "I know he says he's a changed man, and he is. But I also know he has secrets and plans, and that he hates being given instructions. With AC there as well, this could turn into a regular rock and roll circus." He folded a piece of pita bread delicately, and dipped it into the taramasalata on his plate. "Eat. You need to eat." With his other hand, he held out the basket of pita breads to me. I caught his eye, and he smiled, his expression caught halfway between paternal and threatening.

I took a piece of bread, and dipped it into the tzatziki on my plate. "How much influence do I really have though? Suppose he starts using again? Or quits the tour? Or gets into trouble on the road?"

Trevor's expression was extraordinarily calm. "All reasonable possibilities, I'm afraid. But I'll be a phone call away, and then I'll be there. As backup. Honestly, Lily, and please take this as a compliment, you seem to be managing him very well."

"But I'm not doing anything," I blurted out.

"Then it seems to be working wonderfully through intuition. An excellent strategy."

"I don't plot and plan."

"Then you're the only one. But you don't need to, my dear. You're clever, you don't take his shit, and most importantly—you seem to actually care for the difficult bastard."

I blinked at him, a little shocked. "Tristan? A bastard? He's the last person I'd tag with that description. Difficult, yes. Even perhaps a little diva-esque, at times, but…"

Trevor interrupted me. "He can be fairly demanding, at times. You've noticed that, certainly. Luckily it's a short tour. Preliminaries. Everybody getting back in the saddle." He took another sip of wine. "Lily. That's just it. You'll defend him. God help you, you'll even disagree with me." He stopped to put a grape leaf and some calamari on my plate. "You've got considerable power, Lily. Especially where he is concerned. I'm grateful that you use it for good." He gestured with his fork at the array of small plates in front of us. "Now eat. You're going to hate yourself when you're at the truck stop looking at the microwave meat sandwiches. Then your saddest memory will be of all the nice dishes you didn't touch."

I laughed and raised my glass. "To touring."

Trevor clinked our glasses together. "To touring. You poor thing. You have no idea what you're in for. Now eat."

* * *

The next day, I arrived early at the townhouse where Trevor had his offices, and settled in with a cup of tea in one of the corner chairs in his large office. I had done my best to look like a PR person, statement necklace and handbag, flashes of bright color. Sarah, my oldest friend in London, had helped. I was staying with her, and she seemed grateful for the diversion. She was marrying my old boyfriend, now very much hers, later in the summer, and I had the impression even she was sick of the planning. It wasn't a huge wedding, but she was nothing if not precise. Her house was covered in fabric swatches and seating plans. She was very good at putting things together, including me. Despite our differences, I did love her dearly, even if she kept teasing me about whether Tristan was coming to the wedding or not. I didn't really want to admit I had no way of guaranteeing what the future would bring.

The prospect from the record company in the States had just been shown in. I was introduced quickly, and dismissed quickly, which was fine with me. It gave more time to study him. He was terribly shiny. Broad features. He looked like he should be selling oil wells, or machinery. The copy of his CV showed a suitable range of internships, the right college, high-ranked business school. But Trevor got him talking, and within minutes, he had managed to get him to reveal what was behind his resume. The real story was that his uncle was a well-known A and R guy from the 70s who had first gotten him interested in the business. Eased his way in, more like. But everyone had connections. He admired Justin Timberlake. And he seemed pleasant enough, sitting there, getting ready to impress Trevor. I wasn't keen on the double breasted suit. And I had the impression that somebody stateside had told him this was a done deal, which made me feel almost sorry for him. Underestimating Trevor was never a good plan. I had another sip of tea, and pulled out my notebook. Time to decipher the meaning from the words and watch the show. Trevor was already in full flow.

"I would say that we have passed postmodern. Now we are in to what I like to think of as post-honest." Trevor hesitated. "Clearly, we expect honesty from our icons. That's why we follow them slavishly on Twitter, take their battles as our own, and insist that they share each and every portion of their lives with us. We say we want the truth. But that's not it. We want the simulacrum of truth. We want it to look real, and as Camus demonstrated so ably, reality, and the appearance of such, are two totally different things." He paused in the midst of his explanation to drink some tea, and studied the person in front of him, as though he were really considering hiring him.

"I disagree," said the young man, whose name was Steven, and who clearly didn't realize his time was ticking away.

"When a musician tweets something, it shows a piece of his day to day concerns. He shows that this is his life. His soul. That translates into a better connection with the broader-based fan demographic. The key is to find the toleration level, and keep the energy high. Dropping moments of day-to-day life is the best way to do that. Impromptu pictures, quotes, favorite foods."

"Jesus Christ," Trevor interrupted. "Impromptu? When you and I both know you set it up in advance to drop the message at a certain time? Favorite foods? Likes and dislikes? It sounds like a teenage girl's diary. I do recognize that this is supposedly the age of complete narcissism, so the fan base likes to see itself replicated on a grand scale. But...," here he paused to drink more tea, and look over with longing at his box of cigars, "there has to be some consideration of authenticity. Something that sets the artist apart from everyone else."

The young man nodded vigorously, apparently in complete agreement. "I just read a fantastic article on authenticity." He thought for a moment, then said, "Not Camus, but Sartre. It's a perfect example of how our actions must be in line with the image. But image is a starting point. What we are trying to do is not only get the conversation rolling, but make the moments that inspire that conversation. For a fan, watching a video, or knowing a celebrity or musician actually said something, means that they have something to bring to the water cooler."

"Using Sartre to sell? Isn't that a little like using a chain saw to clean out a wound?" He finally opened the lid of the box. Trevor was clearly trying not to smoke, but he was finding it difficult to stop himself from at least rolling one of the Cubans between his fingers. He was feeling the weight of it, the calm and pleasure it would bring. He dropped it back in and shut the box abruptly. I jumped at the sound.

Trevor began again, slowly. "Look, Steven, this is all extremely interesting. Certainly on point. But tell me what your suggestions would mean if we were to promote someone say, like…" Trevor looked out the window, appearing almost distracted, then turned back suddenly, his eyes fixed on his target. "Tristan Hunter? You're familiar with him, of course?" Steven nodded again. "Good. What would you do?"

Steven had the appearance of someone who was about to tuck into a good meal. "Great. Just great. I love a challenge. Some people really dislike him. Fantastic. And he doesn't have a good solid media presence. After all that bad press. Weren't there rumors going around that he was heavily into kinky sex, S and M?"

Trevor looked at him, his gaze level and steady. "We are trying to sell music here, not sex toys."

"But that's just it. His demographic has limited itself to older fans of the first band, and people who are drawn to the rumors. Very limited. If you want the younger teenage demographic, he's going to have to tone down the image somewhat. A lot."

"And what would you suggest?" Trevor asked blandly.

"It wouldn't be too hard. First, clean up the public image. Get some 'candids' of him exercising," here Steven made the air-quote gesture, as if to underline the obvious staging of these scenes, "running, shopping, walking the dog. Normal things. Getting a coffee. Then mix that up with some close-ups from the studio. Playing instruments. Looking intent on the music. Clothes—always important. Nothing too fashionable. Everyday. A little less black and tight. And maybe some pics of him out at restaurants, going to juice bars, meeting other celebrity musicians. Does he have a new girlfriend? We can find a companion for him. Shared interest in getting publicity. I can put in a call to a friend. Always some new actresses happy for the exchange. Controllable situation. Establishing him as…"

Trevor interrupted. "As a nonthreatening mainstream brand."

"Well, yes, to a certain extent. That healthy lifestyle is very appealing now. No one wants to see people falling out of clubs, under the influence. Even smoking. Very Lindsay Lohan. Gives the impression of failure. If he's embracing the moment, then we can reposition him as a star for today." Steven looked thoughtful for a moment. "Hey now, didn't he have a big gay following? Would he be willing to do some charity work? Outreach? That would draw in a lot of people. Explain his outsider status. We could go the other way with clothes at awards shows, that kind of thing. Cleaning up elegantly for events. And we can get quotes from people saying how good he looks—fashion-icon kind of thing. Some best-dressed lists. Suits. Designers. Might be interesting to see if he could model for someone. Keep that demographic interested. Probably would work better in Europe."

I reminded myself to move the tea cup to my mouth from where it had frozen in midair at his words.

Trevor's mouth was a tight line. "I'm sure he would be willing to help with any charity, as he has in the past, but I doubt he would want it publicized or tied into the album."

Steven seemed surprised. "He has? But he hasn't publicized

it? That's a waste. Even a small name drop makes a big difference. Usually spike in donations too. Win-win on both sides." He smiled broadly. "Symbiotic."

"Can I just make a point here? You do know he isn't a pop star?"

"He wasn't a pop star. Before. Now, it's a zero sum game. And pop is where the money is. So if he wants to position himself, he is going to need to do it that way. Look at Coldplay. Alternative to mainstream. Though Chris Martin's arms, crazy, am I right? Someone's been to the gym." He laughed. "Incorporating the hip-hop and rap style. Electronics. Who saw that coming? But he's following the trends."

"And the money," Trevor responded drily. "Though Chris is a very nice boy, really. Talented. And yes, a lot more savvy than people give him credit for."

Steven was momentarily thrown, but he regrouped quickly. "Can we get Hunter to go to some more parties? Charity events? Photos with established names. No one is crazy about the *Daily Mail* or *Just Jared*, but they do get the hits." Steven had a thoughtful expression. "A duet. What does he think of Katy Perry?"

Trevor was silent. "I'm not certain that he ever has. Let me just ask you. Do you actually know anything about him? As an artist?"

"To a certain extent, but I don't always think that's the best way to go into a client situation. I like to see the problem fresh. As a marketing challenge. New ideas first, then we see what we keep from what went before."

"What happened to actual reality? Authenticity." Trevor laid a hand on the cigar box. "Charting a course by what he wants to be."

"Limited by the outdated image. He is a brand, and the word is that the brand needs a reboot, ASAP. Have you thought of some giveaways? Meet the band? VIP tickets are very popular, although he wouldn't be playing venues big enough to make it worthwhile. Maybe if this takes off. Autographed merch?"

"Yes, we have." Trevor had made his mind up, and opened the box, taking out one of the cigars and rolling it between his fingers. His nostrils were slightly flared. He glanced over in my direction, his face expressionless. I knew that didn't come without effort. He turned back to Steven. "And for the merchandising?" The flame shot up as he finished his words. Small puffs of smoke emerged, and Trevor leaned back, taking the cigar out of his mouth, and contemplating it. He waved it at Steven, before returning to producing another few small smoke clouds. With his attention focused on the cigar, he no longer appeared quite as formidable.

Steven looked alarmed, but managed to stop himself just in time from fanning a hand in front of his face to keep away the smoke. He crossed his leg over his knee, and pulled up a neatly creased trouser leg, just short enough to show a slice of his colorful, expensive socks. "I did go to a TTT concert a few years ago, and they had no product. It was such a wasted merchandising opportunity. There were people waiting to buy. They finally came out with some t-shirts, but for such a big concert, it was lackluster. Everyone had those shirts already. They were expecting commemorative items to celebrate that concert. We can't miss out on those opportunities."

"Interesting," said Trevor. "But basic."

Steven carried on. "So I think it's a clear sell. Attract the female pop listening audience, who have the most reach on social media. Tumblr blogs, got to love them. Get the fans to share the transformation. A new haircut, color, mentions of clothes, tweet after the morning run, that sort of thing. Link to fashion blog. Make him harmless. Picture of him walking with a tray—two juices—easier to spot in the photograph. Holding just one in your hand hides it. Could be anything. Juicing is so popular now. A story on his new morning rituals." He stopped for a minute. "I wonder if we could get him on *Ellen*."

"And Tristan's exercise regime will sell records? Fill seats at concerts?"

"If it's energetic, yes, it's great. These are the present day concerns. Body image for women. Youth and strength for men. It's projection and identification. Something that shows he looks after himself. We better not mention age though, what is he, 35? 37? Let's not remind them. Thank god for Photoshop. Comeback can be a dangerous word."

Trevor removed the cigar from his mouth and examined it closely. It appeared as though his greatest concern was whether to relight it. Then he placed it carefully in the ashtray, and stood up. His sudden movement startled me, and he shot me a look, before walking to the window, staring out at the street, and turning back to face Steven. "So, let's recap to make certain I am understanding you correctly. In order to 'reboot the brand,' as you put it, my client needs to share the aspirational fashion and beauty concerns of a new generation of fans, to make them feel that he is one of them. He does this while presumably creating music that he and his listeners have a stake in. Or, would you suggest that the songs reflect these preoccupations of the demographic you have so neatly descrambled?"

"In fact, that's a brilliant idea, Trevor." I winced. "Brilliant. He could write a couple of love songs? Folk-influenced sound is so in these days. Maybe a cover? If he could find a female artist to duet with, that would be ideal. Has he ever thought of doing a dance record? Nod to the 70s, to disco. This way he could show he's still in touch. With that kind of willingness to really experiment, I could salvage his career."

Trevor smiled. "Excellent. Just what we need." He walked over, and extended his hand. "I'm sure you could. Fascinating summing up. Where are you staying again? Make sure Alina has all the details. We'll be in touch." His smile was more of a grimace than friendly, but Steven was shaking his hand, while handing him a small flash drive with the record company name etched into it. "This is a slideshow of some of the people I've worked with. Just to keep you in the loop. I'll let the office know what we've decided."

Trevor pocketed the drive. "Thank you, but I'll call them when and if we make any decision. You know the way out, of course." Steven was staring at him. Then he went over to where he had been sitting and began rearranging files in his bag. I had the impression he thought there was more coming. I knew there wasn't. Trevor sat back down, and began the process of relighting the cigar, finally blowing out a large cloud of smoke. When he saw that Steven was still there, organizing his bag, his voice was crisp. "Have you lost something? Let me have Alina help you." He buzzed down and gave an order.

The man zipped up his computer bag. "I think you're making a mistake. The money you are wasting while you wait. Those lost sales, sales that may not come back. What you want to do..."

Trevor spoke over him. "Ah, Alina, excellent. Mr. Hill was just leaving. Could you escort him out? Thank you so much." He nodded to both of them, then turned his chair so that all they could see was the back of the leather seat, and the very top of his head. Another puff of smoke rose, as they finally left and started making their way down the stairs.

"Fucking hell," Trevor said to himself. "Authenticity. Sartre. Camus. Poor bastards." He turned back towards me. "Cigar, Lily? I've just had a shipment of the smaller ones."

I found my voice. "Thank you Trevor. I think I could use one. Very kind." He inspected my unpracticed attempts to light it, and once I'd managed to fire it up, he turned back to the window. We sat there, smoking, watching the twilight sky darken over the London streets.

The smoke was calming my nerves. A strange little encounter. One which left me with a lot of questions, not the smallest of which was why the record company had sent over someone with that point of view. Someone with almost no knowledge of Tristan's output or career, aside from the lurid details. Maybe it was to remind us that there were a lot of people out there for whom Tristan was a footnote in rock history from a few years ago, and times had moved on. Or could. Or did. Without their support.

I shivered. It was a brutal business, no joke.

* * *

The phone beeped. I tried to ignore it, but I found myself squinting through half-closed eyes at the dark room. What the hell time was it? It felt middle of the night late, too far away from the night to be part of it, not yet feeling the distant change of light and wind that would mean dawn. It beeped again. Two were harder to dismiss. I flung out an arm from the sheets and knocked the phone to the floor. Fuck. Eyes shut, I moved over and did a tired sweep of the floor next to the bed. There it was. I grabbed it, and rolled over on my back. I blearily looked at the bright white of the numbers. 3:37. Who was texting me? I pressed the little green square with the 2 in the corner, like an angry exponent.

The message window opened and I froze. *Watch me,* said the first text.

Then I tapped at the picture to make it fill the whole screen, and it still wasn't big enough. Tristan. Taking a selfie. I wondered for a minute if the phone was wet, as wet as he was. He was leaning against the tiles in the shower, the water splashing on to his torso, which was sleek and shining, rivulets flowing down the muscled core of his body, to land and hover in the neatly trimmed tight curls that partially hid his balls from view. Nothing else was hidden though, and the blood-flushed tip was coated lightly with water, and something else, something that showed his excitement in posing like this. Pressing send. Knowing the effect it would have. On anyone.

The phone beeped again, and the next picture scrolled into view, his hand firmly grasped around the hard flesh. His eyes were less amused now, dark circles, slightly unfocused. A minute passed. The phone beeped. This time the photo was blurred, his eyes closed tight, his hand another blur within the photo, movement. I felt my face grow warm, the familiar sinking heat spreading down. He was a statue, the muscles taut and flexed in his shoulders and arms, the dip of the lines by his hips a rigid indent. Another minute, a beep and the new photo appeared. His eyes were wide open now, and his lips were wet and full, slightly open, as though he had been taken by surprise. His hand was still tight around himself, pulling out the last tremors of furious pleasure. The evidence was captured as it struck him, adding to the sticky wet sheen that covered his heated skin.

I shut my eyes for a moment. It was almost too much. Then the phone beeped again. It was a text this time.

Your turn.

chapter two

New York

The tour bus was both smaller and larger than I had expected. Parked on a rancid street of warehouses near the entrance to the Lincoln Tunnel, the remnants of cobblestones stuck out from the badly smoothed-on patches of tar. The warehouses that lined the street looked deserted and desolate, the multi-paned windows gazing down blankly on the empty street. It hardly seemed believable that a place could be this empty, only a few hours after the rush hour blitz heading west through the tunnels, past the boundary of the Hudson River, separating the city from the rest of the country. Like in that old *New York* magazine poster, New York City seemed as big as the rest of the country, with only the Hudson, that narrow strip of water in between it and all the rest. And even that had been shrunk down, another obstacle to get across until you reached California. Everything outside of the concrete and steel of the city seemed slightly unreal. But we were about to head out, and see just how real it all was. Adventure. The thrill of starting a trip at night, heading into the unknown.

Tristan and I got out of the car, and the driver turned off the engine. He quickly came around to open the trunk, and pull out my suitcase. Tristan's gear was already on the bus. He had a messenger bag with him, slung over his shoulder. He shook his head when the driver went to take it from him, and he left my suitcase by my side. Tristan nodded. We stood there. There was something strange about it, after everything that had happened, to be on this dirty street as a starting point, looking at our rolling home for the immediate future. And we were sleeping on the bus tonight, then waking up in Montreal, where the tour would begin for real.

I watched as Tristan shook his driver's hand. "Keep in touch with Trevor. Let me know the situation." I frowned at the pair of them, but when Tristan turned back to me, his face was calm.

"Trouble?" I asked.

"Nothing. Just keeping an eye on things. Cat's away," he waved a hand though the air. "That kind of thing." He fixed me with a stare. "Not to write about, in any way, Lily. Not even as a metaphor. Understood?"

I nodded, again filled with a strange kind of fear before this man who did indeed control his entire empire—yet never spoke of it, never mentioned the hours of work that went into all of it. Again it struck me that no one really did get anywhere without the secret effort, control, energy that had to be hidden, precious and guarded. "Understood," was all I said. No time for explanations.

We walked up to the bus, and he knocked on the door. He stepped back as it swung open, and we could hear music and the sounds of people talking. Tristan shook hands with this driver as well, and I gave a wave as we walked into the living room of the bus. It was like an extended motor home, a trailer, a gypsy caravan with a flat screen, a rolling picnic basket filled with beer and wine. The windows were large, but tinted, and the world was sucked away as the door hissed shut. Despite the size, it was a little claustrophobic. I took a deep breath. I'd get used to it. I had to. The sofa was already filled with the three people in the band. There was Jack, the bassist, who I'd met and spoken to in London. He raised a hand in greeting, as Tristan said hello, and introduced me. "You all remember Lily, right?" At the end, legs extended and covered in worn jeans, the skin visible through the slits in the thigh, one stretched over the end of the sofa on top of the built in table, the other ending in a laced up black boot firmly planted on the floor, was the drummer, Pete. His head was leaning against Jack's shoulder. And there, at the edge, was AC. He extracted himself from under Jack, causing him to fall over and knock over the drummer. They all laughed.

AC launched himself at Tristan and wrapped him in a big hug. Tristan squeezed him back, and ruffled his hair. I stood there, and AC looked up at me, a question in his eyes. I wasn't sure what he meant. Tristan clearly was relieved to have him there. That much was obvious. I waved at AC, smiling. He flashed a big grin back and opened his arm, leaving space for me to join in. He nodded his head up and down, a small gesture of encouragement, and as I stepped in to the hug, Tristan moved and squeezed us altogether. It felt quiet suddenly, then Tristan kissed the top of AC's head, then the top of mine, and moved away. "Structure and harmony," was all he said, as he stepped back, opening up our trio, my arm still around Tristan, AC's arm still around him on the other side, and stood like that, watching Jack and Pete who had started fake punching each other. They stopped when they saw us watching.

"Yo! Tristan!" Pete called out. "Fucking come sit down and have a beer. Grab me one too while you're at it." Tristan laughed, and went over to him and gave him a big hug as well. "Get your own you lazy fuck," he said, smiling, and I watched as AC pulled out a six pack of Heineken from the cooler, and open them one by one and hand them around.

"Dude, you're here. Excellent! Let the show begin," said Jack. Tristan began to speak and he interrupted him. "Yeah, I remember Lily from London. Lily from London!" He reached out and clinked beer bottles with me. "Nice to see you. Maybe you'll be a stabilizing force on this bunch. It can't just be me all the time." The drummer and AC snorted with laughter. "Shut up you two. I'm extremely stable."

"Yeah, and we won't tell Lily you were just watching porn with us," Pete murmured, then shouted, "Whoops! What have I said?" And they all started laughing again.

"You two are assholes." AC looked at me. "Night one on tour Lily. Where anticipation still fuels the party."

"Instead of being tired," Jack said.

"Or wasted," added the drummer.

"Or bored."

"Or sick."

"Yo, shut up you lot. It's a bus, not a resort. And the last time I checked, you all liked depositing the checks from life in music. I'm sure the call center misses you fuckers. 'How can I service you today?'" Pete punched Tristan on the arm.

Tristan laughed, and drank some of his beer. "Keeping them in check. Thankless task."

"I've got to see what they're up to. Otherwise I won't be able to feel their pain," AC smirked.

Jack thrust his hips up. "Come over and feel my pain. Check out how deep it goes."

AC shook his head. "Oh man. Just like the old days." He leaned down and whispered to me. "It's not their first tour, but they're always like this. Don't let it get to you."

I laughed. "Not yet, anyway."

Tristan glanced around. "How many weeks of the circus?" He gestured to us. "Come see what passes for paradise on the bus."

Pete pretended to whisper. "Oh good, they're leaving. Turn the porn back on."

Jack said, "Where'd you put the remote, you fucker?" Then his voice went lower. "Can't we just listen in? It'll be live."

I wondered if Tristan had heard. I wondered if they cared.

We started walking towards the back of the bus, but Pete called Tristan and AC back. I turned around to see the driver going out. I guessed he was doing a final check around the bus. It must be time to go, I thought. Driving through the night. The Tour. Really beginning. I was examining the bunks, when I heard the bus start up and a loud cheer came from the front. I could feel my heartbeat in my throat. As a kid, I had always dreamed of being rootless, driving around the country. Different day, different town. And now we were about to do it.

Tristan and AC came back—apparently the guys had wanted to apologize for being a little rowdy—and we made it to the end of the skinny corridor, past the bunks with their curtains, looking a little like an old fashioned train. The modern mirror and glass effect, trimmed with little fairy lights, distracted the mind away from the reality that it really wasn't a huge living space. Tristan turned the handle of the door to the back of the bus, and we entered a room that had a queen size bed, a flat screen TV, and a lot of mirrors. I took a deep breath. No wonder people looked forward to the hotel part. This was like camping, with glitter. I looked down at my small suitcase, wishing I had brought a backpack and a Swiss Army knife.

AC seemed happier though. "Hey man, this is pretty nice. Did you request that they kit it out like this?" He stretched out on the bed, his arms behind his head, taking up space like a dog being allowed on the couch.

Tristan sat down on the bed, and shoved AC and his legs over. "Yeah, I did make some requests. Experience tells." He laughed. "Remember that tour up the California coast? When we stopped at that winery?"

AC winced. "I remember some of it."

Tristan looked at me. "We had a big concert—well, not that big. In a vineyard. Complete with hotel. Really nice place. People go up for the outdoors, the tastings. It usually turns into a kind of party. Always a few extra rooms available in case people thought they'd really be spitting it out, and planned to leave afterwards." Tristan laughed, and looked over at AC, a slight indulgent smile tracing across his face. "Some of the ticket holders had big rooms as part of the package plan. They were good people, really. And a couple of the nice ladies had invited AC here back to their room. They got some of the staff to carry him back to the bus when he finally passed out. 4 a.m. I hear this banging on the door. They won't go away. I finally open the door to the bus, and there are these two guys, in hotel uniform, with AC trussed up between them. They carried him in the room—it was a bit like this one—and dumped him there. He lay there like the dead for 12 hours. But we woke him up in time for the next show—still hungover as shit." He looked over at AC. "What were those ladies' names again?"

AC looked sheepish. "Fuck knows, man. They exhausted me, what can I say?"

Tristan smiled. "I hope they named their first borns after you." He laughed. "After all, they'd all be related."

"Hey, I'm careful. Any accidents weren't mine, man." AC winked at him. "Don't worry Lily. Shouldn't be any mothers chasing us in Montreal." He rolled over on his side, and looked up at Tristan. "So here we are, again. Are you glad to have me? I've missed it. Missed you."

Tristan looked over at me, his eyes still and wary.

AC laughed. "She's cool. We had a long chat in London." Tristan frowned.

I finally spoke up. "True enough. We did talk for quite a while. Not sure what we said though."

They both watched me for a moment. I didn't say anything else. Tristan sighed and came to stand by my side. Then I felt Tristan's warm lips on my cheek.

"That's what is so perfect about you Lils. You notice everything and say nothing. Well, except what you're going to write for the magazine."

I kissed him back, gently. I looked Tristan in the eye, then walked over and gave AC a kiss on the cheek. Tristan let out a deep breath. I didn't think he realized it. "Yeah, well, again, like I said before. What you want out there. With extra sparkly fan girl sprinkles." I looked around. "Bathroom?"

"Outside. No, kidding. One door is a closet, the other is a

bathroom. Water only, doll. Unless you're desperate." Tristan grimaced. "Not to be crass, but…"

"No, that's cool. I've been camping. This is just like a mirrored tent." I went out shutting the door gently behind me, but just in time to hear AC saying, "You trust her, Tristan? Are you sure?"

Then Tristan's voice, warning, "She never even told me you two talked. So she kept your secrets. She's kept mine. Now she'll have to keep ours."

I moved away from the door. Whatever their secrets were, I had a feeling that after a couple of weeks in this gilded tin can, I'd know them all.

chapter three

New York to Montreal

The bus had stopped for a break at the truck stop before the border, so we wouldn't have to all wake up in the middle of the night for the passport check. As it was, 5 a.m. seemed painfully early. But the Canadian border patrol apparently liked to put a face with the ID, especially for a rock band in a tour bus. The local promoter in Montreal had faxed them the paperwork. No emails for this. The officer in charge of our passage had already accused us of being incompetent, and Tristan had called James, who had woken up the promoter, who had given us the details. They had all the paperwork for the permits, it had been confirmed by an A. Antoine. That name was enough to get the guy to go back inside to hunt down the passenger manifest. So we all stood there in the early light of the morning, outside the bus, while the guards walked around the bus with a tired looking German Shepherd, who sniffed hopefully, while the one of them examined our passports, looking for errors. A third one, without dogs or passports, had asked for Tristan's autograph.

After he'd moved away, Tristan whispered in my ear. "Do you think it's a technique? Or just poor social skills?" He laughed. The guards glared at us. I gave Tristan a sudden passionate kiss. Let them think we were giggling over sex. Better than thinking we were taking the piss.

The driver looked bored. He'd mentioned briefly last night before we left that if anyone was carrying he'd leave them at the border, so anything better get used up. I saw Jack poke around his shower kit, and triumphantly pull out what looked like a Xanax, and swallow it down with a gulp of beer. Apart from him, I wasn't sure if anyone else had been listening. His pronouncement seemed too serious for the start of tour party atmosphere, but standing here, in the cold grey light, my sneakered feet very small against the freshly poured black tar parking lot, surrounded by broad men in uniform, holstered and booted, I realized what he was talking about.

Finally, the papers were found, and luckily the spelling matched our passports. Tristan had an American and a British passport, due to his American mother and British father, but all the paperwork was for the American one. The permits were granted. It seemed a lot to go through for what was going to be only two nights in Canada, but I'd been through enough crossings to know this wasn't the time to start questioning the politics of it all. Especially the border patrol, who were there to do a job, rely on the easy power a uniform and a gun gave them, then go home. Not there to question the system. I'm sure they missed the days of waving through Americans on a driver's license and a smile. It had probably always been tougher for musicians though, those irregular leather-clad creatures making a mockery of everything decent. I jogged in place to keep alert.

I felt like I could drift off. But the surreal sensation of feeling like we were under arrest even though we had done nothing wrong was unpleasant enough to keep me awake.

After a check which involved another series of questions on the merchandise we had brought to sell, and an examination and count of the t-shirts and posters and CDs, with a tax form to fill out if they were sold, and one more mirror check under the chassis, we were free to go. Canada. As with so many land borders, the landscape had changed. We had left the mountainous forests leading down to the lake, to a long flat plain. The horizon was blocked from a clear view with round European-style road signs and long stretches of farmland. The bright colors of the houses and the billboards in French and English felt weirdly foreign, as though we'd left New York City on another planet somewhere, rather than mere hours away down a highway. Then the land began to fill in, more houses closer together, more signs, the highway widening. The first bridge over the river seemed longer than usual, held up in the middle by an island that held the remnants of a distant world fair. The highway curved around, and we were there—following the river, past the Molson Beer Factory, the uneven skyline of small modern buildings scattered among the older factories and houses.

Finally we turned off, and there were traffic lights. Streets. Apartment buildings. Shops. One café raising its metal bars over the windows. It looked quiet. Too early for much activity on a Sunday, except for a few people who could be going home, or going to work. I was the only one on the bus who was up. The driver expertly pulled into a large parking lot, and stopped. The lack of motion and background sounds echoed in my ears, and I felt a little dizzy. I stood up and suddenly the bus seemed very small, even for someone my height. I sat down again, breathing.

The bus driver climbed out and stretched quickly, then patted his pocket for his wallet. He nodded to me. "What's your name again?" I told him. "Lily, that's right. Look, Lily, I'm going out to pick up a coffee, something to eat. Can you stay with the bus please? I'll be 20 minutes, maximum. I appreciate it. Thank you." And he was already opening the door.

I was just quick enough to follow him down the stairs, a Canadian five dollar bill in my hand. "Sure, fine. You're Hank, right? Nice to meet you." I extended my hand. He shook it, quickly. "Listen, can you leave the door open? I won't go anywhere. Bit claustrophobic. And would you bring me back a coffee? Milk sugar? I'd really appreciate it. Cheers." He took the money, shrugging, and turned towards the exit. I watched him walk away, and turn past the metal chain link fence, and disappear down the strip of beige sidewalk that bordered the lot.

I stood there, looking at the collection of cars and buses, then back down at my feet on the dusty ground. I kicked a pebble. The milky sky meant it was full daylight but it was like a ceiling over the city. There was a bright spot that was the sun trying to break through, but mostly the no-color sky matched the concrete buildings. The bus stood out—silver and black, an energetic stripe of metal that promised a lot. Sound check was at 3 p.m. I looked up at the sky again. The color of very milky coffee. I shut my eyes, and leaned back against the bus to wait for mine.

chapter four

Montreal and West

The first night went well. One cock-up when the bassist started playing the wrong song, having skipped one ahead. Tristan had turned around and made a small motion with his hand, and Jack turned towards the drum kit, and played a couple of gliding notes to put himself back in the right key, the right bar. It was reasonably skillful, but Tristan's expression was one of frustration. When static started to come out of the keyboard monitor, his howl in the lyric felt like it was coming straight out of his blood. One of the roadies rushed out and replaced the cord, and the other half of the bass sound suddenly burst out into the mix. AC quickly threw in a howling whine of bent notes and arpeggiated chords. The explosive energy with which he attacked the strings brought the first smile to Tristan's face all night.

I was there to watch. Take notes. Be there. I looked at the crowd. Plastic cups of beer in hand, swaying along to one of the new songs, a few mouthing the words. The usual throng of the obsessed down the front—a few devoted fans, a few good looking girls who felt justified by their looks to try and catch the eye of the band members. Fuck, you only live once, why not, I thought. Even so, it wasn't a pretty sight. I wondered if they knew the words. Not like the guy over by Tristan, who had the look of the recently blessed, a sort of holy passion and peace on his face. He was fun to watch. When Tristan and AC stood back to back and Tristan slid down halfway, supporting AC, one large hand twisted around and pressed against AC's slim waist, one hand in a death grip on the microphone, his thighs taut with the effort, the effect was electric. I glanced over to the guy. He was frozen to the spot, his mouth slightly open. I was close enough to see that a vein in his neck was slightly pulsing. It was like watching an animal come alive, leaving everything that held him back behind. At the end of the concert, when Tristan bent down to slap the hands of the fans, I watched as he reached out. Tristan's expression changed in a moment, from the rock star performing a necessary part to that of a priest performing a rite that would link the clamoring soul to the divine. His face grew serious, and Tristan reached out and grabbed his hands, delivering a small kiss to the blessed fan's forehead, seemingly unaware of the maze of hands that were reaching out to touch his thighs, his arms, any part of him that they could reach. AC was at his back, smiling down at them, ignoring the pleas of the fans. Then it was all over, and Tristan and AC walked off, waving to the crowd. The guy watched them go off, then pushed through the crowd, as though now he was in a hurry to get away from them, to be alone with his thoughts. And I wondered about the power on both sides of this moment. This connection that would never be repeated for him, but might be only the first of many for Tristan.

After we returned to the bus, we sat for a while in the bedroom, while Tristan and AC worked out some guitar parts and revised the set list. I lay back on the bed, and closed my eyes and listened to them play and hum out parts and make notes to share with the rest of the band. It was soothing, listening to their voices talking, then suddenly bursting out in bits of song, then singing it differently. It was a lullaby, the calm focus of work. The bedroom was starting to feel less like a container, and more like a change from everything, a chance to get away from the world, while strangely going further into it, tires rumbling underneath us, miles passing by us. I dozed off, and Tristan woke me up, asking if I wanted some of the catering that had been provided for the first night. AC had disappeared. He brought me a sandwich and a bottle of water, and kissed me.

"You'll stay here tonight, right?" I nodded, sleepily. "I'm going to go hang out with the band. You'll be ok?" Tristan frowned at me.

I stretched. "Yeah, I'm tired actually. Is that ok? You probably want some time with them anyway, but I wouldn't mind just staying in here."

He gave me a big hug, and found the necklace he had given me under my shirt. Lifting it up, he kissed it. "No worries, sweet Lily. Get some rest. It only gets crazier from here on."

I held his hand to my lips, and kissed his fingers. "Yeah." Tristan pulled me to him, and held me close, his lips leaving soft kisses in my hair, murmuring what he would do if he wasn't working. I held him close, and breathed in his scent, slightly strange, the traces of a hundred fan caresses on his skin, flavored with the soap from the dressing room.

He kissed me again, and went out the door, but turned as he closed it. "Don't worry Lily. You'll see." I smiled as I watched him leave.

The sudden silence except for the rumble of the tires on the road was slightly unnerving. I raised my fingers to my lips, trying to recapture the feeling of his touch. Gone so soon, and wanting it again, more and more as it faded. I lay back on the bed, and looked at the little recessed lights. Thinking about it wouldn't help. Quickly changing out of my clothes, I threw on a t-shirt and leggings, and cleaned my face with the toner from my makeup bag. I felt more comfortable wearing something, even though I didn't usually. I didn't want to go wandering about the bus half-naked in the dark. I crawled under the covers, which smelled of fresh laundry soap, and even though they were scratchy, they were perfectly flat and clean. I rolled over and stuck my headphones on. "Keep on Truckin'" by Eddie Kendricks, his first hit after leaving the Temptations. Perfect. I looked suspiciously at the chicken wrap Tristan had brought. I had to eat. I left it on the table. Maybe later. Or not. I took a few bites and I wrote a bit, and finally fell asleep listening to music.

Around two, according to my phone, Tristan came in and undressed down to his briefs. I watched him sleepily shake out his jeans and lay them on the chair, stripping off his shirt, his leather bracelets dark against his white skin. The tattoo at the top of his ass had turned out to be a tiny figure rolling up the world. It was there, peeking out over his pants, a little joke, glowing in the half light of the fairy lights around the room. When I had asked him why he had chosen that for a tattoo, he laughed. "Have you ever played that game? I played it in Japan when we were touring there. So trippy, so bizarre, and so wonderful. A little like the place. Rolling up increasingly bigger pieces of the earth. It's like a summing up, a metaphor of expanding your mind. Perfect." I patted the tattoo when he got in to bed, and he pulled me up close to him. "I like this," he said, "you keeping the bed warm for me." He kissed me and we settled in together. It felt good. The big scary rock star who wanted a hug. Not so scary anymore. I had a feeling we were both happy about that.

* * *

The rumbling of the bus finally broke through and I crept to the bathroom. I couldn't tell exactly what time it was, but it was early. Or late. That time. I really hoped I wasn't waking anyone up, but there was no way to avoid it. The only privacy that the beds had was a heavy curtain, and they were fairly thick, a sort of cross between canvas and velvet, like a thin theatre curtain. Good, but not perfect. I could hear one of them snoring. I wondered who was where and where AC had landed in the bunk positioning. I had the feeling that he wasn't entirely used to sleeping with the band—unless it was his band.

I opened the little door as quietly as I could, and clicked it shut behind me. Looking around, the bathroom was pretty incredible really, considering we were only on a kitted-out bus. There was more recessed lighting, and a sink that was like a grey granite bowl, resting atop a darker colored granite counter. The shower had a neat pattern of grey and speckled tiles, a hand-held shower attachment, and a glass sliding door. The toilet was black. There were mirrors everywhere. It was all very modern, and clean, and if you ignored the absence of windows anywhere, it was pretty sweet. I washed my hands and brushed my teeth with the bottled water. I wasn't sure if the water was potable, but I figured I wouldn't take a chance. I wondered how quietly I could make a coffee in the front kitchen. There was a constant sort of background rumble from the road anyway. Maybe it would drown things out. I went back to the bedroom to grab my stuff.

Tristan was fast asleep, stretched out on the bed diagonally. His skin was so beautiful against the pillows, the sweeping curve of his shoulder muscle sinking down to his arms. He had been working out—in preparation for the tour. The results were still pretty subtle, but the carved out effect of his muscles was more pronounced. I followed the line of his body, half under half out of the covers. There was the strange little Japanese tattoo above the slight rise of his ass, the other tattoo, a line from one of his favorite songs, stretching out over his ribs on his right side, under his arm, so it was generally invisible unless you got to see him without a shirt, which didn't happen often to the rest of the world. His private message to himself. I admired the view for a moment, then blew him a kiss. I threw on a pair of jeans, and headed out to the front of the bus.

The kitchen was as glossy as the rest of the setup. The stove looked brand new. I opened a cupboard and there was a collection of gleaming white hotel room cups and plates. I sighed. Suddenly being domestic in any way lost its appeal, and I grabbed a bottle of iced tea from the refrigerator instead. The steady snores of the band, and a vague smell of socks and sweat was already beginning to fill the close air in the bus. I sat down, and looked out the big front windows of the bus. There were still bits of fog hovering in the low-lying bushes and patches of forest they had left alone when they blasted through the highway. There were a few cars and vans, but it was still a calm introduction to the morning. There were the lines of trucks heading west, catching the jump on the traffic, sleep not as much of an incentive compared to an early breakfast and the chance to make up some hours before the main part of the day. I felt I should say something to the driver, but it seemed rude to interrupt his intent stare down the yellow lines leading through to the other coast, to the other side of the world. It wasn't so hard to imagine them peeling right down through the sand, into the water, and into the strange half-light under the sea, not so different from the thin early morning haze the two of us were driving through, with our precious cargo of men sleeping childlike behind us.

I was about to say something, even hello, just to break what was beginning to seem like a weird silence when we both knew we were there, when his gruff prison warden voice broke through my thoughts. "Lady on a bus, like a lady on a ship. You're a Jonah, aren't you?"

I laughed. "A Jonah. It's been a while since I heard that expression. Can't imagine you meet too many people who know it, but maybe you do. Do you?"

"Not a lot of women on the bus. That stay." He fell silent.

"I'm not leaving though. Think you'll be ok with that?" I thought I saw him grimace. "By the way, thanks for the coffee the other day. I appreciate it. It's got to be weird, right, this constant change. But you must get pretty close to the bands you drive, right?" He said nothing. I drank some of my tea, and found some music to listen to while I wrote up yesterday's notes. I couldn't stop thinking about that fan, that kiss Tristan left on his forehead.

I looked over at the bus driver. Friend or foe? Or nothing. Hard to say. I thought I'd push it a little just to see. "You know, I knew someone once, a woman, a lady, if you like. She was a boat captain. People said the same thing to her. But she stayed afloat. Maybe she didn't have enough of what you would call feminine to make it count. But maybe I don't either. Am I making you nervous?"

"Women don't usually come on the bus." His voice was flat, almost robotic.

"So, the nice bathrooms are just for the girl in us all?" I laughed. "Really, dude. Don't worry."

He stared at the road. "Some people like to be lied to."

I shrugged. "Most people, maybe. So, you like driving?"

He grunted, non-committal. And I went back to looking at the road.

After about 20 minutes of us sitting there, me lost in my thoughts, watching the day rise, he spoke. I jumped, slightly surprised. "We'll be at the venue in about two hours. You might want to give your boyfriend the warning. Not sure if the manager is here. He's going to have to take care of the check-in too from now on. Wasn't sure if he didn't come in last night."

"Oh, ok. Thanks." I wanted to ask him more, like how many times had he done this, and who hired him for this run, and did he know the band at all, and did he care, but he had already pulled himself in. There was time. At least he was talking.

I walked back through the bunks, and a hand reached out to grab me. I nearly screamed, but managed to choke it down on a gulp. A face peered around the curtain. "Jesus, AC, you scared me," I whispered. "What's up?"

"So, Toronto in about two hours?" AC said. He looked drawn. I wondered if he'd slept at all.

"The driver said so." I replied. "You want a coffee or something? You look wiped." I felt protective of him. That image I had of him, sitting in the hotel room, ordering another bottle of Barolo, that night I'd fled the tour in London, and he'd tried to hit on me, came to mind. There was a sad look in his green eyes, now bleary and swollen with sleep or lack of.

"They always say that. They mean two hours, sometimes three. Staying positive. Keeping us sweet. No, Lily, thanks, but I think I'll wait until we're on solid ground." He paused for a minute. "Say hi to Tristan for me."

"Yes, ok. You can come in and tell him yourself, if you want." A flash of interest lit up his face, but only for a moment.

"No, that's ok. I imagine he'll want to wake up with you, first." He winked and gave me a wan smile, then pulled back the curtain with a flourish.

I looked at the spot where his face had been and kept heading to the back of the bus. I opened the door. Tristan was still asleep, and I crawled onto the bed, carefully, staying over the covers, placing my head on the pillow next to his where I could see him. His dark eyelashes, delicately shaped mouth, the slight darkness around his jaw from not shaving. The vulnerability of sleep. And he allowed me in.

That trust, that incredible trust, so fragile, unmentionable. Something you couldn't say to anyone, ever, not out loud. A silent understanding. If you had to ask, something was wrong. To me, anyway. I watched his chest rise and fall for a while, the steadiness soothing. For a moment it was though I was guarding him. Unconsciously I looked towards the door leading to the front of the bus, the rest of the band, the world. A sudden fierce protectiveness made me want to hold him tightly, tell him it was all going to be ok. Instead, I lay down gently beside him, closed my eyes and tried to sleep. I had a feeling these quiet moments were going to be rare.

chapter five

Heading West and Toronto

The next thing I knew, I was being gently kissed by Tristan. "Lily? Are you awake?"

I nodded sleepily. Then I sat up with a start. "Wait, what time is it? The driver said we'd be there in two hours. How long have I been asleep?"

Tristan laughed. "So responsible." But he picked up his phone. "Only 9. You were up early then. When did he tell you?" Now he was sitting up well, a crease between his eyes.

I tried to pull my thoughts into line. "Around 8, I guess. So we've got another hour."

Tristan rolled his eyes. "At least. They always give you shorter times. I think they think it keeps morale up. I think it has the same effect as setting your clock for the wrong time. You just start subtracting." He lay back down. "So how are you this morning? Getting used to the bus?"

I shrugged, and lay down next to him. "I talked to the driver a bit. Not very talkative."

"They're a strange bunch. All different. All a bit mad. I

suppose you've have to be, to agree to drive a bunch of lunatics through the night for weeks on end."

I curled up next to him, feeling the warmth from his body heating my skin. I closed my eyes. This was nice.

Tristan moved closer to me. I could feel his whole body now against mine. He was very awake now. He took my hand. "I imagined this," he said. "I imagined us together, just the two of us, like this." He laughed. "Isn't that stupid? But I could see us, holding hands, lying on the bed, on the tour bus." He rolled over and carefully draped a long leg over mine. "Maybe not just holding hands, though." He rocked against me, slowly.

I looked at the little door leading to the rest of the bus, out to where the bunks were. I frowned at him. "The rest of them, can they hear us? You've done this before?"

Tristan ignored my question, and instead kissed me, his soft lips tracing the line of my cheekbone. Then he looked up at me, teasingly, from under his long eyelashes. "Why, are you shy? They know what we're going to do." He ran his finger slowly up my bare arm. "I'll be very quiet, if you will." He caught my hand and brought it up to his mouth, covering it, his eyes flashing with amusement.

It went beyond understanding how Tristan made each moment feel like this, like we were starting over, right from the first desperate need to be touched. I closed my eyes. It felt good, so good to feel the weight of his body on me. His hands were warm and strong, and soon I forgot about the people on the other side of the door, the bus, the tour, and everything except the feeling of his fingers exploring my skin. I gasped when he finally entered me, easing in.

"Shh, love." And he smiled, then pulled my hips up and

hard against his. I bit my lip. He thrust in again, then again, pushing further inside, raising me until he held me entirely in his arms. I turned and buried my face in the pillow as I gave up my body to him, trying to muffle my cries. He pulled me tighter to him and then it was too much, and I couldn't tell who was moaning. "Lily," he whispered, "now love, now."

* * *

Judging from the slightly stunned look on AC's face when we finally emerged, I didn't think we'd been very successful at being quiet.

chapter six

Toronto

Coming in on the bus, Toronto looked a little disappointing. Another industrial waterfront, ruined by a big freeway, with patches of greenery that looked like they had been thrown at random. A few plants and trees to distract the eye while the city planners figured out how to reclaim what first had been ruined, and then left to rot. As we followed the lake, and drew closer, the effect of driving under the big highway overhead was claustrophobic, like a video game where you're trapped in a big machine, a big virtual universe of lines. The one where you're driving a car and you've got to jump across to another highway, while floating in space, before the one on top of you and the one you're on come to an abrupt end, like some trick of drawing out the horizon to a point on a piece of graph paper. Wasteland seemed to be a theme of the trip so far. Leaving or coming in to a city or town, as on a train line with only one good track among the rusted spurs and shunts, we were following the line of industrial growth become overgrowth. The tangled mess of neglect and dropped ideas, newly cut through with a six lane highway.

I'd heard such good things about Toronto. Initially, I'd been sorry we weren't spending more time here. Now I was glad we were leaving again tonight. I supposed this was wanderlust—the feeling of freedom, of not belonging anywhere. It wasn't a bad description of how I'd lived my whole life anyway. Maybe I'd turn out to be one of those people who just couldn't stop touring. A top that couldn't stop spinning, on the road again. For now, the reward of six hours of driving was slowing down to the sound of the indicator, ticking out our plans to the cars and trucks we were leaving behind out on the highway. I watched through the window as the bus maneuvered down the street and into the big lot behind the Kool Haus, tonight's venue. It was breathtakingly ugly. Grey. Blue. Plastic and concrete. And amazingly enough, there was a little tangle of fans waiting. They looked very excited. One girl was jumping up and down, holding a vinyl copy of the new album aloft, looking a bit like one of those people that guide in the planes to the gates, if one of them had lost their mind mid-shift. I wondered how long they'd been waiting.

It was the no sort of time, end of morning, beginning of afternoon. I guessed it was around 12:30. The plan was to hang out here all day, do the sound check and the gig, then head out again. The outside beckoned, even if it was nothing more than watery sun reflecting on the faded lines in the parking lot, but I didn't want to deal with the fans. I felt for them, but. Soon enough. Everyone was still asleep, or pretending to be. Tristan and AC were talking on the phone to James. The driver had already gone off. At least he'd asked me if I wanted anything, but I shook my head. I did, but I didn't think a burnt coffee and a road sandwich was going to do it for me right now. On the other hand, it would be nice to get out, clean up a bit. It depended on how bad were the showers in the dressing rooms. I sniffed my clothes. I smelled like Tristan. I couldn't help the smile that instantly spread across my face. After all, touring was like camping. Perfectly clean was for home.

I was making some notes, and listening to the moody intricacies of Recoil, trying to get the blog written. Nothing seemed to link together. I finally threw my notebook aside and stretched my arms out. I really needed some fresh air. I glanced over at the bunks. They couldn't all sleep forever, could they? But they had crashed later than I did. A few more yoga stretches confirmed that I couldn't stand being cooped up any longer. I went to the fridge and grabbed a beer, and opened the door to the bus, breathing in the air of a new city. Fortunately, the driver had shown me how to close the door and open it up again from the outside. So I went down the steps, latching the door carefully behind me. The last thing we needed was to have some excited fan pushing on to the bus. I tried to walk away before I was spotted, but the fans were on the alert, watching for any signs of life. Two of them ran up to me.

"Hi, excuse me, is this Tristan Hunter's tour bus?" At least they were polite, but to be fair, most of his fans did seem fairly respectful so far.

It felt oddly embarrassing to be his representative. I couldn't lie though. "Yes, they'll be out in a while for the soundcheck. If you can wait around, they'll probably do some autographs." That sounded good.

They squealed out a thank you, and ran back to the group. You could see the news spread as different people reacted. It was really kind of cute. I walked away from the bus, not going too far so I could keep an eye on it and its precious cargo. I was the guard, making sure no one bothered them. I looked at my phone. Nearly 1. They'd all be up pretty soon. I walked around in circles, making patterns on the ground, drinking my beer. Hanging out in parking lots by the freeway. Let no one say that touring isn't glamorous, I thought. I drank some more beer. Day three of touring, and I was already a little restless. "Idiot," I said out loud. The trucks going by weren't interested.

I was attempting a labyrinth pattern, in an effort to create some calm, when I felt my phone vibrate. I managed, though I nearly dropped the beer, to get it just before it stopped ringing. I didn't even look at the caller ID. "Hello?"

"Lily, Dave here." His voice was instantly recognizable. I didn't need the introduction.

"Hello Dave, how are you? I knew it was you the minute I heard your voice." I laughed.

"Is that so? Well, I'll take that as a compliment." Dave paused, "I want to catch up and hear about life for you on tour. Right now I have news. Good news. Is Tristan around?"

"He's in the bus. I can go get him."

Dave chuckled. "Up until dawn and coming alive in the afternoon. That's ok. Just have him call me. Where are you?"

He wasn't leaving me hanging like that. "Walking around. I'll get him to call but wait a minute. News?"

Dave hesitated. "It's going to be everywhere in a second anyway. Go ahead, you tell him, but still have him call me. It's the album. It's been nominated for Best Alternative Album at the MUT awards. Shall I read the press release to you? 'Showing us all that the second act might be better than the first, Tristan Hunter, former lead singer with Devised, is nominated for his solo album, *Some of Us Remember the Future.*'"

I let out a shriek. The little group of fans all looked over in my direction. I waved my beer at them.

I could hear Dave smiling. "Thought you'd be happy. Of course, more work for you. We'll most likely do a focus on him and, of course, the tour, next week. Ton meilleur effort, s'il te plait." *Your best effort, please.*

"Comme toujours, chef." *Like always, boss.*

"Good to see you remember your French. Wouldn't want the tour bus lifestyle to lower your standards." Dave was teasing, but there was a serious note to his voice. It was a simple sentence. On the surface.

"Absolutely not. Of course it is early days yet. I'm sure I can still manage to fall out of a limo half-dressed."

Dave cleared his throat. "Yes."

I had no idea why I'd said that. I chalked it up to the edgy feeling I had standing by a bus next to a highway. "I'll check in with you later or tomorrow on the blog. I'm going to tell the band."

Dave's voice, was low, almost kind. "Tell Tristan first. Before the others. Trust me on this."

"T'a raison. Comme d'habitude." *You're right. As usual.*

"Bien sûr. Ok. Chow." And the phone went dead. *Of course.*

It was funny to think of him looking out for me, sitting at the head of his empire, while I went to talk to a half-naked rock star, ruling his world from a mobile bed.

* * *

It was a little crazier tonight, which I put down to the announcement about the nomination. Outside the venue, there were people hoping to be able to pick up tickets, along with some enterprising people selling bootleg Devised and Tristan Hunter t-shirts. I didn't see James doing anything about it. Peter Grant, he was not.

And Tristan was brilliant on stage. He swooped down towards the crowd, luring them in, taunting them with distance, before coming close enough to touch, falling to his knees, clinging on to the microphone like a lifeline. Every word wrenched from his throat, twisting through the vowels, the veins in his neck standing out from the effort. AC matched him, knowing just when to lower the volume and retreat slightly, leaving a space that Tristan filled, effortlessly, the notes punching through the darkness. The drummer, Pete, was really very good. He watched them, stuck with the rhythm, following Tristan's cues, happy to be the solid base for what they did. The dynamic range was good. Some drummers bash away at the kit, no matter what's going on around them. Not Pete. The bassist wasn't as strong, but he didn't distract either. It was a nice set up and it sounded damn good. And when Tristan and AC stood back to back, leaning on each other, Tristan's dark hair flowing over AC's shoulder, the piercing shrieks and collective groan of the crowd summed it all up. Whatever the two of them had, and however it worked, together they touched a different nerve, and the response was immediate and blood-at-the-surface desperate. Looking out at the crowd, they all had a similar expression—a kind of wonder, an openness that was intimate and deeply personal—and repeated on almost every face.

Gauging the power and intensity of tonight's audience, I had a feeling the craziness was going to ramp up. What if he won? There would be no stopping him.

It was a slightly unnerving thought.

chapter seven

Toronto to Detroit

I woke up, disorientated from my dream, with a song from Heaven 17 running through my head. I looked over at Tristan. His chest was rising and falling gently, his dark hair a mess on the pillow. The duvet covered part of his hip, but had slid off slightly, leaving the hollow of his stomach and what lay beneath in darkness. I sat there, in the dim light, watching him. His beauty, so casual and careless in sleep, was extraordinary. I wanted to trace the lines of his face, kiss his full mouth, soothe away the dark circles under his eyes that were the only sign now of the stress he was under. But most of all, I wanted him to sleep. I knew he'd start to be aware of me sitting there soon enough. I crept out of bed slowly, and tried to cover him without waking him up. He shifted slightly, and sleepily pulled up the duvet. When his breathing returned to a steady rise and fall, I threw on my jeans and tiptoed out to go sit at the front of the bus.

The driver gave me his usual dismissive glance when I quietly said good morning to him. I stuck in my headphones, and started playing the song that had been running through my head when I woke up, "Crushed by the Wheels of Industry," keeping it low enough that I could still hear the steady thrum and rhythm of the tires of the bus going over the metal seams in the highway. It was just before 5. It was still dark, and there was a slow yellow pink glow in the distance which wasn't the sunrise, but today's destination. We were driving straight to Detroit from Toronto—Cleveland came next. Everything was strange—already. And it was only the beginning. We all had piled in the bus and the band had finally gone to sleep. Tristan and I had retired to the back bedroom, his face pale with exhaustion. We went to sleep, but something had woken me up and I found I couldn't sleep. And after trying for an hour, I'd given up. Now I was up here looking at the lights on the road.

Here we were, the tour bus, running through what was left of the night, us and the trucks, and the highway, straight here, Highway 401—the Macdonald–Cartier Freeway—which, if the guidebook I'd bought was to be believed, was the busiest highway in North America, with over half a million vehicles a day. And I'd never heard of it before. This road, which for some people was their livelihood, their daily routine, was a giant 10-lane slice separating the interior from the lakes, the last vestiges of the industrial dream. It was so flat and wide here. And the only lights seemed to be the high yellow lights adorning the cabs of some of the trucks, the regular service stations, filled with neat geometric lines of tractor trailers, parked at an angle, towering over the cars that were parked in front, the bright lights of the service forecourt serving as a neon invitation to leave the endless ribbon of highway, a plastic and bright civilization beckoning, a refuge from the sense that you could keep driving, forever. An endless giant road, glimpses of factories and houses, turning on their lights for another morning.

I was shocked out of these thoughts by the growly voice of the driver. He really was something out of central casting, his cowboy hat carefully placed in his locker behind the seat, a big silver bracelet on one wrist, an even bigger watch on the other, his huge scarred hands settled on the wheel comfortably. It was hard to imagine him even driving a car—his hands took over half the wheel. But he seemed to own what he was doing. He'd made it very clear this was his bus. His life. We were being tolerated. Barely. So to hear him asking a question seemed as unreal as the distant lights on the plain we were bumpily gliding through, at 70 miles per hour, maybe a little faster.

"Why can't you sleep?"

I didn't think he would want the long answer to that one. Truthfully, I wasn't sure, and I wasn't sure what he was asking for. "Always an early riser, I guess. Once I wake up, I can't really get back to sleep."

"That'll work when you've got a house of kids to make pancakes for. Kids never sleep either." He said it calmly, as he switched lanes to go around a line of trucks and cars that were slowing for the exit.

I thought about it for a minute. It was what he knew. That's what people did. Sometimes things just were what they were. "No kids planned just yet. Not sure they'd like the touring life." I wondered if he'd answer a question. "Did your mom make pancakes?"

He honked at a truck that was drifting into our lane. "No,

my dad did. She was always working. Her pancakes were better though."

Without thinking, I said, "What were wrong with his?"

"Too thin. He was always in a rush. Said they cooked faster that way. Made more. I think he just had a heavy hand with the milk."

I laughed. "It's funny how breakfast means more than just food. Always linked to something."

He was quiet for a moment, focused on the road. "So, what did you eat for breakfast? When you were a kid, I mean. Not this crap you inhale in between drinks."

I looked out the window. One of the lanes seemed to be a steady stream of trucks, one grey rectangle after another, like toys. "I don't know. A lot of different things I guess. It depended on how things were going." I was quiet again. But he seemed to be waiting for more of an answer. "I guess I always think of it in phases. There was the cinnamon toast phase. There was a poached egg phase, but my mother hated doing it, so that didn't last long. Weekends were bacon. Slightly burnt." I laughed. "They used to take away my food if they didn't think it was cooked enough when we went out to breakfast, but that was on holiday. I used to try and hide the bacon or sausage under the pancakes. It's still a guilty pleasure. Diner food. I can never decide if I'm risking death, or being a rebel."

He sat there, silently, for a few minutes, but he didn't seem thrown by what I'd said. "Bacon's good. You really need a griddle with a flattener—a press. I used to do short order cooking when I got out of the army."

"Where were you stationed?"

"Missouri. They trained me in communications. Then Vietnam. Signed up right out of high school. They got me at the end. I was just a kid. Jesus. I was there at the Fall of Saigon."

I started to speak.

"No, don't ask. You've seen the pictures. It was worse. No room for compassion, they said." He paused to switch lanes again. "I like driving. It's like short order cooking. No time for thinking."

He turned off the signal. "I've got a few pins in my leg. They hurt when it rains. That's nothing, when you've seen people holding their arm, pleading with you for help. The look on someone's face when that's happened…" He trailed off.

"Could you get anyone out?" It was all I could think of to ask. It sounded wrong the minute I said it.

"No." He coughed. "No. Hard to forget." He fell silent again.

I wanted to ask more questions, but everything I thought of seemed invasive or superficial. "Impossible." He didn't reply.

So I looked out the window, both of us watching the road. Finally I pulled out my notebook, and started to work. I making notes, and keeping Heaven 17 on repeat. It just seemed to fit. "(We Don't Need This) Fascist Groove Thang" came up, the song that got them banned from Radio One and insured enough publicity came their way to keep going. It had a cold feeling, the sweet vocals with hints of the New Romantics, over what was at the time, state of the art electronica. In some ways, I thought, with fewer bells and whistles at their finger-tips, it actually had more of the hollow spaciousness that made electronic music. That emptiness. I was writing all this down, and thinking about the lead-on band for tonight's show, and if they'd be any good, when the driver called out.

"There she is. Detroit."

I looked up. It was light enough now to see the distant sky-line. There were skyscrapers, an up and down line, like the heartbeat on an oscilloscope, the lines an etch-a-sketch of vertical and horizontal. I was surprised—I'd always thought that Detroit would be like Baltimore—endless streets of half-boarded houses and warehouses. It looked almost thriving. I made a note to myself to never believe anything I read, and sat watching it approach, almost as if we were descending off some highway in the sky, the exits coming closer together now, houses becoming buildings and strip malls and streets. We were still in Canada. I laughed as we went through Tilbury—industrial names imported from England along with the people. We were heading for an exit that led to the Detroit–Windsor Tunnel. It all looked very normal. I don't know why I was expecting a post-apocalyptic wasteland.

The voice of the driver cut through my observations of the approach road. "Here, I'm glad you're up. The manager—what's his name? James? Handed me their passport details and the manifest. Can you make sure they haven't left anything too obvious around? And stay up here when it gets handed over? Thanks. Otherwise we have to stop first. And we've got to wake them all up."

"I'll do it." I nodded to him. Now I was the tour manager. Shit. I looked at my phone, and checked what number speed dial Dave was on. Then I went to the back. How to do this. Loudly, I supposed. I tapped on the door to the bedroom, and went in. Tristan was twisted in the sheets, a fallen god.

I kissed his shoulder. "Darling. We've got to get up. Border. They'll want us all up."

He was alert in a second. "Where's James?"

"Left the papers with the driver. I said I'd help."

"Fuck." He stood up, shockingly tall and naked. He put his arms over his head, and stretched, then reached out for his jeans. "Better wake them all up. Tell them to take what they have." He choked out a hollow laugh. "Not kidding. Tell the driver we need to stop first."

"We're already here."

"Oh fuck. Ok then. Showtime. Go. Go."

I went up to each bunk and shook the curtain. "Wake up, get up. Border. If you have anything with you, you'd better swallow it all or flush it." There was a collective groan. "Look motherfuckers, just do it! Get the fuck up. Thank you. Help me out with this." I had an idea. "Bottle of vodka for the first one dressed. Cases of beer for 2nd and 3rd place. Bottle of champagne if you tell me what you had to get rid of. Let's do this! They have guns!"

AC stuck his head out. "This prize is so mine." He winked at me. "But I sleep naked. Want to watch me get dressed?"

"Love to, but I seem to be in charge of not getting us arrested." I smiled. "Besides, I forgot my glasses. Need them for the small print."

He smirked. "Bitch. Go on. Save us."

I went back up to the front of the bus. I noticed that the road leading up to the Border Control and the tunnel was named "Freedom Way." As I flipped through the packet of materials to be handed over, it all seemed a bit Orwellian. The information we had to hand over looked complete, at least as far as I could tell. And it gave useful details like where we were staying, times for the soundcheck, contact details. It occurred to me that I should always have a copy of all this. Perhaps the boys were happy being carted around, half-conscious, propped up on the stage and coming awake and alive when they needed to, but I wanted to know where the hell we were going. I wondered if Tristan had all this information. I had a feeling that nothing had been chosen without his tacit approval, if nothing else. I'd already seen him flare up at James in Toronto, asking him what he was actually doing for the money he was extracting from the tour, and it was not a pretty sight. It probably explained why James wasn't here. I thought back to what Dave had once said—"He's a hard-ass, your musical hero." Yes, he was. And fairly unafraid of storming into the midst of trouble. The thought made me worry for him. I just hoped we could get through all this quickly and get some rest, and that James had not fucked up the paperwork in any way. Or tonight's gig and hotel.

The bus stopped, and the driver opened the door. The border police for America, in their uniforms with the Homeland Security logo emblazoned prominently, and the double hand guns stationed at each hip made it feel more like we were entering a military camp. I swallowed. Police made me feel guilty, and big men with big guns made me feel anxious. I took the packet, and went over to the man waiting. I tried to be friendly. "Good morning."

"Papers, manifest, passports please. Can you have all the passengers on the bus disembark for identification please?"

"Sure. I'll get them." I handed him the packet. "This should be everything." I tried to smile. He turned away, and went into the portacabin that was the office. Another policeman, soldier, guard came over and stood by the bus. What the hell were they anyhow? Maybe he thought we'd do a runner like in some Grand Theft Auto game. My stomach lurched. I didn't even like passport control at airports, and they weren't armed. I hopped back into the bus. "Guys. Please. Come. Act normal." The drummer was in his underwear. "Fucking get dressed please. Thank you." And I stood there, feeling a bit like the headmistress at some school for delinquents. Tristan emerged from the bedroom, looking better than he had a right to.

"You heard the lady. Let's do this." And he came up to me, and put his arm around me. "Come on, Lily. I've done this before. Don't worry."

"They look incredibly pissed off."

"We probably should have come through Port Huron. Never mind, too late now." He turned around. "If any of you have anything illegal you better swallow it now, I don't care how much of it there is. Or put it down the drain of the shower. Don't flush anything, they'll be in here searching in a heartbeat. And don't tuck it under your pillow, for fuck's sake."

We went down the stairs, the bus driver behind us, then AC. The bassist and the drummer followed after another minute. "I'm going to kill them," Tristan murmured. "Slowly." We all finally stood there, in a line. I felt like I was waiting for detention.

The border control officer finally came out, carrying the packet of materials. I could tell even at this distance that everything had been put back in a completely different order. He held the passports in his hand. He walked up to us, and followed the line. I felt like he was inspecting the new recruits and found us lacking, very lacking. He stopped in front of the bus driver, and studied his features for a moment, then looked through the passports. "Hank…"

"Yes sir."

He glanced at the rest of us. "Well it's a job, isn't it. Do you have your operator's license?"

He pulled out his wallet, and handed his license over. The border officer compared it to the passport, then handed them back. "Thank you. You're free to go."

He looked at the next passport in his hand. "Pete Harley?" The drummer raised his hand. So I wasn't the only one who felt like we were in school. He went over to him. "American citizen. How long were you in Canada for?"

"Three days." He didn't add sir.

He grunted, and flipped through the passport. "Travel a lot, do you?"

"When I can. Mostly for work. Like this."

He held out the passport and Pete took it. The next passport name that was called out was Jack Wilson. The guard looked at the picture, and held it out to him. He took it. No questions. I wondered why.

I was next. He looked at me. "British resident? Why are you here?"

I resisted the impulse to say I was born here, that's why the passport was American. "I was born here. Sir. Working and living here now."

"Why is this number on the permit written in differently on this page?" Again, I resisted the answers that came to mind—a cross between I don't fucking know, and obviously some official was illiterate.

"I'm not sure, sir. Perhaps they read it wrong. See, the numbers are the same, just those last two are switched."

He stared at me. Then he looked at every page in my passport, a look on his face as if he were adding up years and visits. I stood there and waited. I tried to look calm.

Finally he handed it back to me. "Thank you. You're free to go." Then he turned to Tristan. "Tristan Hunter. This is your tour? You're responsible for these people?"

Tristan looked directly at him. He had a couple of inches on the border officer, and I felt like he was using it. "This is my band. But they are responsible for themselves."

The officer nodded to another man who was waiting a short distance away. "Then you won't mind if we board the bus and have a look around."

Tristan looked bored. "Of course not."

The officer looked at his passport again, then back at him. "You don't sound American." He flipped through some more pages. "Why is that?"

"I was raised in the UK, by my father, who was British." Tristan looked very uncomfortable. I knew he hated talking about his past, his family, anything personal.

The officer looked like he'd hit paydirt. "Why do you have an American passport then?"

Tristan's jaw was clenched. I could see the muscles taut under his cheekbone. I hoped I was the only one. "My mother. American."

"And where is she now?"

Tristan snapped. "Is this necessary?"

"Are you refusing to answer my questions?"

Tristan took a deep breath, and looked over at AC for a

moment. "She's dead. So I suppose her ashes are part of the world. Couldn't tell you exactly where." His eyes narrowed, and he looked up at the sky for a moment.

The border guard came out of the bus. "Looks all clear."

The officer looked at the other passport in his hand. "AC Clark?"

AC nodded.

He went through the same ritual of looking at every page. The officer who had just searched the bus was regarding Tristan and AC quizzically. He finally said something. "Hey, weren't you two in Devised?"

Tristan and AC exchanged a brief look. "That's right," Tristan replied.

"Oh man, I used to love you guys. And now you're solo? Can I get an autograph?"

Tristan gave a thin-lipped smile. "Certainly. Would you like one of the new CDs? Or is that against the rules?"

The other officer looked up, then handed back their passports. He held up the packet and I raised my hand, like a good student. He gave it to me. "Technically, yes."

"I'll get some paper for the autograph," I said. "If that's allowed."

He nodded. "You're free to go. Get the bus moving."

I ran back inside, and grabbed a piece of paper, and a CD. I came out holding them and a pen, and Tristan and AC signed, and handed it over. The other guard had returned to the office hut. I let the CD slip to the ground in front of the man. "I think you dropped something, sir," I said.

He bent down and picked it up. "Butterfingers." He slipped it inside his shirt, and winked at me.

Tristan gave him a little wave, and herded AC and me on to the bus, his hand strong against my back. The driver closed the door, and we were moving, then waiting to pull back into the traffic, then gaining speed on the highway.

chapter eight

Detroit

We finally filtered off the bus, staggering a bit, and getting our land legs back in the warm grey sunshine of the Midwest. There, in front of us, was the peach and beige chain hotel common to the outskirts of the industrial parts of cities that always looked the same, the same mini strips of metal gates interrupting concrete balconies, the long windows that pushed out, the metal blocks of soda machines thrown at varying intervals, the cheap room service. But it didn't move, and for the bunk people it didn't have curtains, so they could have a wank and cry to their girlfriends back home if they hadn't been lucky at cards or at pulling one of the fans who waited prayerfully in the back parking lots of all these places. I'd seen it before, but I'd never been one of the dawn patrols limping off the tour bus into the lobby with a bag full of laundry and an eye on the breakfast buffet.

Now I was following close behind Tristan, who, true to form, had ignored the suggestion of the band that he try and call James, who was supposed to be the manager—even if it was tricky to catch him doing his job—who should have been there already, setting up. Tristan wanted in, and he wanted now.

He stood at the desk, while the receptionist finished her call, smiling and raising one manicured hand up to tell him to wait. She hung up, and was about to speak, when the phone rang again, and she held up her hand, and answered the phone with the stock hotel smile and chirpy good morning. Tristan reacted. I didn't think I'd never seen him move so fast.

"No," he said, leaning over and pressing the button that had been lit up with the call so that it went out again. "We've been here waiting, and we're your next customer."

Her cheeks went even redder under the blush. "You're very rude," she spluttered. "You have no right to touch anything behind the counter, no right at all." She picked up the phone again. "I'll call the manager."

Tristan's eyes glittered. "You do that, sweetheart. Then tell him you've just lost his company steady bookings for weeks, all across the country, and your face isn't going to be on the cover of *Corporate Hotel Monthly*." He stood back. "But go ahead. It's a free country."

She had the phone in her hand again, and was pushing buttons, while Tristan asked her if it wasn't taking longer to call the manager than it would have to check him in, when a man in a suit, his tie twisted around, came out from the breakfast room. "Mr. Hunter," he shouted across the 10 feet now separating them, "Mr. Hunter, welcome to Detroit."

The receptionist looked at him. He was looking at us. Jack and Pete were sitting on the ground with their backs against a potted plant, discussing breakfast. AC was rolling a cigarette, juggling a tobacco pouch and his phone. We all looked a bit used. In truth, maybe not the group you wanted your regular guests, who were handling sales for XYZ Company, to find on the way to their coffee and eggs. The manager forced a smile, then carried on in his stentorian tones. "Lucinda here was just finding your reservation." I watched him glare at her, as she gulped, and began to assemble keys and cards.

The revolving door spat out James, who took in the scene and came up to Tristan first. "Traffic," he mouthed, then swung around to shake hands with the manager.

"Mr. Lorimer, is it? We spoke on the phone. Thank you. I'll take over." He looked over at Lucinda. "Thank you, dear." She turned away, huffily, completely unimpressed with his attempt to charm.

Tristan walked over to the wall near the elevators. I followed, grimly. Finally James came over and handed one of the keys to Tristan. He took it, and without a word, pulled me by the hand into one of the elevators, looked at the key, pressed the button for the 10th floor, the top, and punched the door closed button. "Assholes. All of them."

"She didn't know who you were."

"I don't give a fuck. I've spent years doing this. It's always the same. They either suck up so much you want to smack some sense into them, or they take one look at the band and the clothes, and decide you're going to hell, and their cardboard rooms with fake flowers shouldn't really hold such sinners." He slumped down on the floor. "Shit. I'd forgotten how much I hate the day to day."

I started to say "James...,"

Tristan cut me off. "He's a fucking jackass as well. I would have sacked him if I had the time, and he knows it." He stood up, and gave me a half-smile. "Life on the road." He picked up my hand and kissed it. The tinny bell announcing we had arrived made us both look at the door as it opened. He took my hand and led me down the red carpeted hall. "I'm a diva, darling. Life on the road brings it out in me." He laughed. "There will be a couple of good moments too. Bound to be. Come on sweetheart, I need to sleep some more." He swatted my ass, and gave me that predatory look. "Then we can work on stress reduction." I laughed. "You think I'm kidding." His voice dropped an octave. "There's only a few things that work...and you're really good at every one we've tried so far."

He opened the door. There was a view of the flat endless suburbs of the Midwest, a wide-screen TV, a king size bed with chocolates, and a bottle of something resembling champagne in a bucket on the table. "Nice. Come on, Lily, a shower, a glass of whatever swill they've given us, and bed." He ran his hands through his hair. "Day whatever day it is stress. I wonder where the fuck AC is."

I went over to him and put my arms around him, and listened to his heartbeat, fast, erratic, against my chest. "It's ok. I understand."

He looked at me, quizzically. "Do you? Maybe you do. Well, nothing like a couple of weeks in a bus to really get to know someone." He whispered in my ear. "Think you're up for it?"

I laughed. "Going to find out."

"Yes, we are. First, soap and hot water. Dirt needs clean to land on properly. I think." He kissed me, and stripping off all his clothes and dropping them on the floor, headed to the shower.

* * *

When we woke up again, Tristan decided we needed to walk around some. So we slipped out the back service entrance of the hotel without being spotted. Tristan seemed to know where all the possible exits could be, and had no worries about pushing open doors that said "Authorized Personnel Only." I told him about a park down by the lake that I'd read about in the guidebook. So we headed in that direction, and wound up walking out to the end of the park, by the old dry dock area. Out here, on the edge by the water, you could see what it really was—industrial waste land with the wet dreams of a few developers half a mile away, a Miami on the river that was so out of place next to the low-level brick buildings that had once housed factories and businesses, that you had to wonder. The wind-blown trash stuck to the barbed wire fences. This was the only accessory. The bits of plastic and Styrofoam that would eventually wind up in the picturesquely named off-shoot of the lake that was doing its best to hide its heritage as a glorified sewage runoff, and making it hard for people to re-member what it had once been, the resting and nesting place for shorebirds and fish, a wild and beautiful land.

Tristan leaned against the wire fence, his leather jacket protecting him from the worst of it, and beckoned me to come closer. I'd been taking pictures—I thought they would go with the article, and maybe the eventual documentary. Naturally, I wouldn't be filming it, but I'd be amused if they used some of my angles to set up the background shots. I kept snapping away as I approached him, watching his face go from confused to delighted. It was hard to describe the feeling that was running through me watching him, suddenly enjoying the illicit pleasure of being on the fringes, the metal storage tanks and the grey-green water of what used to be an inlet before mankind had the idea to pour tar down right up to the edges, and suffocate everything green and growing, so different to his skin, golden and dewy, shimmering in the fading light of the afternoon, in sharp contrast to the roller-skate silver metal color of the chain link fence, the tiny stones coming up through the uneven pavement. Tristan laughed, a carefree musical sound that drifted on the air, wrapping around me, tickling, until I had to laugh with him, my finger on the button, snapping away, every angle he threw at me.

"You're too good at this."

"What do they say? 'You've got to love the camera?' Give it up for a piece of metal, a blank eye. A little like music. Fuck me with that thing…like taking the guitar and pointing it at the crowd." And he started to bend his knees, leaning backwards, mimicking pointing his guitar at me. I kept getting closer, snapping away, until he was nearly to the ground, and I found myself straddling him, a leg on either side of his thighs, closer, a straight line between the two of us.

He lifted himself up, the muscles in his thighs visibly straining against his jeans with the effort as he raised himself higher and finally threw an arm around me, steadying himself, his body tight against mine. He had all his weight pulling against me, and I was struggling a bit with the effort to keep all six whatever feet of him from dropping to the pavement.

"Yeah, babe, why haven't we done this before? Where do you want me?" He started posing. A hand on his hip and one out, a little like Mick Jagger, he thrust his body dangerously to one side. I kept taking pictures, trying to focus. His smile widened evilly as he watched me moving around him to get a different angle. Then, quickly, he changed the rhythm, raising both his arms over his head, and started swaying, slowly, to some unknown beat. It reminded me of someone. I wasn't sure who. My brain had gone blank. Then he was taking off his jacket, winking at me, stuffing it between his legs, and started stripping off his t-shirt, doing his best Iggy Pop imitation. "Don't get the jacket," he ordered. "That'll spoil it."

"Who's running this show? Me or you?" I retorted, a little more out of breath than I would have liked.

He grinned dangerously. "Don't know yet." And he started running his hands up and down his long torso, reaching out over his skin with his fingers outstretched, singing "I Wanna Be Your Dog" as he did it. His tongue darted out, and wetting his lips, he ran a finger around his mouth, and stuck it in, pulling it out, glistening. His hand dropped and he was circling his wet fingertip over his taut nipples, then rewetting it, and running it again and again, over the hard point. "Like it, sweetheart?" he taunted. "Come on then, get a close-up." He was teasing now, his hips making slow shapes in the air, and as he turned at an angle I could see the backs of his muscled thighs, reaching up to the perfectly defined round muscles of his behind. He changed the song he was singing, now humming, to one I didn't recognize, emphasizing the beat. "Come on, don't get tired yet," he called out. He dipped down, his knees bent, his fine ass sticking out slightly and rose up, very slowly. Then he did it again, his thighs tense with the effort to lift all six foot two of him smoothly from the ground. I kept snapping away. I'd never be able to use these, but I didn't care. If Tristan was going to give it all up for the camera, I was fucking going to do my best to try and capture it.

Now one hand was slipping down his body, starting at his chest, and slowly making its way over his stomach. He took a deep breath in and his abs tightened, his hips cambered out to the rear, then back again, almost seeming to meet his hand in a dance, as his fingers slipped past the waist of his jeans, just low enough that his last two fingers reached out and skimmed over what was between his legs. He smiled again, that dirty smile, and closed his eyes, only for a moment, as he pressed in, so slightly. Then his hand was up by his waist as though it had never happened. He stared at me. I wasn't sure if he was actually seeing me. He was on stage, in performance mode, lost in finding the right combination. What made him a star was the ease with which he could share the pleasure he felt, was feeling, in teasing the audience. The back and forth, the pull as he played them, knowingly. I could only watch, mesmerized.

My camera hung uselessly over my shoulder, my hand gripping the lens so I wouldn't drop it. Tristan swayed his hips back and forth, then raised his arm. His long fingers pointed at me, then curved over, beckoning me to him. I walked very slowly towards him. I felt drugged. Being the target of all that magnetism, those dark eyes dancing with amusement, his body giving off a force that couldn't be normal, had left me weak. I could hear my pulse beating in my ears. It couldn't be right to want this much. I didn't care.

Tristan reached his hand out, and caught mine in his larger one. It didn't help that it had been the same one he had been teasing himself with moments ago. My breath caught in my throat as a wave of half-formed ideas on what I'd like to do washed over me. He smiled again, as though my thoughts were completely open to him. "You stopped taking pictures," he said, drawing me closer.

"Yes," I murmured. "Should you do that on stage? I mean in public?"

He laughed. "What, this?" And he pulled me up to him as he repeated the same swaying motion, the same almost figure of eight movement, his hips rising up, but now coming firmly against mine.

I shut my eyes. "Yes, that." I could feel how warm his body was.

He sank down a little. "Like that, do we? Maybe I should do it again." And he repeated it, again, once more, then reached around and placed his hand on my ass, and pulled me sharply towards him.

At the touch of his hand, my body melted into his. My eyes shut, and I let myself follow his movements. My mouth was dry, and I tried to lick my lips to wet it again.

"Nice," Tristan's voice rumbled through me, and his lips brushed lightly against mine, then pulled away. I let out a little groan. "Need something to do with your mouth, is that it? I can think of a few things."

Before I could answer or do anything, his mouth was on

mine, his tongue looking for mine, opening me up. We fell back against the wire fence, leaning on it, as his hips continued their dance against me. Supported by the fence, Tristan moved a leg between mine and slid it up, his hip firmly against the center of me.

I moved against him, his voice a low dark encouragement going through me. "That's it. Lils. Use me, use me." His kiss was becoming more intense now, and his head slipped down to my neck, biting the skin where it joined my shoulder.

"Tristan…" I breathed.

We were lost in each other. The heat of his skin, his hands on me, his mouth was relentless, moving first with delicate care, then letting the intensity rise between us, until we were both breathless. His mouth moved to my ear. His voice was ragged and deep. "Lily. Lily. Make me come." He looked around. "Touch me. No one is around, for now. I'm so close…" And he took my hand and pressed against him. "I'll keep watch." He laughed, brokenly. "I'll try."

I didn't even question it. I knew it was crazy and I didn't care. I unzipped his jeans, and gripped him firmly. He gasped. "That's it, like that." It was easy to make him slick. He was wet and hard, and I knew we had moments before someone would come along. I wanted nothing more to take him in my mouth, but we needed all the cover that two bodies could provide. His breathing grew more erratic and I could feel him tightening up. The heat coming off him was incredible. His mouth was against mine, but more for appearances than anything else. His eyes were tightly shut. And he suddenly gripped my arm, and pulled me to him, his head falling on my shoulder, as his body tensed up. His voice was broken. "Yes, fuck yes, yes," Tristan hissed, a flood of warmth erupting over my hand as I tried to catch all of it.

A truck rumbled past behind us. Two lovers, holding each other. Having a moment. Nothing to see.

Tristan took his shirt and wiped us off, before flinging it into the marshy wasteland on the other side of the fence. He shrugged on his leather jacket over his bare chest, and throwing an arm around me, started walking us off back in the direction of civilization. His eyes were unfocused and he didn't say anything as we went past the warehouses, putting space between us and what had happened back there. When we were nearly back to the main road, he stopped, and held me to him closely. Only I could hear what he said.

"We're mad, Lily. Mad. But I love it. And I love you."

chapter nine

Cleveland

Our arrival in Cleveland was uninspiring. It hadn't been a long drive from Detroit, only around three hours, but we'd left around 4 a.m., so it had the feel of an overnight. Seeing the sign for I-90 as we came in made me irrationally wish we could stay on it, go east, and get the hell out of here. A light drizzle was falling. It was early, I needed a coffee, and the excitement of showtime seemed a long way off. Tristan went in to check on a few things and even James had actually gone inside and done some work, checking on the softgoods, and arranging for our new backdrop to go up. Finally, a couple of vans came to take us to the hotel from the bus, which was going to stay parked out by the venue.

A few days in and the routine of dealing with the public had already become just that—routine. Emerging from vans to the disorientating strobe effect of repeated bursts of flash going off, whether it was from a camera belonging to professional paparazzi or a hopeful fan's cell phone, there was a sense that you had to make it past a gauntlet of excited people.

They were all very close. Very close. I felt grateful for the large bodyguards that eased our way through in each place. Tristan didn't like them as much, but he recognized it was a necessary evil. "Sometimes the protection can get a little carried away. You should be able to tell the difference between an excited fan and someone dangerous, and not all of them can, or do," he had said as we were getting ready to emerge to this new group of waiting fans.

"How do they know we're going to be here?" It seemed to me that the fans knew our schedule better than we did. "I never managed to get this close to people back in the day."

Tristan smiled. "It doesn't take much. One person mentions it casually to a friend—usually it's hotel staff. Once the information is out there, pretty easy for it to spread." He looked out the window at the small crowd. "Could be worse, really."

We watched as James emerged from the car ahead of us, and came over to the van. The bodyguard moved through the crowd from the hotel, and James nodded to him. Once he had made a small path, James turned to the crowd and said something.

Tristan looked at me. "Autographs. Why don't you go first, and I'll follow."

I nodded. "I'll wait for you at the door."

Tristan frowned. "You don't have to do that."

"No, I want to see how these people ask for autographs. Besides," I teased him, "only one bodyguard."

"True," Tristan nodded. "James definitely doesn't count."

The bodyguard pulled open the long door to the van, and instantly the crowd surged forward, phones up, already beginning to take pictures. I came out first, and they still took pictures. I turned to look for Tristan, and watched him emerge from the van. A little cheer went up from the crowd, and as all eyes were now on Tristan, who was adjusting his sunglasses with a big smile, his hand raised in a wave, I managed to slip through and wait by the doormen, who were looking on, somewhat bemused. We were staying overnight in one of the better hotels here, so they must have seen this kind of thing before. But I had the impression that they were wondering what about this particular man, however striking he might be, was drawing this kind of attention. It was a fair question. If I was unable to answer it in a detached way, I could still see how this world of musicians, autographs, and crowds must look to the outside world, even though I was part of it in my very own way. When I watched a young woman go up to him, and let out a little shriek as he took her hand, I could understand it. There was just something about Tristan that made you want to let go, with an almost painful burst of energy.

You could spot the slightly obsessed, wearing the latest t-shirt, holding up a poster or a CD cover, nearly crying when Tristan looked their way. The guys were the same, without the shrieks. But they wanted to be noticed, singled out, just the same, and go home and tell everyone about the day they shook Tristan Hunter's hand and got his autograph. Tristan wasn't stupid. He knew how important this was to people, and he made a real effort to be as positive as possible whenever he had to interact with the fans. That didn't stop him always approaching the crowds a bit gingerly, as if they were each made of possible explosive materials. The fans, for their part, were thrilled, but manically determined, pushing various pieces of paraphernalia to sign at him that could include, like that fan back in NYC, arms and breasts. Part of the process was that Tristan never had a pen. One of the fans always handed him a Sharpie, like a little ritual. He always tried to hand it back, but sometimes with the movement of the crowd and the need to keep moving, it wasn't possible. He'd sign, then sign again, sometimes looking up, asking a question, otherwise fairly methodical, almost businesslike, with the intent of getting to as many people as possible in a short time. He smiled, that guarded but beautiful smile. But it was important to limit exposure. After about 10 people had various CDs and body parts signed, the bodyguard moved between Tristan and the crowd and herded him up to the hotel. He nodded to me, and I went in. There were enough photos of me out there already. Tristan had reminded me, "Be careful Lily. Keep your eyes open. Most people are ok, but those who are not, can be actually very dangerous." I had shivered when he said that, and he'd pulled me close to him. "It's fine, Lils. We are always surrounded by people. But best be careful, yeah?" He didn't need to add that I was probably not everyone's favorite person, for obvious reasons.

The check-in was smooth and the room was nice. I walked around the suite, and wound up in front of the window. It was a view from above, rather than a view of anything in particular. It conferred superiority, but over nothing. I opened the minibar, and shut it again. Too early to start on the little bottles, cute as they were. I sat down on the bed, which was hard, and listened to the sound of the shower coming from the bathroom. Tristan wanted to clean up and rest before the soundcheck. Today was a day without interviews, as he'd done a brief promo over the phone from Detroit. I wondered if I should call for some food for him from room service. I jumped up again and walked to the window. That's where Tristan found me when he emerged from the shower, in one of the hotel bathrobes.

He glanced over, questioningly. "Not tired?"

I sighed, and hugged him. He smelled of soap and shampoo. "I am, but. I don't know. I think I need some air."

Tristan nodded and gave me a kiss. "Sure, go ahead. Go out. I'd go with you, but I really want some down time. Anywhere in particular?"

"I thought maybe I'd go visit the Rock and Roll Hall of Fame." I kissed Tristan softly on the mouth. "You have sound check. Besides, Dave suggested I could mention it in one of the blog pieces."

Tristan grimaced. "Dave. Yeah, well, he knows his business. Have you ever been there?"

I shook my head.

"It's ok. Looks better on TV. Don't we all?" He held my hand and walked me over to the bed. "I'm exhausted. Think I'm coming down with something. Already." He pulled down the ugly bedspread and climbed in. "Wait. Have you got money? Take a cab for fuck's sake. Maybe I'll see you at sound check. I don't want to see myself at sound check." He pulled the covers up and I kissed his forehead. He was a bit hot.

"I can stay..." I started. "I'd like to see it though. But if you want me here, I'm here."

Tristan held me to him, and kissed the top of my head. "Rock music's not a religion, you know. It doesn't have to be a pilgrimage. You could just stay here, order up some room service, get a massage..." He trailed off as he caught my eye. "Go on then. You will be disappointed."

I laughed. "I'm frequently disappointed. But that doesn't mean I need to rush there."

"No, doll. I need sleep and you're jumping out of your skin. Don't need a nursemaid, just some sleep in a bed. That doesn't move. Text me if you need me." He leaned back against the pillows and shut his eyes. I switched off the table lamp by the bed and walked out to the front door of the suite, grabbing my jacket. I felt a bit guilty, but it wouldn't make him sleep better if I watched. I shut the door as carefully as I could and put on the Do Not Disturb sign.

The doorman got me a cab. I didn't think he even remembered me as a part of the crowd scene in front of the hotel not more than an hour or so ago. That wasn't a bad thing, but it did remind me how easily I could slip back into obscurity. Tristan didn't have that luxury, or curse, depending on how you looked at it.

We crossed over the Cleveland Memorial Shoreway, which seemed a grand name for an urban throughway, and the train tracks, and approached the lake. The taxi made some turns and there we were—in front of a gaudy glass pyramid. I paid the driver and got out, taking some pictures. A group of tourists were standing in front of a state historical sign, and I went over to have a look. I took out the small notebook I always carried from my bag, and I wrote down the words on the sign:

"Birthplace of Rock 'n' Roll"

When radio station WJW disc jockey Alan Freed (1921–1965) used the term "rock and roll" to describe the uptempo black rhythm and blues records he played beginning in 1951, he named a new genre of popu-

lar music that appealed to audiences on both sides of 1950s American racial boundaries—and dominated American culture for the rest of the 20th century. The popularity of Freed's nightly "Moon Dog House Rock and Roll Party" radio show encouraged him to organize the Moondog Coronation Ball—the first rock concert. Held at the Cleveland Arena on March 21, 1952, the oversold show was beset by a riot during the first set. Freed, a charter inductee into the Rock and Roll Hall of Fame, moved to WINS in New York City in 1954 and continued to promote rock music through radio, television, movies, and live performances.

It was just a small sign. But it ended on a high note. No mention of the controversy that dogged his last years. The irony of "payola"—considering that now every awards show, every blog with a budget, every record company gave away swag in large amounts. Seemed a bit unfair, I thought. It was something that he was acknowledged at all, but with members of the Beatles crediting you for introducing them to rhythm and blues, it was a little tricky to sink him into obscurity. Anyway, his legacy was why this was here, and why I was here. I paid for my ticket and went in.

There were some interesting exhibits, but everything seemed a bit dead and pinned down, like a butterfly on display paper. It was odd, for a cultural phenomenon this vibrant, this diverse, that it all seemed lifeless, behind glass. In many ways, it represented the uneasy relationship between music and sponsorship, the top of the charts and the genuine groundbreaking acts. There were some interesting curatorial choices.

I wasn't really certain that Janis Joplin was best represented by the R. Crumb drawing of her that was due to be a blotter sheet for acid, but it was curious. Women didn't really get much of a look in. They were there, but generally in ones and twos alongside a list of men. 1986, the first year, there were none at all. Then it began. Maybe someone had said something. 1987—Aretha Franklin. 1988—The Supremes. 1989—Bessie Smith. 1990—Ma Rainey. 1991 had Tina Turner—with Ike. Ruth Brown and Dinah Washington in 1993, more "early influences." Then Janis in 1995 with Martha and the Vandellas. Gladys Knight and the Pips and The Shirelles in 1996. Joni Mitchell and Mahalia Jackson in 1997. 1998 had Fleetwood Mac and the Mamas and the Papas. No one on their own. Dusty Springfield and The Staple Singers in 1999. Billie Holiday and Bonnie Raitt in 2000. Brenda Lee and the Talking Heads in 2002. After that, women had to wait until 2005 and the Pretenders. And although I knew that Chrissie Hynde had always talked about being part of the band, seeing as it was her band, and she was possibly the most important member, certainly the survivor, made it slightly less significant than it could have been. They hit Blondie in 2006, and finally made it to Patti Smith in 2007, along with the Ronettes. Madonna in 2008. Wanda Jackson in 2009. 2010 had Abba. And two songwriting teams—Ellie Greenwich and Jeff Barry, and Cynthia Weil and Barry Mann. I stopped then. All very worthy individuals, but I felt there was so many more that could and should be mentioned. If the Sex Pistols made it in, why not Siouxsie Sioux? Part of the quote about her from *Rolling Stone* came back to me: "But only one woman had the style…and she spelled her name with an X." Why had that lodged in the memory banks? Maybe it was the Native American reference that threw them. Carole King presented awards, but where was she in their lists? Doubtless faceless executives could come up with "reasons," but whose reasons? How about The Runaways? Joan Jett? Groundbreaking. And for everyone I could think of, there were certainly others who were loved and respected. What about The Slits? The Pixies? PJ Harvey? The Cocteau Twins? Annie Lennox? Portishead? Suzi Quatro? Kaki King? Guesch Patti—French, obscure, amazing. Bjork. Shit. Kate Bush. Where was fucking Kate Bush?

I stomped out, past the families and the aging former high school band members in their pressed light blue jeans, and grabbed a cab. Was I any better? Writing about Tristan? Hanging around like some lovesick puppy? The "Jonah"? The "girlfriend"? I got the cab driver to stop as soon as I spotted the hotel, so I could walk around a little. After a couple of blocks, I stopped and looked around. It struck me suddenly that all of Cleveland seemed to be sculpted in different tones of beige. Light beige, dirt beige, orange beige, yellow beige, reddish beige. A range of non-choices. I was sure that there was character somewhere, but I couldn't see it and I didn't feel like looking. I took a picture, curious how all the non-colors would show up on a photo. Fuck, I did not want to be here. I marched over to the clichéd blue awning in front of our supposedly nice hotel and pushed open the side door without waiting for the revolving door. Almost immediately, a hotel employee was at my side.

"May I be of some assistance?" he intoned, while looking me up and down. I followed his eyes, and looked at myself and my outfit. Black leather jacket, boots, short skirt in geometric print, silky t-shirt. Hair messy. Bag, also black leather.

I looked back up at him. "Yes, thank you. Could you direct me to the hotel bar?"

His face tightened, his mouth thinning into a line of displeasure. "Are you a guest here?"

That confirmed my suspicions. I decided to run with it. "Isn't the bar open to all potential customers?"

He looked as though he was about to call for backup. "In theory yes, and in practice we do all we can to insure a calming atmosphere for our hotel guests."

I smiled. "Excellent. That's what I'm looking for. A calm atmosphere. And a drink. So I can write my article on discrimination against women in public spaces." He looked alarmed. "But perhaps, just to be on the safe side, so you're sure I'm not a sex worker, you'd like to see my room key?"

He paled slightly, but recovered. "Is it madam's key, or did a guest give it to you?"

I was bored with him. It wasn't worth it to wind him up, but it was tempting. Ah, why not. "It is madam's key. Perhaps you saw madam arrive this morning. Does Tristan Hunter, the musician madam is following on tour and about whom she is writing an article for *The Core* magazine, ring a bell? Unless it's a policy decision you've just taken on your own to insure no future musicians stay here, or women, which I have to say, is a brave judgment that is bound to merit some kind of future reward. Otherwise, I think showing me where the bar is would be a good idea at this point." I smiled at him.

He nodded, and mumbled, "Right this way." When we reached the bar, he escorted me to one of the booths, and mumbled an apology. On his way out, he exchanged a few words with the bartender. I got out my iPad and keyboard and wasn't very surprised to see a server approaching with a bowl of different salty snacks and an ingratiating manner. "Your first drink is compliments of the Manager. We hope you are enjoying your stay here in Cleveland." You could hear the capital letters in his voice.

"I'm beginning to," I replied, and after glancing at the wine list, promptly ordered a very expensive glass of Barolo. I'd call AC when I was done writing. Maybe he'd like to pass judgment on one of their wines.

An hour and a half in, and after a plate of quite acceptable amuse-bouche—little fancy savory snacks—compliments of the hotel, and another glass of the admittedly excellent wine, I felt slightly more relaxed. I read through part of the blog piece I was about to send to Dave. There was so much to say, but this would have to do—for now.

Research unveils a lot of hidden truths. What it doesn't reveal are the unselected people along the way, who regardless of their contributions to science, music, revolution, you name it, were dropped from the story. Who was it who decided to rewrite a bit of history to make it more mainstream? As they say, "History is written by the victors." Maybe. Maybe not. Because information is out there if you look. So the best weapon they have to stop us from looking is to try and convince us that whatever we find on our own is wrong, or incomplete. In an emergency, it could be said that all the choices made for us were for our own good. That we already have all the information we need.

Interesting then, that privacy and information are so closely linked. What they know, is private. What you know, isn't. Everything depends on whose information, whose need for privacy. Personal everyday privacy, like yours and mine, may be under threat, but the decisions are taken by those in charge are carefully guarded. Even seemingly unimportant choices, like who to screen at the entrance of a hotel, or who to reject from a list of musicians, are still beyond scrutiny, obscured under a heading that could read "Obvious Decisions." Who makes these choices? And how do these half-truths have such a long half-life?

Back to my research then, on the apparently superficial and non-political world of music. For instance, I'm astonished to find that although Kate Bush really was the first one to use a jerry-rigged wireless mike, she gets no credit for that innovation. That honor usually goes to the more visible Madonna. The fact that Kate Bush was the first woman to reach number one on the British charts with a self-penned song, is also low down on the credits of time. Did she shift Madonna from the number one spot in the UK? She did. Ignored. She was interested in the use of production, so was accused of over-producing. She wanted a family, so she was described as putting a desire for children above a desire for making another record—some weakness she was incapable of resisting. Her fellow male musicians manage to produce offspring without being subtly accused of the chronic illness of irreversible nesting. Her wish to retreat is seen as a flaw, some incomprehensible absence of ambition, despite everything she achieved. Her desire to disengage from the madness of the music business, becomes only female, not rational. Her music and her breakthroughs, like those of many other musicians who happen to be born without a Y chromosome, or the more evocative description of "meat and two veg," are held to different criteria. That might explain why Kate Bush isn't in the Rock and Roll Hall of Fame, and probably will never be.

Before we are accused of leaving out that other 50 percent, let's *remember that this caging-up does happen to people in a whole range of other, awkward, finally human categories. Even men get told. I read a blog post once about a song written and performed by a musician who happened to be a man. The post said something like, well, he used to be great, but no one is ever good once they get married and have a child. A list of people who have done their best work after that dreadful event formed in my mind. So many rules out there. But nothing beats getting us to police ourselves. All those limits, usefully applied to people we admire. It's preventative— maybe. Preventing disobedience, just in case the artists we love do have real power, and can inspire us to do what we really want. Because normally, they do their thing, and we do ours. We stay within safe limits, while baiting them, begging them to really go wild. Drag us where we wish we could go. That could actually be dangerous. It might even make a person research the rest of history.*

It's a difficult question. Can't we just discuss the art? The music, not the person? Sure.

I make no claim to speak for everyone; it'd be insulting to even try. But I wasn't that keen on the Rock and Roll Hall of Fame. It feels a little like someone Photoshopped history. I'll let Kate Bush sum it all up better than I can.

"We'd give you a part my love but you'd have to play the fool."

I read it again, and emailed it off to Dave. I flagged down the server, and ostentatiously taking out my room key to read the number, signed for the glass of wine I did have to pay for and left a nice tip. At least I could show I wasn't an asshole. I looked at the time. 3 p.m. They were probably all at sound check. I suddenly felt drained. Maybe I was coming down with something too, or maybe the feeling of being itinerant and under observation was getting to me. I packed up.

The lobby was busy with people checking in. Mostly conventioneers, it looked like. I wondered for a moment why they were all there, then decided I didn't care. I needed a shower, and some down time. Guiltily, I wondered if I even had to go to the show tonight. The elevator pinged and the doors opened on our floor. It felt like a lifetime since I'd been here. I reached for the key, and almost on cue, my phone started buzzing. I managed to answer it before it stopped and without dropping it on the carpet covered in fleur-de-lis pattern. Dave. Fuck.

"Dave. How are you?"

"Lily. How are you? Testosterone overdose, it looks like. Do I need to send you on an Indigo Girls tour? Ani DiFranco?"

"Yes, Dave, you do. How pleased I am that you've heard of them." I snapped.

"I've heard of everyone. I think." He paused. "So. The tour. Going ok? You seem a bit…"

"Yeah, Dave. It's fine." I suddenly remembered he wasn't all bad. And he was my boss. "Thanks for asking. I think Tristan has a cold, and I'm a bit tired, but otherwise all good. I'm not even really doing anything, though, and it's still a lot. This touring thing."

"Yes." I could see him nodding on the other end. "Some bands manage to cope with these huge, grueling tours. I'm not sure how. But this is your first one. You're doing fine. You haven't passed out naked under a table yet."

I laughed. "Yeah, but. The hotel staff thought I was a hooker today. Tried to keep me out when I came back from the Hall of Fame. Still, silver lining. Got a free glass of incredibly expensive Barolo out of it. They had to open a new bottle."

Dave was laughing. "Ah, Lily. Well, that partially explains

the ranting blog post. But you know—you seem to have a little fan base of people that like your acerbic view of the world."

"Fucking miracle." I sighed. "Dave, I'm really tired. Do you want me to edit it? That's fine. Not the best thing I've ever written, I'm sure."

"No worries. I'll do it. Editorial mandate, man—date, get it? Such wit."

I groaned. "Dave. Really? And are you going to carve it up?"

"No, just fact check it and simplify a few things. Nothing too major."

"Fine. I trust you."

"Giant mistake. Now go enjoy hotel life. I think you're coming up to a couple of nights on the bus. My advice—stay in the tub and order room service, if it's decent." He sounded concerned.

"Good advice. Not sure I like it here. I may not even go to the show."

"You get a pass for one. Maybe two. Don't abuse it," Dave said. "I'll talk to you tomorrow."

"You got it boss." And I hung up, and managed to get the key in the door after only three tries. A bath. That sounded good actually. But not for the first time, I wished we were getting back on the bus tonight and getting the hell out.

chapter ten

Chicago

Tristan and I came back from a light dinner together to find that backstage was the usual tangle. One of the roadies had been sent on a last-minute dash to get a new rack effect, and the crew were giving each other worried looks, in between checking the wiring and pounding on the drums, while someone tuned the guitar. I popped out to look at the crowd filtering in to the concert hall, measuring how many rows back the crush of the most serious fans went back. Six. That was pretty good, considering the rest of the place was still filling up. I had planned on watching from the front, but Tristan had, oddly enough I thought, put his foot down. "You're going to be back here, so I know where you are, and I know there is someone to look after you." I quizzed him, asking if he was worried about what I'd do. He looked at me oddly, and kissed my forehead. "Whatever you want to believe. But I think your crowd days are coming to a close, Lily." He wouldn't be drawn on any explanations, other than to repeat, "It's best, please believe me."

So I did, and here I was, wandering around backstage, watching the final approach to a concert. A lot of pieces to be put into place, in just the right order. It was a little strange to be on this side of the stage. And everyone knew my name now, not just because I was there following the tour as a journalist, but because Tristan had apparently pulled everyone aside and let them know in no uncertain terms that we were together. I supposed it was inevitable that he had to make it clear I wasn't a passing fling. Yesterday I'd been somewhat invisible. Now everyone tiptoed around me. I figured it would wear off with time, at least I hoped so. Everyone stopped talking the minute I came near.

I stepped carefully over the wires, and around the cases, and made my way back to the big room with the food, and the sofa, and the TV, where everyone was hanging out. The drummer, Pete, was demonstrating his moonwalk, while Jack tapped out the rhythm of "Beat It." He was really pretty good at it, then he dropped to the floor, and spun around on his back. Everyone applauded. He jumped up when he finally stopped spinning, and grabbed one of the beers from the tub filled with ice. "Dancing. Shows you got rhythm. You should try it sometime, Jack."

"Hey fuck you too. Dance on this," he shot back, and did a few pelvic thrusts that a pole dancer would have been proud of. "Did that last night. You seemed to like it."

"It didn't wake me up, so maybe, maybe not, sweetheart."

"Yeah, suck this…" and then Jack fell silent. The drummer gave him a filthy look and flipped him off. It seemed a little more than the usual banter.

I glanced around. AC had just come in. He waved at every-one, then walked over to the table and poured a glass of the organic red from Oregon. I had been wondering who had put that on the rider. The two musicians pulled each other over to the TV, and started flipping through channels, and I walked up to AC. He looked a bit lost today. We'd been on the road for a week, and he didn't look that thrilled. He smiled at me though, as I approached. We'd never really sat down again for the talk that we joked about, the follow-up from our moment in the hotel room, AC with his bottles and red wine, and his attempt to seduce me, and my anger and flight from discover-ing Tristan doing drugs with his ex-wife and the other gui-tarist from Devised. It had been an interesting conversation, in retrospect. And coupled with everything else I'd overheard AC and Tristan saying, it had the potential for a pretty com-plicated situation. But I didn't want to blow it up. Danger was like a big balloon—easier to burst open than you expected. I did want to talk to him though. And I needed to write some-thing up about him, so an interview was on the cards. I didn't want AC to think of me on the other side though—doing what was necessary to get the information I needed, a parasite feeding on its host. I didn't think I came across that way, but people were easily confused. I'd seen that happen, and with my position straddling tour girlfriend and tour journalist, it only seemed to be getting worse.

"So, you going to give me a taste guide to the wine?" I held up a red plastic cup. "My goblet is all ready."

He laughed. "Nice euphemism. Oh, you meant the wine." And he punched me lightly in the arm, and went to pick up the bottle, when we both heard Tristan's voice, and we both turned around to look for him at the exact same moment.

I waved at Tristan, and he waved back at both of us, AC raising the bottle to him in salute, like he'd been meaning to all along. The bass player and drummer had turned away from their TV show to watch the commotion that had changed the atmosphere of the room. They both looked over at Tristan, then at AC, then saw me looking at them and turned quickly away. I caught the bassist's eye for a minute and he looked guilty.

AC interrupted my thoughts. "So, cup, cup. Give me your cup. We'll toast," he said in a kind of sing-song. He poured and we each had a swig.

"It's good," I said. "Even in plastic. And healthy."

AC snorted. "Yeah, more or less. More or less."

I touched my cup to his again. "You know we still need to talk—and do an interview."

AC gave a hollow laugh. "Aren't they the same? Everything I say will be used against me?" He saw my face, and raised his hand in apology. "I'm sorry, Lily, but you know it's a little awkward, not knowing what you are going to write." He lowered his voice. "You saw them." He nodded over towards Pete and Jack. "This is more…uh, complicated, I guess. Than you know." He glanced over at Tristan again.

"Look, I'm sorry," I started to say, but he stopped me.

"More wine? Just a little. We're going on in 30 minutes. I want to be buzzed, not angry. Lily, it's ok. I'll just be glad when you're not a journalist anymore. Or I trust you." He toasted the air. "Whichever comes first."

I looked up at the pipes and air ducts that criss-crossed the ceiling. It made me feel boxed in suddenly, so I looked down at my feet. I wished I didn't agree with him. It wasn't exactly the dream job at the moment. It just seemed to be causing a multitude of problems. I observed him. His green eyes seemed softer, but there was an emptiness there that made me worry. I wondered if he was using again. "AC, I know you haven't known me for very long. But what you said in the hotel room in London..." I stopped. He looked very uncomfortable. "Look it's fine. Forget it. I have a very selective memory, that's all. And I try not to fuck over my friends. Let's talk when you have a chance, right?" He finally smiled, and we watched the group.

James had come in. Tristan was talking to him about how long he was willing to spend outside afterwards signing autographs—"You go out there James, bring the band, tell them I'm doing an interview but I'm supposed to come—hell, I pay you, invent your own lies—and I'll go out for a bit." James looked put out, but Tristan put his hand on his shoulder, and leaned down and said something to him quietly that made him nod, and leave the room. It was probably nothing, but it seemed that there was something in the air, something up. I looked over at AC, but his face revealed nothing. We talked about the hotel, the room service, whether the towels were better in this one than the last one. We were on the bus for the next few nights, so the fact we had gotten used to having things done for us, showed we were about to be schooled in how to deal with road camping.

"I actually like the road better," he suddenly burst out. "It's good. You're not attached to anything, any place. If you're pissed off, it doesn't matter. You're leaving."

I nodded. "I know what you mean." I swept my arm

around. "All this, the waiting. The playing around. There's no more waiting on the road, you're going."

AC laughed. "Yet all people do on the bus is kill time, waiting. Forgetting they're living."

"Yeah, I guess. I like to look out the window. Imagine what my life would be like if I lived in that town, wonder why people are taking the exits. And I've even become used to the windowless bedroom."

"Yeah, it's rough for you, in there. With him."

I looked at him, quizzically. But AC didn't say anything else. Neither did I.

Luckily, the prep call for the band had just come in, which meant that the lead-on band were on their last song. I excused myself, and thought I'd go watch them. I squeezed Tristan's arm as I passed, and he held up a hand to the music tech, and followed me out of the room.

"What was that with AC? You two looked pretty serious over there." Tristan was standing over me, his arm against the wall. I could hear the final chorus of the band—it was too late now to watch, and I suddenly felt both a little guilty and a little trapped.

"We were talking about the road, the towels, life in a small town."

"AC? He's never lived in a small town in his life. I think he feels a bit alien sometimes, when we're not in a city, like he's going to be captured and examined. But Chicago," Tristan did a wide sweep with his arm, "is a pretty big place. Of course, we're leaving after the show."

"Does he feel strange? He hides it pretty well. But you know him better than I do." I paused. "A lot better."

Tristan gave me that searching look, the one that sometimes made me burn, sometimes made me feel like I was being examined. "Does that bother you?"

I shook my head. "No. Not really. Except he doesn't trust me. Should it?"

That little smirk appeared at the side of his mouth. "It depends." Then he leaned down, tall against my smaller frame, and all I could feel was the strange softness of his mouth, the sweep of his tongue, insistent until it all kicked in and then there was nothing but his heartbeat strong against me, and the dark curtain of his hair, brushing against my face, thick and soft,. He pulled me closer to him and I could feel him hard, growing harder. "So good, Lily, so good," he whispered, as his mouth slowly descended down my neck, his touch so light it made me want more of him, now. I couldn't explain why this happened, or why it happened every time, or why I didn't care who saw us. It was though his hands were tracing all the nerves in my body. Now his mouth was up against my ear. "You're more than I ever thought you'd be, Lily." His tongue traced the edge of my ear, and I shivered, eyes shut tight. "I fucking trust you. I don't say that to many people, so please remember that, no matter what anyone says or does, ok?"

I started to wriggle, wanting to see him, face to face, but his hands caught me and pressed me to him. The shirt that he was wearing, the strange small cheetah print he'd found in a thrift shop, the one that I had questioned the wisdom of buying, was now like silk over his muscled skin, leaving his arms bare and draped over his shoulders. All I could imagine is what it would be like to feel him, me naked against him. His kisses had turned into small little licks, and his hand drifted between my legs from behind, making me jump and making him laugh, darkly. He breathed into my mouth as he continuing kissing me. He laughed and pulled away, then stretched against me like a cat, his cock making a very noticeable shape down his leg. I looked down at the bulge. "Go on stage like that, they'll love it. The picture that burned up the internet."

"You mean it doesn't have its own Tumblr page yet? Now that's a travesty. Well, maybe we can change that tonight." His eyes were suddenly filled with that strange fire. And as he moved against me against I lifted my shirt for a minute, after I looked around. Miraculously there was still no one around, but I was starting to feel like I wouldn't have cared even if there was. I rubbed against his chest, against that softness, the smoothness of his shirt, so thin I could feel his skin. I shuddered. This was getting out of hand, and I could hear the muted applause greeting the end of the set. Any second now, the lead on band would be here—I didn't care. I dropped my shirt but launched myself at his mouth, with little finesse but a strange desperate feeling. I suddenly wanted him inside me, burning me, making me take all he had, all he was about to show to an entire crowd. I slipped my hand into his pants and managed to get it as far down as the solid base of him and squeezed it.

He groaned.

"Fuck, girl...you're killing me." We both heard footsteps and the other band was coming towards us. I slipped my hand back out as furtively as I could and ran my hand down his arm, he had goosebumps. My legs felt weak. He waved at them.

"Nice show lads. Getting ready here. Beer's in there." They laughed. One of them winked at me, letting his eyes trace down my body, but they passed us, laughing. And as if on cue, the door to the room opened, and everyone poured out. The bassist and the drummer gave us a look and followed the sound techs going ahead to do the final adjustments to the stage set-up.

Then AC was there. He had a sort of wry smile on his face. I looked up at Tristan, but all his face revealed was a sort of devilish merriment written all over it. "AC," he said, outlining the shape of his balls with his hand. "Come have a look. We're going to get my pride and joy its own Tumblr tonight."

"We are? Yeah, of course. Shouldn't be hard—or should it?" he said. "This your work, Lily? Nice." He questioned me with a nod and wink, then suddenly reached out and squeezed Tristan's still hard cock through his jeans.

He had meant it as a joke, but I saw the look on Tristan's face, as his eyes fluttered shut for a moment. Then he opened them, looked directly at me, then smacked AC on the ass with a laugh. "AC, you're not just hung like an elephant, you've got a memory like one. That's it exactly."

"I'm your man, babe." AC leaned in quickly towards Tristan, then suddenly turned and kissed me, hard, on the mouth. I had the impression that he was tasting me, looking for traces of Tristan. "It's not so bad, really, is it?" he said cryptically. Tristan followed with his own kiss. Soft, and sweet, and oddly reassuring, it was in clear contrast to the fast little kiss AC had just given me. But there had only been a heartbeat between them, and I didn't think it was only my mouth they were after.

I stood there for a moment, touching my lips with a fingertip, and watched the two of them head toward to the stage,

Tristan's arm draped over AC's shoulder. I thought I heard AC say "Nice shirt. Silky."

I laughed.

Watching the show from the sidelines was an experience. With the VIP cord now permanently around my neck, one of the roadies actually brought me another beer when he noticed mine was finished. It wasn't the first time I'd seen a concert from the sidelines, but it seemed like the first time I'd noticed that my status had permanently been altered. People fell in behind me, not wanting to block the view, almost hesitant if they bumped into me.

Pretty different from the mosh pit, I thought, watching the frenzy that was going on in front of the stage. People didn't realize how different. You were there, in front of the crowd, controlling, leading, making it look easy, when in fact almost every last thing had been blocked out and rehearsed. It was a show, but the trick was to make it look like you'd just rolled out of bed, had a beer, then strapped on a guitar, ready to roll, dripping sex. And the boys hadn't been kidding. If there wasn't a Tumblr devoted to either what Tristan was packing or bromance by the end of this, it wouldn't be for lack of trying. The songs were killer just by themselves, but did they get a little more intense every time AC sidled up to Tristan, leaning his head on his shoulder, Tristan's arm slung around his shoulders? Then AC dropped to the floor, wailing out a solo, on his knees. As Tristan approached him, he leaned back, and Tristan straddled him, as AC ran over the strings, increasingly frantically, his face inches away from Tristan's cock, staring at it, as Tristan thrust his hips out, towering over him. So close to what everyone was imagining, what everyone wanted them to do.

The crowd was shrieking, a wall of cell phones capturing the moment for eternity. The song screeched to a halt, and AC stood up slowly, swinging the guitar out of the way, and gave Tristan a full body hug. Maybe I was the only one that saw the moment of serious pressure he put into it. Maybe not. By that time my ears were ringing and my heart was beating. They were quite the double act. It struck me what I hadn't seen before was how comfortable they were with each other. I wondered if I should feel jealous, and I wondered why I didn't.

The rest of the concert went by in a blur. They were playing brilliantly—really doing justice to Tristan's songs. The temperature was blistering. The crowd up the front were pushing up the barriers, and the bouncers holding them back were having a hard time keeping the frenzy in order. So when AC spun his guitar around to his back, and rubbed up against Tristan, I wasn't surprised really when Tristan dove in, and slammed against him with a fury that looked long-repressed. AC flailed for a moment as Tristan forced his mouth open with his tongue, and kissed him, hard, as the seconds went past, and the crowd half-groaned, half-screamed with the sense of relief their contact brought everyone. They finally pulled apart, AC glancing down noticeably at the swelling that made his jeans look as though they were going to pull apart at the zip, and gave him the dirtiest, most knowing smile I think I'd ever seen on anyone. It made me blush, there was something so intimate about it. And in a flash, it was all over, and the band was blowing the crowd kisses, throwing guitar picks and drum sticks, and scooping up the teddy bear with a leather jacket that someone had thrown on at the end.

I felt dazed, and I looked around to see a couple of people

who had obviously been watching me turn away a little too quickly. I raised an eyebrow at one of them who was slower than the rest. If they thought I was going to be a train wreck, they were going to be sorely disappointed. I had no idea what was going to happen next, but as the band ran off the stage, I had a feeling I wanted in, center stage, no matter what.

We all filed back into the room with the food and drink, feeling the high the band was on. They were all hugging each other, and the bassist and the drummer were waltzing around the room singing "I want to rock and roll all night and party every day." Kiss. I had to laugh. Even James was smiling, as he reminded us we had to be back on the buses in a couple of hours for the overnight drive to Minneapolis. Someone put on some music, and the whole atmosphere was this kind of crazy party. There was the usual contingent of pretty girls, and some enterprising souls from the guest list. The usual hangers-on, basically. I was ducking grapes the drummer was throwing at me, trying to throw them back without getting hit, when I realized that AC's organic wine was getting to me, and I felt a bit dizzy. Figuring I just needed some air, I slipped out of the room, and headed to the bathroom. As I walked down the grey breeze-block corridor, I passed by one of the dressing rooms. The door was just slightly ajar. I glanced around, and pushed the door open slightly. Then I stopped, frozen to the spot.

They hadn't heard me, and I stood there, unable to decide if I should back out quickly and quietly, or stay, transfixed at the sight. Tristan and AC were leaning against the far wall, letting it support them from the side. They were looking at each other, faces nearly touching. My eyes traced down their bodies. Tristan's shirt was pulled up slightly, showing a line of skin. Their jeans were unzipped, hanging open on their hips, belt straps dangling. Tristan's large hand was between them. His long fingers were wrapped around both their cocks, stroking them together. AC reached out and gripped Tristan's shoulder. His eyes were tightly shut, and he let out a gasp as Tristan began to speed up his movements. AC's low whisper broke through the sound of their breathing. "I'm so close, please, Tristan, please." Tristan moved closer and finally kissed him, his mouth on his, a fierceness in his movements as he moved his hand. A moment later, AC broke away, then his voice shattered, repeating Tristan's name as he clung to him, trying to stay upright as a series of shudders ripped through his slender body, letting out a final cry. Almost immediately, his hands dropped to cover Tristan's with his own, finally pushing Tristan's hands away completely so his hands were sliding over Tristan, pulling at him slowly, teasing him. Tristan gasped, and thrust against him, their mouths tangled. Then suddenly he was still, his voice a twisted plea, "oh fuck, AC, so good, fuck, now" and his dark head fell back, their hands now moving together, as Tristan came over both of them, AC intently watching him finally lose control.

I silently backed out, pulling the door nearly shut to hide them, while they were still dazed, and headed, practically tiptoeing, to the bathroom. Once there, I leaned against the counter, and splashed water on my face, trying to stop shaking. The sensation thrumming through my body was intense. I could feel my heart beating hard against my chest. I was powerless. I just stood there, letting the electric pulse run through me, hip bones jarred up against the counter, arms straight, holding myself up against the cold edge of the sink, wishing they'd both come in and find me. I turned on the cold water, and leaned over, thrusting my hips out into air. I placed my head very slowly under the cold water, until the chill hurt, and the feeling of want seemed to run through my whole body, as though I could touch my skin at any point, and find the pressure unbearable.

I finally stood up, shaking my wet hair, and pulled out some paper towels from the dispenser and squeezed my hair dry. I looked at myself in the mirror, and my eyes were wide and black, endless holes where my pupils had taken over all except a thin ring of color. I looked like a wild animal. Who knew what the rest of the band was going to think—I could only imagine the state Tristan and AC were going to roll up in. Maybe they would go right to the bus. That suddenly seemed a good idea. I didn't want to see anyone but them, and they'd have to draw their own conclusions.

It was a hell of a secret, and now it was mine too.

chapter eleven

Chicago to Minneapolis

I had gone back to the bus, once I'd calmed down a bit. No one else was there yet, and I was glad to be alone, at least for a little while. I switched on the light in what passed for a living room, and made my way past the empty bunks to the very back. The first thing I saw was a bottle of Wild Turkey that someone had given to the band. Somehow, it had wound up back here. I stared at it. Sure. The plastic seal on the top came off easily, and bottle in hand I looked at myself in the mirror. Standing there, lit by the little fairy lights that ran across the top, the disconnect between seeing my face and hearing the thoughts hammering at my head made me turn away. I didn't want to see myself. I didn't want to think either. I didn't even have to look at the bottle. Nothing was easier, so easy. The first swig went down, slowly, burning a line through my chest. The second was longer, and sent warmth shooting into the rest of my body. I suddenly realized my feet were cold. The third one felt good, almost too painless. I put the bottle down by the bed so I could undress. I fished around in the suitcase and put on the short, lacy nightdress I'd brought. Then I lay down on the bed, staring at the ceiling. I didn't know what I was thinking, exactly. It didn't matter. I finally pulled myself up, and took another drink. Sitting up was better, and cross-legged, bottle in hand, I stared into space. After a while, I got my phone, and putting in my headphones, just set it to shuffle. I couldn't choose. And propped up by the pillows, I sat there, in the dimmed light, listening to music, pulling the bottle to-wards me when it seemed like a good idea. No one to stop me. No one to say something pointless. Nothing made sense. Except it did. It really did. How could I be surprised? All the signs were there, right back to when AC and I had first talked, sitting in that hotel room in London.

I wondered if I was supposed to be jealous. The idea kept floating around the edges of my thinking. So I tried it out. "But he's mine now," I said out loud to the half-light of the room. That sounded stupid. We were together. I didn't own him. "I love him," I whispered. That made more sense. I said it again. But that other thought was still there. I had another drink before I spoke again. "He wants someone else," I stut-tered. That hurt a little. But it wasn't someone else, it was AC. But what did he want? How much? I thought back to the two of them together, the pure pleasure over both their faces. "I don't mind," I murmured.

"Oh, fuck it," I said to the room. Silence followed, like a shadow in the corner that had been waiting its turn. I took an-other burning sip to fill up the gap. Talking to myself in the back of a tour bus wasn't going to help or change anything. I loved Tristan, I cared about AC. They were rock musicians. On tour. I didn't think rules applied. Maybe those rules never had to apply. Maybe we could make up new ones. That made me feel a bit better. I grabbed the bottle and swallowed until I began to cough. Then I placed it very, very carefully on the side table, so it wouldn't move, and wiped my mouth. Nothing mattered. So much better this way. Much better. I pulled the covers up to my chin. Finally warm. It didn't matter so much anymore what I'd say to him when I saw him. I closed my eyes. I had no idea. Nothing seemed clear. Nothing. Nothing.

* * *

The first thing I noticed, after the slow rhythmic breathing of the body next to me, was the rumble of movement, the feeling that you get on a plane but slowed down, with the odd bump in the road. I lay there, and everything that had happened came back to me, along with a vague dizziness, and a pounding in the center of my skull. I must have had more to drink than I thought. I guess I'd finally passed out, headphones on, and hadn't even noticed their return, or the bus leaving. I rolled over carefully to look at Tristan. He was so striking just lying there, with his back slightly exposed, showing a long curved creamy expanse of smooth skin. Tristan had beautiful skin, especially for a man. The color of it, that pale yet honey tone, the ripple of muscle visible underneath, alive and warm, was crying out to be touched, to be admired. In a smaller man, it might have made him look softer. On Tristan's six foot two frame, it gave him a slightly otherworldly air, as though he had been sent to us from a planet where everyone was naturally graceful and sleek, like fine race horses. For a moment I wanted to pull down the sheet that was covering him, and slide my fingers over that expanse of skin, going further down, until I reached even more silken skin that would be warm and cool at once to the touch. It wouldn't take long to feel him grow hotter and harder under my touch, still dry and smooth except for the slight bead of wetness at the top waiting to be smoothed over the aching hardness, sign of more to come, that would soon be everywhere. Unless he was spent from being with AC. I took a deep breath. That was a complicated feeling, and it made the pressure in my head worse.

I reached my hand out to pull the sheet away then stopped. No, it wouldn't be fair. He was only just now getting some sleep. He was in the middle of a tour, with more still to come. Exhausting him, or worse, testing him, wasn't going to help. I crawled out of bed slowly, before I could change my mind. I wanted him to be happy. I needed to see how he was going to act, without my prompting, or demanding explanations that I already knew didn't really exist. There was only one explanation. There was only ever one. He wanted to do it. And if exhaustion and stress meant he was more likely to start using again, then I would do whatever it took to help him, even if that meant AC helped too, even if it hurt. Which it did, a little.

I managed to extricate myself from the sheets without waking him, and putting on my leggings, a t-shirt and a big sweater, padded across the carpet to the bathroom. Looking at myself in the mirror, I could see my own lines of stress. I was worried about him, worried about us, worried about the tour, worried about the blog that I was dutifully writing up every day and sending over to Dave. Dave. For a moment, I thought about calling him. No. Dave was not an answer to this. Dave was work. Work was a good thing, giving me something else to think about. Or not. I shut my eyes. AC's face as he watched Tristan come flashed across my mind. The two of them. Unbound.

I took some painkillers for my head, and sprayed my face from the bottle of Evian that I kept in the bathroom, fresh pure water at a premium on a tour bus. I needed water. Stumbling out past the bunks, the snoring and sense of warm man heat told me they were all asleep. I turned on the kettle, and boiled water for a cup of tea, then went over to the sofa. The rays from the rising sun were just starting to arch into the bus, stripes of warm yellow light that lit up the small living room and made a pattern on the wall, as the sun shone through the skylights and windscreen and tinted windows of the bus. I had my notebook with me as I sipped my tea and watched as the glow through the glass became clearer and whiter, and the sky turned from pink haze to bright blue space. Sunrise was over so quickly. It seemed to me that once, long ago, dawn had lasted longer.

Later, when the boys were up, drinking beer, watching DVDs, and trading insults, everything would seem normal. Normal for a tour. I closed my eyes for a moment, and thought about enjoying the calm. But it didn't take long before I had reached for my notebook with a sigh. I traced the soft surface of the lined pages. "Nothing," I whispered, "matters." I stared into space.

What had Dave said? "Just send what you see, and let me worry about the structure." I had thought it odd at the time, but I had a feeling he knew what was coming down the road better than I did. He'd been pretty insistent. "Just observe. Write down what you notice and send it along. Every day. I know how tours get. You're going to get wrapped up in the stuff on the road, no matter what you say now." So every day, I had been sending him something, however small. It was a lot like a tour diary. Fuck, it was a tour diary. And I would have to keep sending him my little observations, now even more heavily edited. I wondered how much he knew, and if he would work out what the hell it was all about. Maybe one day I would even be able to tell. When it was over. Because Dave hadn't been wrong. I was right in the middle of it, and I couldn't see anything.

Normal. For a tour. The band had called it a night probably only a couple of hours ago. It was 6 a.m. The end of the day for them, the beginning of the day for the rest of the world. The real world, which apparently was out there somewhere. People going to work. Getting up, making breakfast, waking up reluctant children, putting on their masks, preparing themselves to face the day. Off to work, waiting for the weekend, which was...when? I realized with a start that I had no idea how far away the weekend was, because I had no idea what day it was. I flipped through the book to see if I'd written down dates but in the collection of notes and description, but that had stopped pretty much right away. It hardly mattered, my life was here on the bus. I put down the pen, and buried my face in my hands. Maybe I did need to call someone. But my phone was in the bedroom. And I didn't want to think anymore. So I got up and sat down closer to the front, so I could look out the window at the road.

"Good morning Hank," I said quietly, not wanting to startle

him, although I knew from experience he had an eerie sixth sense of when and who was up in the bus behind him. I guessed it came from a lot of practice driving a behemoth of a bus, containing precarious and volatile cargo, and judging from some of the experiences he had told me about with other bands, a necessary precaution.

"Good morning Lily. Up early, as usual."

"Went to bed early."

"You were the only one. What's up, road fatigue?" His voice sounded friendly, almost sympathetic. Or maybe I just needed a friend.

"I guess." I took a deep breath. "I guess it's harder than it looks. Touring. Moving from place to place."

"Ya think?" He chuckled. "I think you're a natural. Like a duck to water. Looking at you, I thought, she'll be off like a shot, once she hears the talk, sees what goes on. She's a nice girl. But look at you. Still here." He stopped talking for a moment, to pass a truck towing a car. When we were back in our lane, he started again. "Smarter than you are nice, or so it seems."

"Smart? Smart enough, I guess…" I trailed off.

He looked at me in the rear view mirror. "Smart enough to have seen enough. Not to judge. Not really."

"I suppose I want love though, just like any nice girl." It felt like a confession.

Hank didn't seem to mind, and treated it like the question it was. "It depends how much love you want. How much you need. How much you're willing to ask for."

"But…" I stopped myself. "It's hard to ask." I glanced over at him, and caught his eye in the rear view mirror.

Hank looked back at me. His expression was stern, but his eyes were soft. "My advice, Lily, is this. Don't ask for what you're not going to get. Be happy with what is in front of you. Don't do things because you're supposed to."

I sat up, surprised. He smiled at me, before his eyes went back to the road. "How did you know?" was all I said.

"You're not the only one who keeps their eyes wide open. Eyes open, mouth shut. It's kept me alive this long. I recommend it to you. You'll never know what people think unless you give them a chance to tell you," he said.

A wry expression twisted my mouth into a small smile. "Eyes open, mouth shut. Ok."

"That's the ticket. And I don't mean that fool writing you do. No one pays attention to writing. They know it's all lies anyway. But say the right thing at the wrong moment, and that's all you get remembered for."

"Is that what happened?" It popped out before I had a chance to think.

Hank didn't seem bothered. "Yeah, close enough. Close enough. But you know, some things aren't worth fighting for." He jerked his head towards the back of the bus. "Him, I don't think you need to fight. That's the one good thing about these free spirit types. If they want to go, they do."

"I guess that's true."

"He's the kind that will always do what he wants. He'll hate you if you make him choose. Don't do it, girl." He chuckled again. "Unless you want to learn to drive a bus."

I laughed. "Now you're talking." And I asked him some idle questions about gears, and the test to be a driver. It wasn't what either of us was thinking about.

* * *

We'd been sitting in silence for a while, Hank watching the road, and me going between writing a few lines, and turning up my headphones, gazing out the window. There was a steadiness to it, the exit signs at regular intervals, the switching back and forth between the lanes, all the while going forward, the lines ribboning out beside us. It was hypnotic.

I hadn't realized that I'd dozed off, but I was suddenly conscious of a warm body next to me. I opened my eyes, slowly becoming aware of everything around me, where I was, what was happening. I looked up, and there was Tristan, looking a bit sleepy himself, wearing only a white t-shirt and a pair of boxer briefs. He seemed larger than life, slightly unreal but still skin and muscle and blood pulsing through his veins. It was hard to reconcile everything I knew with his physical presence. He smiled at me when he saw I was awake.

"You can only sleep on sofas now, out here with Hank. I told you this would happen." He grinned. Lower, he whispered to me, "Are you all right? You were really out when we crawled in last night."

I curled myself up against him. "I'm ok." It didn't sound convincing, even to me. "I guess I didn't sleep well, for all that."

Tristan held me to him, softly, like he was taking special care. I closed my eyes and leaned my head on his chest. He was so much larger than I was. I just wanted to feel his arms wrap around me and hear his heartbeat, steady and solid against my ear. Until this feeling stopped. Wanting wasn't getting though, and I knew he wouldn't sit still that much longer, off to make phone calls, coffee, something. So I held on a little tighter, and curved my legs over his, so I could feel his thighs against mine. Hard muscles, soft skin, the slight scratch of hair. The closest I could get to having him wrapped around me, keeping me safe. For a while. I breathed in, a big shuddering gasp, and I closed my eyes again. I wasn't going to think. He was here, and I was here, warm in the grip of his strong arms. It was good enough.

Hank's voice broke through my thoughts. "She's good company, Tristan, that Lily girl. I've decided. I'm going to keep her on the road with me." He stopped for a moment. "I think she's got a taste for it."

Tristan laughed. "Is that so?" He kissed the top of my head. "Queen of the road, then." But I could feel his whole stance change. He tightened his arms around me, and pulled me up on to his lap, and now he really was cradling me, almost possessive. "I think you'll have to find your own, Hank, mate. I'm holding on to this one."

Hank let out a low whistle. "Is that so? Well, if you're sure. Don't forget, Lily. Offer still stands. Not many like you in this world."

I smiled against Tristan's chest. For a moment I loved Hank just as much. "I'll never forget."

chapter twelve

Minneapolis

The hotel in Minneapolis was a welcome change from the bus. Climbing down the big stairs, out on to the road, I felt like I'd disembarked from a boat—the ground still seemed as though it was humming and shifting under my feet. The hotel itself was nice enough, the usual collection of bad paintings, marble facings, and armchairs that looked more comfortable than they were. But we took one look at the room, another TV behind a fake mahogany cabinet, another pair of tasteful lamps, another polyester bedspread covered with the carefully handwritten welcome and pair of chocolates and decided we needed some sunlight and air.

Tristan had slipped us out the service entrance for a walk. Now he was laughing at my complaints of feeling seasick. "That happens sometimes. But you probably won't be able to sleep now either, not that you've gotten used to the movement." He stopped and winked at me. "Then you'll become a real tour rat, unable to sleep, dozing off during the day, up all night." I swatted him. He caught my wrist in his, and pulled me to him. "Then you'll have to tour forever, with me, and we'll never sleep. You'll have to sing with me in trucker bars, telling stories of the road."

"Will we have a trailer?"

"No, we'll have a truck, and sleep on a mattress. When it's clear and warm, we'll put it on the roof, and look at the stars."

I shook my head. "You'll miss the city life."

He took my hand. "I don't know. Maybe I would. I like this though." He waved an arm at the wide straight street, headed for the outskirts of town. "We could disappear out here. No one would find us."

I linked my arm through his. "I think you're pretty easy to find in a crowd. Look at you."

Tristan frowned for a moment. "True. True. Easily solved. When we're on the road again, I'm getting a trucker hat. Stuff all my hair underneath."

"What about the leather jacket?"

"I haven't gotten that far yet." He stopped and turned me to face him. "You know, you can't exactly go undercover anymore."

I shrugged. "That's because I'm with you. People stop to look at you. No one knows what I look like anyway. People might know my name from the writing, but there's no face."

Tristan frowned again. "Well, not anymore."

"What? Why?" I tried to make a joke. "Am I super famous now, like you?"

Tristan didn't look happy. "Didn't Dave talk to you? He said he was going to call you."

Now it was my turn to make a face. "I didn't...I saw he called." I looked away. "I didn't feel like talking much. I've been emailing him with blog updates. It's been all right, for the moment, anyway." I didn't mention that I hadn't trusted myself to talk to him this morning. One soft word from him, and I might have been telling him all my worries. "I guess I should have called him."

"You know, you didn't do anything wrong." Tristan smiled. "But he's still your boss. Mostly, anyway."

I thought about the other reason I didn't always want to talk to him. That direction seemed a safer option. "Sometimes when I talk to him…I don't know. No one likes to be reminded they lost. Especially not someone like that. Especially not Dave."

"The ego of man. He'll live, trust me."

I looked up at Tristan. "I'm sure he will. Anyway, I know I made the right choice."

Tristan gave me a little shove. "Are you sure?" Then he bent down and kissed me, his tongue teasing the corners of my mouth.

It just felt too good. I let my mind go blank, just feeling the width of his back under my hands, his skin, warm and with the faint smell of the cologne he'd tried out when we were out shopping yesterday on North Michigan Avenue still lingering on his hair. "Spray perfume in your hair, that's what my grandmother always told me women did. I figured it would work for me too," he'd said as he sprayed a little cloud of it around his head, and walked through it, while the saleswoman gazed at him like he had come to rescue her from a tower. He'd bought a bottle, and signed a card for her. The scent suited him, a complement to the way his skin smelled, sweet and salty, the smell of grass on a summer day, the smell of dark skies in the middle of the night.

The warmth of him, his quiet strength, the way he gave himself up to the kissing. Some people walked by, and he slowly pulled away, remembering we weren't alone. "We could go back up to the room," he whispered. I was about to answer, when he stopped me from speaking with another small kiss. "No, wait. What I was about to tell you. Dave. He saw the picture on *Just Jared*, and he told me he was going to run your pieces with a small headshot of you from now on. They're updating the link on the website too." He ran his hand through his dark hair. "He'll talk to you about everything."

"What picture?" I asked, slowly. "When did this happen?" I wasn't sure I really wanted my face everywhere, but it looked like it was too late for that.

Tristan looked annoyed. "This morning. They're quick. I told James to show you. Never mind—here. Look." And he pulled out his phone, and starting pulling up a photo. He enlarged it as much as he could, so you had to scroll down to see the entire thing, but there it was. A picture of us coming out of the restaurant in Chicago, Tristan opening the door to a cab, me looking around as always, slightly wary. It was a very clear picture. The caption was pretty definite too. "Tristan Hunter, former lead singer with Devised, out in Chicago with his new girlfriend Lily Taylor, a writer for music magazine *The Core*. Hunter is on tour, promoting his new solo album, *Some of Us Remember the Future*."

I stared at the photo. Then I looked up at Tristan. "Seems a bit of a coincidence."

"Which thing in particular? It all does."

I smiled at him. "That's why you're wonderful. Exactly. How did they know we were there…"

He finished my sentence for me. "…and how did Dave know about it practically before the picture was run?"

I nodded at him. "It's a bit of a mystery. Either he's having us followed, or they contacted him first before they went with it."

Tristan shrugged. "He's got friends everywhere. And enemies. It wouldn't take a lot for someone to realize the connection between me, you, and the magazine, and think to call him for more information."

"He probably bought the photo himself and sold it for more to *Just Jared*."

Tristan laughed. "I wouldn't be surprised." He grew serious. "But it does mean we need to keep an eye out." He looked up at the sky. "It was only supposed to be a small tour." He took my hand again. "Lily, I don't want you to go out without someone with you, ok?"

I sighed. It was nice to be looked after, but I didn't want to be guarded. "Tristan, I'll be fine."

"It's a good idea. Really. Lily, listen to me." He looked around, suddenly edgy. "Let's keep walking, ok?" He stood up and pulled me up with him. We walked for a few blocks in silence. Suddenly everyone on the streets seemed to notice us. Maybe it was just that we were giving out some kind of electric charge on the energy we were producing. Or that Tristan, tall, dark, and always looking like a rock star, even in a t-shirt and jeans, was attracting attention, as he did. Used to standing out in the crowd, Tristan seemed to take up more space than everyone else. He noticed I was looking around, nervously. "Hey, Lily love. Please don't worry. It's fine. It's just that no one really knew what you looked like before, and now they do."

"I know. I know. It's ok. I'm famous. Can't do my own shopping. But I'll finally get a good table at the last minute."

Tristan laughed. "Yeah, it's got perks. No doubt. And most of the crowds are really good people…"

I finished his sentence for him. We'd been doing that a lot lately, I suddenly realized. "…but some of them aren't too thrilled to see you hooked up with someone."

He looked straight ahead. "I get threats too. You just ignore them, mostly."

I stopped short, then looked around, and started walking again. We probably looked like we were on drugs or something, I thought. Not really walking with a destination. "Threats?"

He sounded so casual. "Sure. Mostly things about the lyrics or the evil of drugs, or the way I look, or just attention seekers. You know, like the people on Twitter who ignore everything you say, but respond to every announcement, every tweet with a plea for you to follow them." He put his arm around me. "Some people just have their obsessional moment, it passes." He pulled me closer to him. "But some are a little more insistent, say crazy things." He shook his head. "It's a little weird. You get used to it. Mostly. But for right now, I want you to be careful."

"Ok." I shrugged.

Tristan stopped again. "Ok? That's it? No arguments?"

"No, why would I argue? You've been doing this longer than I have. You're probably right. So now, I'm freaking out a little just walking around Minneapolis. In daylight. Hardly a war zone. No, whatever you want." For some reason, one of the lyrics from a Pulp song came to mind. "What exactly do you do for an encore? Cause this is hardcore."

Tristan took my hand. "Come on, let's walk." We headed down Hennepin Avenue towards the river. Tristan wanted to get to the water and see the warehouses, if we could make it that far. I was starting to feel like we were on the warehouse tour of North America. It was amazing how many beautiful, desolate brick buildings still existed, even here. But for once, I wasn't sure I felt like walking in some half-populated fiction of industry.

He wrapped his fingers around mine, and pulled me closer to him. "Don't go crazy on me now." We walked a bit further, then crossed the street. It was a normal day, in a normal town. All around us, people were getting through life, answering calls, kicking off their shoes surreptitiously under their desks, fighting for little successes, mostly wishing they could go home. And here we were, out in the daylight for what felt like the first time in a while, an anomaly in the normal order of life. Tristan put his arm around me. I stopped holding my breath, and leaned into him. He kissed the top of my head, and hugged me. "You get used to it, Lily love. And if you get a little more careful, a little more wary, then that's the price you pay."

I hugged him back. "It'll be ok. I'll be ok. It's what I want, remember?" And I twisted a finger around the necklace that I wore all the time, that I hadn't taken off since the night in that Lower East Side bar, where he'd found me again, and we'd vowed to stop fighting what we so obviously had together. I thought of AC. And then I didn't.

Tristan smiled at me, that blazing grin that literally seemed to dissolve my vision, and reduce everything to a corridor of energy running between us. "You're smart, and watchful and so am I. Although I might get Rick over here. Remember him? He frightens everyone. His network isn't quite the same on this side of the pond, but he's still a big guy." He laughed. "Did you know he once pulled me out of the crowd and up onto the next balcony? The crowd was getting a little too excited."

I gazed at him, all 6 foot 2 of skin and muscle and leather. It didn't seem possible. "That's kind of unbelievable."

"Yeah, I didn't quite believe it either. But he was worried. And when we're worried, we do amazing things sometimes." He pulled me up to him and touched his lips gently to mine, the faint scratch of stubble grazing my chin, before moving around my cheek, where he kissed me again. "I'm looking after you. Don't worry. Don't go anywhere."

"I won't. I promise."

He turned us around and we started walking back the way we came, the large concrete blocks of the sidewalk making our steps seem slower, less productive than they would be elsewhere. The distances out here were starting to get to me, the endless landscape. "I really wanted to drive us out by Paisley Park. I would have liked to see it. But we've got sound check, the show, then dinner with the band, then the bloody DJ set. I promised them I'd be there."

"It's ok. We'll come back. Or maybe we'll steal the bus and drive out there. It's like half an hour, right? They can all camp out while we're gone."

Tristan smirked. "Are you going to drive?"

"Damn straight. Just try me. Besides, Hank's taught me everything he knows."

He stopped again and kissed me before I had a chance to

breathe. "It what makes you so incredible. You probably would do it," he said, as he broke off the kiss. "But don't." He winked at me. "I'll be watching you. No bus theft. It's not on the rider."

"Can I have our hotel rooms painted pink?"

"I've already asked for them to be painted black, sorry."

"But no one can look at me as I walk by."

Tristan laughed. "That already happens love, they're all terrified of you. You vixen."

I shook my head. "No, doll, that's you. You've frightened them all off. You and your very tall, very angry, very crazy self."

"I have no idea what you are on about. Speak to my manager. Actually don't. He's fucking useless."

And we both started giggling like a bunch of kids in class who'd been told not to laugh. We kept bursting out laughing as we walked. I was sure that some of the people giving us filthy looks thought we were laughing at them. But we were just happy. And we turned around and walked all the way back like that, past the cars, the buildings, the people doing their everyday tasks. Then we found ourselves in front of the hotel. The outside was a strange sandstone color, with bars on one of the big windows—it had apparently been a bank. I thought it looked a little like a jail.

We went in. It was only us, and AC had begged for a room too. The other two were staying on the bus. Tristan had told James he wanted a little private time away from it all, especially as we were about to do a five day long haul on the bus down to Texas. But even though the place was supposed to be a bit nicer, it was still a typical chain hotel, the big yellow diamond shapes on the polished white floor repeated in the oddly colored gold grey carpet around the edges, dotted with chairs where you could sit, if you wanted to hang out in hotel lobbies. I looked around, and saw a couple of hopeful fans notice that we were there, and start to approach us. I nudged Tristan, who looked up from asking the front desk staff to send up some sparkling water and a bottle of champagne. "For later," he whispered in my ear. Out loud, he said thank you to the man behind the desk, and turned to face the four girls headed our way. He glanced around to see if anyone else was heading over, or noticed, and he advanced a little ways towards the elevators, watching them slow down, uncertain if they should approach him. He finally stopped. Taking this as encouragement, they came rushing over, as though this was their last chance. Which it possibly was. He moved me behind him, ever so slightly, as the first girl approached ahead of her friends, turning around to make sure they were still there.

"Is it really you? Tristan! Oh my god, I've wanted to meet you for so long. Oh my god! Shari, get over here, quick!" She stopped to catch her breath for a moment, her hand on her chest, which was rising and falling with an incredible rapidity. I hoped she wasn't going to hyperventilate and pass out on us. I looked over at the people at the front desk, who were watching, somewhat amused. That reassured me—at least they were there, they could call someone, or act as witnesses if one of the girls passed out from the excitement. It had actually happened twice so far, once when he was signing autographs, and once when he had leaned down to touch hands with the fans pushed up against the stage. They had fainted dead away. I couldn't really blame them. I knew what it could be like.

The girl was talking really fast now. "Tristan, Tristan,

can we all get a photo with you? Please?" He nodded and she squealed. When he put his arm around her, her eyes closed in sheer ecstasy and she said, "Oh my god, he's touching me. Shari! Andi! Melli! It's amazing. Get a picture, get a picture." Tristan smiled his killer grin at them, as one by one, they all came up to tuck themselves under his arm, as multiple pictures were taken on their phones. Nothing was real anymore until you had an Instagram of it. Tristan asked them all if they were coming to the show tonight, and they were. He signed a couple of mini-posters, and an old 7 inch from the first band. Tristan's face lit up. "Where did you get this, and what's your name, so I can sign it?"

The girl with the record was quiet, almost slinking back into herself, while her friends squealed and bounced around, showing each other the pictures, coming up to touch his arms again, then backing off. Melinda, for she was telling us that was her real name, stared at him, her eyes wide. "I don't like Melli. But she always calls me that," she said, approaching Tristan very carefully.

Tristan smiled at her. "I'll make sure to write Melinda then. And where did you find this one? Are you sure you want it on this? It's pretty rare." She looked up at him, blinking, like she couldn't really believe that Tristan was speaking to her. She opened her mouth, then closed it again, then shut her eyes. I wondered if she wouldn't be able to get the words out.

"It's my brother's—he's overseas now—I promised him I'd come tonight and get it signed." She sighed. "He played your music for me all the time, and now I love it too. But I don't know when I'm going to see him again..." She broke off, and wrapped her arms around her thin body, her pale hands and fingers covered with rings disappearing into the pockets of a worn blue sweatshirt. Tristan was by her side in a second, pulling her arms out so he could take her hands. He squatted down and she followed him, and they seemed to be away from the others, who were now watching, curious. "What's your brother's name, Melinda?"

"Neil," she replied.

"And where is he?"

"Afghanistan. He's been there a long time. I'm really worried. Mom and Dad said he was right to go back again, but he looked so sad. They told me not to worry so much." It was though the words were tumbling out now that the dam had been broken. Tristan frowned.

"Of course you worry. You care about him, right? Your big brother. Naturally."

She nodded, a couple of tears slipping out and down her face. Tristan smoothed her hair away from her face. He suddenly looked older, and I could imagine him, just like this in years to come, giving out wisdom that he had won hard.

"That's why you're so brave. You're being brave for him. And you know he's proud of you, right?"

She nodded again, watching him with a kind of wonder on her face, her eyes big and sad. Another tear dropped down her cheek. He stood and pulling her up with him, wrapped her in a big hug. I was close enough to hear him whisper in her ear. "You come backstage after the show. Come up to the stage at the end, and I'll send someone out to find you. Ok? Then we can get the whole band to sign stuff for you. AC is there too. Remember him? Ok? Don't forget." He kissed her cheek, and gently took the album from her, signing it to Neil and Melinda.

She took the record from him, and looked up at him, standing up a little taller.

"That's right. Braver than the rest." And he waved at the group, and took my hand. "Sound check. See you ladies later at the show."

We walked off to the elevators, I held on to his hand. "You're amazing, you know that, right? That was incredibly kind of you."

He walked into the elevator and punched at the button for our floor. "No, it wasn't. It was normal. That poor kid. Who knows what could happen." He looked at me. "It was human. That's what I want to avoid. Not being able to do that. I mean, it's crazy that I can, and it's wrong. I'm nothing special, just a person. But I would have liked to have a brother, and if I can do something that means something, makes her life and maybe his a little less painful, then I will." He kissed me. "Five minutes of my charmed life. That's all it took."

He took my hand as the doors opened and we walked down the hall to our door at the end. "But you. Thank you for staying there. For watching." He hesitated. "She wouldn't have done that. Alixe. She thought the fans were an annoyance." His mouth tightened in a hard line for a moment, his eyes focused on a moment that was far away and out of sight. "But you. Are different. And. Should be careful. Now a quick shower, and it's back to work."

He unlocked the door, and started removing his clothes the second the door shut. "I'll only be a few minutes. Will you get the door when the room service comes?" I'd already forgotten that he had ordered a bottle of champagne from the front desk. After that whole scene with the girl. And I watched his long streamlined body cross the carpeted floor over to the green and blue tiles in the bathroom, his legs a series of hard, flexing curves up to his perfect ass, his back a long stretch of tight muscles and smooth skin. As I watched him move, watched him shut the door, and heard the sound of the shower starting, I realized that he never stopped working. That even now he would be thinking of the sound check, and what to ask for, what to tell the band, remembering to get someone to fetch the girl from the front of the stage. And he hardly ever shared what he was organizing in his mind, and he never asked for help. All that thinking went on in that beautiful head. And the kindness he had shown was so simple and straightforward, like he understood. But it was something that she might remember her entire life.

Not for the first time, it struck me how lightly he carried the enormous responsibility that he placed upon himself, to get it all right.

* * *

The sound check went well, and I watched them fool around with a cover of the Blondie song "One Way or Another." I had no idea why they had chosen that one, but it was amazing to see Tristan stop them and explain what he wanted the rhythm to do, actually taking off his guitar to play a couple of bars on the bass, before heading over to the drum kit to show Pete how he wanted more high hat, and a steady beat except for the last two beats of the 8 beat section. I just watched. As usual,

I saw a couple of the roadies keeping an eye on me. When I caught them at it, they just turned away. I had the feeling that even though I here doing a job as well, writing it all up, they still saw me as the girl. They thought I was only there because that's what the band girlfriends did. The girlfriends brought beer, they held things, they found wallets, they watched the men in adoration. I did have the last one down, I thought.

But things had changed, were changing. And even though there were still plenty of women out there ready to be picked up and taken advantage of in exchange for sex with a famous, or even not so famous musician, that really wasn't me. Not really. After all, I'd spent a lot of time, back in the day, trying to convince people that I was actually listening to the music. There were a few times I'd been severely disappointed by someone I'd been able to meet, who wanted one version of woman. On the other hand, it took such incredible devotion and dedication to get anywhere, to put something out there for the critics and fools to jump on, that you had to cut them some slack. Just because someone was an artist didn't make them a saint, sadly. Realistically. But there were a lot of fools out there.

Tristan was very different. I thought of the way he had acted with that shy young woman. His sense of compassion, of connection, was incredibly strong. I watched him as he got the band to go through the last song of the encore one more time before finally calling it quits, and letting everyone relax before the show. He was a perfectionist, but the rare kind who made himself work too, fighting off his own inner brutal criticism to try and reach something transcendent. He was flawed— obviously. When he threw an arm around AC, and squeezed him tight, his easy smile lighting up the stage, I already knew

I'd keep his secrets forever. Tristan was something special. An artist, strong enough to know the depths of his own heart, and brave enough to sink into that darkness. And come back.

Because the tour was off to a good start, and to celebrate the unexpected nomination, Tristan had told James to organize a dinner after the show somewhere different than the hotel dining room, or the inevitable catering in another backstage room. He had been looking forward to coming to Minneapolis, and happy that we were playing First Avenue. And he was doing the DJ set there later tonight as well, which he thought would be fun. It was one of those places in rock history. Tristan thought Prince was a genius, and deeply admired his determination to carry on, to stand up for what he believed in, to follow his own vision even when people and the record company said, no, too much, not right, won't sell. Perseverance. To keep going and follow your own path, despite the odds.

The last time I'd spoken to Dave, I'd mentioned that it might be good to go out to Paisley Park, get some comments from Tristan on the legacy and continuing legend that was Prince. Dave offered to make some calls. But Tristan had shut it down completely, saying Prince probably didn't know who the hell he was, and he wasn't going to make a legend like that think that he was trading on his name to get publicity for the tour. Dave tried to talk to me, told me to mention it again, which I did, because I thought maybe Tristan was being a little too careful. But he was adamant. He wouldn't do it. On his own time, maybe. Prince didn't need his shit. He'd maybe try to meet him at a concert. Someday. And so on.

So here we all were, at the restaurant, instead of getting

a tour of Paisley Park. I watched Tristan chat to everyone, trade jokes with drum and bass, as he had started to call Pete and Jack, tell them not to drink too much, his arm casually thrown around the back of AC's chair. AC always sat next to him now. I was on the other side. Especially after what I'd seen in Chicago, it made sense. They had this indelible bond, and it was clear to anyone with the eyes to see. AC really was a kind of fragile soul, quick to react, his emotions scratched across his face, a second later hidden, his dark stare into the distance, the open wound flushed out later with a bottle of wine. Unfortunately, all the wine seemed to do was sew up the top, and leave a big gaping hole underneath. Tristan seemed to know this, and once he realized that I wasn't going to come between him and his friend, gravitated instinctively towards AC when he was hurting, and finally, as he had done for me, made it clear in a number of ways that AC was under his protection, and to hurt him was to risk seeing Tristan at his worst.

So I wasn't expecting anything but a nice dinner, a couple of glasses of wine and some of Minneapolis' best cooking. Everything seemed calm, Tristan and AC sitting side by side, the focal point despite the round table, me next to Tristan, facing the drummer and bassist, James next to the drummer, and the PR person from the record company who had flown out to see the band, sitting on my right. The food was really good, and everybody seemed relaxed and happy. The show had gone well and the Blondie cover had received a rapturous reception. AC was coming up with a list of potential covers and singing pieces of them in a ridiculous voice. Tristan was cracking up. I was half listening to the PR person, Annie, talk to me about the response rate to the tour blog, and the tracking numbers they were getting from the new followers, and how surprising it was that the numbers held steady across various age groups. I had just been thinking about how things were changing. That considering you now had a few generations of people who had been listening to rock music their entire lives, it wasn't that surprising. It was almost as if the record companies were acting like the parents from 30 or 40 years ago, claiming you'd grow out of it, surprised when you didn't. Maybe. I was just telling her that it might be better if the companies didn't act as though the entire market was born in the 21st century, when we both stopped.

What made us both turn to look at the head of the table? I can only imagine it was Tristan, whose entire posture was that of a wildcat about to pounce on its prey. What the hell had happened? I'd tuned in to their conversation for a minute, when demographics had started to get to me. They'd only been talking about sports, about football—soccer over here. Suddenly I realized exactly what was going on. Tristan and I had been chatting earlier about the news of the 25-year-old soccer player, who had quit his team, and then come out as gay, finally doing an interview about it. Tristan had mentioned that it had taken a lot of courage, but that he wished the guy could have kept playing, even though he understood why he stepped down. I had looked at him, wondering if he was going to say anything else. But Tristan had just muttered that the music business wasn't quite there yet, and hadn't mentioned it again. But it must have come up.

The bassist was looking at Tristan. "Of course he left, man. It's not natural. It's against what the Bible says. No one wants a fucking fag on their team." He laughed. "Looking over your shoulder all the time. If I thought somebody on my team was a gay boy, I'd carry a weapon. Man's got to defend himself."

Tristan looked stunned, then furious. "The Bible? Really? That's your reason?" He put his fork down, very carefully. "So you think you don't know any gay people?"

"If I do, they know better than to get to know me. Otherwise maybe I'd have to persuade them they need to stop their sick behavior." He took a swig of beer. "My friends and I used to be very persuasive back in high school. No limp wrists in our town."

I looked at my half-finished dinner. A skin was forming on the cooling sauce. It all suddenly looked glazed, the wrong colors, the meat like a bloody wound. I look a sip of water and prayed not to be sick. I glanced at AC. He was sitting there, gripping his wine glass.

Tristan looked at his hands. "So you like beating up gay men. Or maybe just anyone who's not like you." He lifted his head up, and his eyes were black. "Why don't you start with me then?"

There was nothing I could do but watch what was about to go down. Annie, next to me, whispered in my ear, "What? What's going to happen?" I waved at her to be silent. She carried on. "He can't do this. Not here. I don't know who's out there. I'm going to run damage control. Text me what's happening. I'm getting the car. I'll tell you when it's safe to leave." And she jumped up from the table. Tristan and the bassist were still staring each other down.

"Look man, I don't want to fight you. I don't like being around gays. That's all."

"Say it again," Tristan said slowly.

The bassist shrugged. "Tristan, dude, I didn't mean anything by it. Gay people do what they want. Just not around me. If I don't want Adam Lambert sleeping in the bunk next to mine, it's my business."

Tristan laughed. I knew that laugh. I winced.

"Except this is my tour. So everything is my business."

"It's wrong, man, that's it. Anyone will say the same thing."

Tristan relaxed his posture slightly. Jack thought that meant he was off the hook. I knew it meant he'd made his mind up. He crossed his arms. "So that's what made you say if someone gay was on your team you'd carry a weapon?"

I couldn't even look at AC.

My phone buzzed and Tristan called over to James at the same time. "James—take care of the bill, please?" He stood up, and shook out his arms, and put on his leather jacket. It looked like he was suiting up for battle.

Tristan walked over to the bassist, and stood in front of him. It forced Jack to tilt his head right up to see him. Then he said, "This is the way it is." The bassist raised his arm and started to get up, but Tristan stopped him with a look. "I suggest you think of your future. I'm happy to say you left for a better offer. Provided you play the next four nights and keep your fucking stupid ass mouth shut. Or not. Leave now. Right now. Say what you like. Publicity won't worry me."

I looked down at my phone. The text from Annie said she had a car waiting outside the kitchen. Tristan looked over at me, and I mouthed "kitchen" at him. He waited for me to get up, nodding to the drummer, who was still sitting there, slightly open-mouthed. He started to head towards the back of the restaurant, clearly thinking that we were following. But

AC was frozen in his seat. I came up behind him, and rested my hand on his shoulder, bending down to whisper in his ear. "Come on my friend, I've got a bottle of Barolo that needs an opinion."

And as he stood slowly, I put my arm around him, and we walked tentatively towards Tristan, whose tall frame was nearly to the doors. Then Tristan turned around, checking we were behind him, and caught sight of me, supporting AC, who was clearly upset, though doing his best to hide it. Those eyes took in the whole picture, my arm around him, his arm slung over my shoulder, his pale face. His eyes grew dark, and his hands balled up into fists.

AC noticed as well and roused himself from where he had been leaning on my shoulder. "Dude. Tristan. Forget it. He's an asshole. I just…" He squeezed my hand, and went over to where Tristan was holding open the door to the kitchen, his shoulders set against an invisible army. "Leave it mate. He's just ignorant. And Tristan—you know this isn't just about me." Tristan stood there, rigid, as the clatter of pots and pans and tickets being called out went on behind us. AC went up to him and forced him to look him in the eyes. "Tristan. You've got my back. I know that. I wouldn't be here except for that. But I've got yours as well. So forget it." He repeated it more forcefully. "Forget it. Let's get the fuck out of here. We've got a tour to finish and we're bigger than this."

Tristan nodded silently, and turned to walk through the kitchen. We followed him, a small line snaking over the big red floor tiles, skirting the line chefs who were getting meals out while glancing around at us, clearly wondering what the hell we were doing back there, so close to boiling pots and flaming pans. It smelled good, but I had no appetite. I was drained by the whole thing, the fight and the tour, and I just wanted to get the hell out of there. We finally reached the doors to the outside, and walked past the dumpster. Annie was there waiting. She looked grim, and it was strange to see one of the support team at the wheel of a car, instead of the usual drivers. She must have jumped in her rental car and come right over. The engine was idling, and the bitter smell of car exhaust made me feel sick again for a moment. She gave a brief wave when she saw us. The locks popped up on the door a moment later, and AC got in, followed by me, then Tristan, who slammed the door with a fury.

"Is everything ok, Annie? Any press downwind?"

She shook her head. "No, checked it out, made it look like we had an announcement. Told them you'd be available tonight after the DJ set, answer a few questions. Threw the dog a bone. Don't think our boy will go to the press. Nothing happened, right?"

Tristan was silent. AC had his eyes closed.

Annie asked again, but this time her voice had gone up an octave. "Nothing happened, right?

Tristan's voice was his usual lazy drawl when he was holding back some huge emotion. "Depends what you mean by nothing, Annie."

We were waiting at a light, the steady click of the indicator expanding the silence. The light changed, and we turned across the traffic. I wished we could just drive away and disappear. Annie finally spoke. "Tristan. Throw me a bone. Not that kind. If I've got to get on the phone to the label, calm them down, just tell me what you did. I can't do damage control if I get the story last."

Tristan laughed. "You mean, did I come out? Or did I punch someone? Was there blood? No, no, and not yet in no particular order to all of the above, Annie." He ran his hand through his hair, and flicked an invisible speck off his red jeans. "All publicity is good. You, of all people, should know that."

Now it was her turn to be silent.

We got out of the car in front of the hotel. Annie handed the keys to the valet and said she'd be back in an hour, and we headed inside. AC and Tristan walked through the lobby, looking neither to the left or right, while Annie glanced around, glaring at anyone who looked like they were heading in our direction. We made it to the bank of elevators, and she jabbed at the button. "Listen, Tristan. Be careful out there. There are people following your every move." AC looked pale.

He came and stood very close to her. "Two answers to that. That's nothing new. And I'm not changing my life."

Annie turned to me. "Please make him understand. And be visible. Talk about the female fans. Romance. Music. Keep posting, but try to have a delay of a day or two from where you are."

I looked at her. "I usually do anyway. Do you really think there is something to worry about? And what?"

Annie shrugged. "Sex, drugs, and rock and roll. The usual. But he just had a public fight about gay rights. We don't know how many people have something on their cell phone, but we've got to figure at least one does. And you're about to head through the Midwest, down into the South. Most of what people do still has a statute on the books somewhere against it. You've read the stories. Tour buses being boarded. Hell, even

Willie Nelson gets it, and you guys don't have anywhere near as much country cred. Just keep it clean."

I really did roll my eyes then, and grabbed Tristan's hand. "No sodomy, no drugs. Got it."

Tristan squeezed my hand. "Annie, thanks. Let me know if you hear anything, and send me the interview questions for the Kansas City radio station. Thanks again, see you later. Text me if I'm not where I should be for the press."

Tristan, AC, and I got in the elevator, and as the door shut, AC started talking nervously. "Tris, look. This is nice, the being on tour thing. I love playing with you, you know that." The elevator stopped at the gym level, and two women in bathrobes started to get on.

I held up my hand. "Sorry, we've got a sick guest here. Please take the next one." And I pressed the close door button as they stood there, open-mouthed.

Tristan was leaning against the back wall of the elevator. "Nicely done, Lily. Think I'll hire you as the tour manager. Couldn't be any worse." He looked stricken. "That's not what I meant. You know. No. Fuck this. AC. You're not leaving the tour. You won't break my stride, career, or whatever else you're thinking. Do what you need to. I'm there. But leaving isn't an option." He had a funny look on his face. "Didn't you just tell me that this wasn't just about you?"

AC glanced at me. "Did I?" He gave a weak smile. "Fine, I'll stay. But I hope you're still saying that when you can only play state fairs and two-bit casinos."

"Shut up. We'll all go live in Berlin. I'll sing cabaret. You can dance. Lily will tell fortunes, there will be absinthe and opium and the nights will be long and sweet." He laughed as the door opened. "In fact, let's fuck up the whole thing. That sounds fairly tempting."

AC did smile then, and he turned to go down the hall to his room. Tristan pulled at him. "No. Don't trust you. You stay with us. Quick clean up, then we can face the music. Literally."

We got ourselves ready, and headed back out. I was a little nervous about the whole thing, but was trying to put on a brave face for Tristan's sake. AC just looked numb. I didn't hold out much hope for tonight. It was supposed to be a fun idea, Tristan playing some of his favorite music. Now everyone was too distracted, too tired. But he was used to this, putting it all to one side to be in the spotlight. Me, not so much.

The doorman got us a cab, and the driver took us to the side entrance for the venue without a word, thankfully. Not a fan. Just a normal person. Tristan tried the door and found it locked. He banged on the door in annoyance, and when no one came after a minute, he pulled his cell phone out of his pocket, and pressed the speed dial. "And where is James in all this mess? Seriously, I've got to sort this shit out," he said, more to himself than to me.

Another minute passed, and the door was opened by a chastened looking venue employee. James was a foot behind, pretending he was annoyed. Tristan gave him a look. "Where the fuck is the VIP room here? Can we go there? Now? Thank you very much." James looked like thunder, but Tristan ignored him.

AC slipped behind me. "You've got to love him when he's like this." He pulled me back slightly so we were a few steps behind. "In this game, Lily, someone's got to play the diva. Better that it's him than anyone else."

The VIP room had the catering, the red velvet sofas, the local rich kids. But the music sounded tinny, and the paper tablecloths were already ripped and soggy from melting ice. People were drinking, talking in their groups. They'd all looked up when Tristan came in, but they were playing it cool. I had already spotted the two women who would definitely be coming over at some point, trying to get Tristan talking. Tristan gave a quick look around, then whispered in my ear that he was going to check out where he'd be doing the music, and left. On the other side of the room the drummer was sitting by himself, a bottle of beer and a shot in front of him. The bass player was there too, but sitting with James, who I imagined was trying to get him to stay. I looked away, and went and asked for a decent cold beer. Clutching it, I sat down on one of the sofas, under the ducts for the ventilation system. It hit up against what looked like a drain pipe and there was a patch of grime where the two connected. But it was dark, no one cared. I didn't even notice I was holding the bottle of beer against my head, until I felt a hand on my shoulder. It was AC.

"Hey," I said, and we clinked bottles. "Are you ok?" I gave him a little one-armed hug, which he didn't return.

He shook his head. "Yeah, I'm all right. I'm…it was just a shock, that's all. I don't ever feel…I should be used to it. We don't really have to talk about it, yeah? But I'm fine. What about you? Are you ok?"

He was giving off a weird vibe. I didn't like it. But there wasn't a lot I could do. "I'm ok. Felt a bit sick before." I took a couple of deep breaths. "We're out of here tomorrow, thank fuck."

AC lent over. "Sick? Why?" His face was very tense.

"What he said. It's disgusting. I mean. That there are people who are so ignorant. Cruel. Prejudiced. Still. And that he could be so fucking clueless about Tristan." Shit. I looked at my beer, then back up at AC.

AC raised an eyebrow. "Yeah, not realizing how Tristan would feel on that issue. When he's so…"

I looked at him. "Open." I tried again. "Well. On stage." I drank more beer. "Performing."

AC gave me a look. "Performing. Exactly. Playing to the crowd. Being outrageous."

This was not going the way I had thought it might. Of course AC would never say anything. Not without Tristan on board. The loyalty between them ran deep. Everything I was saying sounded wrong anyway.

"I wish we were going now. I feel like every place we stay I want to leave."

He grimaced. "Yeah—and we're on the bus with bass boy."

I finished the beer. The end always sucked. I needed a shot. And another beer. Maybe they'd cancel each other out. The bus. The fucking bus and all of us on it. I'd forgotten all about that in the interim luxury of hotel life and separate rooms. Well, that wasn't going to work. "Look, AC, I know Tristan won't care. He can get them to do this. We need another bus. I'm going to go talk to him. Hang on." AC looked startled, but I mouthed at him "be right back." Getting up, I went and dropped my empty bottle off at the bar, and picked up two more. I looked down at the main room. Tristan was over on the other side, chatting to the guy by the decks. They were nearly ready to start, so I didn't have a lot of time. I quickly found the exit to where the regular people were, and went down the stairs to the main floor. There was a lot more air down here. Sliding in between the crush of people, I made my way through the crowd over to the stage. One of the bouncers approached me, but I flashed him the laminate, and waved over at Tristan. He waved back, and I hopped up onto the raised area where the computers were, and walked over to him.

His smile was quick and brilliant, and just as quickly hidden. He glanced around, like he was looking for someone, but turned back to me when he didn't see anyone. "What's up, Lily?"

I handed him one of the bottles. "Brought you a beer. AC's upstairs. He knows I'm down here. I'll go get him for the set, not to worry. But can I talk to you for a minute?"

"Yes, of course. Yeah." He excused himself and we went out to the little back hall at the side of the mini stage. "What's up?"

I didn't want to waste time. "Look, can the tour afford another bus?" He looked surprised, but remained quiet. "AC really doesn't want to sleep in the same space as Jack." Tristan raised his hands to stop me, but I didn't want to be interrupted. "He won't tell you. He doesn't want to be a burden, believe me. But he is more than a little unnerved by what was said."

Tristan looked serious. "I'll ask James. It's a little last minute, but we might be able to get one to meet us tomorrow. Or a driver and car until they sort it. It's only another week, not even." He was thinking out loud. "People will party tonight while they are doing the load out. Then either crash right away, or hang out. AC can come sleep in our room. Or not sleep. Watch some movies or something. An all-nighter.

Like the old days. Yes." He looked happier. "A car at least. Maybe they have a bus they need to move. Nothing fancy."

We stood there for a minute, and I was turning to go, when he reached out to stop me. Suddenly I was wrapped in his arms, pressed against his chest, his lips on my forehead. He held me like that for a moment, before his hands dropped to my hips, and he made me face him. "You know, Lily, you're an incredible woman. Person. I was wondering if you were going to be jealous, possessive. Most people are. But you're a fighter. And loyal. To my friends too. I like that." He kissed me. "Lovers, and mates." He held me to him again, and whispered in my hair. "I'm fucking lucky, is what I am. And you... are very special."

chapter thirteen

Minneapolis to Kansas City

We were all sitting in the new bus—AC, Tristan, and I, head-ing to Kansas City. After the DJ gig in Minneapolis, the three of us went back to the hotel in a cab. We didn't even say good-bye. James was given the task of telling them we'd see them in Missouri. I had glanced at the drummer's face as we left the club. Judging by his expression, I think he had wanted to say something to Tristan. The bassist, Jack, just looked angry. There had been an unspoken understanding that it would be a good idea to stop socializing with both of them, the bassist and the drummer, despite only one of them being at fault, and only see them at sound checks and the actual gigs. We were closing ranks. It made sense, mostly. As we were all yoked together for a few more days, no one wanted a repeat incident. Looking at Tristan, I didn't think a round two would end as peacefully, despite his calm reassurances.

Tristan's long legs were stretched out, tightly encased in his usual black jeans, his booted feet crossed on the table. The wide screen was playing some car chase movie that he wasn't watch-ing. AC was sitting at the kitchen table, back leaning against the wall, his legs bent, feet on the bench, looking at his laptop. I was reading a book I'd picked up in the last truck stop we'd been through—nothing spectacular, but I was vaguely curious to see how the spy was going to escape his double life. I laughed to myself—life and art mixing yet again. Playing the public role, getting used to the photographers rushing us as we went in and out of hotels, the obligatory night club visits, posing against the backdrop of advertisements, being sure not to block any of the logos, while we attempted to look at once mysterious and approachable. The zeitgeist, the tone of the age. Anyone could reach out to us, ask for an autograph, send a tweet—as long as it didn't say anything, and they kept their distance. As much as Tristan wanted the connection with the fans, and with everyone on the tour, it was time to put up some walls.

Besides, the electronically fabricated closeness was only an illusion. There was some connection to reality, like the tweets that mentioned fellow musicians, or artists whose work we wanted to bring some attention to. We. Actually, at Tristan's suggestion, I had taken over doing most of the tweets. James was delighted to not be burdened with any more work, as sending out press kits to radio stations and checking on us seemed to exhaust him. For my part, I was happy that he had one less instant input to the media circus that was keeping an eye on us. Even so, when we switched from one bus with all of us crammed in, to one for the band, and one for the three of us, someone had leaked the arrangements to the gossip columns. Dave had texted me as I was getting on the new bus. I had a feeling I knew who the leaker was, but then again I now had a choice of enemies to pick from. Why and who was his final question by text. Complicated and not sure yet was my response. Dave hadn't replied, but that didn't mean he wasn't doing some research.

Then Annie had called us frantically from Chicago, and said she was flying into Kansas City to manage the PR for the rest of the mini tour. She suggested we abandon the bus, and fly to Houston from Oklahoma City, then have a driver take us to Dallas, and on to the last date in Austin. We'd kicked that idea around, and finally agreed. That left us with only two more nights on the bus. I wasn't sure I'd miss it. I didn't have the same romantic feeling about life on the road that I'd started out with. And I missed Hank. AC looked anxious, and I wondered if I had been the only one this morning who had noticed that he and Tristan were barely touching, saying "excuse me" if they needed to go anywhere near each other. Considering they had been falling all over each other every time one of them made a joke, or imitated the front desk reception, who seemed to have permanently established themselves as Tristan's least favorite people, the sudden distance and silence felt ominous.

If the traffic was ok, we were due to arrive just before 4. Enough time to do the sound check, then get some air, or come back to the bus. That left three hours to go. I turned a page, then turned it back again. And another. I looked at the words in front of me. I hadn't really been reading, just looking at the type, thinking. Sighing, I started again at the last place I could remember. The book was fine. I wasn't. The tension was making the air thick with unspoken feelings, misery. I gave up on the book, and put it down, breaking the spine with a low crack. Tristan winced. I shrugged an apology. "Anyone want tea?" There was silence. I tried again. "Beer?"

AC threw me a wan smile. "Yeah, I will, Lily. Thank you." He waved away a glass. "No, bottle is fine." I looked over towards the driver, who I noticed was watching us in the mirror. I wished Hank was there. I realized I had come to rely on the moments of weird camaraderie we had developed, watching the road together. I had opened the beer when I remembered that technically, we weren't supposed to drink while the bus was in motion. Usually no one cared. The driver gave us another glance in the mirror, then turned back to the road. Last minute bus and driver. He'd probably been told we were all junkies. Maybe Annie was right after all.

I placed a bottle down in front of AC, then walked over to Tristan and handed him one. He nodded thank you, a frown creasing a line between his brows. AC had turned back to his computer. I went and got one for myself. This was clearly one of those times when tea wasn't going to cut it. We all sat there, nursing our beers. I looked out the window towards the road. Miles and miles of highway, thousands of cars headed somewhere, for something. The clouds moved by. The sky here was bigger, the land flatter. I felt like I could watch a cloud start from one end of the horizon and move to the other. Weather was coming in, and a strong gust pushed at the bus. It seemed like it wouldn't take much to flip us over if there was a storm. Not out here. And almost on cue, the sky began to get darker, and the first raindrops started hitting the windscreen. All of the headlights came on, and the traffic slowed down. I laughed. Too perfect. A dark day to match a dark mood. Both Tristan and AC looked at me, then returned to what they were doing, or what they weren't doing.

Tristan's phone buzzed, and we all jumped. He looked

at it angrily for a moment, then picked it up. "Yeah, hello." There was silence. "Yeah, hey Annie. What's up?" He listened intently. "I don't really think…" He waited. "Yes, record company protecting their investment. That's what they do." His tone changed. "Annie. Listen. Calm down. You haven't been involved in a bit of gossip, but trust me, love, I have. Overreacting just tells them they're right." He was nodding his head. "More sympathy towards the drugs. Yeah, probably true. Shall I go OD somewhere? I'm sure that can be arranged. Change the story." Tristan looked over at us, shaking his head. "Annie. I'm kidding. Have you got any Xanax? It's all going to be fine."

He listened again. "Do I care? No, not really. I care about the music. I care about what people actually think and do in their lives apart from the manufactured truths that they get throttled with from day to day." Tristan was pinching the bridge of his nose as he listened. "Annie. Fine. I will play their game. For now. Mostly because I don't have a better playbook at the moment, and there's more gigs to get through. Then New York. Then L.A." He listened again, and drained his beer. I went to get another one, and Tristan nodded at me gratefully. "I may have a different idea then. But for now, that's fine."

He took a big swig of beer, and nearly spat it out again with a noise that was a cross between a laugh and a shout. AC was watching him carefully. "Is she what? Is Lily my beard? Are you fucking kidding me? Actually, yes, but she's working on turning me." More silence. "No, I won't say that tomorrow. Really, Annie, you're a nice person, I'm sure, but come on." He stood up, holding his beer. For him, the conversation was clearly over. "Text me the details. No, don't text James. He's got a lot going on. Yeah. Right. Tomorrow. See you there then." Tristan tapped the screen, and threw the phone onto the sofa, and disappeared into the back.

I started to go after him, but AC called me back. "Don't, Lily. I mean, do what you want, but I think he's got to process all this."

I came over and sat down at the table, across from him. "Not sure how you process insanity. Yes. You're probably right. I mean. You know him. Well. I do too, but…" I stopped. "Fuck, AC, what's going to happen? And why is this so bad? Am I missing something here?" I tried not to think of what I knew.

AC shot me a quizzical look, then his face softened. "Tristan and I…have a lot of history. You know that. You know the whole story of what happened with him and his ex-wife, Alixe. Paul is under her spell completely. I'm sure they wouldn't mind seeing all this solo success go adrift. And they might not be the only ones. And…," AC looked at his beer, then back up at me, "I'm here. They're not. Tristan probably should have let James go, but he thought that might make it worse. Well, it is worse." He looked down at the table.

"But damage control? It was just an argument. Not even any punches thrown. So what if the guy is a bigoted asshole. At least bassists aren't as hard to find as drummers," I joked lamely.

AC grimaced. "Yeah, true. But…" He stopped. "It's not my…" He paused again. "Look, Lily. You're a smart woman. You can figure this out. Count on your fingers. See how far you get. How many gay or bisexual rock stars are there?

Let's stick to men for the time being. Freddie Mercury, right. There's one. He's probably the most famous. Did you know that Queen initially had a lot of success in this country but no one knew what they looked like." He thought for a minute. "Still. Freddie. Who else? The Eighties were good—Frankie Goes to Hollywood, George Michael. Still, not really rock, right? Not really alternative. Ok, the Nineties, you had Kurt Cobain saying, what was it, 'I am not gay, although I wish I were, just to piss off homophobes.' Nice. Of course he said he wasn't gay, and then he shot himself, so. Bowie. Well, he was a pioneer. Iggy Pop. Weren't they lovers? But wasn't Bowie's biggest success in this country after all that? We've got the pioneers. The people who broke the rules. The artists. Lou Reed. Bowie. Of course, they did wind up partnered with a woman, but they didn't lie about who they were and what they did. That was the 70s. I don't know, there must be more, right? But where are they? Not a lot. A little like sports, you've got to figure the stats alone show somebody's not telling the whole truth." He drank some more beer, and began tapping his fingers on the table. "Tristan. Is a rulebreaker. But he'd also like a career. And he's pissed as hell for being put in a position where he's got to…"

I finished his sentence for him. "Lie, or tell the truth?"

AC met my eyes. "That's about the size of it."

I started to say something and thought better of it. "Beer?" He nodded, and I pulled open the fridge and took out two more. Another hour to Kansas City. I hoped there was something stronger backstage. I flipped open the tops, and came back to sit down. I didn't want to ask, but I could feel the question banging around my head. Dave's face came to mind, looking at me regretfully. Another image came to mind, something I'd promised myself I wouldn't think about. Fuck. Why couldn't I learn to keep my mouth shut? "AC?"

"Yes, Lily."

"You care about Tristan, don't you?"

He shrugged. "I always have done. We started in this game together. It's been a long haul, through a lot of craziness. Sure."

I didn't push it. The other question was still pushing at me, though. I took a sip of beer to try and make it go away. It wasn't going. "AC."

He smiled, amused. "Yes, Lily."

"This is going to sound really stupid."

"That's ok, Lily. If we were drinking Barolo, at least our honesty would seem slightly more noble. But we're on a bus with beer. Hit me up."

I took a deep breath. "This would all be a lot easier if I just knew."

"Knew what exactly, Lily?" AC looked very tense.

"I...what am...AC...be truthful. What am I to him? Am I just a beard? Does everyone know but me?"

AC was smiling again. He chuckled into his beer. "Beard. I can't believe you'd even ask that."

"But is it true?"

"No," said AC and his one word was echoed by the man who was suddenly at my side.

I looked up at Tristan.

"Slide over, share your beer, you must be drunk to ask that. Beard. No. Ok? Believe me. Believe AC. Many things you are to me. Beard, not one of them." He took a swig and emptied the bottle. "Besides. I'm good, but not that good."

AC laughed. "Money. You could always fake it for money. Nothing like cash to guarantee erections."

Tristan laughed, and it was though all the pressure had been let out of the room slowly, and things didn't seem quite so breakable. AC smiled at us. "You bastard," Tristan said. "Revealing my money fetish like that."

AC lifted his bottle. "What any true friend would do."

We all sat there for a few minutes in silence, before Tristan spoke up. "So. Might as well get this out of the way. Annie-who-needs-Xanax-badly has set up a radio interview for us tomorrow morning. 100.5. The Rage." He drew it out. "The home of alternative in these parts, apparently. And we are all to go on. Lily will play beard, I mean girlfriend, and be revoltingly feminine." He turned to me. "Believe it or not, I think Annie will be turning up tomorrow with appropriate record company approved apparel. You will giggle and say you've never met anyone like me, and no, we haven't discussed marriage...yet. AC and I will punch each other, talk about beer," here he raised his bottle, "and AC will mention the model he is looking forward to meeting up with again in L.A. next week."

AC laughed. "Wow. Really? Are you going to do it?"

Tristan's expression darkened. "We. We are going to do it, because reacting is never a good stance." He put his arm around me. "And it protects both of you. From all this crap. And it's true." He tried to smile. "Well, not the model. You can't pull a model for shit."

AC put on a hurt face, then laughed. "What do you mean? That last model I slept with was incredibly..."

Tristan interrupted. "Thin?"

AC laughed. "Yeah. No, Tris, she was a nice girl." He

looked at us. "Just not for me." He got up and headed towards the bathroom, then turned around. "Hey, great idea. Call Trevor. He's got books of models. Get him to line up a few for L.A. Three should do it. Because all real men can get it up three times a night." He walked off singing the KC and the Sunshine Band song, "That's the way, uh huh uh huh, I like it, uh huh, uh huh." His laughter trailed back, then the door opening and closing brought it to an end.

I looked at Tristan. "Really? We're going to do this?" I wanted to ask him a million questions. Tell him I knew why we were doing it. But I sat there, and waited for his answer to a question I hadn't needed to ask.

His eyes were far away. "I don't like it either. But until I think of another way to handle it, we've got five days to get through." He kissed my cheek. "It's not a lie. We are together, and I do care about you. Obviously. More than you realize. It's just no one else's business. But they want happy heterosexuality, I can do that. Rather just do sexuality, but we're halfway there."

* * *

The concert was good, not great, and the bassist seemed to be playing either to the crowd or to the drummer. There was no interaction between him and Tristan and AC. I couldn't imagine why someone would throw away a chance like this over some stupid prejudice, but then again, people did a lot of things I didn't understand. I was happy to get back to the hotel room we'd booked at the last minute, and try to have some quiet time. AC had retreated to his room, begging off the offer of watching some movie. He hugged us both, and winked at me. But he looked exhausted. Tristan headed to the shower as soon as we came in, and I ordered some room service. When the bell rang, I signed for it at the door, and let them push it over the threshold, before I said I'd take care of the rest. The server protested, but I thanked them, pulled out another bill that I didn't even look at, and pressed it into his hand. I shut and locked the door, and pushed the table to one side.

"Table or bed?" I said to Tristan, as he emerged from the shower, dripping wet, a towel slung low around his hips.

"Bed, I think. What have we got?"

"Hamburgers. They look ok."

"After the shower, I barely feel hungry. Too tired." Tristan pulled on a pair of running shorts, and stood there, drying his hair with the towel.

His face was drawn. He looked almost ill, the circles under his eyes becoming more pronounced. I suddenly felt very worried. It'd been stupid to think all this was going to just be a blip on the radar. "Do you want a drink? Try and eat something, maybe."

"Yeah, let me have a look. Maybe a glass of wine or something." He came over to the table, and picked up one of the burgers. "Looks all right." He took a bite, and walked over to the window, chewing. "Nice view," he gave a half laugh. He looked at the burger.

I took a bite of mine. It was ok. Hotel food. "It's all right."

"Yeah, it's ok." Tristan came back over, and put the burger down on the plate, and picked up a chip and contemplated it thoughtfully before putting it in his mouth. He crinkled up his face. "Greasy." He wiped his hands carefully on the napkin. "Maybe a glass of wine. I think I'm too worn out for this." He looked around the room. "Smaller than usual, isn't it?"

I looked at the pale green walls, the prints in their gold frames. It was a box. All I could see were the corners. I breathed in. It suddenly felt more cramped than the bus had. "It's not brilliant, is it?" I didn't want him to see my growing sense of panic, but maybe if we talked a little, lay down. "Tristan?"

But he was heading back to the bathroom. "Be right back. I feel like complete shit, Lily." He shut the door and the shower went on. It wasn't enough to hide the sounds of someone being sick.

I sat down on the bed and waited. It wasn't the food— we'd barely eaten. It was exhaustion. Stress. And nowhere to go with it. The noises finally stopped, and the shower ran a while. Then Tristan emerged, drying his hair with a towel, his skin paler than I'd ever seen it.

"Lily. Are you ok?" It seemed a funny question coming from someone who was obviously ill.

"Yes. Tristan. Can I do something?" I tried to ignore the prickles under my skin. I felt light-headed. What the fuck were we going to do?

"No, it's ok. Look, I'm going to get a sleeping pill from AC. He's always got something." Tristan was putting on a pair of jeans as he said it. "Do you want one?"

"Sure." I was about to ask if I could come too. I clamped it down. I didn't think this was just about the pills.

Tristan paused at the door, bare chested, his jeans caught up at the top of his ankle boots. "I won't be long. I want to make sure he's ok."

"Sure." There wasn't a lot to say. He gave a weak smile and the door closed behind him.

I looked around the room. Then I walked over to the desk, and flipped through the pads, trying out the pen on a couple of sheets. I put the pen back in the drawer, and went back to the table, covering it all with the napkins. There was nothing wrong with the food, but the smell of greasy burgers and fries was making it worse. I opened the door and looked up and down the halls. Nothing. I pushed the table out, wincing at the noise of plates and cutlery crashing together as the table went over the threshold.

I stood out in the hall. This hotel had red pink carpet with a small repeated white diamond shape. The line of sconces lighting the hall repeated, separated by a print, and a door, at neat, regular intervals. The ceiling felt like it was getting lower, and the hall longer the more I looked, like some kind of optical illusion. There was no sound. Even the elevators were still. I shut the door. Back inside, I gave the room another once over. All normal. Green. Small. I went into the bathroom and flushed the toilet and washed my face and hands. I avoided the mirror. Then I went straight to the minibar, pulled out a beer and two small bottles of bourbon, and arranged them neatly on the table in front of the sofa. The remote finally switched on, and I turned down the volume on the Weather Channel, as I watched the outlines of states with pictures and numbers changing in front of them, and men in raincoats standing by highways. I unscrewed the cap on the first little bottle, feeling reassured that there were others in the minibar. Two swallows emptied it, and I opened the beer. And bottle in hand, watching the local forecast, accurate and dependable, I settled in to wait.

chapter fourteen

Kansas City to Oklahoma City

I hadn't waited that long. A couple of hours later, around 2, Tristan had rolled in, looking slightly less sick, but no less pale. He raised one eyebrow when he saw me on the sofa, but hadn't said anything, just beckoned me over. I'd switched off the TV and walked over to him. He smelled faintly of cigarettes and the outside and something else I couldn't quite place but that seemed familiar. He wrapped me in his arms, and we just stood like that. Eyes wide open, but mouths shut, I thought. I had a feeling that if I could have seen his face he would be staring at the wall, the same way I was. He finally released me, and started removing my clothes, and his, carefully, as though he were putting a lot of thought into it. When we were both naked, he looked at me, and holding out his hand, he helped me get into bed. We arranged ourselves under the covers, his arm around me. With his free hand, he switched off the light, as we settled in.

Then we both started talking at the same time. Tristan gave a small laugh. "You first," he said.

"How's AC? Is he ok?" It seemed a safe question.

"Yeah, he's all right. We'll get past this." He ran his hand through his air. "We had some decisions to make. With the radio show tomorrow as well." He held me closer. "You're ok. Right?"

I nodded.

"Fuck, I forgot about the sleeping pill. Too busy doing real drugs. At least I don't feel sick anymore." Tristan gave a low laugh. "Now I just can't sleep."

I stared at the ceiling. "Are you sure you're all right?"

Tristan shook his head. "Don't worry about me. You shouldn't drink so much."

"Maybe I should have a taste of what you and AC are doing."

Tristan was quiet for a moment, then rolled me on top of him. In the gloom of the darkened room, his eyes were remarkably bright. He studied me for a minute. Then he kissed me, a short soft kiss, his mouth fitting to mine comfortably. I felt some of the tension release, and I sank against him, my head on his chest. He stroked my hair. "You're probably right, at that. Let's see what we can do."

And we had stayed like that, his hand idly smoothing over my hair, until I had drifted off to sleep, anyway.

* * *

The interview the next day was embarrassing. The host of the show started off on the right foot by calling the album

"Remembering the Past," then asking if Tristan was worried that his style of music wasn't as popular as the stuff in the charts like Rhianna. Tristan tried his best to be diplomatic, and talked about the fans worldwide, and the loyalty that they'd shown after Devised split up. But the host just carried on. I had the impression that he was hoping for a blowup. Tristan became increasingly sarcastic.

The radio host played the single from the record then announced proudly that he actually had set up a quiz for the guys on football. American football. Tristan smiled politely. "I never watch it," he said, "but you must be a big fan. Is something important happening?" The questions were all about options, and trades, and trophies. We all made terrible guesses. AC kept giving him the names of basketball players. Every time the host said "But that's basketball," AC would answer, "Really?" I tried to answer a few questions as well, but the radio guy made sure to talk right over me after the first few words.

But I had my own segment. The host had turned to me and said, "So let's meet Lily. We don't want to leave out the girlfriend. Look what Yoko did." He turned to me. "Do you feel you're like Yoko, a difficult woman?"

I stared at him. "She's an artist. Difficult to understand maybe, for some people. If that's what you meant, then yes."

The guy gave a big guffaw. "Tristan, you've got your hands full there." Then he asked where I liked to shop.

"Places where things are for sale, generally," I responded. Tristan rolled his eyes. The next question was which celebrity I'd go out with if I could. "You, of course," I said, "But only if we can shop together. I really want to get you some new clothes." AC started laughing so hard they cut to an advertisement.

But Tristan was trying his best to keep it together. After the ad ended, he stepped in right away and mentioned the concert the night before and how great the fans had been, before repeating the correct name of the album. The guy started in again with another inane question and Tristan stopped him. "Sorry, mate. I'm not finished yet," he said in that slow way he had when he was getting annoyed. Then he went on to give the upcoming dates, the name of the album, and nomination for the awards show. "I didn't know you were nominated," exclaimed the host. Tristan smirked. "That's all right—you didn't even know the name of the album when we started." But Tristan thanked him at the end, a total professional, and signed autographs for some of the staff, and he and AC signed stuff for the little group of fans that were waiting outside the radio station.

But seeing as I'd received a text from Dave that morning asking if I was all right, before he asked for an update on the status of the project, I was perfectly aware how fast the gossip had traveled. Now it was out there, I was the official girlfriend. Tristan had even managed to get in the plug for our relationship where he had explained that now that we were a couple, it wasn't really fair to the band to put up with our lovesick antics. Tristan had been grinning, his dark shades giving him a forbidding aura, as he leaned over and kissed me, holding up the microphone for the sound effects, while I giggled nervously. But when we got in the car, Tristan turned to me. "You know that guy was trying to catch us out, don't you? Sometimes it's better to just answer the questions." He saw my face. "Not that you weren't right to be annoyed. The guy was an annoying prick."

I was about to answer, say I'd never asked for this. I could feel all the repressed emotion coming to the surface. All the things I hadn't said. "Tristan, not really fair on your side. You drag me into this, to play a part. I don't see…"

AC interrupted. "You can't give her a hard time for standing up for herself, Tris. You got in a few of your own digs. And you're used to this shit." AC gave me a hug. "Funniest fucking thing ever. Stupid asshole. Football or shopping. For fuck's sake."

Tristan stared at both of us, frowning. Then he closed his eyes and shook his head. "This is what I get. Well deserved." He ran his fingers through his hair. "Fuck, I'm sorry. I'm tired, I haven't really eaten in 24 hours…" he glanced over at AC.

AC laughed. "I hear nothing tastes as good as…," he smirked.

"Skinny feels," I finished for him.

"That too." AC winked at me.

Tristan was trying not to laugh. "Bloody hell. You two. Let's get the fuck out of here."

chapter fifteen

Oklahoma City

Six long hours later, we had arrived in Oklahoma City. We were still in the middle of nowhere, or it felt like it, but it seemed like we were closer to something. It was a day off in the middle, which had seemed like a waste, but now that it was here, was the best idea ever. We'd gone for a walk, got followed, jumped in a cab, and gone back to the hotel. Tristan had ordered pizza, AC had come over, we'd watched two terrible movies on Pay-Per-View, and we'd all crashed out on the sofa. AC finally woke up and staggered back to his room, and Tristan and I had fallen into bed. The sheets were soft, and so was the mattress, and we both finally slept for longer than three hours.

The next morning, the arrival of room service was announced by the knocking at the door. I went and answered it, and was greeted by an excited smile that quickly fell when his eyes took me in. Greg, according to his nametag, gamely pushed in the cart, and set it up, straightening out the white linen tablecloth with precision, testing the heat of the insulated carafe of coffee, uncovering the basket of croissants with a flourish. I had a feeling he would have waited around and offered to feed us. He looked like a sweet guy though, a kind of sick hopefulness still dancing around his eyes. I took pity on him, and gave him a quick smile before calling out. "Tristan! Come sign the bill, ok?"

We heard the sound of approaching footsteps, and the door to the bedroom opened, and out came Tristan, in a pair of low-cut briefs and an Iggy Pop t-shirt. I glanced over at Greg, who looked as though he had just seen a ghost. I hid my smile, and hoping I wouldn't have to catch him if he fell, I prompted him. "Hey Greg, thanks for setting it all up so nicely. Have you got the check? And maybe you've got something you'd like to be signed, if you wanted an autograph—for you, or a friend, maybe?" I tried to be casual. I didn't think I'd read him wrong, as he looked like he was hyperventilating. But I wanted to give him an out, in case he didn't want to.

Tristan was smiling. "Hey Greg, thanks a lot man." He held out his hand. Greg stared down at their hands joined, and then slowly looked up. It was easy to forget, being around Tristan all the time, that he was usually at least an inch taller than everyone around him.

Greg looked like he was having trouble talking, but he finally got there. "Tristan, man, wow, surreal. We…I've…down in the kitchen, drew straws…so awesome to meet you, man." He gasped for air. "I've been a fan from the start, dude…uh… thank you." He pulled out a copy of the first CD from inside his uniform coat, and handed it to Tristan.

"Wow, it's been a while since I've seen one of these. Nice. The Japanese pressing." He signed his name with a flourish. "Are you coming tonight?"

"Fuck yes!" He blushed a bit, and lowered his voice. "Yeah, totally. Really looking forward to it." He stood there for a moment, just kind of stunned, until Tristan spoke again.

"Well dude, thanks so much. Go over to the merch table tonight, give them your name, we'll have a t-shirt for you." Tristan started walking towards the door, and pulled it open. Greg still looked slightly dazed. Tristan put his hand on his shoulder. "Good to meet you man. All the best." And he closed the door, shutting out the image of Greg's face, still looking bemusedly at Tristan and the CD in his hand.

I went and sat down at the cart table and poured out some coffee. Tristan was still standing there. "You want some coffee, Tristan? Sorry about that. He just looked needy."

"Shit, yeah. Please. No, he seemed a nice guy. You usually get a couple of fans in the hotels. Not always." He laughed. "Like the other day. But mostly. I'm glad you called me in, that was nice of you." He sat down and started idly toying with the end of a croissant, dunking it in his coffee, and taking a bite. I watched him swallow. He ate like that, in silence, then shook his head. "Coffee not great."

"No."

"Croissants kind of bready too."

"Yeah, well, it's a hotel," I replied. "The usual."

"Maybe he didn't deserve the t-shirt." Tristan laughed. "No, I'm kidding. That's the trouble with sleep. It gives you energy to complain. But it makes you crazy. The dissatisfaction. You know? I'm glad you're here." He drank some more coffee and made a face.

"You want something else?"

"It's ok. There's always the minibar." He glanced over,

and passed a hand in front of his eyes. "You know, anything I want, I can get it? Someone will bring it? If I want drugs, sorted. Women—almost easier than drugs. I can start doing almost anything, and someone will come and either help me do it, or remind me I need to be on stage—and help me afterwards." He flung an arm out. "Anything. I want. No one will stop me for any reason—except to perform. My fucking contractual obligation. That's it. The smallest portion of the day."

He got up, and before I could stop him, he had pulled open the minibar, and grabbed the bottle of champagne on the bottom shelf. "The rest of the day to fill with anything I want, all the time, and twice on Sundays if I claim I need it to get on stage. Or through the day. Or to write a song." He twisted open the cork, and drank from the bottle, before handing it to me. I looked at it, uncertain. "Go on Lily, I want you to."

"And if I don't want to?" I said slowly.

Tristan came closer. "But you do want to. I know you do. You're here to see it, see it all. You didn't realize that's why you wanted to come along, but I think you know it now. You wanted to see how we change on the road. See what most people don't see." He thrust the bottle at me. "Take it."

"I've got to write."

"Yes, true," said Tristan. "But you want this for you. You want it all. Go on. Take it."

"You make it sound like it's all bad." I took the bottle. "Like it's always too much. It was ok at first."

"It always is. But no. It's not all bad. Or too much. Not at all. And some of the experience you can take home with you. Some of it you do take home with you, whether you should or not." He did a twirl in the room, his hand gripped around an invisible microphone. "For example, I get off on being worshipped. Watching people get nervous around me. Tricky thing to bring home." He stretched his arms over his head. "Drink."

And he watched me take a sip of champagne. It was cold, and slightly bitter, and I felt instantly better having the bubbles pop on my tongue, the familiar sensation. I took another drink. I looked up at him. "Maybe. But you've been through it all."

He laughed. "Have I? I guess I have. But I still want more."

"Not like this."

"Yes, just like this. You don't even realize, but you get it. Most people just read about it, the mix of fantasy and lies. Or they've had it, but they're too fucked up to remember." He knelt down in front of me, his eyes alight. "I think you're able to do it all. Fantasy, lies, and truth. Maybe."

His eyes were almost changing color. There was that strange intensity in his look, as he ran his hand down my face, along my neck, over the rise of one breast. "What do you think?" He slowly untied the cord of my robe, and opened it. The cool air in the room hit my skin, making me shiver. His eyes were locked with mine. "Alone, or together? How do we go down?" I shook my head. "Not sure yet, are we? What can I do to help make a mind up?"

His fingers hooked under the thin elastic band of my panties, and pulled them down over my thighs, until they slid down and came to rest at my ankles. He took the bottle of champagne from me, and took a swig, then dropped his head between my legs. He let a tiny trickle of the champagne spill out over the heated skin there, and the cold wetness made me jump. His hands silently held me down, and another burst of wetness poured over me and down, soaking into the robe. I tugged on his hair, but he didn't stop. Over and over, until my grip loosened, and my head fell back. Finally, he came up to face me. I licked his face. "Like 'Sea of Sin,'" I whispered.

The corner of his mouth twitched, and he poured some of the contents of the bottle into my mouth, until it trickled down my face onto my breasts. I licked my lips. He smiled, and it was a fearful sight. "I knew you'd understand. 'It gets better and better,'" he sang. Then he took another swig, and pulled me roughly up by my legs until my thighs reached his shoulders. Slipping off the panties and throwing them aside, he then hooked one leg over his shoulder, pushing the other one over the edge of the chair. He opened his mouth against me, and the liquid slid out of his mouth. I could feel it, slightly cool and wet, inside, a different kind of wet. His tongue followed, entering me, slowly. I moaned.

Tristan raised his head slightly. "That's it. This is what I want. Control. Don't move. Don't say a word."

I closed my eyes as his mouth touched me again, his tongue insistent. Then his fingers were there, opening me up, until there wasn't a part of me he hadn't touched, tasted. He stopped for another drink, and again the coldness of the liquid startled me. He pulled away and watched me twitching under the slippery roughness of his touch. I felt, rather than heard him say "No." Then his teeth followed his tongue and I jumped. His arms held me down, and I couldn't move. My back was cramped against the chair but every attempt I made to shift was stopped with the pressure of his strong forearm, and I was pinned there, against his teeth, his lips, his fingers, moving.

There was too much to process. My skin felt like it was dissolving beneath him, straight to nerves, blood flowing. He pulled at the delicate skin and his tongue found another part he hadn't explored.

"So close, so close," escaped, and one of his hands stopped what it was doing and slowly slid a long finger into my mouth. I ran my tongue around it. His quick intake of breath went through me like a shock. He started fucking my mouth with his finger, then added another. "Quiet. I'll let you come. Trust me? You shouldn't." And his mouth began an endless series of patterns, slow, fast, circling around in some magical diagram. His hand left my mouth and returned to explore, and I was open beneath him, larger, smaller, a house of rooms I was lost inside. "Now. Now. For me. Show me," Tristan murmured, and something within sped up just enough that I barely realized I'd been thrown over the abyss, the tension exploding as I writhed against his mouth and cried out, unintelligible noises. His voice was a low whisper. "That's it, that's it—let it go, let it all go. Give it to me."

It was the last thing I fully remembered. Then I felt his arms wrap around me and lift me up, carrying me through the door into the bedroom, and placing me down on the bed. Then he was naked, over me, his hand wet from me and wrapped around himself, hard and slippery, and then he was crying out, coming hard. The heat of it hit my skin, and he was on me, in me, liquid, dissolved. He collapsed with a shout, and pulled me to him, and we were both wet with each other, dizzy, delirious with the speed that it had all flooded through us. Breathing hard, he pulled the sheets over us, and buried his head against my shoulder.

The repeated buzz ring tone of the hotel phone finally broke through my sleep, followed by a groan from Tristan and a squawk from me as he rolled over to get the phone. We had been completely stuck together. I rubbed my hand up and down my stomach, as I listened to the conversation.

"What? Oh fuck, that's right. 10 minutes? Well, I'll try." There was a silence. "That's your job. That's right."

It was James, of course, reminding Tristan he needed to be downstairs in 10 minutes—the car was booked to take him to the radio station for today's interview. I knew that. I didn't realize how late it was. Tristan slammed the phone down. "Fuck. Not in the mood. Fine."

I reached out and squeezed his arm. I still felt dazed.

"I'm sorry Lils. I've got to jump in the shower." He gave me a quick squeeze. "We're good, yeah?"

I nodded, but it was clear that his mind was already on the business of the day—interview, sound check, quick signing at a record store in town. I lay back down on the sheets. I had the terrible feeling something had gone wrong, somehow. Or maybe it was just the abrupt shock of reality. The shower had already switched off, and Tristan burst through the door, towel wrapped around his hips, and proceeded to fish through his suitcase for suitable clothes. Except he was throwing it all on the ground. "Shit. Where are those jeans? Fuck." He spun around and pulled a pair of jeans off a chair in the corner. "Right." He dropped the towel, and pulled them on, tucking in his balls, and keeping a hand in front as he zipped them up. He grabbed the Iggy Pop t-shirt, and a leather jacket from the floor next to the suitcase. He scooped up all the clothes and threw them back into the bag, then jogged over to me and kissed me quickly on the mouth. "Sorry Lil. See you later, yeah?" and patting his pockets for wallet and phone, he ran out of the room. The door closed behind him.

The room seemed very quiet after he left. I was tempted to turn over and lie there for the rest of the day. Instead, I made myself get up. There was a little champagne left in the bottle. I finished it. I hated folding, but I took every shirt and pair of pants and tried to put Tristan's suitcase in some kind of order. Then I got in the shower, and washed us off. What was left of the insanity. I didn't know why, but I felt frightened. Like Tristan had moved on to an entirely other level. It was sudden, strange. And I couldn't put together the pieces. Had I liked what we did? Yes and no. Yes. Mostly. But there was something about Tristan, something that maybe he hadn't even noticed.

I kept turning it over in my mind, as I dressed, as I called for maid service to make up the room, as I waited for the elevator, as I walked out the door, avoiding a small group of three women, who were trying to look nonchalant, but one of them had a tattoo and another had a telltale Devised album poking out of a shoulder bag. I skirted the potted plants, fake I noticed, watched the doorman get a cab for a businessman with a shoulder garment bag and a laptop, and watched the buses go down the avenue as I walked past buildings, shops, sandwich places. I finally stopped at a coffee shop. I stared at the cup in front of me as though it would provide some answers. All I could do was watch him. Keep an eye out. But he was on the edge. The question was, the edge of what? Was it just tension, the end of a short bumpy tour? Artistic personality? Me? There was no doubt that the added stress of having me along on the ride was another strain, even as it provided some ways to relieve it. I thought of this morning, and blushed, remembering him, the intensity. Was it quick and crazy like that with AC? How easy had it been before to get that kind of release, without me? I picked at the cardboard of the cup. Abruptly the place seemed small, tight, the line of people waiting for coffee another barricade keeping me from the outside. My chest grew tight, and my throat went dry. Grabbing my coffee and my bag, I pushed my way through the crowd, my eyes practically shut against the lights, against the people that kept coming in. I forced my way outside and walked away as quickly as I could, trying to take deep breaths. Was it just panic? Was that what Tristan was feeling too? I went around the corner, and saw a concrete ledge setting off a pedestrian area. I made my way to it, and sat down, refusing to look around, just trying to get my bearings, to settle down.

I sat there for a while, recovering from the panic, thinking about the small canal and neatly groomed walkway outside our hotel window. Brownfield, no doubt. Perfect. In the center of the shit storm. The stress was incredible. I could feel it. Connected as we were, I could feel him. Feel the worry, even though he didn't like to talk about it. And there was AC. And me. Everyone wanted a piece of him, and he just wanted all this to be a success. It was all like a ticking clock, every second ticking away another chance to make it work, or another minor disaster, like nearly missed radio interviews. It was a business. It didn't seem anymore like you could roll up when you wanted, blaming drugs and a disregard for the rules. Now you were expected to be all that, a symbol of all rebellion, while keeping to a schedule and making sure the band got on the bus and saying the right things, not the wrong things when you were talking to yet another DJ on yet another corporate radio station. Especially here. Only 4 days left. It wasn't that long. Why it seemed like we'd be lucky if we made it, I wasn't sure.

I looked at my phone. Right now Tristan was on the air. Today's radio station. The same questions, the same give-aways, the same smiles, the same handshakes. And I knew. I knew it was too much. He needed an oblivion that music wasn't giving him, and that I couldn't give him. And there was AC, his oldest friend in all this, who had been there in the bad old days, who knew him. He knew how to handle him but he was also blinded by his own needs. Like me. Trevor. Maybe Trevor. I got up and started walking. I'd call him. I needed to clear my head first. I wasn't sure what I was going to say. I wasn't sure I'd know until I started speaking. But I had the awful feeling that I was going to burst into tears the minute I heard his distant, sardonic voice. He had saved him once. Maybe he could do it again. If he even needed to.

The phone rang, oddly clearer than the last phone call I'd made to New York. The woman who answered put me through right away. Perhaps Trevor had been waiting for this call. Knew it was coming, like rain. The phone kept ringing though, and finally it went back to the receptionist. "Look, just tell him Lily called. Can he call me as soon as possible? It's urgent." She wrote down my number, just in case, and I pressed end with a sense of fatality. Where the hell was he?

There was no reason why he should be available, just because I wanted him and Tristan needed him, but I wanted him to be there. I walked for a bit longer, and when the lines of shops and offices petered out into warehouses, and signs for the highway, I turned around. I crossed the road at the next set of lights, and called the hotel for a cab to come get me. There was a diner another block down, and I went in and sat at the counter and ordered a coffee. The cab would have my number. There'd be other cabs. It didn't matter. I half listened to the guy with the Caterpillar t-shirt make chit-chat with the waitress. They would go out. They wouldn't have tortured sex. He wouldn't be on the cover of a magazine, or on the radio, but he wouldn't have to fight the temptation of drugs either. Although there was always the easy darkness of drink, un-faithfulness, violence. I turned away. I wanted them to make it, irrationally. They probably barely knew each other. Were probably married to other people. She came over and refilled my coffee and I tried to smile. It felt like I was admonishing her. Don't let him fail. Don't lose him.

I drank my coffee, grimly. The cheerful bell sung out a welcome for every newcomer who came through the glass and metal door. When the phone rang in my pocket, I ignored it, thinking it was the doorbell. Then I wrestled it out of my pocket, and nearly dropped it.

"Hello?"

The clipped, brisk tones of Trevor came across clearly through the air. "Good afternoon Lily in America. I heard you called?"

For a moment I couldn't breathe. He sounded so calm, so reasonable, so far away from all this. "Trevor. Oh god. Thank you. So glad you called. Hang on a minute, I've just got to pay—do you want me to call you back?" I fished out a five dollar bill from my pocket and threw it on the counter, and slung my bag over my shoulder.

"No, Lily, that's fine. Take your time. I take it something's happened then?" Trevor's voice was like a balm. I was fighting the urge to blurt out everything, AC, this morning's weird sex, the drugs I was now sure were around all the time. I made it outside, but my moment of silence had clearly said enough. "Tristan? Of course. You wouldn't call for yourself, but you sound awful. What's happened?" He waited.

"Trevor. God. Tristan. No. He's fine. Well, no. He's not fine. But nothing has happened. Not yet." I retraced my steps along the street. Damn the stupid cab. "But…"

Trevor interrupted me. "It's the stress. That's why we started with a small tour. I figured you having you on board would help as well." He paused. "But it hasn't?"

"I don't know, Trevor. I'd like to think it has. I'm there, I listen. Eyes open, mouth shut."

"But he's said or done something you don't trust and you're frightened." There was such an air of finality in the way it said it. I hung my head. I'd failed, clearly. I wasn't supposed to be asking for help.

"He's going over the edge. I think he wants me to go with him. Like a test."

Trevor's response was instant. "Then that's a test you're going to fail."

"But I'll lose him."

"Is that what you're frightened of? Or is it that you want to see how bad it gets?"

I was silent. I thought of this morning, and suddenly wished I'd never called. "I'm not going to lie. That doesn't mean I don't want him to be safe."

Trevor was quiet. I thought I heard the sound of a match being struck, at a distance of 5000 miles and a great deal of technology. Finally he spoke. "Fair enough. Bravely said." He inhaled again. "One of your best qualities."

"Thanks. I guess." I didn't feel particularly brave. "What do I do?"

"What do you think you should do?"

I laughed, nervously. "Really? I think I should spend one more night on the fun ride, and then say I've had enough. I think you should come. I think he trusts me enough to use me. And I'll let him. But I shouldn't."

Trevor sighed. "I knew I'd have to come over early."

I tried to reassure him. "Look, it's fine. There's only a few more days…"

Trevor broke in. "And then there's L.A. The awards show. And the reality is that he needs to tour."

"It is about money then." I waited for the light. There was a car rental place on the corner. I was almost tempted to hire a car and just disappear. Get the hell out. While I was still able to drive.

"Ah, is that what he said? Not the old 'contractual obligation' speech? Listen, Lily. It's what he needs to do. What he has to do. No one stops being a musician or an artist. What the hell is he going to do, buy a trout farm? Open a restaurant? Fuck off." He paused. "Not you. I apologize. But you must see that we have to make this work. There is nothing else. It's his life."

I felt the tears start.

Trevor must have heard something, because when he spoke again, his voice was softer. "Lily, love, it's ok. You were right to call. Ticket in place. I just need to move some things around. L.A. already a definite. Seven days. A week. I'll be there. If anything happens in the meantime, call me. Call me anyway."

I murmured a thank you.

"And Lily? It will get crazier. Just hang on, but leave when you can't see the way through—and when you think he'll notice. I'm going to find a new manager. It's time to recall James. Permanently, I think. I'll see what I can bait the trap with. You—just stay close, and stay calm. What did Bob Marley say? 'Everything's going to be irie,'" he chuckled.

I tried to manage a laugh. "Ok." I didn't feel convinced, but the fact that he knew felt like a huge weight off my shoulders. "Thank you Trevor. I will keep you posted, I promise."

"Yes, please do. I'll call you in New York in a couple of days."

"But I'm supposed to be here," I protested.

"We'll see. Talk soon, Lily. Look after yourself." And with that, Trevor was gone.

I walked for a while, in a daze. When I looked up again, there was one of the black and yellow cabs, with the name painted in yellow on the side. Thunder Cabs. He probably wouldn't pick me up, but it couldn't hurt to try. I waved. He pulled over and rolled down the window.

"Can you take me to the Residence Inn? In Bricktown? I'll pay extra."

He looked at me quizzically. "Did you call for a cab about 20 minutes ago? To go to that hotel?"

"Yeah, that was me. Sorry, I had an emergency phone call. Can you still do it? 20 bucks for you on top." I suddenly wanted nothing more than to get back and face whatever was going to happen.

"Yeah, no problem. Get in—I'll tell the dispatcher I found you."

chapter sixteen

Houston

The flight down to Houston had been uneventful, even if it was a little weird looking down and seeing the ground go past so quickly. The spaces that had been overwhelming, almost suffocating in their endless horizons were now divided into different colored sections, like some child's puzzle. Maybe it had been a good idea to get some distance, from everything. Tristan was still jittery. I didn't think it was helped by the double vodka, and two trips to the tiny airplane bathroom. Even if we were flying in first class, I was a little worried that he was being too obvious. On the last trip back, AC had stuck out his arm, and stopped him. It was the first time I'd seen them touch in a couple of days. They'd been so careful. AC put his hand on Tristan's arm. AC didn't say anything, his eyes deep and expressive, focused on him, a slight frown marring his smooth forehead. Tristan looked back down at him. I watched as he shut his eyes for a second and gave an imperceptible nod. The whole encounter must have lasted 10 seconds, if that. AC removed his hand, and Tristan sat back down next to me, staring into space, his dark hair a contrast against the beige seats, and the almost opaque protective paper on the head rest. The front of the plane was shaped into a point up here. If you looked forward, it was like being on a rocket. Headed into space, but unable to see where you were going.

Houston was hot, and the little crowd of fans at the airport were polite, but eager to get a photo of Tristan and AC as we made our way out to the waiting car. They both signed autographs, and posed for a couple of pictures together, their arms around each other like the world was a party and everything was fun. Both their faces changed in front of the cameras, like they both knew which angles suited them best, which expressions gave which impressions. But when it was time to stop, and the airport security guard stepped forward to separate the fans from their prey, they both returned to their normal expressions, and it was if a light had been switched off. They needed it, but it could be a parasitic relationship. The fans fed on their host, and if they didn't limit it, there would be nothing left. Sometimes you felt that the fans wouldn't mind, that they'd like to see them crumble and die, the desire to take everything apart, destruction a part of the passion.

The hotel was pleasant. James had flown down with us, and checked us in, while we waited in the bar. AC ordered for all of us. For someone that outwardly, at any rate, did not give the same impression of command as Tristan did, AC managed very well when he wanted to take control of a situation. Maybe it was the sense he gave off that if it had come to this, it was serious, and he wouldn't tolerate any arguments. Or maybe it was that he knew when to push, and when to let it all go. Watching Tristan look gloomily at his vodka tonic—with extra tonic—

was almost funny. But they had another radio interview to go to before the sound check and a quick record signing at a store near the venue. AC caught me eyeing Tristan's pout, and with an amused expression, he winked at me. "Only one bottle for baby. Even if he throws all his toys out of the pram." I laughed.

"Shut up, both of you," Tristan said miserably. AC and I looked at each other, eyes big, fake shock written over both our faces. AC mouthed "ooooh" at me. I tried not to laugh.

* * *

"His name was always Buddy…and she'd sigh like Twig the Wonderkid." That portion of the line was running through my head over all the other sounds as I walked up and down the street outside the radio station where Tristan and AC were. I turned my headphones up louder to drown out the clank clank clank of the nearby roadworks, the buses going by, the cars, the people. It wasn't even that busy, compared to New York, but it felt like it. There was a guy coming my way in a cowboy hat. I couldn't help it, I laughed out loud, and the man in the hat gave me a dirty look. It was hot, and it was dusty, and beyond the buildings, I knew there was just land, and oil derricks, and cattle waiting to be turned into cheap frozen burgers, and ancient burial grounds, and dirt. Land. And the lizard-like waiting and hot rock heat.

It was almost 2:30 p.m. The day winding down, the interview would be over, and the car would be there to take us back to the venue for the sound check before tonight's show. I felt guilty. I was writing of course, but it wasn't the same as having to spew out the same old set of answers to an endless parade of interviewers, asking the obvious, looking for the hopefully shocking angle that would add nothing to the world's knowledge, but would keep them in bread and butter for the foreseeable future. Now that AC was going along, I wondered if some interviewer was going to get more than he or she had ever wished for.

I'd been politely banned from interviews after Kansas City. It was clear to the record company that it was only my gender they could rely on, and barely that. Trevor had congratulated me when I'd told him the news. "One interview, that's fantastic. Of course, the bloke handed you the Yoko poison pill, so it wasn't entirely your own doing. Still. Well done." Apparently he'd told Tristan that if he wanted any more proof that I wasn't in it for the celebrity, he was out of his mind. And Dave had mentioned that there was now a Tumblr called "We Are All Yoko." I'd just laughed when he told me.

I looked down the street. A tall dark head had just emerged from the building, followed by a slightly shorter blond head of loose curls. They were quickly surrounded by a little crowd that I knew would contain two bodyguards, and a small loyal group of fans who had waited for Tristan and AC to emerge. I came closer. There was the car. They were standing chatting with the fans, posing for pictures, the girls eyeing Tristan for the most part, with a couple clinging on to AC adoringly. He looked amused. And the two more menacing members of the group were keeping a close eye on the proceedings. I was grateful for them, whatever impulse made this their calling. It worked for all of us—they banked on their natural ability to inspire fear and obedience, not to mention their unspoken enjoyment of this power. I banked on the fact that it worked, and kept Tristan safe. And AC.

There had been a couple of instances where a fan had drifted right over the edge into fanaticism. It was almost understandable. Tristan's profile, emerging into the everyday, standing a head above almost anyone in the street, the long lean line of his thighs in the tight black trousers, the leather jacket taunting the heat, his half-smile hinting at a multitude of feelings while coaxing everyone else's to come out of hiding, to come into the light from the dark playground of their bedrooms, the internet sites, their personal blogs, their secret dreams. His hands, actual skin, reaching out for a pen and the album covers, magazines, CDs, tickets, pieces of paper, fan art, t-shirts, clothing, skin waiting to become tattoos, hands, arms, phones, cameras, all reaching out for him, all wanting that piece of the divinity that meant they'd been validated, that some part of their lives at last was bigger than all the rest.

I approached only at the last minute. A gesture from Tristan was enough to tell the bodyguard to let me through, which he did, a protective arm around me. I got in to the car last, and as I sank down to the level of the seats, for some reason I turned back to look at the little crowd. One of the women was inspecting me, her expression a mixture of envy and confusion and want. Sheer want. I wanted to tell her, it's not as easy as it looks, it's not as much fun, it's actually a lot more like real life than you'd think, there's jealousy, and fear, and uncertainty. But she'd never believe it, I thought, not as the bodyguard shut the door with a sharp click, and the car pulled away slowly. Then Tristan took my hand and smiled at me, and I thought, all except for this. His mouth, his strong hands, and mostly the look in his eye when he found me next to him, safe and happy. This didn't feel like real life at all. But maybe it felt like love.

* * *

Tristan was fidgeting on the bed, flicking through the channels, propped up by the three extra full pillows he had asked housekeeping to bring up. Everything was done, the radio interview, the sound check, the record signing, So we were biding our time, watching TV and waiting for the main event. I was working on some voice-over sections for the documentary, the on-again, off-again project, which now, according to Dave, was on again. It didn't seem possible, but with the success of the Stone Roses documentary, hot on the heels of the award winning look at Freddie Mercury, it appeared that the public was ready for more rock history, even of fairly recent date. I was scribbling away, vaguely aware of Tristan's increasingly speed-driven flick through the channels, when the sound of the remote smashing against the wall made me shriek. I had caught the tail end of him raising his arm, but it all happened so fast, I couldn't make out why he had done it, or what it meant. Now we sat there in silence, staring at the black scrape on the wall, and the shattered pieces of the plastic casing half lost in the deep pile carpet.

"Fuck this shit," Tristan said, strangely out of breath. He looked over at me, then shut his eyes tight, flinging his head back against the pillows. "I can't do this. All this domestic."

I stared at him, silent.

"No, that's not what I mean. No. I love you. You know that. But this," here he swept his hand through the air, in almost the same gesture he used to obliterate the remote, "the waiting. The steady meals. Destinations. Fuck." He sat up, his hands brushing through his dark tangled hair, "I want to get wasted. Do crazy things. I don't know if I know how to be like this. Sensible."

I breathed out, slowly. "Maybe you're just bored. Nervous about the awards show. Finding it weird that someone is making a docu-drama of your messed-up rock and roll life." An edge had come into my voice. I thought of that girl looking at me, longingly. I wondered what she'd do, face to face with the ever-growing monster that on-tour Tristan was threatening to become.

Tristan looked at me, surprised. Then his face hardened. "Yeah. I am all those things. But. I want to be the other. I want to write some songs, I want to play, I want to go crazy. I don't know how to do it like this. That place seems very far away, when I'm lying here next to you, ready to order room service, no band mate to put under the shower, no half-naked girls to be escorted out."

"Is that what you want? And the drugs?" I paused. "I thought that was already taken care of." He raised an eyebrow, but said nothing. "Women? It wouldn't take a lot of work to get back there. A quick phone call, and you could have the local talent here in a heartbeat. I was under the impression you were already working at full capacity though." I got up. "Getting there is easy. It's getting back that's tricky. But if you want me gone," I started picking up my papers, "It's easily done. No one said I had to be on tour with you every day, every night." I walked over to the minibar, and pulled out a little bottle of vodka, which seemed to be today's drink, and a beer, and went and sat on the sofa. I rifled through the papers, unseeing.

Tristan got up, and started pacing. Then he stopped by the window, to look out at the 24th floor vantage point. I'd stood there myself when we arrived, watching the grid disappear into the horizon, half listening to Tristan making his phone calls. Now I didn't know if he wanted me to fight him, or let him have his way. Teach him a lesson, or prove love by acquiescence. What I did know was that he couldn't feel that I was holding him back from anything. That would be disaster.

I thought back to the talk Trevor and I had when I'd flown out to see him in London before the tour had even begun. Now his words seemed oddly prophetic—"don't let Tristan feel he has either the upper hand or the lower. In other words, don't hesitate to remind him that he has made all these choices." He had laughed. "Nothing a rock star loves more than to risk, to threaten to give it all up. Make sure when he wants to go there, he knows that no one will stop him." Trevor had gazed at me. "It's not true, of course. We'll stop him. But god help us if we fuel him by restriction."

I had turned towards Trevor then, really uncertain of what he was telling me. "But your story? Tristan crying…"

Trevor shood his head. "If we want to keep them, we raise the alarm—but we get out of the way. Then we pick up the pieces." He saw the look on my face, and carried on. "There's nothing we can do but pray they listen."

"But you...you practically staged an intervention. How can you let him go, if that's what he is going to do?"

"Because Tristan will dance his own dance. Be the music—not the steps." He had reached out for my hand. "You're sensitive—as he is. I trust that you will respect his demons as you do your own, my dear."

And here was the moment Trevor had warned me about. I hadn't really understood what he had meant. Now I did. Tristan. Always wanting more than he had, feeling that insane pressure, needing to act, to do, to make something happen, almost anything. Trevor's voice echoed through my head— "respect his demons as you do your own..." I took a deep breath. How many times had I felt trapped? Those long, late night walks home alone, where the silence and the isolation had been what I wanted, when I didn't know how to deal with what people wanted. Their idiocy. The want. It seemed to me it was the same problem. This didn't need to escalate. Maybe. I opened the beer and drank half of it before I answered him. I hoped he couldn't tell how much I was holding back.

"Maybe you aren't sure what I want. Or what you want. But you'll never figure it out watching reruns of *Ellen*."

Tristan smiled finally. "I like Ellen." His voice lowered. "I was hoping she'd give me some help with the whole gay thing." He smiled. "What was it you said? 'Working at full capacity?' Nice." He smirked.

I wasn't going to be baited. Keep it light. "I don't think you need any help. You seem to be doing just fine." If he expected me to say anything precise, he was very wrong. But I still tensed every muscle in my body I could feel. Letting go. The hardest thing for me. My demons. "But you probably need some space.

That's fine." I had my phone out, my finger on speed dial. "It's the last nights of the tour. I've seen the shows, had the bus experience. Next week L.A. I'll see you there." The voice on the other end of the phone was cool. Dave's secretary. Used to the sudden emergency. "Ginny. Lily here." We were on first name basis now. Would that still hold true if I wasn't fucking the star? Didn't matter. But given my part in the whole production, I'd have to insure that held true. Ironically, continuing to fuck the star now seemed to depend on not doing it. Yin Yang, I thought. It's balance. "Can you book me a ticket out back to New York tonight? Houston, that's right. Yes, I will hold."

Tristan watched me, a slight flicker in his swirling eyes. I pretended not to notice. This game depended on me holding my ground. "Yes? First flight out tomorrow morning at 7? Sure, that's fine. Ticket in my email in an hour? Great. Cheers, Ginny. Appreciate it. Say hello to Dave for me. Thanks again." I pressed the end call button with a bit more ferocity than usual. "Ok, tomorrow a.m. I'm out of here. And now I'm going to do a little shopping." Tristan raised his hand as if to stop me. "No, it's fine. I'll see you later— either at the show or after." I went over to him and hugged him, as though I was heading for a shower, rather than leaving. "Have a nap. I'll get someone to give you a call when it's time to head out."

Tristan leaned his head into my neck. "You scare me a little, you know."

I laughed. "Yeah, me too." I kissed him and grabbing my bag, I headed for the door. "It's all good, love." I blew him a kiss from the door, and shut it carefully behind me. I walked down the hall, made it to the elevator, then collapsed against the wall. I had to do it. He had to make the choice, not me. I wasn't going to jail anyone against their will. Before I could think any more about it, I pressed the button for the elevator. I rode down in silence, making up my mind. When I got down to the lobby, I asked the concierge to get me a taxi to the mall. I didn't think I'd need 5 hours in the mall, but then again, I didn't think I needed to hang about watching the show either. Probably the moon-eyed wonder had gotten old. It didn't matter. I sat down in one of the big chairs by the doors, waiting for my ride, and pulled out my phone again. Another speed dial button, and it struck me that it really was true, when you really loved someone, you did want them to be happy. Mostly. Even if that didn't always get you everything you thought you wanted. But it also didn't mean you gave up yourself. What a fucking moment to learn that lesson. At any rate, I'd had enough of half-measures in my life. I wanted the passion, I wanted the truth. I listened to the voice answer the phone.

"AC? Lily here. Yes. Look, he's alone. And he needs you. No, everything is fine. But I think he's freaking out a bit. I have a feeling you'll know what to say. No, really it's ok. I'll see you both later. No, I won't be at the show. Taking a break. Going to eat some ribs. Shop for luxury goods. Be good to each other, ok?" And I rang off. Outside, a black town car was pulling up. The doorman waved to me after getting the nod from the concierge, and as he opened the door to let me slide into the air-conditioned darkness, his deep voice said, "Have a good evening, Miss."

Well, I'd started something. Now to see whether it was good, or not.

* * *

I'd turned off my phone in the film. I didn't want to look. But now that I was outside, trying to remember the title of what I'd just seen, determined to distract myself and kill time, weaving my way through the crowd of people laughing and talking, I had to. I wanted to. I'd been good. I switched it on, and watched the emails and DMs add up, a little like the spinning wheels of a slot machine. Then the voice mail—only three. I pressed it and watched as it went to the list—it was AC, not Tristan. I pressed play before I had a change of heart or a chance to think about what that could mean.

His voice was clear. "Lily. Come home. He loves you, so much. And so do I, and not just for being that constant in his life. You're rad. Seriously. Touring really gets to him. He thought it'd be easier this time around. He didn't tell you. And someone was trash talking the band. He's got to sack James, he's a fucking time bomb. Now he's spending time chatting to Jack. No good will come of that. Fuck it. But come back. Come now. Ok? Please?" I listened to it again, walking towards the exit of the mall, watching the couples and the high school kids strolling by, heading home. I called for a taxi, and stood outside, breathing in the warm air, the dark sky, watching the headlights come on the different cars as they started up and headed off. But it wasn't until my cab had turned up, and I'd given the guy the name of the hotel, which luckily I'd saved on the phone, that I texted AC. *On my way.* I added the next part more slowly. *For now.* And hit send before I had a chance to change my mind.

It took about half an hour to get back. It was before midnight. I figured I had time for a shower, and a chance to collect my thoughts before I needed to deal with either of them. I could pack. The flight left at 6:40. One stop, no plane change. Seemed fair. I was thinking about what I'd say to both of them. I was hoping it wasn't going to be too hard to leave. Or too easy. I turned my feet away from the elevators, and towards the bar. I needed a drink, and to try and remember what it was like to be on my own. Watching. Thinking. On my own time.

I sat near the end of the bar, and ordered another vodka tonic. There was a part of me that wanted the medicinal taste of a straight shot, the burning feeling of alcohol like a cleanser, cutting away the extra. The emotions. The feelings. But I wanted the anonymity more. Nothing says look at me more than a woman ordering shots in a hotel bar, and I could already feel the late night men circling around behind me, trying to get a read. I literally shook my shoulders, involuntarily, as though I could make them all disappear with a quick gesture. The bartender chose that moment to bring me my drink. He gave me a funny look. I returned a level gaze. Life shadowing a rock star on tour had taught me a few things, I could see that. "It's a little cold in here. Can you turn down the AC? And bring me some peanuts, or snacks—whatever you serve? Thanks." And I turned away again. I ignored the shiver the coldness of the frosted glass gave me, my warm fingertips melting away neat little ovals on the glass, and I tried to ignore the taste of the tonic, chasing instead after the bitter absent coldness of vodka. I did finally notice that I'd tipped down half of it almost immediately. There goes anonymity, I thought, and when the bartender came back with a little tray of nuts and mini cheese crackers, I ordered another one. Then I ignored the way his lips pursed slightly, and the quick look he gave me to make sure I wasn't about to fall off my chair. The second one came, and I was pleased to notice it was a little stronger. Maybe he figured he'd get rid of me that way.

I was staring into space, and counting to a hundred every time I thought about taking a sip, and doing my best not to listen to the conversation the two men at the other end were having about the overlap between sales techniques and sports prowess. It was 12:30. I figured I'd head upstairs after this one. I doubted we'd sleep tonight anyway. Hadn't Tristan said he was tired of domesticity? Nothing more domestic than sleep. I'd just called for the check, when someone sat in the chair next to me. I looked straight ahead, and waited for the return of the bartender. A hand settled on my arm, and I looked down, startled. I knew that hand.

AC grinned at me. "I thought I'd find you in here. Getting up some liquid courage before you face the diva?" I started to reply, but he shook his head, and took my hand. "I don't blame you. And I won't blame you if you leave, or if you hate me. But you shouldn't. And I don't want you to."

I did speak up at that. "I don't hate you. I never have. And…"

AC interrupted. "…we need to talk?"

The wry expression I could feel twisting my lips into a half smile said it all. "Yes. I guess we do. Probably overdue. But that's not it, you know. I'm not blaming you for him. Or what the two of you have."

AC rolled his eyes and tilted his head back a bit. The bartender came with the bill. AC stopped him. "Sorry mate. Can we get two more of whatever that was? Thanks. Put the whole thing on this." And he handed over a black card, like a magician pushing forward the most important card from the deck, effortlessly. The effect was pretty magical, too.

"Nice one," I laughed. "Now you're just trying to impress me."

"Sure," AC smiled. "Took you long enough to notice. Besides," he shook out his hair, "you haven't admired the natural set of curls life has gifted me with."

I reached up and twisted one between my fingers. His hair, the gold side of yellow blond, was incredibly soft. "Cute."

AC winked at me. "Now you're just flirting. Heartbreaker. And your man is waiting for you." The drinks came, along with another bowl of snacks. There were three different kinds now, I noticed. "But I recommend you let him wait, at least long enough to have a drink with me."

I narrowed my eyes. "Isn't that just going to piss him off even more?"

AC took a sip, and grimaced. "God, tonic. Lily. Yes, probably will. But damn if it isn't good for him." He raised his glass. "Don't try to be everything for him, Lil. Or give him everything he asks for. You'll exhaust yourself, and create a monster in the process. Push back. Relax." He drank some more. "Don't you feel better having walked away, even a little?"

"You told me to come back."

"Yes, I did. Because it's the right thing to do. And he cares. A lot. Let him. Now make him work for it."

I looked at his face, the green eyes, the quiet confidence that was there. And trust. Something like faith. "And you?"

"And me." He kissed my cheek. "We'll have that chat soon, I promise. With Barolo. But now it's diva time!" And he laughed, the moment of seriousness gone as quickly as it came.

I turned around at the entrance to the bar. AC was still watching me. He shooed me away with his hands, a big smile on his face. I waved, and turned the corner. I had a feeling he was going to be there until the bar closed. I glanced around, looking for fans. Amazingly enough, none of them had managed to sneak past the entrance. I pressed the button for the elevator. I had no idea what I was going to say. Maybe we wouldn't say anything.

I slid the key card into the lock and the green light glowed. I turned the handle, but the room was dark. Maybe he wasn't here after all. He needed to sleep, but I couldn't imagine he'd gone to bed already. I switched on the light. It didn't even look like anyone had been here. I had the sudden thought that maybe he'd left first. Maybe he'd only told AC he was coming back. AC didn't know everything. I swallowed down the feeling of panic, and dropped my bag, taking off my jacket, and draping it over the arm of the sofa.

Then I pushed open the door leading in to the bedroom, and gasped. The lights had been turned down, but there in the half-lit room, the curtains open to show the night 24 floors below, lay Tristan, sprawled out on the bed. His dark hair was fanned out over the pillow, his long legs still in tight jeans splayed out across the white sheets. His feet were bare. I could just make out the tattoo across his foot that said "plus jamais," never again. He'd gotten it to match mine—to keep me company, he'd said. His body seemed longer than ever, a slash of dark color against the sheets. But he was still wearing his leather jacket. One hand was balanced lightly between his legs, long fingers stretched out from hipbone to hipbone. The other arm was stretched tautly upwards, but this time the long fingers were firmly pinned to the headboard, a metal cuff circling his wrist, a silver band on his pale skin. The other section was locked firmly on to the railing.

Tristan opened his eyes when he heard me gasp. They were focused on me intently, and I felt the weight of his stare so keenly I nearly turned my head away in embarrassment.

His voice was an inky drawl, scratching itself through all my hastily constructed barriers. "Like what you see, then?"

I felt my face grow hot. His next words were a direct challenge. "Shy? Afraid of what you want? You weren't earlier." He looked me up and down. "What if I couldn't move?" He pulled at the cuff to demonstrate. It rattled loudly in the room. I had the feeling everyone in the world could hear us. Tristan's voice brought me back. "No? Not enough incentive? I could try and read your mind, tell you what you want." He stared at me, I consented to meet his eyes. "You fall into it so easily. So good." He smirked, and looked down. I saw his free hand was unbuttoning the top of his red jeans, and slowly lowering the zipper. He adjusted himself, and sighed with pleasure at the release of pressure. "Fuck these things are tight. Are you still there? I need some help here." I was still standing still. "Unless you don't want to. Then I could do it myself. Would you like that? Or do you want to help?" I made myself move forward. I was dizzy, my vision clouded. I had the half-formed thought that only Tristan could inspire submission while tied up.

He stroked himself slowly through his half-opened jeans. His gestures were painfully slow. My skin prickled, as though he was touching me himself. Everything felt heavy, drawn out. It was though I could feel my blood racing through my limbs, pulsing steady and light-filled. It was impossible that any touch could cure this. It felt like a sickness, the first stages of fever when lights hold a halo and every nerve is raw. I kept staring at him, steadily, unable to stop. His hand sped up ever so slightly, and with a long sigh, he stopped and looked at me. "You're still nervous. After all this time."

I tried to shake words into my mouth from somewhere, anywhere. "I'm...not...I'm a bad top."

"Who told you that?" His eyes glittered in the half-light of the room.

"I just know it." I wrapped my arms around myself. "It started well, but then...I don't know..."

Tristan smiled, a crazy kind of smile, that managed to both reassure and alarm all at once. "That's not you, love. That's them. A top needs a bottom. It's not a matter of just lying there, it is trust. Submission. Willingness to be led. Signals exchanged to help you do that. Otherwise...," he trailed off, "... it's just confusion. Only signaling that someone doesn't know how to play." He smiled again, and this time it felt like a punch to the gut. "But I know how...to play. So. Let's play."

My eyes shut tightly. I couldn't feel this and see at the same time. Everything hurt, felt hot and swollen. It didn't seem possible that anything we could do would make it better. I found myself approaching him, in a daze. I wanted to touch him, feel the silky hardness of him under my fingers, watch him come apart.

"That's it love. Come closer. You need this. Something else within you. Watch it happen." He pulled at the cuffs again. "I can't move. I won't move. Now—think about what you want. Let go." He nodded his head to the left. "The minibar is there, with my key. It's a choice, like anything. Go over there, pull out something you want. Remember how to choose. Remember how to enjoy it. I'm waiting." And he stopped his hand, squeezing at the base of his cock, stopping the feeling as I watched. "Go on." His voice was low, encouraging but soft, like he wanted to be touched, wanted something else. I walked over to the minibar, and pulled out a half bottle of Champagne, then thought for a moment, and added a small bottle of Remy Martin. I held them aloft, like some prize. His face didn't change expression. "You chose. Now take." His dark eyes remained fixed on mine. "Take what you want. It's that easy."

I looked at him, laid out there, a fine sweat beginning to bead on his forehead. I could smell him, sweet and piercing, that strange smell of a man aroused beyond the point where he could go back, a wet, cold, white smell, mixed with his sweat, the warmth of his skin under his leather jacket, I closed my eyes tight again. It hurt. This painful desire, with no clear steps to relief, and the overwhelming feeling that relief was actually the last thing I wanted. I unscrewed the top of the tiny frosted dark green glass cognac bottle, and upended it, feeling the burning pour down my throat, burning its way into my chest, offering another pain that was a welcome change from the pain under my skin. His voice came again, teasing, whispering, slow. "What if what you want is what I want as well?" He breathed in. "What if I know how to let you?'" He shut his eyes again. "Come on." He pulled at the metal bracelet, then let his arm go slack. "I trust you. You'll know how to treat me."

I stared at him.

"Please," he murmured, "I've been waiting for you." And that undid me. If he needed it, then I could admit to the desperation I felt, the heat. Maybe it would be different. I shook off the fear, and the bad memories of the last time I had the upper hand. I wanted it. Wanted him. And he lay there, his eyes closed, waiting. Mine. I ran my hands over my breasts. It was though everything was hot current, the shock at the sudden rush of feeling almost too much. I could even not touch him if I didn't want to.

But I did want to. So badly. I needed to feel his warm skin on mine, tease the hair on his belly, turn it into torture for him, the way it was so often for me, when I saw him, and all I wanted I couldn't have. Again.

"Come on. Please." That voice, dark and pleading, hinting at desires I barely admitted to myself. I was scared, so scared. I knew all too well what it felt like to be disappointed. I didn't want to risk it. My mind scrambled for a way to play it safe.

"Don't." That voice of his, again, slowing down the air around us. Like he knew. "I'll help. Let me help. Haven't I always helped?"

He let his hand fall away. His cock jutted out, hard and swollen. There was a glint of smooth metal at the base. "Take what you want. Tell me what to do. I won't move."

* * *

I missed my plane.

chapter seventeen

Houston to Dallas

We stumbled out of the hotel the next day fairly early for the four hour drive to Dallas. I could only guess, but I had a feeling I finally looked the part. Virtually no sleep, sunglasses to cover up that fact and ease the pain of bright lights. Add to that a ripped leather jacket, high heeled boots, and a floppy brimmed black hat to hide my face from the sun and the fans, coupled with the fact I could barely walk. It felt like every muscle in my body had been pushed to the breaking point. I did not care. Remembering how I got this way kept me smiling mysteriously at everything and nothing, an occasional blush leaving me warm and slightly embarrassed. Tristan had his usual leather jacket and shades, the usual tight jeans, and a smirk that never left his face as he casually signed a few autographs. AC was waiting by the limousine, signing a few autographs of his own. When he caught sight of us, he let out a howl. The fan standing next to him jumped back and nearly knocked over three of the girls waiting their turn. Tristan just turned towards him, the smirk firmly in place. AC signed their autographs quickly, and advanced towards me, extending his arm. "Does Madam require assistance?"

My mouth twisted into a tight smile. "Madam requires you to fuck off." But I took his arm, and we strolled over to the limousine, Tristan following closely behind, signing a few more autographs. The driver helped the doorman add our bags to the trunk, and Tristan and AC turned to wave to the crowd before they got into the car. I turned with them, and stood there as the cameras went off. Then Tristan dove in, pulling me with him, and AC gave a final wave before following us.

The driver asked if we were comfortable and if we needed him to stop anywhere before he hit the highway. I just needed water, but there was a bar, bottle of champagne, and two large bottles of water already in the car. I had the painkillers. Tristan and AC said they were fine, and with that we headed out to the I-45 for the straight shot to Dallas. I was pouring out a glass of water, and about to take something when AC placed his hand on my arm. "Hungover?"

I nodded. "A little."

He smiled. "Sore from last night?"

I blushed.

Tristan threw him a warning glance, but AC just laughed. "As it should be. But I think champagne should be our cure and our celebration. Seeing as it's here, and all." He held up the bottle. "Looks fresh. That's good. Quality company, this. No recycling. I've seen limos where the bottles look like they've been sitting in the hot car for much too long. But not this one."

Tristan rolled his eyes. "The wine connoisseur speaks."

AC slapped him on the back. "Come on, Lily didn't leave. That's worth celebrating." He started unwrapping the foil.

"And I hate waste. You know that." He twisted off the cork. "So dangerous to let a cock, I mean a cork loose in a car."

I laughed. Even Tristan was smiling. He took the glass AC handed him. "All right, then. A toast, at least."

AC raised his glass. "'To everything, and all the rest.'" It was a Devised lyric.

Tristan echoed his words. "'To everything, and all the rest.'"

AC nodded at me. "Now you." He leaned over and kissed me on the cheek. "You're one of us now. You didn't leave." His eyes were soft and encouraging.

I looked over at Tristan. I didn't think I'd ever seen that expression on his face before. He leaned over and kissed my other cheek. "That's because she's different. Go on, then, Lil."

I raised my glass. "'To everything, and all the rest.'" We clinked glasses. I took a sip, and glanced at the other two. It was apparently necessary to finish the whole glass. I quickly returned the glass to my lips and followed suit.

AC refilled our glasses, and we leaned back against the seat, together.

* * *

We'd been quiet after that, looking out the window. Tristan looked at messages on his phone. AC had put in his headphones. I just watched the road go past, the exit signs giving names to the places we were leaving behind. It was greener than I had expected, but the low buildings and big wide skies gave me that same feeling of being trapped in some kind of bell jar. Some of the buildings were covered with vines that looked like they would grow over you overnight, like Sleeping Beauty. You could imagine waking up, covered with green ropes like snakes. Tristan pointed out a tree filled with large birds. "Buzzards," he said.

AC pulled off his headphones and peered out the window. "What's the difference between a buzzard and a vulture?"

"An interesting question." One eyebrow went up. "One you will regret asking." Tristan swiftly grabbed his arm and pretended to try and wrestle him out of the car. "Here, nothing. That's why they're waiting for you. You just have to die first."

AC raised his arms, his hands falling forward. "I am dead." His voice came out in a croak. "I am the undead. And you. You will join us." He lunged forward and caught Tristan off guard, knocking him flat on the long seat. "Join us. Aha, the beating pulse of youth." And he fell on him, trying to bite his neck. Tristan tried to push him off, but AC was remarkably persistent. And stronger than he appeared. Finally, he was straddling him, pinning him down with his wiry arms, his mouth fused to his neck. Tristan stopped struggling, and stretched out under him, just long enough for AC to drop his guard. Then he flipped him over, so that he was above AC, victorious. It was remarkably effective. It occurred to me I had been on the receiving end of that move last night. And the look of triumph on Tristan's face had been similar. But their bodies were still touching, and AC's face was slightly flushed. Exertion, anyone might say. Except then he turned his head, slowly, deliberately, towards me, and winked.

"He's one of us now," AC grinned. "See? He's dazed. Sure sign of the undead. Or something."

Tristan sat up, legs bent, sitting back on AC's ankles. "You're such a prat." He had his hands in his lap.

AC, however, did not. He stretched back, and crossed his arms behind his head. It only made what was very obvious even more so. I giggled.

Tristan frowned, and climbed off his legs. "My god, AC, you're such a show-off."

AC smiled. "I do love an audience." He glanced over at me, then turned back to Tristan. "And you're a natural performer." He paused for effect. "Or so I've been told. Might pass the time for Lily here. Beats buzzards."

Tristan laughed, but he didn't say anything, just grabbed the bottle of champagne we'd opened and poured each of us another glass.

I watched. But nothing happened. And the rest of the ride was very quiet.

chapter eighteen

Dallas

The concert was going pretty well, all things considered. With everyone suffering from some kind of ailment—colds, stomach problems made worse through no sleep and drink, to a sprained ankle the drummer had gotten when his foot caught on the steps leading down from the stage, and that was now taped up, the professionalism was really starting to kick in. They sounded tight. Problems in the songs were getting worked out. Timings were even more exact. The bassist, to his credit, was playing really well tonight, and even attempted some onstage interaction, walking around to each member, during a small bass line prominent in one of the middle eight sections. He stopped at Tristan and AC. AC had been standing slightly behind Tristan, almost looking over his shoulder at him. The bass player inclined his head slightly, and AC shrugged, and then smiled, playing a little flurry of notes to compliment the bass line. Tristan just stood there, legs apart, the microphone swallowed up like a toy in his hand. They stood there, facing each other, for a moment. I doubt anyone noticed. Then

Tristan raised his arm for the beat to begin the chorus, and he gave a brief nod to the bassist, before starting on the lyric. It was as close to an apology as anyone was going to get.

Tristan stayed there for a moment, both hands clutching the microphone, the dark head bent over, hair covering his face, the veins sticking out in his neck with the effort, the passion he was putting into the lyric, before he came forward, leaning into the crowd, the shrieks increasing in volume every time he moved closer to a new group. It was stupid, it was cliché, it was predictable—and it worked. The same way a kiss works, even though you know what's going to happen. The same way coffee wakes you up in the morning, even though you've had it before. The same with any ritual. The structure is always the same. The passion behind it creates the power. The emotions on the faces in the crowd, their energy as they pushed forward, trying to get closer to their hero, their imaginary lover, their idol, their secret dream, were enough to keep the spark going. That's what made every night different. Everyone in the audience, everyone in the band, all came in with their issues, their fears, their hopes—and the outcome of the mix could never be predicted. I watched Tristan hold his hand out to people in the front row. Everyone who could was reaching for him, stretching out their arms like a lifeline, hoping for a touch that they would never forget, a bit of magic that might even change their lives. There was no way anyone could say that real live performance wasn't important. The kind where musicians played, and worked for it, and sweated it out. For the people watching, it was a moment that defined who they were.

Tristan was now leaning back against AC. Their spark, whatever they had together, indefinable, created its own excitement. If they could share a little of it, it couldn't hurt anyone, could it? AC's guitar was piercing through the air. I looked at him again. He wasn't as beautiful as Tristan, he didn't have the warm physicality Tristan possessed so easily. But there, in his half-closed eyes, his face lost in concentration, pulling the sounds together and flinging them out into the world, he was beautiful. Then he opened his eyes wide, and you could see it, the pleasure at his skill, at feeling Tristan's body on his own, the impossibility of this happening again and again. The knowledge of pain, of loss. And yet there was a pride there, a survivor instinct, a certain defiance. I watched as they finished the song, and Tristan held his arm up, and said into the microphone, "Please give it up for AC Clark! And his magic guitar!" The crowd cheered. And there was Tristan's real beauty. He could not only share the spotlight, but he would make sure it shined on those who deserved it, using his considerable power to make sure it happened. He saw what others couldn't, and he helped everybody else understand.

AC grinned at him, and waved to the drummer, his arm punching the air to start off the pulsing beat of the next song. And it had been an ok show before, but now it took off. The two of them were on fire, invincible. Maybe because they had remembered there was only one more show left. Maybe because you just didn't know when the lightning would strike. You kept at it, waiting for divine intervention. And they looked like gods up there on the stage. Otherworldly. Invincible. And up there, they were.

It was when they came off stage, that the vulnerabilities returned. The irony of the situation—that I was there to write about them, write about the tour, and I knew all the secrets, even the one they didn't fully realize had escaped, even if AC kept hinting at it. And I knew I would never write about the two of them, even if that one story would be enough to ensure my future success and notoriety. Regardless of my personal interest in the matter. No matter what happened. Never.

I always used to wonder why there weren't more stories out there about what went on backstage, the relationships. Maybe because when you got close enough, you did feel a kind of extreme loyalty. Or maybe because no one would ever believe it. If you were in, you protected the pack. If you were out—it just sounded like whining. There had been a couple of tell-alls. Despite some interest, they generally came across having the same effect as spray painting a marble statue. Making something ugly. And there were some bad stories out there that had never seen the light of day. I thought of the engineer who had described to me being told to call home with excuses to the wife—not his, but the keyboardist he was working with. The people who made the music weren't perfect. But the dream thrived on illusion. So the question underneath was always there—why are you doing this? Why are you spoiling the dream?

The band was starting the encore. The whole thing had gone by so quickly. I looked around. The usual complement of roadies, girls who had managed to get backstage, local celebs who liked the band, taking selfies with the stage as backdrop. There'd be a party after the show, some contest winners, autographs, drinks, the customary crowd. I watched them wrap up. Then the whole band came together and lined up for a bow. There was something about the way they were all waving, the way even the bass player was finally acting like a part of the band, that made it feel more like the last night of the tour. A final wave, and they separated, drifting off the stage, AC handing his guitar over to the roadie looking after the instruments, while taking a towel from him. Tristan got his towel too, and gave me a little wave, as they went past the onlookers, smiling, but eager to get back to the dressing room, and decompress before they had to face another crowd at the after-party.

I followed, and when the band bifurcated into the two dressing rooms, I went with Tristan and AC. They were the big names, and because of that, no one really questioned the hierarchy of the larger dressing room going to them. Whatever else anyone might have been thinking, they either didn't say or kept it very quiet, especially after the blowout in Minneapolis. I don't think anyone doubted Tristan when he had made it known "that he would sack the next person outright who hadn't reached the 21st century." The whole thing seemed very far away now. The energy had changed. Everything was about tonight, this moment in time. And tonight, it was one more party to get through, one more concert. The promise of some time off before hitting L.A. still seemed a distant idea.

Tristan was stripping off his shirt. He wouldn't take a shower here, but he always washed the sweat off his face and torso. He always said, especially on nights like tonight when he was wearing leather trousers, that it was more trouble than it was worth to take everything off and start again. So he stood there in the middle of the room, peeling off the sweat-soaked shirt, revealing the fascinating expanse of skin, the line of dark hair leading down, his chest displaying his new tattoo. I glanced over at AC. He was watching, his expression blank. It was all in his eyes. The slightly raised eyebrow, the intensity of his gaze. It was the look of someone whose imagination was at work. But he felt me looking at him, and turned in my direction. He winked before I could look away. I smiled, almost blushing. But he was quicker than me, more used to the quick cover-up. "Shall I take mine off too, Lily? I'm sure you didn't only follow us in here for an interview." And he pulled off his t-shirt in one quick motion, and circled his nipple with a finger, sticking out his ass, a near picture perfect imitation of a 1970s era Mick Jagger. "Fuck, I'm hot. Shit, girl! Yes!" And he did a little shimmy.

I couldn't help it, I collapsed on the sofa laughing. AC was funny. But he also made me nervous. There was something about the two of them there, standing there, looking at me like that. I didn't even want to think about it.

Tristan sniggered. "AC, you killed her. Your stripper act is too much for the girls, I keep telling you that."

AC smacked his ass, hard. The sound of skin connecting with leather rocketed through the room. "Not often enough." He went right up to him, striking a pose, and stuck out a hip, looking for all the world like some androgynous fighter, ready to start something. "Like what you see, darling?" We both looked at Tristan to see what he'd do.

A flicker of something crossed his face. He opened his mouth, then shut it. Then he moved to circle around him, slowly, as though he were inspecting the goods. He stopped when he had made a full circle, and looked him in the eye. Then without warning, he spun him around and pulled him up hard against him, and held him tight to his body. One hand went to his nipples and pinched, relentlessly enough that AC finally let out a small yelp. But the look in his eyes was melting, as much as he was trying to keep from showing anything. Tristan did a slow grind against his ass, then pushed him away roughly. "I'm sure I told you not to tease me." His voice was low. He turned to me and smiled. "Performers on and off the stage. It's in our blood." And he walked off to the bathroom. But leather pants don't hide much.

"Bastard," AC muttered. But he laughed and strutted over to the table to get a bottle of water. "Want something, Lily?" That tone in his voice.

"No, I'm fine." Except my voice came out as a croak, my mouth was so dry. AC stared at me. "Maybe I do. Thanks."

AC came over and handed me a bottle. "That's right. When you're thirsty, you drink."

I didn't say anything.

* * *

They had closed one of the smaller stages in the venue for the party. It was feeling more and more like the last wrap-up, the final cast party for the stage show. Everyone was in a good mood. Tristan mingled and signed some autographs for people, chatting to the record company people like they were lifelong friends. The cynical side of me wondered if they had news on the winners for the awards show. If he was going to win, they would want to be nice to him, their cash cow. If he was going to lose, they'd want to be nice to him so he wouldn't throw a tantrum and do something to sabotage the tour.

Besides, even the nomination had increased the sales. That's how it all worked. Nothing like telling people something was popular to get them all to rush out and buy it. I studied their faces. It was a business. Even with everything I knew, I tended to forget that, seeing it all more solidly from the side of the artist. These were people mingling, enjoying the perks of the job, happy to keep up with the meetings and paperwork tomorrow if they could get drunk with some stars tonight. An ocean of selfies, pics with the band, who would stand closest to Tristan, AC a close second. I shook my head, and headed for the bar. Positivity. There were worse things. And it wouldn't kill me to be more positive.

As I ordered a bourbon, figuring even if Texas wasn't the south, it was close enough, I was surprised when the bartender started flirting and chatting, asking how I liked Texas, was there anything I wanted to see. I laughed. Then I realized it was the first time anyone had apart from Tristan, or maybe AC, had actually spoken to me in weeks. And Hank. Fuck I missed him. The entourage circled me warily. I avoided the outside world, the fans, the staff. It wasn't as though you could speak to them anyway. No one was really to be trusted, unless they were on the inside. I could feel myself shutting down. I smiled, warily, and made some comment about wanting to ride a horse, which made him laugh, as it was intended. He probably didn't know who I was. Anyway, it really didn't do any good to let down your guard. I was part of the tour. Who knew who he was, really? There would have been a time when I would have been happy to talk with him. Now I felt like I needed to protect myself, keep all my knowledge my own. If that was partially because I usually liked to talk to people when I was drinking, and partially because I couldn't stop thinking of something in particular, I couldn't tell. It could be paranoia, it could be self-preservation. Whatever it was, I didn't want any secrets to slip out. I was drinking, not drunk, not yet, but I was getting there. Loyal to the group and part of it. Passing by the rest. I said thanks, maybe a little more curtly than I had intended, and moved away.

I wandered around a bit, listening to pieces of conversations. The usual mix of nonsense, flirtation, and business. I spotted AC, and relieved, went over to where he was was standing. They were lowering a screen, and someone was setting up a projector. One enterprising group went over to one of the low red brocade covered sofas, and showing admirable teamwork, all pitched in and managed to carry it over nearer to the screen for a better view. I whispered to AC, "What the hell is this? And is there popcorn?"

He looked at me. "You'll never believe it."

"Try me," I laughed. I looked at my glass. Nearly empty.

AC put his arm around me and we walked back over to the bar. "Devised home movies. And videos." His voice went down a little lower. "Tristan is pissed off."

We got to the bar and I ordered a beer. Time to slow down before I said anything I'd regret. After we turned away, I leaned over to him. "Why? The videos everyone's seen. What are these home movies?"

AC smiled. "That's what he's finding out right now. I think—probably—James." He looked at the ceiling. "Hopefully they're not too bad. I told him he shouldn't make a fuss—looks worse."

I thought for a minute. My brain seemed to be working

slower. "No. It's not a good idea. Especially with the possible documentary. Dave will have a fit. He's going to want this exclusive for himself. Can't they just show the videos? Shit. Tristan. Where is he?"

AC nodded towards the backstage. "Back there. I think he wants to see them first."

"Ok. Let's go tell them to just show MTV, or something that actually plays music. Keep the crowd happy while we deal with this." We walked over to the guy with the laptop and the projector and gave him instructions on what to do. Then we started heading backstage. I already had my phone out. Panic was making me remarkably clear-headed. "I'm calling Dave. It's—fuck, what time? Christ it's 1 a.m. there." I listened to the ring. "Can't be helped."

The ringing stopped and Dave's voice came through loud and clear. If he'd been asleep, I couldn't tell. "Lily? What's the problem?"

There was no time for pleasantries. "Dave. Yeah. Look. We're in Dallas, and some mug down here from the record company has got ahold of what he's calling 'Devised home movies.'"

"And?"

"And no one's seen them, but they want to show them to the after-party. As in now." I gulped a sip of beer. "Tristan's trying to find out what they are and where they came from. AC thinks maybe James."

"Yes, well that's always the main source. No one's seen them? Is AC there with you? Can you put him on the line?"

"Sure." I passed my phone over to him.

AC started to speak, but clearly Dave had interrupted him.

He was listening, and suddenly his face went white. "Oh, fuck. Those. Of course." He listened a bit longer, then walked a couple of steps away. "Does she?" He tried not to look at me, but I had the impression they were talking about me. "Not sure, but that's not the problem. Yeah, I'll go find Tristan. We'll call you right back."

AC waved my phone at me, and nodded his head towards the backstage, and started walking to the side door at a rapid pace. I caught up with him and took my phone. "So it is trouble."

AC looked grim. "Yeah, a bit. Nothing that can't be solved. Like blackmail." He laughed, but there was no humor in it. "Come on, we've got to find Tristan. Now."

We pushed through the door, and went down the long hall that led to the backstage area of this part of the hall. We could hear voices, getting louder as we approached. We turned the corner, and there was Tristan, looking murderous, James, who was holding a couple of DVDs in his hand, and a record company suit, who genuinely looked confused. He was speaking.

"We thought it would be fun. No, I haven't seen them, but I was told they were outtakes from the videos and some backstage interviews. Nothing crazy there." He turned to Tristan. "But if you don't want them shown, that's fine." He looked nervous.

A muscle in Tristan's face was twitching. Otherwise, he was dangerously still. "Tell me one thing. How many copies of this are there?"

The record company guy swallowed. "Well, I made a copy—as a backup. You never know. It's in my desk. At work."

Tristan looked at him. "Go and get it and bring it back here."

The man had a shocked expression. "It's 1 in the morning."

Tristan took a step forward. "If you can tell time, you might keep your job. Go get it. Now. Thanks." The man nodded, and backed out, before Tristan could say anything else.

Then he turned towards James. AC caught his arm in mid-air with a surprising amount of strength. "Don't do it mate. Look at the scum. That's what he wants."

I started dialing Trevor. This needed the big guns.

Tristan pulled away from AC, who grabbed him again. The look in Tristan's eyes was deadly. "You fucking prick. How many of these do you have?"

"Enough. Enough to insure my safe passage out of your employment and on to someone else. What, you didn't think I knew you were about to fire me? Send me off blacklisted? You're too caught up in yourself and your...," he spat out the next words, "dear friend."

"Leave Lily out of this." Tristan moved closer. AC was leaning on him.

"Not Lily I'm talking about." The look on Tristan's face altered, and he threw a glance in my direction. "You thought no one knew? You're not as smart as you pretend." He handed over the DVDs. AC grabbed them before Tristan had a chance.

I was on my third message to Trevor. "Please Trevor, pick up. Tristan is going to kill James. He's blackmailing him. Shit." I hung up, and redialed Dave. He picked up right away. I looked over at James who was still talking.

"What's on here isn't a lot. But it's enough. And coupled

with the way you've acted, should be enough to stop a promising solo career. Or slow it down. Get all those stories back up in the press again."

I held the phone to my ear. Dave had been talking. "Dave. What? Look. Tristan. James. Is blackmailing Tristan. Something about the DVD. Stopping his career. What can I do?"

It sounded like Dave was punching numbers into another phone. "Did you call Trevor? Yes? Ok, I'm trying him again. We're ready to run with something, I just need one more answer from him. Hang on. Look. Get their attention. Then repeat exactly what I tell you."

"Ok," I said. "Hang on." I took a deep breath. And I let out a shriek that was probably going to get the whole party in here. At last then there would be more people to keep Tristan from going to jail for manslaughter. They all turned to look at me.

I marched up to James. "I've got a message for you, you fucking worthless piece of shit." I spoke into the phone. "Ok." I had a feeling I shouldn't say his name, though it probably didn't matter. "Go ahead."

Dave spoke slowly. "Swiss IBAN number. Starting with CH 93. Contact Idute." He paused. "Hang on, I've got Trevor. Yes. Go ahead." He repeated each part separately, and I spoke the words as though it were a magical formula that would make James disappear. With any luck it would.

James was scoffing at each one, though. "IBAN numbers, so what." After the next part he muttered, "The Swiss ones all begin with CH." At the name "Idute" he froze. "You're bluffing."

I heard Dave laughing. "I'm sure you thought of this, but ask him if he wants to take that chance."

I did.

"I will release these. You can't prove anything."

Dave had heard him. "Don't tell him this, but it was a set-up. People Trevor knows. They gave him some hacking information to see what he'd do with it. Then tested him by having a fake contact offer him money." He paused. "Tell him it wasn't really the FBI he passed it on to. He never left their network. And that they know where he is."

That did get a reaction. A stream of swear words that was the most energetic statement I'd heard from him the entire tour. Then he said, "I can still do this."

Dave laughed again. "Tell him to go ahead. Ask him where he wants to be buried when they find him. They don't like traitors."

After I'd repeated Dave's question, James looked nervous. "If you're bluffing, I have enough copies of this to make a difference."

Tristan said, slowly, "I don't give a shit what anyone else wants with you. We will follow you. Look behind you from now on, because it might be in 5 years, or 10. Who knows. Now. Get the fuck out of my sight. Now."

Dave was listening. "Take the DVDs and get Tristan out of there. AC too. Go stay in a different hotel. Actually just get your bags and get the driver to take you to Austin. Get a new hotel there. Don't stay where you're booked." I was listening, but I stopped when I heard James.

James had a vindictive glare as he spoke to Tristan. "And your sweet lady there. How long will love last when she knows," he jerked his head towards AC, "about your bit on the side there? True love. She'll like the sex tape scene." He spat on the ground.

AC grabbed at Tristan again, who was looking between the three of us, faint panic in his eyes. Dave was silent on the phone.

I stepped up to James, taking each step slowly, fists clenched. When I was close enough to smell his breath, I started. "Did you watch it on repeat? You and the remote. Your only friend. For the rest of your sad life." Then I was shouting in his face. "But guess what? I already knew. I already know. And I don't care. How about that." I stepped back. The temptation to take a swing at him was too strong. "Fucking loser. Go die somewhere." I backed away from him, pointing at him to stay where he was.

AC looked like he was about to grab for me as well.

I tucked the phone under my ear, and linked arms with AC, who yanked at Tristan. The three of us walked away. I didn't turn around. I just wanted to get the hell out of there. Dave was talking.

"What Dave? Sorry, yes, we're going. Car should be outside? Brilliant." I listened. "Ask me tomorrow." When I pressed the end call button, I realized I was shaking.

We said good night to the few people cleaning up at the bars. Like nothing had happened. The rest of the people had already left. As we got outside, the record company guy came running up to us with a bag. "10 DVDs. This is it. I swear."

"Good," Tristan muttered. "Because you're the only one left who could have copies. And if there's a leak, we'll know it's you. Time to go home now. Party's over." He hesitated, as if he were going to say something, and Tristan broke away from us, and took a step forward.

"Tris," whispered AC. But the guy had already turned and was walking quickly back to his car.

Tristan looked at the DVDs in his hand. "I only have two," he mimicked, horribly accurately. "You lying sack of shit. Fuck you. Fuck all of you," he yelled out into the night.

AC had him by the arm. "It's ok mate. It's ok. Come on, let's go." The sound of his voice seemed to calm Tristan down, and we kept moving towards the car.

Tristan turned to AC. "Fuck, let's score. You must know someone here." He threw his arm around me. "Everything's going to shit anyway. So much for keeping it on an even keel."

AC was silent. Then he finally said, "Remember. Just not today. And—I don't want this great evening to finish up in jail. I don't think they like us round these parts." His sudden twang in his accent made Tristan smile, but we both held on a little tighter.

We finally made it to the limo, and AC went in first, with Tristan in the middle, and me at the end. I was looking around to see if anyone was watching, or following us, but it seemed very quiet. Too quiet possibly, but I couldn't see anything. I didn't want to get paranoid. But all of us were completely on edge, and very wired. I didn't see how we were going to get through the night, but then again, we really didn't have a choice.

Once we were settled in, and the car had picked up speed, AC started poking around. "What, no minibar? Well, that isn't going to fly. Lily. When we go up to get our stuff, remind me to pull out some drinks from the room."

Tristan was just lying there, his head back against the seat, eyes closed. He looked completely drained. AC studied his face. "Tris. It's going to be ok."

Tristan nodded, but didn't say anything.

AC carried on. "If you promise to be good, Lily and I will pack up. You can stay here. Fair enough? But no running off to the kitchen to score."

Tristan coughed. He sounded exhausted. "No, I better come up with you. Maybe I'll jump in the shower." He sat up straighter. "I can't believe how close I came to smashing that fucker's face in."

AC gave a bark of a laugh. "Yeah, mate. Neither can we." He looked over at me, an uneasy smile on his face. I wasn't convinced he was as in control as he appeared, but his air of relative calm was soothing to me as well. "Yeah, Tris. It's all going to be fine. Of course—there is that one thing."

His eyes were closed again. "Only one?"

AC pretended to look out the window. "It's going to be hell to do the thank you videos for the regional record company PR people."

Tristan opened his eyes, and then burst out laughing. "Fuck. You are so right."

* * *

At the hotel, it was all business. We all went up to quickly pack. I'd barely unpacked, so it didn't take long. Tristan jumped in the shower. AC did a sweep of the minibar, and stuck the bottles in my purse.

"You carry those. I'll go down and do some quick checkout thing. I want to get out of here before the news goes very far," AC said. "Wait for Tristan."

I glanced at him from where I was arranging the bottles in my bag so they wouldn't make so much noise banging together. "Well, yeah, of course."

"I think it's all drained him. We're going to need to keep an eye on him." He came over to me and put his hand on my shoulder. "He's not as tough as he looks."

"You've known him for a long time."

"Yeah, true. But you were brilliant back there."

I caught myself smiling. "I was pissed off back there."

The sound of the shower stopped. AC squeezed my shoulder. "Lots of questions, yeah? But not now. But...did you? Know?"

I picked up my suitcase. There wasn't a short answer for this one. "Will you take my bag down? Later. Ask me later. I won't lie."

AC gave me a quick hug. "See you down there. Hurry his highness up."

"Not a problem," I said.

AC stopped at the door. "No. It never is with you. I can't understand how he found you."

I stopped rearranging the bottles and shrugged. "Simple. I fell at his feet."

"As we do." And he was out the door, dragging our suitcases behind him.

chapter nineteen

Dallas to Austin

Once in the car, a couple of mini bottles from the minibar better than we'd been before, talking didn't seem like a good idea. Tristan wrapped his arms around both of us, and we both moved closer to him. It felt like he was keeping us warm, but I had the feeling it was a little bit the other way around. He needed us to hold him together, so he wouldn't spin out of orbit and lose his center. The edge had felt very close back there. And talking seemed a waste of time. Why question what was obviously working? What really needed to be explained, after all? Particularly at the moment. No one asks why animals stand together for warmth, or why people reach out for someone's hand when it's dark. It could be as simple as that, our pile of bodies in the back of a limousine providing more comfort than we could on our own. I kicked off my boots and put my feet up on the seat. I looked out into the night. If it was slightly more complicated than that, asking a lot of stupid questions wouldn't help.

I woke up a couple of hours later. I thought I'd heard

something. The driver's voice was coming through the intercom, very quietly.

"Is anyone awake?"

I pressed the button to connect. "Hi, yeah, keep it down. What's up?"

"We'll be there in about half an hour. It's still early." I looked at my watch. Ten past five. Yes it was. "Do you want to go right to the hotel, or get some breakfast first? There's a decent 24 hour diner folks like, I can take you there if you want."

My stomach grumbled at the mention of diner food. What had I eaten for dinner? Bourbon, champagne, and whiskey. Yeah. Maybe eating first wasn't a bad idea. It was very early. "Hang on a sec," I said to the driver, and took my hand off the intercom. My neck was stiff. I'd moved along the seat to get to the controls, and now I turned around to look at Tristan and AC. Asleep still, though Tristan appeared to be moving slightly. They looked angelic, AC with his curls, and Tristan stretched out, his legs looking even longer in the confined space, the circles under his eyes and pale skin making him look like a lost child. I didn't want to wake them up. They needed to shut down, forget about everything. But food wouldn't hurt. If Tristan didn't want to deal with the public, we could always get takeout.

I pressed the button again. "Sure, why not? They may decide not to, but let's head there. Thanks." I shut off the intercom in the middle of the driver's "thanks." I didn't want to bother the two of them any more than I already had. I crawled back to Tristan's side. He sleepily pulled me to him.

His voice sounded dry. I wondered if he was getting sick. "Is everything ok?"

"Yes, no worries. Diner food soon."

He leaned his head on mine. "Good, think I'm hungry. Bit more sleep first though."

I closed my eyes, and leaned against him, feeling his weight on mine. Another half an hour in our cocoon.

* * *

We managed to get a parking space in the lot for the nearby shops, although it was a little tricky to maneuver the limo around. But I supposed the driver was used to that. I hoped so. Tristan offered to bring him some breakfast, and then changed his mind.

"Come in with us, man," he said. "You've got to be hungry, driving overnight. And you've still got to go back, right?"

The driver shook his head. "No, I'm due to stay here with you, until after the concert. Then back."

Tristan looked surprised for a minute, then nodded. "Shit, I'm losing it. That's right. Even more reason to come have breakfast. Otherwise, I'm going to get offended and think you dragged us to some tourist place with awful food."

The driver looked a little embarrassed. "It is a tourist place. But the food's good. All right, I'll come. Very gener-ous of you, sir."

Tristan tapped him on the back. "Don't start saying that around me. The press'll pick it up."

AC let out a howl of laughter. The driver just looked con-fused. It took me a second to figure out what Tristan meant.

Then I glanced over at AC. He just winked and shook his head.

Tristan smiled. "Don't worry about it. And ignore him. He's always like that. At least I can see trouble coming. Come on, let's go before anybody turns up."

We went in. It wasn't exactly what you thought of when you imagined a diner, even with the counter and big clock. I couldn't put my finger on it. Maybe it was the strange stainless steel bell-shaped lights and the green walls. The circular banquette seats around a table made it feel more like a dream from a TV show in the 70s than a modern restaurant. I couldn't decide if it was the lack of sleep, or food, or just everything, but it all seemed like a set, just a little surreal.

The food was decent. AC was thrilled they had a vegetarian breakfast with homemade sausages. The driver had chicken and waffles. I had a hash brown sort of thing with real sausages. Tristan ate half of mine, and the frittata he ordered. After a long night of stress, it felt good to be somewhere else, eating some decent food. There was always that odd feeling from being in a new place, on the road, of not really existing. We could all just get back in the car, and take off for somewhere else. In less than 24 hours, we'd be able to do it. One more show.

Finally, we staggered out into the milky sunshine. Rush hour was beginning, like it did everywhere. I wished we could have a few hours of 5 a.m. lack of pressure. But the day was here, and so were we, and it was time to get back into the world. The driver held open the door for us, waving Tristan away. "Ok boss. Hotel next. Unless there's somewhere else we need to go first?" Tristan had grudgingly tolerated being called "boss" instead of sir. "Hotel St. Cecelia, that's right, isn't it?"

AC whistled, and looked at me. "Ask Tristan. His idea," I said. He'd actually called them directly, himself, after he'd gotten out of the shower in the last hotel. That we'd left. Or never really got to. Last night. This morning. Everything was really starting to blur.

Tristan bowed his head in acknowledgement. AC looked pleased. "Nice. Haven't been there in years. Good choice, Tris. Don't tell me—surprise me. Bungalow or piano suite?"

Tristan grinned. "You'll find out soon enough."

AC reached across me and tapped him on the arm. "Wait. Did we get thrown out of there?"

Tristan frowned. "Was it that place? Fuck pool sides are all the same." He ran his hand through his hair. "You know, I honestly don't remember. I don't think so. They seemed happy enough to take the reservation. I was lucky to get it—they'd had some last minute cancellation thing. Unless it's just a plan to get us to pay for…what was it?"

AC smirked. "I think it was a chair we threw in. And the woman behind the bar."

Tristan looked at us, wide-eyed. "Oh shit. Maybe it was there. Never mind. We're older and wiser now. It was an ugly chair, anyway."

AC looked out the window. "Older, for certain. I'm tired."

We pulled into the hotel a few minutes later. The entrance looked like a private home, except for the strange shield-shaped neon sign. We pulled in, and there was someone at the door almost instantly. Nothing like a limo for attracting attention. The car stopped and the door swung open. The man welcoming us looked a bit like he'd been lost in the sun for a little too long at some point, but he was perfectly friendly.

"Checking in, Mr…?"

Tristan smiled, and ran his hand through his hair again. "Mustang. Reservation for one of the bungalows in the name of Mustang."

The guy did a stellar job of hiding the smirk just enough. "Mustang. Yes, I believe we have that ready for you now. Let me get your bags."

Tristan nodded. "Cheers mate." Then he gestured to me, a bit panicked. He came over. "Lily? Do you have any cash? I wasn't prepared for all this. Forgot about the liquid asset part."

"Don't worry, I've got it." I fished around in my bag, but AC was already there, slipping the man some money. He waved at us. Tristan looked instantly relieved.

AC came up to him. "Living in the bubble too long, man."

Tristan laughed. "Yeah, yeah, tell me all your problems by the pool."

We all went inside and stood around awkwardly while Tristan signed for things, keeping an eye out for curious guests, then Tristan went out to arrange the pickup with the driver for tonight. Finally, the same man came to lead us to the bungalow. Tristan was about to wave him away, but AC grabbed his arm. "Don't let them know you remember this place. They might remember you," he whispered dramatically.

Tristan rolled his eyes. "Fine." So we followed the man to the windowed building, and let him describe the amenities, the bar, the outside seating, which towels to use for the pool, and how to call for the concierge at any time, day or night. When he got to showing us the DVD player, AC exclaimed,

"Perfect. We have some DVDs…" Tristan glared at him. "Of the tour. The tour. To watch." I was trying not to laugh, but at the same time it was the only way to deal with the weirdness we'd had to put up with over the past 24 hours. Giggling, I pulled AC to come show me the view of the pool, and we watched Tristan thank the guy and shut the door behind him.

"How much of a tip did you give him? For fuck's sake. The DVD. Fuck." And he started laughing. "How the hell did we get to this point? Do you remember how it happened?"

AC sat down on the sofa. The view out the floor to ceiling windows was of the pool, a collection of unfamiliar trees, the other shaded bungalows. He had a thoughtful expression on his face, even if the fatigue made him look more dissolute than usual. He shook his head, and pushed back an escaping curl. "We're incredible?" He breathed in. "Honestly Tris, I try not to think about it too much. That way lies madness. After Devised split…" He trailed off. "I'm just happy to be here. Life doesn't like it when you ask why. Full of reasons why not." He stood up. "I have a fast metabolism. And the wet bar is calling my name. Anyone else for a bottle of wine and a drunken float in the pool? Come on, we made it this far."

"Living the dream." Tristan's voice was teasing but he looked sad, like he'd just been reminded of all things he wanted to forget.

"Damn straight. And you better lock up those DVDs before anyone gets curious. Promotion, my second skill. No, third. Now what goes well with vegetarian breakfast, at," he looked at his watch, "9 a.m? I think there's an amusing little white in here calling my name. Lily?"

I jumped up to help him. I didn't want to think about what had been left unsaid either.

* * *

So here we were. The last show of this leg. I'd made it, through secrets and Tristan's unpredictable behavior. I'd had Trevor encouraging me to take a break, and head back to NYC, and AC asking me to stay. And I'd stuck it out. And I'd had that one moment in the limo, with the toast to the line from the Devised song, "to everything, and all the rest." Devastatingly simple words, which in that moment transformed a lyric into an indelible bond between the three of us. A long, long road. 3500 miles of it. And I felt like I'd worked every mile. But now, watching them at the end of the encore, bowing and waving to the crowd, it really did seem as easy as they made it look. One of the roadies ran out on stage with two bottles of champagne, and gave one to Tristan and the other to AC. They popped the corks to general cheering, then like a couple of leather-clad race car drivers, shook the bottles hard and starting spraying the audience and each other. The people in the front must have taken a direct hit. Everyone was shrieking. And the two of them stood there, brandishing the bottles, side by side, simply watching the crowd. Tristan coaxed another few cheers out of them, then went up to the mike. "Thank you Austin! You've been beautiful. We will see you next time."

Dripping champagne, they both waved to the crowd and started walking off. AC stopped, drank from the bottle to more applause, and threw an arm up in the air behind him in a final wave as he walked off stage, the last person to disappear into the wings. I stood there watching as the die-hard fans kept cheering until the house lights came up. It broke the spell, having to squint into the light, the black floor sticky with beer and discarded cups. The ones that always left a little bit before the end never saw this. They would already be in the parking lot, away from the crush. The audience filed out, shuffling along, revealing more of the floor, except for a guy and a girl standing off to the side, still gazing at the stage. They were holding hands. For a minute, I thought it was Melanie. I blinked to clear my vision, but when I looked again, one of the staff had asked them to move on, and I couldn't see her face. I hoped it was her. Whoever it was, they had found someone they could share their passion with. I turned away from the brightly lit theatre. I knew that wasn't an easy thing to find.

The after-party seemed to be starting already, the backstage of the venue filled with people drinking and laughing. This wasn't even the official one. Tristan had promised to attend everything, after a short conversation with Annie on the phone a few hours before the show, while we were relaxing in the room. Apparently their biggest worry was that the star would self-destruct one way or another, or worse, not do any promotion. So Tristan had sworn to sign everything that was put in front of him, and shake everyone's hands. Kiss all the women. Whatever they wanted. I could tell he was tired, and sarcastic and slightly bitter about the whole thing. But Annie obviously didn't do sarcasm, and whatever he had said, she'd taken at face value. Besides, he'd meant it. Most of it, anyway. AC had dragged him out to the pool after the phone call, Tristan's posture a little more tense than it had been before. But now they were doing the rounds, fixed smiles on both their faces.

Watching them I remembered I needed to check in with Dave. A quick phone call over the noise of the party, and I'd found out what the hustle they'd run on James was. Apparently it was all Trevor. I wasn't surprised. It seemed Trevor had mentioned to his PA that he needed some likely lads to play a part. To set a little trap for someone that needed to learn a lesson, learn his place in the scheme of things. When he'd mentioned James' love for hacking intrigues and easy money, she had told him that she had some friends who would be perfect. So he'd taken them all out to a good dinner, they'd figured out the details of the scheme over the brandy and cigars, and Trevor had provided the seed money, and a small fee. I knew, or I hoped, I'd get more of the story out of Trevor directly but I couldn't resist asking Dave. "So it was a scam? They weren't even hackers?"

Dave had chuckled. "Lily, who knows. Trevor told me that her friends had seemed extremely knowledgeable. But they claimed they were pretending. All in fun. Trevor's no fool. If he said he didn't want to know, that's your answer."

He told me to hold on, and I heard him speak to someone in the background. Then his voice was back. "Anyway, you made it. Congratulations. Enjoy the last night. And relax. Call me when you're back in New York. Ciao. And give Tristan and AC my best." I was about to say something when the line cut off. I was left with the silent phone in my hand, and the sounds of clinking glass in the distance. Dropping my phone in my bag, I took Dave's advice and went to join the party.

I got a drink, and said hello to a few people. But the proper after-party was in some club somewhere. So after Tristan and AC had gone to clean up, we all headed outside. They appeared and signed autographs for the crowd of the faithful waiting. One of the security guards helped us to the street, and we climbed in the limo.

The intercom came on. "Good evening boss."

Tristan laughed. "Have you moved to Austin now? I thought you were heading back to Dallas."

The driver didn't seem surprised. "They said you still needed a driver out here for another day. I'm in a motel. I figured what the hell. Nothing much going on at home anyway."

Tristan shook his head, even though the driver couldn't see him. "Well, good. Nice to know who's up front. I appreciate it. I'd invite you to the party, but that's the whole point—you're not supposed to be drinking."

"It's ok. Thanks boss."

AC looked at Tristan. "Another day."

Tristan grinned at him. "Yeah. I figured another night of poolside living couldn't hurt." He put his arm around me. "You're staying, right?"

AC shrugged, but his eyes were bright. "Maybe I will at that. That model in L.A. is going to be so disappointed."

Tristan put his hand on his knee. "As your physician, I recommend a day of rest if you're going to be shagging three models a day. Or one model three times a day. Or two models one and a half times a day. Wait, that's wrong. No wonder I keep losing money."

AC put his hand over Tristan's. "Good advice doc. Now tell me. What's a half-shag?"

"There's a joke in there. Give me time."

AC leaned over and kissed me on the cheek. "All the time you need. I'll be over here."

"Bastard."

AC lay over us. "My real name must not be spoken. Now remind me what crap I'm supposed to spout tonight if we want more hotel nights. At this point, you've got me where you want me. I'll say anything."

"Just the usual. I'm wonderful, a genius, best thing that ever happened in your life…"

"Usual lies, full version. Got it. Invoice you in the a.m."

Listening to them, there was a part of me that almost wished for one more insane night on the road.

chapter twenty

Austin to New York

The last day in the hotel felt like a long goodbye. Tristan and I were due to head to NYC for a few days before going out to California. AC had always planned to go directly to L.A. He spent most of his time, apparently, these days, on the west coast. I realized I had no idea where he lived, if he had an apartment somewhere, or if he drifted from place to place, staying with friends for a few days, before moving on. It hadn't mattered before, not that it would be an easy question to ask. But I had a feeling I knew the answer anyway, from something he'd said. We had all been sitting at the table in the morning having breakfast. AC had looked at both of us, before stabbing a bit of French toast with his fork. "This is nice. Something new and something old."

Tristan had glanced at him. "Ok, I'll jump. What's new and what's old? Don't say me. Or Lily."

AC kept cutting little pieces of French toast, but didn't say anything else. Once all of it had been carved up into small squares, which were remarkably uniform, I thought, he impaled one on the end of his fork, and twirled it in the air. "No, not that. Just it's nice having breakfast with people I've known longer than a few weeks. A few days. Hours. That's new." He chewed thoughtfully.

"So what's old?" Tristan asked.

"Knowing I'm leaving tomorrow. Not being entirely sure where I'll be after that."

A terrible look crossed Tristan's face. "Shit, AC. Why didn't you say? I thought you were heading off to see that woman, what was her name? Heidi? Heather? Heather in leather? What happened?"

AC laughed. Now he was making two little stacks of the French toast squares. "Helene. Heidi. Really?" He picked up two squares with the fork and examined them carefully. "This food is really pretty good. No, I am seeing her. I think. Not sure I'm in the mood for your average model star-fucker, though. How jaded is that?"

Tristan quickly put his hand on AC's forehead. "Are you sick? Damn. One day off. That's all it takes." He ran his hand through AC's blond curls. "Come with us then. A couple of days in New York. Cure you. No dragging anyone back though, mind. A home's a home."

AC raised his eyes and the two of them exchanged a silent communication. AC broke away first, and looked over at me, then back at Tristan. "No, you two need some time. And I did promise. Besides, I've got to sort out some shit in L.A. Think I need to store my stuff somewhere more permanent than some junkie guitarist's garage, you know what I'm saying?"

Tristan shrugged. "Fine. After the big show crap, you're

coming back with us to the city. Don't say no. We'll arrange it later." He looked him up and down. "Now stop playing with your damn food and eat it. You look too skinny. I'm going to start having to look for your coke stash, and you know how that ends up."

"Yeah, up your nose. Besides, you like me skinny." AC winked at me. "But what about Lily here? Don't you think you should ask her first? She does, you know, like live with you. Might want her opinion on this."

I jumped in before Tristan could say anything. "No, it's cool. We don't need any of those couples' talks in the bathroom." Tristan snorted. "You are very welcome as far as I'm concerned—and it's not my house, anyway."

AC leaned over and picked up my hand, and kissed the top of it, gently, theatrically, while gazing at me from under his long eyelashes. "Nomads, isn't it right? To our soft landings."

Tristan grabbed my hand away. "Don't make me change my mind. 'Nomads.' Drama queen." He kissed the same hand, then pulled my arm around his neck. "Don't make her leave."

AC shook his head. "Not a chance." He pushed at his plate. "Come on, last day. Let's go hang out in the pool for a while. All this talk of the future is making me anxious. And you know what happens when I get too anxious. I can't swim if I drink too much."

And we spent the day doing nothing. Swimming. Sitting by the pool. A couple of the other guests definitely recognized us, but whether they wanted to protect our privacy or keep their cool and their distance, I couldn't say. It was hard to believe only a couple of days ago, we'd been constantly surrounded by people, most of whom either wanted something or were there to keep too many from wanting too much. We all regarded everyone else warily, were happier when they went away, and even more pleased when we retreated back into the bungalow for a bottle of wine, the door closing tight behind us.

We wound up ordering dinner from somewhere the hotel recommended. I didn't even pay attention. It was good, without being memorable, but the idea that we had nowhere to rush off to was the real draw. Tristan inspected what AC was eating and told him he had to eat more. He even picked up a forkful of food and sang a little song about hungry birds until AC obediently opened his mouth, chirping, and ate it. Tristan laughed, pleased.

Somewhere out there was the real world, some hard place, with its details and demands. But for the moment, in the soft warmth of a room we probably would never see again, none of it mattered.

We opened another bottle of wine and went over to the living room area that faced the pool and the trees. AC picked up his guitar, and began strumming some soft chords. I stretched out and listened to him sing a couple of Neil Young songs, my eyes closed, wondering how life could really get this easy. Tristan suggested another one, this time Simon and Garfunkel, and the two of them began to sing together. Their voices, away from the stage, and the demands of singing over the electronics, and the crowds, and the drums, were more subtle. Still powerful and rich, but with overtones and a warmth that could never be transmitted over and through the speakers. Part of me still wished I had something to record it that would do it justice. But some moments are just that—

ephemeral, born to be experienced, and not captured. I sat up and poured more wine, and sat cross-legged on the sofa, watching them as they tried to figure out the exact chord for a Nirvana song, watching them laugh as they teased each other. "You're diminished, you muppet," Tristan said, giving AC a one-armed hug and a quick thump around the head, as he went off to get some water.

At one point they started trying to think of any song they had ever liked. One of them would sing the first few lines, before deciding they couldn't be bothered to work it out, and moving on to the next one. Then AC picked out a few notes and said, "Kate Bush. You like her, right, Lily? Come and sing on this one."

I felt my face go red. "Yes, I like her. No, I can't sing."

AC stood up and pulled at my arm. "Come sit on the floor next to us. You'll hear the notes better through the vibration of the guitar. Makes it easier. Come on. You've sung before, everyone has. Come play with us." He pulled at me again, and grabbing my wine glass, I got up and followed him. He sat down in the chair, and I knelt on the floor by him, Tristan on my other side.

Tristan smiled and leaned over to kiss me. "Good. I'll still love you if you can't sing, you know."

AC smacked his head. "For fuck's sake, Tristan, that's not much of an incentive. Either way." He took my hand. "Ignore him, Lily. A little too much Saturn in this one sometimes. Killjoy."

Tristan stared at him, open-mouthed.

AC thrust out his arm and stuck his finger in between Tristan's lips, moving it to punctuate his words. "It. Is. True.

Chill. The. Fuck. Out." He removed his finger, and placing it in his own mouth, swirled it around. "Not bad. I think I need another glass too though."

I started to jump up to get the bottle and their glasses. AC put his hand on my shoulder. Tristan nodded to him. "Stay there, Lily. I'll get it." Tristan slid up off the floor, long legs unfolding. "Do you need a pillow?"

"Yes, please," I answered. AC smiled, an approving little smirk on his lips.

Tristan came back with the wine and a couple of pillows. It was getting late, and you could feel the silence coming off the windows, almost as if the absence of sound was shaking the glass. The lights in the other bungalows and rooms were scattered now, and the overhead illumination on the pool had been turned off. It was very quiet.

AC drank some of his wine and put down the glass, and picked up the guitar again. "So which song? 'Wuthering Heights'?"

I thought for a minute. "I don't know. I guess I know the words to most of them. 'Babooshka'? That's a good one."

AC smiled. "That is a good one. Tris? We can work this one out right?"

He was leaning back against the sofa, his eyes closed, his full lips slightly wet from the wine, his neck long and curved. "Sure," he murmured. "You guys do this one. I'll listen."

AC nodded. "Ok." He began something that sounded so much like the first three piano chords, even on guitar, and then ran out the tripping upwards notes that followed, and began to sing. In the middle of the third word, he stopped. I'd been sitting there, silent. "Come on, Lily, help me out here." He gave me that slow smile he had, the warmth in his eyes liquid and intuitive. Both he and Tristan had eyes that seemed to have seen much more than the average person, wearing the scars of having existed in places most people weren't able to survive. He nodded to me, as though I'd said yes out loud.

AC began again. The chords wanted to foretell something serious, weighted and measured. He started singing the first line, "She wanted to test her husband..." and I took a deep breath and joined in. "She knew exactly what to do." And we were off. Thinking of the words took my mind off Tristan. I could almost feel his intensity, the concentration he brought to the music, to anything. Then the next verse was already there, the story and the song spinning together. Finally it came, the "uncanny how she," the climax of the song. AC caught my eye and wouldn't let go, and the feeling hit just right, the strange rhyme, and our voices, and his careful strumming on the guitar. "I'm all yours, Babooshka ya ya." Foolish, serious words. We both let the notes carry as AC precisely hit the un-expected power chords at the very end. I could feel the hair standing up at the back of my neck as the sound finally died away.

I looked up at AC. He grinned at me, then looked over my head to Tristan. I turned to follow his gaze, and finally faced Tristan. He had this odd expression on his face, halfway be-tween confusion and something almost like the tightness right before the tears. He bowed his head, his dark hair partially obscuring his eyes, before he ran his hand through his hair as usual, his lips a thin line. He blinked. He started to speak, then stopped, and just reached out for my hand, looking back over my head for AC.

AC played a little arpeggio. "I told you, mate. Not even the surface." Then he bent down, the guitar flat on his thighs, and kissed the top of my head. "And you. You can sing. Who said you couldn't?"

I looked at the window. More lights had been extinguished now. I wondered what time it was. A memory of another night, long ago, came without warning. A girl looking out the window on to a dark road, wondering how long it would be before a car came along once more, yellow headlights a quick triangle of light brightening up the darkness, the red lights the eyes swallowed up in the distance. Another set of words chasing her up to the cold, unfinished room, words always said so low. That girl had been days away then from escape, days away from packing up what little she had, and taking her chances far away, somewhere else. Trying not to look back.

AC couldn't have known what he was asking. Between Tristan's decisive insistence and AC's gentle intuition, the two of them could open up every wound I'd tried so hard to plaster over.

AC's voice cut through my thoughts. "Lily? Are you ok?"

His eyes were green, so green. Like the Northern Lights on a cold, star-filled night, or forest ponds filled with moss, or the last of the light in the sky before a momentous storm. I rubbed at my eyes. "Yeah, yes. Sorry. Been a while I guess." I tried a weak little smile. "Another one? Now that we've started, and all?" I felt Tristan take my hand, and squeeze it. I squeezed back. He knew. He always knew.

We sang a few more songs, and finally Tristan joined in, and it felt good. Weirdly good. We were just finishing up a medley of 80s classics, when Tristan looked at his phone. "Fuck. 3 a.m. Car coming at 7. Maybe a couple of hours of sleep?"

So we all hugged, and Tristan and I headed to the bedroom, while AC made up his little bed on the sofa. I washed my face, carefully avoiding looking at myself in the mirror. Too much had happened. I didn't need to see the traces of it all scrawled across my face. I threw on the nightdress I seemed to be wearing to bed these days, and crawled in under the sheets, next to Tristan, who had already flung himself into bed, naked except for his silky underwear, uncovered. He was already half asleep, but he pulled me closer to him. "You have a wonderful voice," he whispered. "You must sing more." Then he turned on his side, his face on my shoulder, his eyes closed. "My mother used to sing to me, all the time. My father hated singing, once she died." Then he rolled over on his back, his eyes suddenly open, staring at the ceiling. "He wasn't all that keen on it before." I knew how much it had cost him to say those words. I placed my head on his chest, and let it rise and fall with his breathing.

"These memories. That we think we are over. Dealt with. Then the ambush." I sighed as I said it.

Tristan pulled me up to him, and then we were lost in a kiss, loss and pain and life there, his warm skin, his mouth on mine. All that couldn't be said.

And there was a little cough. We broke apart, and looked at the end of the bed. There, standing in his boxers, the light from the living room making a halo of his tangled hair, was AC. Tristan sat up. "Mate? Are you ok?"

He came a bit closer to the bed. AC looked pale and blotchy, like he'd been crying. "Tris. I just can't. The last night." He coughed again. "Lils, it's lonely out there. But say no if it's too weird, ok? You'll tell me the truth, right?"

There was something in his voice that brought back everything I'd been thinking. I couldn't swallow. I couldn't speak. So I lifted up the covers next to me. Catching his eye, I managed a little choking laugh. Then I moved my hand so I was holding up the covers next to Tristan.

Tristan flung down the covers all the way, exposing his long legs against the white sheet. "I guess it's all decided then. Get over here." And AC climbed in next to Tristan, who lay back down against the pillows and pulled me next to him, his other arm circling AC, who was clinging to Tristan like he was a life raft. We settled in, small adjustments. AC's arm was next to mine, and he moved it so it was pressing against me, gently. Tristan was breathing softly beneath our skin, nearly asleep, holding us both up. I thought of how different AC's skin felt, and how strange it was to feel them both at once, comparing. I remembered a picture from a book I'd had as a little girl, showing three lost children trying to sleep, leaning against a big tree in the middle of the forest, the dark line of the tall tree bisecting the triangle of their heads, huddled together for warmth, praying for protection. I hadn't thought of that book for ages, but I could see all it now, the fraying blue cloth cover, the faded gold embossed printing on the cover, the picture of a cottage on the front, gripped in my hand as I felt asleep. Right before I fell asleep I realized I was holding someone's hand tightly, and they were clasping mine.

* * *

The next morning and the wake-up call found us all occupying our own sections of the king-size bed, but the bleary looks we all gave each other once we realized where and who we were filled with a kind of contented understanding. A knock at the door made AC jump out of bed. He retrieved the coffee and croissants that Tristan had arranged for the day before, and between getting ready and packing up the guitars and suitcases, there was no time to talk. It was probably just as well. I wanted to think, to feel. I didn't want to have to explain anything. I had a feeling that none of us wanted to break this strange fragile thing we had created.

Then the car was waiting outside, and I took another look around the room. To me, there were traces of magic in all the corners, across the unmade bed, its white sheets still shaped in the pattern made by our bodies. I was sure if I looked closely enough, I'd even be able to see the imprints of our warmth on the carpet where we sang together.

I blew the room a kiss and shut the door. Nothing was the same, and never would be again.

We said goodbye at the airport, under the eyes of the staff of TSA and the check-in desk at AC's flight, and anyone else who might have noticed or cared on the way to getting their own flights. Tristan watched him head down the steel box ramp. AC turned and saw us looking, and a big smile illuminated his face, and made him seem bright, very bright indeed next to all the early morning passengers rushing to get space for their carry-ons, and he waved at us, and was lost in the flood of scurrying heads. I squeezed Tristan's arm. "He'll be all right, won't he?"

Tristan looked down at me, his eyes slightly red. "Jesus, I hope so Lily. I fucking hope so." He kissed me. "Come on, we've got our own flight to take." His mouth moved close to my ear. "I didn't think I could love you more." He grabbed my hand, and we headed off to our gate. We were nearly there, when a fan came up to us, wanting an autograph. It was the first time I'd seen Tristan say no, even if it was with an apology about being about to miss a flight. We hurried on. At the gate, Tristan gave me the tickets, and put on his sunglasses. "I might as well enjoy the perks of the cliché. I'm really not in the mood. Do you mind, Lil?"

"Not at all. Gives me something to do. Let me." I took the whole shoulder bag with all the ID and info in it from him. He still had his guitar, which would go in the carry on in first class. We checked in, and went through. I had one hand on his back, the other arm out keeping people away, I suddenly realized, in bodyguard stance. It amused me to think I'd been watching that closely, that I could just step into the role, despite needing at least another foot and a hundred pounds of muscle to really make a difference. Still. Don't fuck with the mother bear. On the plane before take-off I texted Dave and asked him to get us a person to get us through and a car. "Tired" was the only explanation I offered. Let him make of that what he wanted, I thought.

We didn't really talk during the flight. Tristan fell asleep for a while, his head against the plastic wall of the plane. I tried to tuck a pillow in by his neck. I stared at the map of our journey, looking at the outlines of the states, wondering how you could come so far, and then go even further than you'd expected. I tried to write a postcard to Hank. I'd gotten his name and address from the bus company. I'd never said goodbye properly, but I figured he knew why. I hoped he'd be pleased to know I still thought of him. Except I couldn't think of what to say. I wanted to tell him everything, everything that had happened, but I knew I couldn't do that. Even if he would have understood. I wished there was someone I could tell all this to, but there wasn't. I put the card back in my bag. For later. When I could remember how to talk about things that didn't cut quite so deep. I asked the stewardess for two glasses of cava when she came by on her regular round to stare at Tristan. I figured if I asked for two, I had a better chance that she wouldn't spit in it. She looked at him again. "He must be tired," she said quietly.

Quietly, or not, I didn't want her to wake him up. "That's right," I replied. "Thanks for getting the drinks." I tried to smile. So did she. Neither of us looked very convincing. When she returned with the two glasses, I had my own set of sunglasses on. "Thanks again."

I looked at the map. We were about to go through Ohio. Another hour or so. I sipped at the cava. Tristan was starting to wake up.

"You ok?" I handed him the glass.

"Thanks." He drank the entire thing. "That's better. Can we get more? I'm all right. Bloody exhausted, I guess."

I waved at the stewardess, and whispered to Tristan. "She wants you. Autograph?"

"Sure," he squeezed my hand. "Hi," he read her name tag. She stuck her boobs out a bit more. I didn't think now was the time to mention to her that if they were any closer to my face, I'd have trouble breathing. "Maryann." He held out his hand. "Nice to meet you. Thanks so much for looking after us. Can we get some more of whatever this is? And we've got a CD in here, if you want one."

She beamed. "That would be great." She was back in moments with four of the little bottles of cava. She opened two and poured them, and gave the others to Tristan. She gave him a big wink. "Don't tell on me now."

"As if I would." He was signing the CD. "To Maryann. Thanks so much, sweetheart. Really appreciate it." He blew her a kiss. I thought she was going to faint.

We sat there, plastic cups in hand. "That was nice of you."

"Not really," Tristan said laconically. "Going through the motions, to be perfectly honest."

I didn't say anything, but he took my hand, and pointed out the window. "Above the clouds," he hummed.

"It looks pretty from up here."

"All the nonsense, down there. And then... Are you sorry you came along?"

I looked at him, wide-eyed. "Never."

Tristan smiled then, for real, but his eyes were intense. "No going back once you've been on tour."

"No going back. I wouldn't want to, anyway. Even if I could."

He intertwined his long fingers with mine, and raised our hands to his lips, and kissed my fingers where they were linked with his. "Stay with me, Lily."

"As long as you want me. Maybe longer."

He kissed the tip of each finger. "No matter what."

"Everything matters."

He turned to look at me. It was the first time I'd ever seen real uncertainty cross his face. He studied me, as his eyes hardened again, ever so slightly. "It does." He took in a gulp of air, dropped my hand, and looked away, out the window. It was almost as though he was talking to himself. "There's more to this. I know that. I won't ask you to do what you can't." He shifted his entire body until he was facing me. "But I will ask you to be honest with me."

It hurt to not be touching him. But I knew what he was doing. I would have done the same. "I can't lie to you. I don't want to either. I've…" I stopped. Just words.

"What?" Tristan's face was serious. "Tell me."

I shut my eyes. I couldn't keep all my thoughts straight, with him staring at me like that. "You were there. You know." I grabbed at the cup, and sipped at the contents. Tasteless. It could have been anything. I forced my eyes open and stared back at him. "The song. Singing. Sharing the bed. It meant something to me too. Whatever it is."

His eyes were endless. "And AC?"

I smiled. "You want words. That's so unlike you. Wouldn't you rather hear me now and see if I keep to my word? That's what you'll do anyway."

Tristan couldn't help the twitch that teased at the corner of his mouth. "My god, Lily. You weren't supposed to figure me out like this. Ok, fair enough. But now I want words. Tell me."

I drank some more, and tried to think of what to say. Everything coherent was gone from my head. "Tristan. I'd love to say this beautifully." I swallowed. "But we're on a plane, and I can't think, and oh, fuck. I don't know. Tris. I love you.

For real." I felt my voice drop to a whisper. "It scares me a little. A lot. Fuck." I looked at my hands around the empty cup. "Now it's a speech. I want you to be happy." I lowered my voice even more, until I was practically breathing the words. "Fuck it, he needs you. I need you."

He repeated his question. "And AC?"

I wasn't sure what he wanted me to say. "I care about him."

"That's all?" That piercing look had returned. There wasn't a place to hide from that.

"I...he...understands you."

"And does he understand you?"

"Sometimes. Maybe yes. It seems that way."

"And how do you feel?"

"About him?"

Tristan inclined his head. I was about to speak when the announcement from the captain came over the speakers. We were on our final descent into JFK. I peered around Tristan to look out the window. Only ocean. I'd barely noticed that we had been losing altitude. The stewardess came around to check we were following the instructions, and we gave our bottles to her. She tried to touch Tristan's hand. He smiled, politely, raising an eyebrow at me after she left. We adjusted our seats, returned everything to its original position, buckled in. I leaned into the seat back, trying to pretend I liked flying. Or this part of it.

Tristan's voice was a low whisper. "How do you feel about him?"

I shut my eyes again.

His hand was on my arm. "Tell me. I need to know. Please. No lies, ok?"

I took a deep breath. All this could have remained unspoken. At least for another day. But Tristan was there, breathing steadily, his hand firm on my arm. My heart was racing. The plane was moments from landing. Putting it off now would be worse.

"I...he...I don't know. Yes. He is. Strangely fascinating. There."

I looked over at him. Tristan's mouth was turned up at the corner, a look of irrepressible glee removing a tension around his eyes that had been there. For a while, it suddenly struck me.

"Well?" I put my hand over his.

Then the grin spread across his whole face. "I was convinced you didn't like him. Thought you were putting up with all this for my sake."

Now I was smiling. "Martyr complex?"

"Something like that."

"Damn I'm good."

"Cards close to the chest." He looked down. "I like that."

"So, brakes off the train then?"

The serious look returned. "I don't know." He took my hands again. "You really did know."

"I really did." The plane hit the runway and bounced, and touched down again. I clutched at Tristan's hands as the engines roared into full reverse.

"How?" he whispered in my ear. The squeal of the engines almost drowned him out. I looked around. The closest person was across the aisle. They were just a little too far away to hear.

I leaned towards him, my mouth touching his ear. "Chicago. Dressing room. Door ajar." I could see the whole scene again, their bodies against the wall, Tristan's face lost in pleasure. I pushed it from my mind. "I didn't mean to spy. But. Quite a show. Lucky it was just me, really."

"The night you were passed out."

"The very one."

"You were upset."

"I was a lot of things. I couldn't really...I don't know. Untangle it."

He gripped my hands. "Lily. I didn't mean to hurt you."

I leaned even closer. The engines were powering down. Our whispered conversation would have to end. "You didn't. You are you. That's it. That's all I want."

The plane started to bump over the seams in the runways, heading towards the gate. We passed by the planes lined up, waiting their turn to head out, to speed down the runway into the sky. We were going towards the buildings. Back to civilization. Back to New York. And it really struck me. We were home. This part of the tour was really over. And now all this new information was going to have to be part of real life. Which meant that life was going to change.

I wondered how.

chapter twenty-one

New York

We were only going to be in New York for a few days, so it had felt strange to return to the apartment, almost like another hotel room. I supposed it felt more like home to Tristan, although he didn't seem that happy to be back either. I felt itchy under my skin. Tristan, pacing while he talked on the phone, gave off that aura of a wild caged thing he had at times. We thought about going out, which probably was what we both needed. Mindless activity. But Tristan didn't want to deal with the public, and there was nowhere either of us really wanted to go. Instead, we indulged in the small luxury of ordering food to be delivered, the one thing that New York could always provide, the ability to stay shut inside. We made more phone calls. I checked in with Dave, but it was really just to thank him for organizing the car and driver to extract us from the airport. There was nothing to deal with at the moment, and for that I was very grateful.

I strolled around the apartment, gazing over all the places that now held memories for me as well. Our short, intense history together was leaving its traces on his home. I wondered what Tristan could see, that I couldn't. That was the trouble with mysteries revealed. The state of wonder the revelation brought on reminded you of all of the secrets, all the other things that you didn't know. I found Tristan in the kitchen and approached him carefully. After a moment, I gave him an awkward hug. We were standing by the kitchen window, where I'd made that fateful choice to stay. Was I making it again? In some ways it seemed that way. Tristan kissed my forehead, and we gazed at each other, and within all the uncertainty and unease, there was that little feeling that yes, we did know each other. Deeper understanding, wordless, silent, not spoiled by some inane rush to explain. His eyes were dark, and bottomless.

He frightened me a little, all the same, and I gave him a half-smile, which he returned, shaking his head, all the irony, all the complications, all the possibilities of the situation in his look. He kissed me, and returned to his phone calls. I stood there, and watched the streets below. So many moments in relationships were acceptance, and quiet, and storing away confidence in the future because you hadn't fucked up the present, even if all you did was nothing. Nothing was a choice too.

Dinner came, and over sushi, we watched a film. Tristan idly tapped his foot as the woman in the French film found her way to the house in the hills, and it was all too late, because the lover was going to jail. She wailed, then was silent, as the gendarmes pushed him into the car, and you knew they'd never see each other again. Her final reflection, facing the rock faces of the primitive mountains where they'd hoped to hide, was an acceptance of simple tragedy. FIN came up, and Tristan got up to throw out the containers. It was utterly banal, and very domestic, and we were playing house. Remembering how life went. Tristan showered, then I did, and there were glasses of water by the bed, and the lights were switched off. Finally we went to bed, and the bed itself seemed big and strange, the distant constant roar of movement and traffic outside providing a lingering music that crept between you and the pillow like little needles keeping you from sleep. I kissed Tristan's shoulder, and turned over.

The next day rose thick and warm, with the kind of heat New York City used to only have in August. The heaviness of the air around us didn't bring any comfort. It wasn't a soothing blanket of warmth—instead, the air was thin and hot and empty. Tristan slung his arm around my shoulder and dropped it almost immediately. "Sticky," he said. I shrugged. We had decided to go for a walk, and then get the ferry over to Williamsburg, in Brooklyn, hoping for a bit of fresh air on the river. Tristan said he had an errand to run over there, and I was happy for the distraction. We walked past the traffic lined up at the entrance to the Holland Tunnel, the cars revving their motors in their excitement to get through the light and wait on the other side for more traffic. Two men behind us talked about sales and their niche market. I looked over at Tristan, who was almost amused, but as he swept a hand through his dark hair, and pushed it off, away from his skin, I could see that he was tired, and not really enjoying this, our slog through the downtown streets. "It will be better when we are by the water." I muttered. He threw me a weak smile. The traffic poured slowly across Canal Street. A little girl next to us screamed and pulled at her mother's arm, as the mother patiently tried to calm her. She pointed, hysterical, at the gutter.

We looked down, and there, slightly squashed, lying across the metal bars of the drain at the corner, was a half-grown rat. It wouldn't have scared anyone while alive. The girl's reaction seemed almost cruel, except that she was genuinely scared. Tristan looked away. He really was tired. Even the short tour had taken it out of him, the setbacks, the success. His silences, more frequent, and longer, seemed menacing somehow. Except behind his eyes, when you looked, his big eyes, floating between dark and light, seemed to be begging for something, release maybe. And as soon as you looked again, they were flat, still, a pond in the afternoon light waiting for someone to drown.

We got a taxi, and reached the ferry terminal, and waited with the tourists, the workers heading home, the mothers who had been out on a day trip with their children, the few wanderers and ramblers headed back or out, it was hard to tell. We showed our tickets on my phone, and walked down the gangplank, a weird little commute. Most of us walked onto the boat and headed for the stairs that led to the outdoor deck. Tristan and I commandeered a corner, and looked out across the water to the Brooklyn Bridge, to the reclaimed land where the docks and the ships slotted in used to be filled with activity. The boat headed across the river and docked at the base of the hill leading up to Brooklyn Heights. The old buildings looked fake, the new ones looked empty. A group of children got on, all holding ice cream cones from the shop by the ferry dock. It should have felt like the joyful end to a summer day. The ferry left with a shout of the horn, and a gasp of cooler air from thick green water of the East River came to us.

"Let's stay on to the end, then come back," Tristan shouted

over the roar of the engines. I nodded agreement. He pulled his hat further down over his forehead. With the sunglasses, the hat, and the plaid shirt, he looked like all the other inhabitants of the new Brooklyn. You'd have to have very sharp eyes to catch those memorable features, the sharp nose, the finely cut mouth. I had my sunglasses on as well, my hair pulled back. Two arty people disappearing into the crowd on a very hot afternoon. The boat stopped, then headed further up the coastline, to the new unmemorable towers taking over the former brownfields of Long Island City, north to the Queensboro, now Ed Koch Bridge. Looking west, there were the old apartment and new business buildings of the East Side of Manhattan, still marked, but no longer dominated by the fishbowl blue green of the United Nations building, a polite but imposing monolith on what had once been another forgotten piece of unwanted waterfront land. Tristan suddenly reached out for my hand and squeezed it, and I held on, the warmth and softness of his skin a strange contrast with the strength and size of his hand, clinging to me tightly.

We stayed on the boat at 34th Street, and no one seemed to mind. The people disembarked, and the new group refilled the boat. The horn went again, giving notice, and the ferry quickly left land, heading across what seemed a mere spit of water, to dock hurriedly at the Long Island City port. Letting off a few brave souls reclaiming the factory lands overlooking the grey offices of midtown, it roared off again, reversing into the river, heading at a fast pace through the now calm waters of the East River. An inlet went by, its banks almost retaken by foliage, green against the brick and concrete walls of the warehouses just beyond, a shadow of what once must have been a watery and fertile land, quiet and waiting. Tristan still had my hand in his, as we both looked out at the passing scenery. "Do we get off at the next one?" I asked.

"No, let's stay on until the first stop in Williamsburg. This is good." Tristan murmured, his lips again parting the hair just over my ear, getting much closer than he needed to be. I leaned into him, the rounded muscle of his shoulder just brushing the top of my head, his arm around me, close and protective. The boat stopped again, at the end of a long dock, and headed out once more. We watched the shoreline pass by, the overgrown tangle of plants and half trees and weeds giving way to the three blank white tanks containing some mysterious substance, surrounded by a yard full of trucks and other vehicles, looking like they had been there always. A dock appeared, the boat did its quick maneuvering, and we got into the line waiting to jump off the boat as soon as the gangplank hit the concrete pier. Tristan looked around, slightly nervous, the way he always was the minute he was in a crowd of people with no immediate exit. We followed the line out to the park. He pulled me over to a line of wooden benches that looked out on the skyline. "Lily. Come with me." I squeezed his hand again, and followed him to a bench.

We sat there for a while, my hand small within his grasp, watching the kids play on scooters and the Williamsburg hipsters with cash to burn walk their dogs in the shadow of the new condo buildings all around us. A couple of people who looked like they pre-dated all this new transformation, sat around, not fashionable, enjoying the sun, a can of beer in a paper bag day. Another ferry came and left. Finally, Tristan turned to me.

"Lily, you remember all the things I told you about my family?"

I nodded, not sure what to say, wanting to listen before I ventured anything.

Tristan's eyes were dark as he looked out over the water. "I've done a lot of crazy things I guess. Trevor's pretty pissed at me." He turned towards me and kissed my cheek. "But you. Are you angry?"

I thought about all the things I wanted to say, and all the things that it was pointless to bring up. "I'm not angry. You've always been honest with me. I'm not expecting perfection." I looked into his eyes. "I don't even know what that is. You. You're perfect for me. All I want is you. The way you are. For real."

Tristan ran his fingers through his hair. It was such a familiar gesture I felt like I was doing it myself. "I want to tell you things. Ok?"

I pulled one of his hands towards me, and held it between mine in my lap. "Anything. Really. I mean that." I tried to smile. "Tell me."

Tristan looked at his hand in mine, then up at the sky. He breathed in, and turned to face the river again. "Lily. Talking. I guess I'm not used to it." He turned back to face me, and took off his sunglasses, and quickly put them back on. "Let's walk." We got up from the wooden bench and started down the path, avoiding the mini scooter riders and bicyclists, before heading out on the cobblestoned streets. "Trevor said I should trust you," Tristan finally said.

I nodded. Nothing I could say would make it easier, or better. But Tristan looked like he was waiting. "You should," I finally murmured. "You can."

Tristan's face was in shadow, the sunlight blocked by the tall building, his silhouette sharp lines on the hazy background of smog filled air and green junk trees creeping through the chain link fences. "My family. They…I don't know. Trevor made me go to some therapy sessions. After. That. With the drugs, right?" He hesitated. "After the first time. I didn't think it helped. But maybe it did. I never thought about it much. I never wanted it to. What it all meant. Being left alone like that. As a child. I thought I was very grown up. To look after myself so much." He laughed, a bitter choking smirk that cut through the soft summer air. "It seemed normal for a long time. A very long time. After all the things that happened. It still feels normal."

I nodded at him. "Time. Makes some things better. But anything like the same thing happens again, even a thought, it's just like it's on repeat."

Tristan put his arms around me. "Repeat. That's it, Lily. I don't want to repeat. I want it to be new. I want it to be right. But I feel like I keep fucking up."

I didn't say anything. This wasn't the time to say things. Stupid words.

"I know what it is, Lily. I know it. As long as I have something else to go to, it feels like I can get out. I can escape. Before it's too late. But I still love…people." He pulled his arms away and punched one fist into the other.

The smack of skin on skin made me jump. It felt like he was hitting me. Himself. Everyone.

"But I can love, Lily. I do love…It's just…" Tristan trailed off. He looked towards the south, the lowering sun hitting his features, every outline traced by the light, his skin pale yet golden in the swirled afternoon sunlight that bounced off every particle, a prism in the polluted air. He was so beautiful, it almost hurt to look at him, and I did, I had to look away. I forced myself to look back. I wanted to want him for all the right reasons, but sometimes just looking at him tore away all my resolve and I just wanted him, so badly. For any reason.

"I know..." I ventured.

Tristan gave me that look. "Do you?"

I made myself stare back. "Don't I? Really? Then tell me. Talk to me. Please Tristan, please. Don't do this."

His face was hard, his eyes cold. It was easy to see how he'd gotten to where he was, the unwillingness to back down. "Lily. I'm not going anywhere. Even if you hate me. Even if Trevor hates me. Even if AC hates me. I'm not leaving. That's what I always did before. I didn't stay for the final act. Because that's what I thought it was. The end. I couldn't ever see a way of resolving anything—because everyone left. Don't you get it? Everyone left. Even if they were there physically, they weren't there in spirit. Someone said to me once—your family and friends—they must all want a piece of you, of your time. And they didn't. They didn't really care if I was there or not. Unless they were lonely. Then I was company. But I could have been anyone. Anyone at all. Alixe reminded me of my father. I guess." He laughed again, that horrible tinny sound that meant nothing was funny. "Success. That's why people want success. At least that's why I wanted it. I thought it would make that empty feeling go away. But it didn't. It made it worse. I had more people to be betrayed by. Sounds so fucking melodramatic, doesn't it? Ah, whatever." And he was silent.

We walked by another little park by the water, and went

in. There was an empty bench on its own, away from the others. We sat down. I held his hand, examining his fingers, the calluses from the guitar playing. "I'm still listening." I didn't look up.

"Drugs. Drinking. So easy. All that empty space and there they are. You buy them. For a while, they're yours. No excuses to be made. The edges get softer. Like the women. They're around. So easy. Easy to pretend no one cares." He crossed one leg over the other, pulling at his jeans for a moment. "I didn't care. All that mattered was how I felt. I'm not proud of it. But I'm not lying either."

I stretched out on the bench and rested my head on his thigh, and looked up at the clouds. Anywhere but his face. I had the feeling that if I looked at him, everything I'd been thinking would betray me, and he'd stop talking. That was the last thing I wanted.

He rested his hand on my head, and began stroking my hair, tugging a little at it when he found a tangle from the ride over on the boat. It felt good, so good. I closed my eyes, and hoped he would start talking again. His hands were soothing, gentle, yet held so much of me at one time that it was a matter of either fear or surrender.

"AC." Tristan's voice was low, but I jumped all the same. I'd been dreaming, dreaming of everything being ok, of his hands on me, again and again. I tried to smooth out my breathing before I spooked him. He was going to say something. "AC," he repeated, and breathed out heavily. "I've hurt him, and I've hurt you. And Trevor. "I should probably just leave."

I reached up and grabbed the hand that had been stroking my hair. "Don't stop. Don't leave. I don't want you to. Talk to me."

"You're beautiful, Lily. You deserve more."

I gripped harder. "I don't want what you think I want. I want you. Talk to me."

Tristan was silent again, but he left his hand in mine. Finally he started up. "AC. I…" He pulled his hand away. "I… he's…he's my oldest friend, Lily. He's been there. Through everything. He stood by me when I fell apart. When I fucked up my life, he tried to be there. I wasn't there for him." He took a deep breath, and I realized that he was crying. "I love him, Lily. I love you, and I love him, and I just don't know how to make it work. I'm sorry. I thought I did."

My eyes were open now, and I watched him rub the tears away with the back of his hand. "Tristan. I love you. I've been with you now. I know you. Better now. It's time, that's all, it's time that we need. I need to learn you. You need to trust me. And I'm not going anywhere. You don't have to explain. You can. But don't apologize. Please." I swung my legs over and sat up, cross-legged on the bench, my head buried on his shoulder. "Tristan," I whispered, "I'm here. I'm not running. Usually I do. This time I'm not."

He leaned his head on mine. I played with one of the strands of dark hair that fell against my skin. "I love you. I'm here. We're going to change and think and do what we want. It's a journey. Give me time. Give me the same time you've given AC. I'm not going to run." I took a deep breath. "Please."

He lifted my head, and stared at me, his eyes dark and light and sea-colored and earth-colored. Then his lips were on mine, gentle, measuring the shape of our mouths together, his tongue tracing a line at the corner of my mouth, teasing, soft, waiting for me to ask for more. "I love you," we both murmured at the same time, and then he took my mouth, commanding, trembling, both of us soft and hard on each other. He ran his fingers along my sides, almost ticklish, until he drew a straight line across my stomach to the center. It was like every nerve ending was concentrated there, fanning out in a beating pulse that reached to my toes. I felt weak. "Tristan," I managed to say. "I think we need to get out of here."

Tristan laughed, that dark, dirty laugh this time, the one that made me want him more. He wrapped a long finger around the chain he had given me, and tugged gently. "You want me," he smiled. "Still. After everything I've said. After all you know about me."

I was still faintly trembling from his kiss, and his touch. It seemed a ridiculous statement to make. But he meant it. He didn't trust easily, and neither did I, and that meant I needed to be careful. As careful as I wanted him to be with me. I just kissed him, and leaned my head on his shoulder. Tristan put his sunglasses back on, and pulled me up to my feet. "Come on, love, let's walk around. Otherwise I'm going to tease you all day."

I looked up at him. "So we're together, right?"

Tristan nodded, smiling.

"You're going to give me time to become an old friend?" I asked.

"Friend. Lover. Girlfriend. Partner. Whatever you want to call it."

"And AC?"

Tristan smiled. "Can he be all those too?"

"If he wants to be. He can be what he likes. What you like."

"Ok. That's ok then." Tristan studied me. "You mean this, don't you?"

"You know, I really do. But."

Tristan stopped, his hand on my cheek, smoothing away the little frown by my eye. "But?"

"But I don't know what I'm doing. I mean…how."

His face lit up. "Neither do I, love. As long as we keep reminding each other. But we seem to pick things up quickly." He leant down and kissed me, softly breathing into my mouth, tender and calmer.

Then he wrapped his arm around me, and we strolled down North 7th Street until we reached Bedford Avenue. It took only a block before there were two girls ten feet behind us, giggling. The word "autograph" came through the noise of the crowd, along with a muffled shriek.

Tristan looked at me, and actually rolled his eyes. "Shit. I shouldn't have come down this street." He looked around. "Come on, we're almost there. There's a shop I want to look at. Maybe they won't follow us in there." I caught his eye. "I'm not in the mood. I just want to be with you and remember what's it's like to be a person. Or invent it, possibly. Anyway. It's just across the street."

He grabbed my hand, and we crossed over, in between the cars waiting at the light, and after another look around to see if anyone else was following us, ducked into the little store. The musty smell of old belongings and the half-light reflected off the dark wooden floors filled the small space. Tristan was looking at a vintage typewriter. I gazed surreptitiously through the curtains and plant stands in the window. Sure enough, the two girls were still out there, phones in hand. One of them spotted me, and raised her camera to take a picture. I swung away, trying to look as though I'd just seen something I wanted to look at. I didn't want to make it obvious that neither one of us were in the mood to deal with the fans. We'd been lucky to have an hour or two where no one paid attention. Now, I felt like I was back in the zoo. I couldn't imagine how Tristan must feel—never having a moment away from being on display, his every action scrutinized for signs of debauchery or headline-worthy notice. The constant observation would make anyone crazy. I watched Tristan as he carefully picked up a Tiffany style lamp as though it weighed nothing. That got the shop owner's attention. The one constant in trendy neighborhoods was for shop assistants to ignore anyone who came in. I watched as the woman approached him, shoulders back for a confrontation, recoiling slightly in shock when she realized who it was, then softening, as Tristan turned his warm smile in her direction. Charm was supposed to be the ability to get yes before you even asked the question. If that was true, he was nothing but. A vague sense of protectiveness overcame me, and I couldn't resist. I wandered up and stood nearby, just managing to keep myself from threading my arm through his, possessive and visible. She gave me a brief once-over and carried on.

"I'm so sorry I didn't see you when you came in! It's been so busy in here today." Tristan smiled at her.

"No problem, no problem at all. I'm just browsing. Looking for some rad stuff for gifts, you know?" He rested his hand on the old wooden and glass display case, looking down at the trinkets cradled in silk on the glass shelf within.

She stumbled for a moment, then regained her composure. "Can I help you find something? Are you looking for anything in particular?"

Tristan didn't respond, but was staring intently at a group of necklaces. He glanced over at me, then went back to studying the jewelry. Without looking up at the shop keeper, his voice rang out. "Those three. Could you take them out. Thank you." It wasn't a request. She opened the back and taking out each one individually, she laid them out on the glass. She rested her hand nearby, but Tristan just looked at them, and waited for her to retreat slightly. Then he reached out, and with a crazy delicacy, lifted up each one, and held them up to the light. They were old—enameled silver pendants surrounded a flower-like shape of what looked like sapphires and pearls. The two others had no stones, but continued the shapes on tiny drops of silver. They were beautiful. I stood there, admiring the beauty of the two together, his strong sculptural features intent on his examination of the finely worked pieces. I couldn't imagine how he had spotted them, in the midst of all the mid-century modern bric-a-brac and tables that filled the store.

"When did you get these?" Tristan asked. There was a certain tension in his voice that surprised me.

"Last night actually. A box of things I had been promised finally turned up." She looked apologetic. "Another store closed, down in Bed-Stuy. They'd promised me first rights on their antiques."

Tristan said nothing, but turned the necklaces in his hands. I noticed he was holding all three at once, as though he was reluctant to put them down. Finally he spoke. "How much?"

"For one?" she asked, rather stupidly I thought.

"No, for all of them. All three. What do you want for them?" Tristan looked out the window. The girls were still there. A flash from a cell phone camera broke the dusty light in the shop. Tristan glanced over at me, and I gave him a quick nod. He turned back to the woman, and waited for her answer.

"They are beautiful pieces, aren't they? Art Nouveau, I believe." She hesitated. Tristan pulled himself up and looked down at her.

"Don't sell me. Just tell me. Then I'll tell you. Yes or no. How much?"

She turned and opened a ledger she had by the cash register. I felt certain that she already had a price in mind but was buying time. She spoke in to the book. "I have them down for, all of them, would add up to 6, but seeing as you are you," she turned back to face him, "let's say 5800."

Tristan smiled. I knew that smile. She obviously didn't. His voice was a slow drip. "Did you know these were stolen?"

She went pale and looked at the floor before she could stop herself. "I never know where things come from. By the time they get to me they've been through several people."

Tristan simply looked at her. "I imagine that's true. I also imagine you know some of these people. Let's say 3000, and you tell me some names—before someone comes along with a warrant."

She turned back to the book. I felt Tristan go rigid next to me. "I won't be..."

He interrupted her. "You will be. You ought to learn to lie better if you're going to be in the stolen goods trade. But...if you don't think that's fair, let me just call my bodyguard who's circling round in the car. Do you know he's an off-duty cop? Old friend. I'm sure he'll be able to advise us on a good price. Maybe he can ask one of his friends who's on duty to help. But that seems like a lot of trouble, doesn't it?"

She slammed the ledger shut and I stepped back, startled, into the rack of dusty sports jackets and dinner jackets behind me. I flinched at the touch of the scratchy wool on the back of my neck. She thought I was backing off. That wouldn't work. I walked over, very precisely, to stand by the display case, my arms crossed. She glared at both of us.

I looked over at Tristan, a question on my face. He inclined his head, ever so slightly, and stood up a little taller, one hand behind his back. I knew it was clenched tight, ready to fight, wanting to, holding back. I caught the woman's eye. "Money is money. And this is going to be a great part of the article I'm finishing up." She ignored me. "For *The Core*." That got her attention. "I'm sure everyone will see it as human interest. I'm sure no other reporter will be interested in a hipster joint fencing stolen goods. It makes a good headline, doesn't it? 'Vintage Turns to Violence,' or 'Hipster Hung Out to Dry.' Of course, 'Bitch Should've Known Better' works for me, but…"

Suddenly the woman was in my face. "You don't know what you're talking about."

Tristan was there in an instant, looming over us. His expression was volcanic; there was a dry violence crackling through him like a fuse ready to ignite. "Bring it on, doll. Not a problem. Assault and theft go together. But if I were you— I'd take the money and forget about all this. Just like we're going to." He pulled out a wad of money from his front pocket, and peeled off ten one hundred dollar bills. "I'll send someone around with the rest. You might want to have some names for him—he'll be expecting some information in return for the rest of the cash." She didn't move. "Good. It's a deal then." He looked out the window, and spotted the small crowd outside. Then he turned back, and gave her a big air kiss on each cheek, visible to everyone watching. He put his hand on her shoulder and leaned across the counter again, and spoke very slowly. She blushed in spite of herself at his proximity. He gave her a cold smile. "There. We're friends now. I'm going to tell my fans outside with their cameras what a great place this is. You'll be in all the blogs. What great publicity."

He gave me the necklaces. I wrapped them in some tissues that I had, and pushed them down carefully to the bottom of my bag. Tristan turned back to the woman, who was now angrily pulling out a small box and a receipt book. "No, we don't need a box, but thanks for asking. A receipt though. That will be great. Be sure to date it." He watched her. "And stamp it, that's right, name of the shop. Your name at the bottom. No point lying," he shrugged towards the window, "they've been photographing us the whole time." She finished writing and pushed the receipt over to him. "What, no phone number? Darling, don't forget to add that. And your personal cell." He winked at her. "I might need to get in touch." He pocketed the receipt and put his arm around me. "Thanks again." His grip around my shoulders was firm, bordering on painful.

At the door he murmured, "Lily. We're going to sign some autographs. You're going to stay for a couple of minutes then find a cab. Get it to stop out of sight." We went out the door, the tinkling bells marking our passage. Tristan went right up to the girls and posed for pictures, his arm around their shoulders, big hugs for all of them. He gestured to me then, almost imperceptibly, and I smiled at everyone, then started down the sidewalk, keeping a lookout for a taxi. I'd walked two blocks before I saw one coming towards me. I flagged it down, and texted him, while I told the cabbie I was waiting for someone. I stood outside the cab, one hand on the door. Tristan came strolling down the street, both girls still hanging on. When he saw me, he extricated himself. I got back in, as he looked around the street for any other onlookers, and the cab pulled away. Tristan gave him an address in the West Village.

He pulled me to him. "I like your tough side. All that repressed anger. We'll have to explore that." He smirked. "But it was the perfect distraction."

I shrugged, making a face at him. "Very angry. Tristan. What the hell is going on?"

He glanced out the window. We were just going over the Williamsburg Bridge. The sun was nearly down, but there were the lights of the buildings shining on the water, and the reflected rays of the last of the day made the colors wet and shimmering, even if only for a moment. It was very changed from a few hours ago when we were in the park, trying to sort everything out.

"Lily. Those necklaces." He rolled down the window and let the wind blow his hair around his face. "I didn't tell you. We were robbed when we were away. Your stuff is still in storage—there wasn't any reason to worry you. They didn't actually take that much. Some gold records in frames. Pictures. These necklaces. Carefully curated. It looked like it might have been an inside job. Only a couple of people know where some things are." His mouth was a thin, tight line, and he shook his head. "They only took a few items. I think they knew what meant something to me."

"Tristan! Why didn't you tell me?"

He looked at me, his eyes suddenly vulnerable in the fading sunlight. He looked very tired. "Lily. I didn't mean to hurt you. I'm used to dealing with all this crap on my own. Don't hold it against me, please. I don't need that now."

I started to say something, then thought better of it. I took his hand. "I just want to help."

Tristan nodded, thoughtfully. "I know. I'm sorry. Of course you do. Anyway—I thought they might turn up. I finally got a tip that they could be here." He turned to me. "I wanted to get them back, if I could."

"They are very beautiful. Fragile."

Tristan shook his head. "They are. But that's not why." He stared at me, eyes still holding traces of the volcanic rage I'd seen briefly in the shop. "Those necklaces. They belonged to my mother." His voice faded away on the last word.

I whistled. "But no ordinary thief would have known that."

His voice was unnaturally quiet. "I've trusted...the wrong people. Sometimes. Sometimes people can be very...deceiving." And he turned away, but his hand reached for mine.

His mother had died here alone, living in a hotel. Tristan had told me that one night. We had been in bed, afterwards, and he suddenly said he wanted me to know more about who he was and where he'd come from. So he'd described some of his childhood, and his mother, who'd been a great romantic, and very beautiful. She had met the slightly cold and distant, but extremely intelligent and icily good looking man who was Tristan's father when she barely out of her teens. But the fairytale match she had dreamed of hadn't worked out. She'd finally left his very British father, and her 8-year-old son, tired of all the infidelities, tired of having to play the role of a conventional middle class Englishwoman that she wasn't suited to. Apparently she had thought she could remake her life back in the States, then return for her son, and show him a little bit of the country she had left behind when she had fallen in love with his father. The irony was that Tristan's father had just brought him over to New York for a visit, looking for her, hoping to coax her back.

When he thought of his mother, or the last time he had seen her, it was an image of her sitting at the very end of a neighborhood bar, where everyone knew her name, surrounded by warm-hearted drunks all delighted to meet her sweet and polite child. No one obviously had an inkling of what was coming, only a week later. Apparently the strain of an uneven life, with too few kindnesses and too many drinks and too many pills, had weakened her system. They had found her, unconscious on the front stairs of her building, hypothermic. She never woke up again. It had been very unexpected. After a lonely funeral attended by one other person, a blank room of grief sparsely decorated with some flowers from the bar and a bouquet from the super, Tristan and his father had returned to the UK, and had never spoken of it again.

He had told me half the story that night. I hadn't pressed for the rest. When he finally gave more details, leaking them out like tears quickly swept away, I knew he was grateful that I remembered everything he had told me before. The shorthand was enough. I knew what he meant. I wasn't sure how anyone could forget.

Tristan had the cab pull up on the corner, and we got out. "Come on. There's a nice little wine bar near here."

"Won't they recognize you?"

"Probably. But then again that means we get a seat." He grinned. "I think I deserve a bit of pampering, don't you?" He took my hand and led me to a grey door.

"Turks and Frogs?" I asked.

Tristan shrugged. "Sure. Why not?"

"Cacik and Camembert?"

He laughed. "Something like that. Come on, it'll be fun." He pushed open the door, and sure enough, the second the bartender behind the small wood bar spotted Tristan, he stopped pouring and put down the bottle. Gesturing to the server, he handed her a white plastic "reserved" sign and pointed to the small table in the corner, against the bookshelves. A collection of thick white candles, all burnt down to various heights, were reflected in the big ornate mirror. The yellow light flickered against the red painted wallpaper.

The server wiped down the table, and stopped two people from sitting down. The couple who had been waiting put up a mild protest to the bartender, who shrugged. "Sorry. Oversight. That table's been reserved all night." The man started to get irate. The bartender offered him and his girlfriend a place at the bar, and a free glass of wine. They walked past us, unaware, vowing never to return. Tristan ignored them, and went up to the bartender. "Chris. Cheers. Sorry about that."

He pulled out a wine list and handed it to Tristan. "Good to see you, Tristan. Glad you're here. Hey, they were tourists. The table was already reserved. And a free glass of wine. Who turns that down?" He looked at me. "Why don't you and…"

Tristan stopped him. "Lily. This is the divine Lily. Lils, meet Chris. Pours a mean glass of wine. Can really open a bottle too."

Chris laughed. "Too kind. Nice to meet you, Lily. Mi casa, su casa and all that."

I shook his hand, which was slightly wet from taking the glasses out of the dishwasher. Tristan ordered a bottle of Sancerre and a mezze plate, and his arm firmly around me, guided me over to the small table in the corner. By this time, everyone in the place had seen him, and if they hadn't known who he was before, their friends were telling them in stage whispers. I looked around, and the first person I saw stared at me, then quickly turned away. I smiled at Tristan, and stopped looking around. He was still more used to this than I was.

After a glass of the very good wine, Tristan looked more relaxed. "I got them back. That's what counts." He swirled the wine around in his glass. "A bit of excitement. Probably needed. But I'm glad we got there in time."

"Yes," I replied. "And tracking down who did it?"

Tristan looked tense again. I was sorry I'd brought it up. "I need to speak to Trevor. He's a master of revenge, really." He saw my expression, and reached for my hand. "No, kidding. Really. But he does know how to solve puzzles. An excellent judge of character as well. As I've learned."

"He's a complicated man."

"Trevor? He is that. But underneath it all, he knows what counts. I'd trust him with my life." Tristan laughed, quietly. "I have."

I didn't know what to say to that. "We'll see him in a couple of days. In California."

Tristan smiled, that dazzling, flirty smile that was designed to get him everything he wanted, and usually worked. I'd learned it could also be his way of changing the subject. Making people forget what they had asked. "One more day of rest. Fortunately. I'm not sure I can keep up this pace."

I winked at him. "I'm sure you can keep it up as long as you like."

He smirked, his eyes alight. "At least now I know."

"What?" I asked.

Tristan leaned back in his seat, his body suddenly elongated and very much on display. He raised his glass and gave me a sideways glance, a half-smile playing around his mouth. "What we're doing tomorrow."

chapter twenty-two

L.A.

L.A. It's like the garden of the kings in mythology. An un-tamed paradise of long boulevards and tall palm trees, bunga-lows carved out of hillsides, desert and mountain and sky, all leading down to the sea in a ritual of primeval worship. Except the gods are money—as usual, and sex—the airbrushed, oddly buoyant kind, and power—the silent kind, everywhere, like oxygen, and exerting its pressure just like the emptiness in your lungs when you don't breathe in. It's in the shortcuts that are available to certain people, there to remind you of a differ-ent track than the one you're on when you look up, exhausted, from your so-called honest ways. It's where a child grows up in privilege and is handed the keys to the kingdom, along with your dull obedience. Some do work for it, determined to make second or third generation success be more than just an acci-dent of birth. And a few simply wind up there, out on the far coast, having fought their way to the top on the colder side of the country, any country. The pleasures of cruelty insure that once the fortunate ones dance on the top of the big candy mountain, we get to hear any reversal, amplified, the sound of their fingernails ripping out as they desperately cling on. Others just open the big candy store and we finally hear the real story after the ultimate failure of their last trip to rehab. It is the land of fantasy, even—or especially—if that fantasy is a disaster. Drag it out now, entertain us.

Tristan leaving to lick his wounds elsewhere, depriving the media machine of the joys of watching him lying in the gutter, hadn't endeared him to the place. His ex-wife and her contacts, and whatever vendetta she might wish to conjure up now that we were both on her turf made me very wary of what we were going to find here. I crossed the arrival hall slightly behind Tristan, and listened for the first salvo. I didn't have long to wait. The photographer we came across in the airport yelled out over the echoing floors and walls to look his way. When that didn't work, he came closer, snapping away. When we didn't pay attention to him, he called out to me. "Lily, Lily, come on sweetheart, you know how to smile." We ignored him. He followed. Then he tried a different approach. "Lily, how are you going to stack up against the ladies out here? They all know how to work it." The giant bodyguard the airport or airline had provided, I wasn't sure which, placed himself between us and his mouth and the lens. We carried on, once again reminded that sunglasses only block the light.

Walking through LAX, I thought how sometimes the pictures of a place are like the trailer—only the best parts, and the rest is fairly dull. So far, it didn't feel like Hollywood. I didn't know what I was expecting—it was just an airport. But when Tristan noticed how on edge I was from the encounter with the sleazeball camera hound, he squeezed my hand quickly, and murmured. "You're doing fine. Try not caring—they smell fear. It's a lagoon of piranhas out here." And he winked at me. I tried to relax my shoulders. I'd signed up for the whole funfair ride. The drop was only a part of it.

The bodyguard led us out to the front, and handed us over to the not as large but almost more intimidating rent-a-cop-slash-driver, who looked a little bit like he'd been a Top Gun and survived a crash of some kind. He was menacingly good looking, with a scar that peeked out the top of his mirrored shades, and ran down his cheek, across his lips, and disappeared under his chin somewhere. He and the bodyguard nodded to each other, and the exchanged look of mutual respect that they took the time to engage in, was very different from the one the driver proceeded to give us. Tristan was, as usual, in black jeans, a leather jacket, a white t-shirt, a collection of necklaces and bracelets of different colors and materials circling the smooth veined skin. And there was me, my look now incorporating most of the rock star girlfriend clichés. The boots with a heel. My own collection of necklaces, including the one Tristan had placed around my neck that fateful night in the LES bar. A chiffon blouse under a new leather jacket that Tristan had bought for me in New York. Blue tinted metal framed sunglasses. And a self-protective air of both arrogance and irony that seemed to be rubbing off on me. Judging from the stares that met me every time I looked around, apparently I was getting better at the act. I wondered when it would stop being a game of pretend. Maybe it already had.

Tristan introduced himself and shook hands with the driver, smiling in my direction as I gave a little wave, which seemed to unfreeze the atmosphere somewhat. After the driver put our

bags in the trunk of the 1960s convertible Caddy Tristan had insisted on renting—we climbed in the back seat, and the roar and
rumble of the old 8 cylinder engine felt like the ignition stage
of a Saturn V-5 launch. I adjusted my sunglasses, and braced
myself.

"Freddy, we're ready for take-off," Tristan laughed, and
pulled me closer to him, as we pulled out of the loading zone.
"Let's do this right. First stop—In N'Out Burger. Something
on the way." Tristan had rented a place out in Silver Lake,
the hipster paradise on the other side of the 101 from West
Hollywood. We were due to spend two weeks out here while
Tristan did promotion, played a couple of invite-only acous-
tic shows with AC in conjunction with some radio stations,
and hopefully get to relax a little before the big awards show.
Tristan had been emphatic. "Yes, I'll get a driver," he had said
to Trevor on the phone from New York, "and a limo for the
appearances, naturally, but we're not going to sit at home and
wait for party invitations. L.A. parties," and he made a face,
"don't make me do nothing but. I'd like to try and actually
have some fun." Trevor had flown out the day before, but he
was staying in a hotel, even though Tristan had tried to convince him to stay with us. We had both been on the phone
with him on a conference call so he could speak to us about
this promotional section of the tour. His response had been
classic Trevor.

"L.A. isn't a place I come to often enough to cushion
the blow. When I'm there, I want to feel the poison. All of it.
Running through my blood. Speeding up my heart just to slow
it down, fatally. Clearly, I need a hotel."

Tristan had just laughed. I thought it was a little too close to home. Trevor was joking—mostly. But so much tempta-tion—it couldn't be denied. I wanted to resist asking Tristan what it was like to be back here. But driving around the end-less loops of concrete off-ramps filled with a steady stream of cars each containing one impatient person, I couldn't wait.

"Tristan." Then I faltered. The last thing I needed was to sound like some jealous, worried girlfriend, busy laying down the boundaries, secretly wondering what happened when she wasn't around, if the appeal was still there. Honesty. Right. Mostly.

"What's wrong, Lil? You've got that look on your face again." He squeezed my hand. "It's going to be fine, really." He looked at me again. "Let me guess." He looked up at the sky for a moment, and ran his hand through his hair in that way he had, his long fingers twining with the dark strands. Against the backdrop of unfamiliarity, it made him look more like an image, the icon he was. I didn't know why that made me feel better. It shouldn't have. "You're worried, that here, where it all went a bit tits up for me, I'm going to be tempted. And indulge. And stray. And with Trevor here, and AC, it will be easy to give all of you the slip, and go say hello to some old friends of the chemical sexual kind."

I glanced down, then away. A Mercedes convertible was passing us. The blonde woman with her gloved hands on the wheel looked like an advertisement for every excess California promised.

Tristan followed my look. "Exactly. That's it. All promise. All of it. And for people who haven't been there, and seen into the black heart of it, it's extremely alluring." He took my hand. "I'm not going to lie. As far as the drugs go, it's always going to be there. That tug. In fact, out here, where it's so easy, just too easy, I've got to be careful."

I frowned. "Tristan…"

"Lily, I'm not a saint. I'm a person. Surrounded by people who want things, who are ready to offer me whatever they think I want, or whatever they want to give, as a way of getting what they want or need. Sometimes they guess right." He squeezed my hand again. "I have you. That's what I really need. I trust you to remind me of what's important."

I shook my head. "Tristan. Gatekeeper and girlfriend. That's a tricky combo." I took a breath. "You're expecting a lot of me."

He smiled, in that way that was both reassurance and challenge, the slight crook of his mouth balanced out by a certain darkness around his eyes. "Yes. Yes I am. And maybe it's not fair, but here we are. In the looking glass, down the rabbit hole, whatever it is. And you've been there too, so you know what it's like." Tristan pulled me towards him, and I rested my head on his shoulder. "I can't do it without you."

I stayed there, and he kept his arm around me, and silently, we watched the road, and the cars going by, the rolling stop-start of the traffic locking us into the rhythm of the city. Tristan only held me tighter when the motion of the car made me shift position, and we moved together. It was a silent conversation, and the warmth of his body seemed a little like a guarantee.

After a while, we turned off the highway, and we were on roads that still were like freeways—car-controlled stretches always leading away, never towards. Then we were right in the heart of it, and everything looked familiar because it was.

Wherever you looked it seemed like it had been in a movie or a TV show, or maybe some music video. The total picture made you wonder what would happen if you leaned on the surface, if everything would fall backwards, revealing dust, scaffolding, discarded paint cans.

And then we were driving on Sunset Boulevard, and the big sun was going down behind us, and the artificial lights were coming up. I was driving in a convertible, with a beautiful man, the background of the deepening sky bringing out the sharp lines of his nose and his jaw, solid, strong, the sparkling lights reflected in his dark sunglasses. The twilight smelled warm, faintly like dry sand, the crisp acrid smell of old car exhaust adding a strange urgency to the coming night.

Even the little red palm trees on the packet of French fries, and the neon glare of the burger place, in all its garish glory, didn't erase that image from my mind.

* * *

Trevor, amazingly enough, was waiting for us at the little bungalow Tristan had rented, standing at the door, with what looked like a gin and tonic in his hand. Tristan went up to him and gave him a huge hug, while Trevor looked over his shoulder at me. He raised his eyebrows, and pointed to Tristan's head with his free hand, but his crooked smile was real. Tristan whispered something in his ear, then kissed his cheek, and Trevor laughed. "But you don't like gin," he responded to whatever Tristan had told him. He came over to me and awkwardly bent down to wrap me in a hug. I squeezed him tightly, and I felt him relax, pleased. We kissed, half cheek, half ear. But we were done with the air kissing.

The driver brought the bags up, and we all went inside. We sent the driver home—it was unlikely we were going anywhere tonight. Trevor had a bottle of champagne out, and an oddly shaped rectangular pizza covered in artichokes, olives, capers, and arugula salad was on the dining table. That part of the house looked like it used to be a porch, and had been covered over with windows, like a greenhouse. The sliding doors were open, and it was warm, but not unpleasantly so.

Trevor smiled. "All organic. Thought you needed something healthy."

"You know me too well. We just stopped at In N'Out. But this looks fantastic." Tristan glanced up at Trevor. "You're staying here tonight, of course."

Trevor shook his head, and a momentary flash of worry crossed Tristan's face. "I'm...," Trevor gestured to the outdoors, "staying for dinner. Naturally. I picked it out. And I will be back in the morning. We've got some logistics to work on, I'm afraid." He walked over to the champagne and began to unwrap the top. "But you two need some space, and I'm a creature of habit, so." The cork came out with a satisfying pop, and Trevor poured it out into three flutes that were waiting by the ice bucket. He handed them out, and raised his glass. "To success. Without stress."

We clinked our glasses. Tristan looked relieved. But he downed his in one go. "Oh, that's good. How can champagne go so well with hamburgers and pizza? How did they know?" He laughed. "I'm going to go wash off the plane. Be right back." We both followed his long form as he headed back to the door. "No, don't tell me. I'll find it." And he went around the corner and out of sight.

Trevor turned to me. "He doesn't look too bad. Any drugs?"

"Maybe. But not a lot. He wants to, but so far I think he's managed to restrict it to mostly drinking. He asked AC to score for him that night in Dallas, but I think that was down to the events. No visible signs, but he knows how to hide it."

Trevor looked thoughtfully at his glass. "I'll find out. And AC?"

I glanced at Trevor. Then at my glass, which was suddenly empty. I walked over to the table and refilled it. "Which part?"

Trevor gazed at me, a deep line between his brows. "That's all you needed to say, my dear. Are you all right, that's the next question…" he looked up. "For the guest of honor. Come drink some champagne. Are you going to surf? That's really what the fans want to know."

We all sat down. Tristan drank another glass, almost as quickly as the first. "Surfing. There's an idea. It's been a while."

Trevor cleared his throat. "Good exercise, of course. I don't think it's on the list of excluded activities that allows me to insure your body on the tour, but just in case, wear a hat, and don't get recognized." He drank some champagne, adding, "And don't break anything, naturally."

Tristan punched him lightly on the arm. "Naturally. Money. Must be made."

Trevor gave a choking laugh. "Money paid for this adorable little house." He glanced around, blinking. "Beautiful." He raised the bottle. "And this champagne." He smiled, that somewhat thin movement of his lips that made him appear slightly less dissatisfied than usual with his surroundings. "But. Tell me about the tour. And AC. How is it all working out?"

Tristan bowed his head slightly, as if he were being called up before the headmaster. Then he raised it, almost defiantly. "He's a great guitarist."

Trevor narrowed his eyes. "He is. Without question. And of course, your oldest and dearest friend. Apart from me, that is."

Tristan was alert now. "And Lily."

Trevor's voice was even. "Lily is somewhat more than a friend. But then again, so is AC."

Tristan was silent.

Trevor laughed. "You need to come back to the old country, my lad. Focus on your work, not the shock value. Let's be professional here. The bassist is gone, obviously. We need to interview some new ones, but I think I might know someone in London who might fit the bill. I'll talk to him, then you can talk to him." Trevor turned to me. "Lily. How are you? You survived the tour, so good job. Made of tougher stuff, as I'd always thought." He waited a beat before carrying on. "So. Tristan. Are we using?"

Tristan remained stubbornly silent. Trevor tapped his foot. Tristan looked at him.

"Do we have to do this now? In front of Lily?"

Trevor's face was immobile. Then he spoke, very slowly. "Yes. Yes, we absolutely do. Because we are your friends and we need to know. We need to know how close we are to trouble. It's our business as well." He placed his hand on Tristan's shoulder. "Lily loves you. As do I. And she knows it all. Or most of it. As do I. If you must hide from us, at least let us have the luxury of knowing where you were the last time we really saw you. Tristan."

Tristan remained silent. Trevor waited. Every so often his foot would tap. "I do want my pizza tonight. But there is another bottle of champagne. Shall I get it while we wait?" Trevor stood up, and he was tall, taller than Tristan standing, much taller than Tristan sitting, and his angular dark frame cast a shadow in the room.

"Fuck. Fine."

Trevor sat back down, and pulled one leg up over the other, neatly arranging his trousers. "Excellent. I believe you Yanks say 'spill.' So let's have it then."

Tristan looked uncomfortable. "A bit of coke, here and there. Other than that, nothing. I was offered some smack. I turned it down."

Trevor remained in the same position. "From AC?"

Tristan changed position in his chair. "I…yes. Just the coke. The smack was from a roadie. But I did ask him, AC. For it."

Trevor said nothing, but got up. He stopped next to Tristan, and put his hand on his shoulder again. "Let me get the champagne. Thank you for being honest. It wasn't that bad, was it?"

Tristan looked relieved. "No. Not so bad." He looked like he wanted to say something, but he stopped himself.

Trevor watched him carefully. "That's all right then. Just one more question. Which would be easier to give up, AC or the blow?"

I looked over at Tristan. His eyes were wide with surprise.

He clearly had not been expecting that. "You're not going to make me choose, are you?"

Trevor looked grim. "I might. I just might, at that."

Tristan looked at me. Trevor saw his expression. "I think Lily just wants you to be happy and well. She's quite resilient, but as you know we all have our limits."

Tristan rubbed his eyes. "You're a bastard. The drugs. The coke. Of course. Fucking hell, Trevor."

Trevor's face was lit up with a sort of menacing glee. If there had been a candle held under his strong features, the effect could hardly have been less alarming. "Excellent!" he exclaimed. "Correct answer, and I'm sure Lily will agree. Let's toast to your ex-junkie's reclaimed heart." He started walking off to get the champagne, and he turned back after a few steps, and faced both of us. "And I am a bastard, like everyone else in this fucking trade. However, I have a kind soul. Don't bloody forget it." Tristan and I both laughed, nervously. "Children," Trevor spat. "Now let me get this bottle before it freezes."

The rest of the night was relatively calm, and we sat together, rehashing the tour, talking about the future, nibbling at the cold pizza, which did go more elegantly than might be expected with the champagne. Finally, the air coming through the screens started to cool off, the circles under Tristan's eyes became darker, and Trevor finally called for his car.

I watched them talk quietly at the door, Trevor's arm around Tristan, Tristan gesturing with his free hand, but the other firmly around Trevor's suited back. I pretended I was stacking dishes, but really I was watching them. Closely. Tristan looked like he was listening intently to whatever Trevor was saying, then he shook his head furiously. Then they both turned to look at me, and I looked down at the small stack of dishes as though I'd been very involved in my task. When I looked up again, walking the dishes over to the open-plan kitchen, they were deep in their conversation. If they had noticed me watching, they wouldn't say. But I would never be so foolish as to underestimate either one of them. Together—they were immovable, unstoppable.

Then Trevor left, and Tristan stayed in the doorway, the slight breeze from outside coming in the house, and blowing his hair back. Framed like that, the light from the small outdoor lantern casting a yellow glow on his face, Tristan looked like he was facing down a multitude of demons. He straightened his back, still looking out into the darkness filled with curved roads and hills, and finally shut the door. He came over to me, and pulled me up into his arms. My head was against his chest, and I could feel his heartbeat, steady, slow, determined.

"Lily. Now I have a question for you."

I mumbled my agreement into his chest.

"Is your love going to survive the reality? Or are you going to want me to keep things under wraps? Keep the rock star mystique going?" Tristan gave one of his short barking laughs. There was a bitter tone to his words.

I pulled myself away until I was standing at arm's length. "Tristan. Two answers to that."

"Two?"

I gave him my own bitter smile. "At least. But yes. First off, it should be obvious by now. I want you. Not a made-up version. Remember? Give it time. Give me time."

He seemed to relax a little. "Yes. Just with Trevor and his interrogations…"

"He cares. I do too." I paused. "And so does AC. We all do. We just want the chance to keep doing it."

Tristan closed his eyes for a minute, then reopened them. The usual half-smile had reappeared. "Fair enough. And the second part of the answer?"

I kissed him. "There is a difference, you know, rock star, between mystique and lies. A big difference."

He gave a wry smile, shaking his head slightly from side to side. "True. True. So. Mystery, not treachery?"

I kissed him. "Something like that."

"Bed?" Tristan intertwined his fingers with mine.

"Bed."

chapter twenty-three

L.A.

It turned out that the parts of the trip to L.A. that were supposed to be restful, weren't really. Trevor turned up the next morning, and they hit the ground running. Tristan, after some argument, got on the phone to London and spoke not only to the potential new bassist, but also to someone who Trevor thought might be a good replacement road manager. Trevor had been quite insistent that Tristan at least consider getting someone to do the day to day. "It's not realistic, is it, thinking you're going to do everything. Especially out in Asia. You need someone to facilitate." Trevor looked exasperated. "And I know you want it to be me, but it's too much for me now. Those days are done. I'll come out to watch and check up on everyone, but arguing with the staff at 3 a.m. at each load-out, no." His voice turned slightly more cajoling. "You made it yourself with the ridiculous James, but it wasn't a good situation. If you're going to do this, and you are, you need proper support. So try him out. Call it temporary. I think he'll do the job for you though."

Tristan had nodded, and actually seemed to like the guy while he was on phone with him. He handed the phone back to Trevor, who said he'd be in touch, but to get his passport in order, it wouldn't be an official work trip, so no visa, but he'd be paid. Through the London office. He would call back. He then turned to Tristan. "All right? A few days out here. Be good to trial him, especially if the video shoot goes ahead."

We were waiting on the possibility of being able to shoot what would be Tristan's first video for the new album. With the publicity from the award nomination, and the first part of the tour completed without too much mishap, the record company had decided a video was going to be crucial to the next single's success. Trevor had jumped on the chance, and had been pushing everyone to make it happen. There was a fairly new studio out here which had done some interesting, experimental videos, and they were excited enough about the prospect of working with Tristan that they'd rearranged a couple of dates. Now we just needed the permits to shoot on location, and a couple of storyboard edits. The last set had been emailed to Trevor. He had flipped through them on the screen, with Tristan looking on. When they got to the last board, showing Tristan with a snake coiled around his shoulders, they both burst out laughing.

"What the fuck is it lately with the snake in the video thing out here? It keeps turning up. Did you see the one where it crawls on that poor model? She actually twitches. Sexy? Maybe if you're into snakes." Tristan did a little dance that was part snake charmer, part struggle to hold up an imaginary boa constrictor around his shoulders.

Trevor grimaced. "I did see that. Whatever they paid her, it wasn't enough, poor creature. Perhaps it's the end of days mentality." He snapped his fingers. "We could have a flood in your video. You could be stripped down, with a tool belt, building your ark for the genetically gifted."

Tristan laughed. "Hate hammers. Nearly broke my hand once trying to put up a shelf. Besides, didn't someone do that? Some metal band?"

Trevor looked thoughtful. "I think you're right. And you can't break your hands. We need them. What about locusts? Hard to organize, though."

"All that buzzing."

"Fire and brimstone?"

"More permits."

Trevor smirked. "Now you're understanding my life. Well, perhaps we could throw some leather and chains on you, and have you escaping from the prison of convention."

Tristan gave a fake yawn. "Sounds fantastic. Are we going back to the 80s then, when videos had a theme based around some ridiculous setting that had very little to do with anything? Let's find an empty swimming pool. How about a library?"

Trevor smiled. "Absolutely. Unless you'd rather pretend you're a pimp surrounded by dancers who are your stable of 'hoes'. I hear that's popular too."

"Fuck no." Tristan got up from the table. "I'm allergic. And to the whole 5, 6, 7, 8 crap. Useless really." He looked at me. "Told you Lily. Can't put up shelves, and I can't dance. Discredit to both sides." He laughed and went to pour more coffee.

I took the opportunity his brief absence afforded to ask Trevor the question I wanted to get out of the way. "And James? Where is he? Not out here, right?"

Trevor looked around, then lowered his voice. "I believe the New York City cops were less than pleased with what they found in his apartment. Really, these anonymous tips are so helpful to the boys in blue. 1-800-COPS? Something about theft? Grand larceny? I'm so bad with all these legal terms. Did he manage bail? I forget now. Unlikely he will be here though. Not to worry." He turned to take the coffee from Tristan. "Thank you. So are we go on new manager?"

Tristan frowned. "Why is he free?"

Trevor waved his hand in the air. "Your new manager? I know, the best should always be taken, and it's only any good if you steal them away. Generally. My understanding is that he grew tired of his last band. Apparently they were better at getting into fights and smuggling underage groupies on to the bus than actually playing. Always one step ahead of a lawsuit, or worse. Writing on the wall, that sort of thing. He won't be available for long, but I hear he is loyal, so if you wait, you might not be able to pull him away from his new home."

"Fine. We'll try him out. But just a trial. And Lily needs to like him. And AC."

Trevor smiled. "Excellent. I will call him back. And I think you're right about Lily. We would have saved ourselves a lot of trouble if we'd recognized that her fierce right hook was trying to eliminate a problem, way back in London."

Tristan came over and hugged me. "That's true. I'd forgotten about that. Lily, if you want to punch him, let us know.

So we can watch." He laughed. "When is AC turning up, anyway?"

Trevor's answer was short. "He's in Arizona. At a spa." He looked at his watch. "He will be with us tomorrow afternoon."

Tristan ran his fingers through his hair. "You sent him to rehab?"

"More of a detox, really. Just to keep things from escalating. He'll come back, bronzed and fit."

"I don't think he needed it."

Trevor was tapping away at an email. "No? Maybe not. My mother always told me an ounce of prevention was worth a baggie of the wrong cure, or something along those lines."

"You should have asked me first."

Trevor looked up from his email. "Why? You're not his keeper, and neither am I. But he is my investment, and yours, if you'd stop to think about it." He went back to his email, then looked up again, this time at me. "Lily will back me up on this, with her encyclopedic knowledge of the music industry. Lily, tell us. How many great bands imploded due to drugs or vast quantities of alcohol or both?"

I rolled my eyes. "You know as well as I do. Almost all of them."

Trevor had that tight smile again. "And how many recovered from the loss of one of their band members, whether through breakdown or death?"

I thought for a moment. "Not many. I mean, the Stones, but they're a special case. There are a few, but a lot of people would argue whatever they did afterwards wasn't as good."

Trevor smirked. "Hard to get up excited in the morning when you know you're partially responsible for the death or destruction of someone who you once spent all your time with. But I'm just guessing here."

Tristan rubbed the bridge of his nose. "Fine. Fine. I hear you. Both of you. My god. It'd be easier to work with snakes."

Trevor went back to typing. "You got that right, at least."

* * *

AC did turn up at the bungalow the following afternoon, his first stop from the airport. The bell rang and Tristan got up to let him in. I was sitting at the table by the sliding doors. I watched as he dropped his bag, and Tristan wrapped him in a tight embrace, then stepped back to examine him. He ran a hand through AC's curls, and punched him lightly on the arm.

"You look good," Tristan finally said. "Maybe a bit more relaxed."

AC shrugged. "Yeah, it wasn't bad. Except the getting up early part. But I tried to remember the last time I got up early, where I was and all." A small smile played around his lips. "That helped. But it was nice out there. Bit remote. Be a hell of a walk to try and leave."

Tristan drew his eyebrows together, an expression of concern wrinkling his forehead, as he picked up AC's bag and brought it in the living room, AC following close behind. They were out of sight now, but I could still hear their voices. I waited. I knew they'd come in here when they were ready. No point in pretending they didn't need a minute together.

"I tried to call you. But you didn't pick up. Trevor just told me yesterday."

"So it wasn't your idea to put me in detox land?"

Tristan's response was immediate. "Is that what he told you?"

AC laughed. "Oh, come on Tris. Trevor's too sly for that. He just made it seem that way."

Tristan's voice was dark. "I think he overstepped this time."

I could almost hear AC shaking his head. "No, mate. Don't be hard on him. He saved your ass before. He cares. He really does." There was a pause. "Look. I'm alive. Massaged, juiced, exercised, ready for California. Or what life brings."

Tristan's voice was lower this time. "We can do this, you know."

The smile in AC's voice was crystal clear. "I think we can. The music is great. All we need to do is stay upright and get it out there."

"I didn't just mean that."

"I know what you meant. Now give me a proper hello, and let's go see Lily before she figures you're running out on her."

Tristan sounded surprised. "But. I'm not. Not at all. She's amazing. I love her. You know that. And she puts up with me."

AC laughed. "Less of that last one I think, is the key to lasting happiness. I'm not here to make you make her suffer. Don't overthink it, Tris. You've got enough to give. And to do. Come on."

My ears felt like they were burning. I stared at the computer screen, and tried to finish the sentence I'd been in the middle of typing. I deleted it and rewrote the same exact thing three times, before I finally gave up, and went outside to sit in the little garden. A plane flew past overhead. I looked up. The white jet trails were solid, compact, then little by little, they started to spread out against the blue of the sky. Somewhere up there, the air was clean. People were heading to new things. The lure of the untried. The different. I closed my eyes, and leaned back against the chaise lounge. The air smelled half of flowers, and half of exhaust, and heat and dirt, and the racing, throbbing grit of people pushing their way through life. Dusk to dawn. Dawn to dusk. I suddenly felt like I'd been on both sides of that division for too long. The rumble of another jet overhead reminded me of beach holidays, long ago, and the way sounds were different in the summer. I listened to the plane get louder, then slowly fade out, becoming part of the background of all the other noises. I thought about how they all worked together, like a symphony, like the keys on the piano, one hand playing the bass, the rhythm, one hand playing the top melody, everything changing when they moved past each other, or coincided. Chords that came apart and found each other again. Notes that imitated each other, then slipped away.

I must have dozed off, because the next thing I knew there were two shadows blocking the sun. "Lily? Here you are. I wondered where you went." Tristan's voice sounded soft, regretful.

I shaded my eyes. "I must have fallen asleep. I came out for some air." I tried to laugh, but my throat was dry. "Hey AC, you're back." I started to get up, and Tristan instantly reached out a hand to help me up. "How was it?"

"Ok. I don't like eating cactus, I discovered."

I made a face. "Hate the stuff. Leave it in the desert, that's what I say." And then Tristan had his arm around me, and AC did too, and the three of us stood there, bodies touching, my head against both their shoulders. A hand was stroking my hair. It wasn't Tristan. I pulled them both a bit closer. I could feel Tristan's lips softly kissing my head. "I'm glad you're back. And ok."

"Me too," AC murmured.

And we all held on, a little tighter.

* * *

"It's really really hot and it's really really boring." The voice of our new do everything organizer, pitch-in man, and road manager, Adrian, rang out in the hazy and hot L.A. air. Across the street a group of fans watched his every move from their vantage point directly across from the red awning of the hotel. The infamous Sunset Marquis. The band had come together there to prep for the next part. Pete, the original drummer, was still part of the group. He had been quizzed about whether he wanted to stay after everything that had happened, and proved his worth by apologizing, saying he was sorry that he hadn't done more to stop what had happened. Before it happened. He had offered to leave, but Tristan told him to forget it, and that he was glad to know he wasn't the only one who had been bothered by the whole thing.

So Pete was happy to stay on board and happy to meet the brand new bassist, John. Considering he had just flown in from London, knew no one except Trevor, and had honestly admitted to not being a diehard Devised fan, John had already impressed everyone with his musicianship and wary, observant personality. "All bassists are named John, aren't they?" He had joked when he met us. "Unless they're called Flea. I had no choice."

The two of them were there along with the newly re-habbed AC for a couple of days, bonding, rehearsing, teaching John all the parts, while Tristan did a round of photo shoots and interviews. Then they all met up in the evening to talk about the day and plan out the daily rehearsals, ironing out the final logistical details—plotting how the rest of the tour, which had now become a worldwide event, would go. And Adrian, the manager, equally new, but like the bassist fitting in remarkably well. There was still a long road ahead, but so far it all seemed to be working out. Trevor popped in and out, beaming at all of us in his slightly sinister way, to watch the proceedings with an eagle eye.

And Trevor, oddly enough, seemed to be enjoying playing temporary road manager while he guided Adrian. Strolling out of the hotel, the regal, besuited Trevor greeted everyone, then handed Tristan's bag to the driver to put in the trunk of the limo, along with a garment bag containing Tristan's white suit for the video shoot. He was asking Adrian for a break-down of the rental costs and delivery schedule for some extra instruments they were bringing in. Adrian reeled off num-bers, and mentioned one guy who seemed to be a pain in the ass. I watched Trevor twist his face into a quick smile, before throwing another set of questions at him. He didn't even flinch. Adrian was doing very well.

We were all due in the next hour or so down at the club

that was going to be the set, for the usual hurry up and wait that was a part of filming. The interrogation over, Adrian was chatting to the doorman, while taking a picture of the four fans across the street. Three guys and a girl, dressed in their rock star best, standing there, waiting. "Our big fan base," he laughed. "They've been there all morning. There were six of them before. We're going downhill!"

"Has anyone been out there to say hello to them?" I asked.

He looked at me strangely. "You're worried about them too? Yeah, just this morning Tristan went over and brought them some coffee. Where were you?" He laughed again. "I told him not to. The way to keep fans is to torture them. Let them wait. Let them starve. Odd, but effective. Also less wearing on the purse. But he wouldn't listen. You can't boss the boss." He chuckled. "He'll learn. I've only just started."

The band came out. Pete, a small bag slung over his shoulder, and John, carrying his bass in its flight case, both looked a bit dazed in the bright sunlight. "Over here lads," Adrian waved at them, from the side of the limo. He patted each one of the them on the back, whispered into Pete's ear, making him laugh, and finally dipped his head into the limo, looking a bit as though he were tucking them in, even though I had a feeling what he was doing was making sure they only had a certain amount of alcohol available for the ride to the set. They drove off, and the next limo swung up.

AC and Tristan emerged into the sunlight, walking towards the road as though everything on Earth had stopped until their arrival. The fans across the street waved, and called out their names. AC smiled at Tristan, and the two of them stepped into the street. Trevor was by their side immediately, glancing back at Adrian as if to say, look, this is what you need to do when I'm not around. The three of them crossed over, AC and Tristan only looking straight ahead of them, Trevor scanning the road and the sidewalks like an owl looking for prey, his head swiveling. He raised an arm protectively as they approached the fans, and permitted AC and Tristan to sign a couple of t-shirts and CD covers, making sure they weren't accumulating items to sell on eBay. One of the guys said, "It's great to see you out AC. You look really fit."

AC smiled and mumbled his thanks, and then Trevor was herding them back across the street to the limo. "You three get in the back, I'll ride up front." He peered through the passenger window at the driver, and came back towards us. "No, slide over. I'm riding back here with you. He doesn't look very welcoming. How many days do we have of this? That's right. One very long one that compresses two days of work into what will feel like a week."

Tristan grinned. "But there are no snakes."

Trevor turned to look at him. "Damn right. No animals of any kind."

"Only me," AC cut in. "I'm ferocious."

Trevor nodded. "No, I think you're fairly well trained. What is it, Tristan, 'give him a bone'? Very effective."

I didn't think I'd ever seen Tristan blush before.

AC rolled over on his back, and placed his head in Trevor's lap, looking up at him hopefully. "Woof. Never argue with success, isn't that your motto, Trevor? Besides, your bark is much worse than your bite. We all know that."

Trevor put his hand on AC's forehead for a moment, then

pushed him gently. "Go on. You're getting hair on my new suit, AC. Lily, I admire your patience with these clowns."

"Animals," interjected AC.

"Musicians. You're all mad. Maybe I can get my island nation back, exclude the pair of you."

I laughed. AC sat up.

Trevor looked over at me. "Lily understands me. You will be my Evita, darling. First act of business will be to dispense with this lot."

Tristan smiled at me and took my hand. "Trevor, aren't you supposed to be massaging our egos for our moment in the spotlight? Lily does understand, that's just it." He kissed my hand, and winked at me. His smile seemed to make everything right, and I felt the familiar warmth that made me feel like I could do anything, if only he were there by my side.

Trevor coughed. "Not the fluffer, Tristan." He looked down, and raised his eyebrows in mock surprise. "As if you needed one. Be sure to keep that up on camera. And I'll do my part to make sure the cameraman and editor don't go all coy when they film and only show from the waist up. Americans frame men in the shot like they're still shocked by Elvis."

Tristan snorted. "This is why you're the best. Making sure the fans are always happy."

Trevor sighed, theatrically. "But at such a cost."

I knew he wasn't entirely joking.

chapter twenty-four

L.A.

We had been there about a week when the first big invitation came up. Trevor had been putting out feelers, and had finally found a huge party that he approved of. Given by a well-known fashion designer, it had all the trappings—oceanfront home, movie stars, models, fashion insiders, a few music industry people. Trevor sent an inquiry, and it turned out that the designer was a fan, of course, and incredibly delighted to have Tristan and his plus one attend his little gathering. He must.

And Trevor was determined that we were going to attend. "Look, Tristan. You need to put yourself about a bit. Be seen. In the right places. If you're worried, neither of them will be there, Alixe or Paul. We apparently have a truce. Self-interest, I imagine, possibly based on the threat of loss of royalties from the forthcoming Devised Greatest Hits album. All that lovely cash gone if she does anything to damage that little project and the potential success your publicity is bringing." Trevor smirked. "Although I do love a lawsuit. Never mind. And," he paused for effect, "I hear that Paul is trying to write an album. Oddly enough, my server brought me a copy of a couple of the demos when I was picking the kale out of my salad at lunch the other day."

Tristan looked up. "Oh yeah? How is it?"

Trevor grimaced. "As if you needed to ask. Tell me— how is it supposed to be any good, when he's out of practice playing, because there are so many better things to do, and he's still grasping the necessity of song structure? A chorus. So pop."

"That bad?"

Trevor shook his head. "Worse. But people will buy it, because it's him, and some producer will spend three months crying every night at 4 a.m. in an attempt to make something like music out of it. You know. The usual."

Tristan shrugged. "He's a decent guitar player if you tell him exactly what to play and show him how to do it." He glanced at Trevor. "There was a time when I cared. That time has passed. I wish him well in whatever he chooses to do."

"He's a parasite," Trevor spat. "But that's for me to worry about, not you."

Tristan's mouth was a thin line. "Harsh. Possibly accurate. As long as he doesn't threaten what I do, or trouble Lily, or AC, I really try not to think too much about it."

"AC won't see him anymore. He was pissed at how he treated him in London. And you. Reeling you in with drugs."

Tristan gave him a hard look, then smiled. "AC. Doesn't he want to come to this party? He likes fashion. And models."

Trevor patted Tristan on the back. "Good. That means you're going. I'll ask him, but I think he's actually enjoying hanging out with the band."

Tristan grinned. "Road animal. He's probably right—isn't this just going to be a lot of beautiful people comparing personal trainers and bitching?"

Trevor coughed politely. "Indeed. Beautiful people bitching. You'll probably be turned away at the door. Nothing in common at all. Now please stop whining and consider my serious problem—finding a quiet place to smoke a cigar without people making comments, or worse, lecturing me. As occurred only last night. A very lovely woman encouraged me to welcome positivity into my life. Now I have to leave the grounds of the hotel for a simple cigar, and attempt to walk in a city without sidewalks."

"There's always the beach," Tristan said, smiling.

"That's an idea." Trevor clapped his hands together. "However, the thought of spending an hour each way in traffic to engage in an activity whose sole purpose is to relax me seems somewhat pointless."

"True. So give up while you're here."

Trevor looked away. "Touché. We each have our little addictions, don't we? Not bloody likely, as they say. Be sure to give me a full report on the party. I actually think this man may admire your music, or some nonsense. Get a modeling gig out of it. Free clothes. And the record company might just die from the joy. All that PR they didn't pay for."

Tristan ran his hands over his body. "Hello bitches. Maybe I will. Maybe I will."

* * *

So we found ourselves being driven up to an excruciatingly modern beachfront home, the last rays of the setting sun sparking the blueish glass windows that formed part of the sides of the building. It was a linked collection of glass and wood boxes that appeared to be partially suspended in air. The roof hung above the structure almost like a canopy, and the entire creation, dominating its slice of land in between the beach and the road, was surrounded by bamboo plants and greenery. Once admitted inside, the house felt insulated from everything, as though you were on a boat, or some kind of submarine, watching the world through the blue glass, feeling like you were underwater. And then you walked to the end of the house, and the glass and neat strips of wood opened out on to a deck, and the wide expanse of the beach and the last of the sun setting over the dark green Pacific rose up to meet you.

"My god," Tristan whispered, after we had made our tour through the house, and were standing out on the deck, watching the distant lights of the cargo ships out to sea. "Someone's done very well for themselves."

"Perhaps you should model for him," I said. "Perks like hanging out here."

Tristan winked at me. "What do I have to do for him to get a house like this?"

I laughed. "Sex acts that haven't even been invented yet. And you'd need to clone yourself. Probably pick up his dry cleaning too."

Tristan groaned. "There's always a deal-breaker."

"Sucks, I know," I murmured. "But we could get a jump on the inventing part. Be prepared."

Tristan's eyes lit up. "Suddenly this party is much more interesting." He moved closer to me. "Later?"

I was about to answer, when one of the extremely attractive servers came over to us. He was exceedingly polite, apologizing for interrupting us, but our host wanted to meet Tristan Hunter before the hour grew any later. Tristan thanked him and said he would be with him in a moment. The young man smiled, and went and stood over by one of the stone pillars that held up the glass ceiling above us, and waited.

"Before the hour grows any later, interesting. Does that mean you'll be his first of the evening?"

"Heavens, I hope not," Tristan whispered. "That means I'll have to do all the work." He shook his head. "Lily. Behave." Then he leaned over and kissed me. "Maybe I will get a modeling job out of this, after all."

He looked oddly hopeful. I couldn't help but wonder what was going through his mind. "I don't doubt it. You are frighteningly beautiful, you do know that?"

"Isn't that my line?" Tristan smiled at me.

"You can have it back later. Now go—not polite to keep the host waiting. Work it baby." Tristan smiled and kissed me again, then turned to walk over to the man waiting to lead him away. I watched them disappear though the connector leading to the next glass and wood box, then I turned back to the ocean. It was an extraordinary view. One of the servers came by with tuna sashimi. It was delicate, sweet, and melted away to a sea taste that lingered on the tongue, and mixed with the faint smell of the ocean drifting over the sand to the house. The chatter of conversation faded in and out, as people circulated, stood, moved on. They were dressed beautifully or outrageously, above all, expensively. Surrounded by all this luxury, nothing seemed very real. Another server came around, this time with champagne and aged tequila in small, salted tumblers. As I stood there, sipping iced champagne out of a crystal flute, while watching a red carpet parade, the scene was somewhat clichéd, but astonishing nonetheless. I half expected the clock to strike 12, leaving me in a pumpkin pulled by mice. And when two very famous actors walked by, followed at a reasonable distance by someone that looked vaguely like a minder, and at a further distance by people that were trying hard to hide a certain grasping excitement, I laughed. I'd stepped through the looking glass. Fame, power, and money, but so beautifully deployed, it was a little like resenting a Siberian tiger for its superior hunting skills. It was just a shame that you were the prey.

I turned away from the ocean, and headed in, over the partially transparent floors. In the center of the building, there was a reflecting pool now softly lit, the tiny lights against its cobalt blue surface like the stars that would be seen through the skylight directly above it, if not for the smog. It seemed a petty complaint. I stopped a waiter for one of the caviar toasts he was carrying, and I wandered to the back. Even at night, the view of the surrounding area was oddly sharp and immediate. I supposed it was the effect of the floor to ceiling windows. I wondered what Dave would think of all of it, and I laughed. He had probably been here, I would have to ask. I thought about writing up the party for the blog. But it was too alien. Too different from normal experience to be believed. I would have more luck writing about moving staircases. The small percentage of people for whom this was everyday life would find my wonder at it all a symptom of jealousy, or foolish innocence. And maybe they'd be right, I thought. None of it seemed real, anyway.

I headed back through the house towards the ocean, suddenly feeling claustrophobic despite all the lights and glass. With the fleeting thought that maybe Tristan was going to be tied up for the night, I plucked another glass of Cristal off another tray, and settled in on the deck overlooking the beach. The sound of the waves, across the dark sand and water, performed its usual soothing magic. I wished Trevor was there, with his cigars, and utter disregard of anything that wasn't central to his concerns.

I sensed, rather than saw, the presence next to me. I waited. They'd say something if they wanted to talk. The appeal of silence had been a slow lesson to learn, but a useful one.

Finally he spoke. "Are you here alone?"

The voice sounded familiar. "Naturally not," I replied, before turning to face him. I wasn't sure how successful I was at hiding my gasp.

He held out his hand, perfectly polite and very smooth. Yet there was something in his manner, almost apologetic, as though he regretted having this unnatural interaction with most people. I knew about that feeling, better than he could guess, but not the way he did. "I'm Robert," he said. To put in the last name would have been insulting. This made it more intimate. "I noticed you were alone, and I thought I'd come talk to you."

"Lily. Pleasure to meet you."

"Lily. That's an old-fashioned name. Like Lily Langtry? Another famous actress, known for her charm and beauty. A worthy namesake." And he smiled, that famous impish smile, bright eyes under very long lashes. It wasn't difficult to see how he had first attracted attention. And kept it.

"Oh, I'm not an actress," I answered quickly.

"Oh," he said, half imitating my voice, "I think you are. If you're here, you have to be. We all got in here under false pretenses." He smiled that half smile, filled with interesting guilt, the one that usually filled large screens at the multiplex. "But if not, you should consider it. You're really very striking. And any woman willing to stand alone at one of these parties—hard to see how a stage could hold any terrors."

I laughed then. "You could be right. I've certainly been seeing a lot of them. Stages, not parties. Perhaps you're right. Maybe I should try taking a turn."

He grinned. "That's it. Of course you should. Are you here with an actor? We're terrible bores. I hope not, for your sake."

"No, I'm here with…"

"Tristan Hunter," a familiar voice broke in. Then he was there, all long limbs in leather, his hair looking a little more in disarray than usual. It didn't detract from his sudden, intense charm. He stuck out his hand.

"I'm Robert," he replied, and they shook hands. Tristan was taller and gave off an intense presence. Robert shimmered, an invisible spotlight on his smile. It was slightly overwhelming, standing between the two of them. "Lily is delightful company. And I'm a big fan. You've got a solo album out?"

No one, not even Tristan could resist that charm. And it

seemed he really was a fan, reeling off concerts and albums with some enthusiasm. They exchanged numbers.

"I'll have them get you a copy. And we're due to come back for a concert after Japan. Be a pleasure to make sure you have some passes." Tristan smiled.

A phone buzzed, and Robert produced a slightly awkward expression. "Duty calls. That's the trouble with these tight dresses—I hold the phone. Great meeting both of you." He and I exchanged a cheek kiss and a slight hug, and he and Tristan did the guy handshake. It looked for a moment like they were arm wrestling. He was very muscular, under the polished exterior. Tristan's eyes sparked from the challenge.

We watched him sink back in to the crowd, saying hellos as he went, hand on shoulders, before he finally disappeared from sight. The room was filling up. Everyone looked shiny, slightly too perfect, the women balancing on tiny little heels that only emphasized how thin they were.

Tristan smiled at me. "So, I'm going to be a model. And I have an appointment tomorrow for a tattoo with his favorite artist."

"So a success then. You're fairly appealing," I winked at him. "I'm not really surprised."

"Not jealous, are you?"

"Of what, and should I be? Your vast sex appeal? Exchanging little kisses with the fashion world? No. He's clean, and you're careful."

Tristan burst out laughing. "Fuck. Lily." He kissed me. "If this is your way of finding out what I did, I didn't."

I shrugged. "You're pretty hard to resist."

"More than the incredibly famous movie star you were flirting with?"

I couldn't help the smirk that traveled across my face. "Well, I don't know. He gives off quite the sexual aura underneath all that..."

"Make-up."

"I love guys in eyeliner. You should try it."

"Or I'll lose you?"

I danced away a few inches. "You came back just in time. I was negotiating for my first movie role."

"Casting couch?"

"No, sheer talent." I winked. "That was coming afterwards. Form follows function, don't you know."

"Why break the rules?" Tristan was grinning.

"Exactly. I'm sure his couch is very comfortable." I reached out for one of Tristan's hands. "Long, too."

Tristan raised an eyebrow. "Interesting. Care to compare? I think mine is...fairly substantial."

"Really? That's the rumor. But you know how these things get around."

"Want some proof?" Tristan's eyes were amused, but there was a darkness around the edges.

I dropped his hand and turned away to look out to the ocean. It was a beautiful view. I felt him come closer, and stand behind me, one hand on the railing next to my arm. His mouth moved against my ear. "Let me prove it to you. All of it."

I leaned slightly back against him. "I'm not sure I can take all of it," I murmured.

Both his hands were on my hips now, as we stared out to sea, unseeing. "I think you can." His mouth dipped to my neck, and I could feel his throat on my shoulder, his words rumbling through my body. "Let's go find out."

Wordlessly, Tristan took my hand, and we walked back out through the crowd to find our car and driver.

* * *

The drive back was strangely tense. I felt the energy thrumming through him like a drum beat, steady and taut. I had no idea what he could feel from me. Without looking at him, there was no way to tell. This was the time of wait and see. No questions. I opened the window a bit more and let the cool night breeze in. I looked down. We weren't even holding hands. I moved further away, closer to the window. I could sense his dark smile. The extra distance made it worse. Space meant more terrain to cross, more to desire. I had no idea how much longer we had left in the car, but as time passed, and we moved through the miles of cars and palm trees and neon, I could feel him, coiled up and waiting. The noise of the engine grew louder, then faded. My heart beat in my ears, the pulse dense in my throat, my legs. I swallowed, trying to lick my lips. I had the sensation he was watching my every move, waiting for me to break, waiting for the moment when I'd crumble and crawl to him. Prey. All I had was to resist. But I wouldn't. I wouldn't. He would have to come all the way. All the way to me. I shut my eyes. I could hear the blood echoing in my head, and I wished we were in a fast car, a race car, one that could downshift hard, and dip down low, roaring, leaving everything behind. Tearing air and energy out of the sky, one last stand.

Finally, we turned into the driveway, and I pulled at the handle on the door, almost before the car stopped. The sound in my mind was like a long slide guitar sound, slick and wet on the night air, taunting. I walked to the door, silently, and I felt him come up behind me, still not touching. "Here we are," he said. "Ready?" And he opened the door, and swung around. The breath caught in my chest when I saw the look in his eyes.

Tristan backed into the room, beckoning me with his hands, swaying his hips slightly, the energy unwinding like a dance. Like an animal, an athlete, his body obeying, I thought, and then there was the intensity in his eyes. Hypnotic. It might be a game. A very serious game. I shut the door behind me. "Lock it," he ordered. "No more worries about thin walls," he said, with a slight sardonic smile. He kept moving, gesturing me to follow him, out of the living room, and down the hall to the bedroom that held the large bed that faced the garden. Tristan was humming softly. I could barely make out the words. His voice was one long low drawl, a rope lifeline onto a ship of dangerous thieves. The look in his eyes was almost too much. "I've been waiting for this," he murmured, "don't do anything. Just stand there. Like that." Then a lower whisper. "The rush you give me…looking that way. Desperate."

I went to kiss him and he stopped me, his hand on my mouth. "No. Not yet," he said. I tried to bite one of his fingers as he trailed it across my lips. His voice was harder now. "No. I told you to wait." Tristan was towering over me. I stood there, watching him, trying not to tremble. His eyes were softer now, for a moment, gazing at me with a kind of wonder, before he circled around and stood behind me. I leaned back against his chest. The first solid contact. I had to shut my eyes, it was too much. I tried to breathe. I wanted his hands on me. I would never ask. His body was still, unmoving, but I could feel it, every muscle, every curve, every bone. I thought I would scream. But I wouldn't beg, and neither would he. His complications were like my own, they were my own.

Tristan ran his long fingertips down my sides. I shivered. "Do you like that?" He laughed. "Yes. Of course you do." Then he stopped and came to stand in front of me. Close, not close enough. And he slowly began unbuttoning his shirt, his hips swaying slightly to a song only he could hear. I watched as each button came under his fingers, twisted, and opened, revealing with every easy, unbearably precise movement, a naked strip of smooth skin. I let out a little sigh. He smiled. "Like what you see? Too much? Let's slow it down a little bit more. And his body moved as if he were dreaming, as if we were in a fog. I tried to make sense of the glow that came off him, the energy.

Mesmerizing, to stand there watching as the soft shirt moved against his body, a long V of skin revealed, now that it was mostly unbuttoned. He was swaying slightly again, steady. "That's it. I see it in your eyes. Concentrate. Imagine what you want. Want." My body moved imperceptibly closer towards him. He saw it and stopped again. "No." His voice was insinuating, demanding. "No." Then more slowly, in that long drawn out way he had, his voice becoming deeper with each syllable, "Not yet. Will you get what you want? It depends if you trust me to give you what you need." He smiled. Impossible to argue. He was in control. And he began again. Another button fell under his fingers, his eyes on me steady, like a beacon in the dim light. Why did it feel as though even the air around us was becoming cloudy? I wasn't sure if I could move even if I wanted to. It was as though he had hypnotized me, my very soul fascinated by what he was doing. Another inch of skin appeared, now his chest was a strip of taut skin, his stomach revealed by only an ever increasing swathe of slightly muscled flesh, a dark line of hair heading downwards. I wanted to look away and hide from the dark electricity that poured off him, the steady movement of his body. I made myself focus on his fingers, what they were doing. The slight swaying motion of his body sped up, and his hands were at the waistband of his trousers now. He breathed in a raspy pulse of air, a low sigh loud enough to echo through the darkness of the room, lit only with one dim lamp, and with one motion he pulled his shirt out and deftly undid the last button. With a slow dip of his strong shoulders, the shirt slid from his body, becoming a pool on the floor. With another few fluid motions, his trousers followed. There was nothing underneath. He stood there for a moment, his eyes shut, completely naked, revealed, feeling the air against his body.

Then his voice rang out. "Touch me now. If you want to. Start with my throat." I managed to raise my arm, trying to keep myself under control. There was a part of me that wanted to just launch myself at him, rub against him like a wild animal in heat, scream at him to take me, stop all this, make it better, make it end. My hand reached for his neck, and wrapping my fingers around it slightly, I squeezed. He let out another slow groan. His voice was low. "More." I pressed a little harder. That my small hand around his neck, could have this effect. I tightened my grip.

His eyes were shut, he let out a ragged sound. "Touch me." To have all this power. Over him. Over six feet of him, skin like cream and dark haired, his face almost unfamiliar, twisted with desire in the half-light of the room. All this from just the simple pressure of my hand on his long throat. Then I let go and he released all that was left of the air in his lungs as I traced a line down his chest, circled one of his taut nipples, and dragged it down with a painted fingernail. I looked up at him. His eyes were still shut. He looked tense, wound up, yet his mouth was still slightly open, his lips soft and full and curved. I watched fascinated, as his tongue ran a slow sweep of his upper lip. I touched my finger tip to his hard nipple again and watched as his tongue made that same motion, tasting the air, tasting the sweat on his skin. It made no sense. I could feel it when he did that, an electric metal wire from his mouth to mine. He let out a low moan and the sensation went lower. My hand followed a line down from his chest, lower, across the steady beat of his heart, his breathing quickening, his muscles tense with waiting, down, skimming the sheer line of his now lightly shining skin. It felt hotter in the room. My arms were burning. My legs were numb from keeping still, trying to stop the shaking. All I could do was focus on the slowness. He hadn't even touched me yet. But it was though every movement he made, every precise gesture, every finger bent just so, every flexing of the veins in his arms was something I could feel, burning inside me.

Tristan took one of his hands and laid it flat across his stomach. His fingers were long, so long. They stretched across his torso, his thumb jutting out at an angle. I wanted to take his fingers in my mouth, feel them on me pressing, down, slowly, softly. He moved his hand slowly, covering himself, wrapping his fingers around the hard flesh. He gasped slightly. His voice was sultry, rough. That voice. The same, and not the same. His commanding tone. I surrendered willingly before it. "Suck on your fingers." I did, watching him watch me, imagining it was him, wanting to thrust my hands in his mouth to feel him on me. Instead, I reached out for him. Wet, they traced the beginning of a line of dark hair the same color as those tangled in disarray on his head. He didn't stop me. His hipbones, jutting out, my fingers tracing them. He had left his hand where he had placed it, pointing down, covering his length, his fingertips just sweeping his balls. His hands, big as they were, looked comfortable there, finally, touching himself, taunting me. I wanted my hand to replace his. But I could do nothing unless he told me. We waited. His eyes closed.

He breathed out slowly, and as though speaking from very far away, said "Touch my legs. Don't touch my hand." I linked my fingers and ran my hands down over his finely shaped ass, then back in front, down past the v of muscle, over hard thighs, strong legs, solid, unmoving, the muscles firm and defined, down past his calves to his feet. I dropped to my knees, my hands on the front of his thighs, looking up at him, waiting. Tristan stood there, steady, all muscles, a sheen of sweat on his skin, his hand still wrapped around his cock. I watched as he carefully moved his hand, sliding around on the smooth skin. I watched as a slight tremor shook his legs. I stood back up. We were in a dream, like a dance. I waited for his lead. Just looking at him was almost enough. Almost. It was hard to take in so much male beauty in one place, skin and muscles, his face impossibly lost to pleasure. Yet here he was, in front of me, eyes tightly shut, naked, his hand still touching himself, teasing.

His voice, went it came again, surprised me. "Blindfold me." His eyes were still closed. I managed to walk over to the suitcase, and pulled one of the black silk scarves from the small bag of scarves and silk twisted cords that was always in his possession. Usually they were for me.

I had to stand on tip toes to reach around his head, and tie the knot, the way he had taught me. I wrapped the scarf around twice, checked it was secure. I murmured, "It's done."

"Now wrap one around my neck."

I tied it tight, a thin band across his Adam's apple and the muscles in his neck. A vein was full and raised just below the dark line. Tristan's mouth fell into a thin, dangerous smile.

"Now lead me to the bed."

"Tristan," I breathed out. I took the end of the scarf, and walked him slowly over to the bed. Then I turned down the duvet, exposing the crisp ironed white sheets.

"Help me lie down." I knew he could do this without me, but he held out his hands and I helped him lower his body, then moved him until he was in the middle of the bed. He stretched out like a mountain cat, slow, strong, his stomach muscles taut, his glossy dark hair spread over the pillows, the expanse of his burning skin against the coolness of sheets, a line of pulsing muscle all the way down to his finely shaped ankles. The man was a sculpture. I had never seen anyone like him. Every bone carefully made, every muscle a fine sweep of curving power. He pulled his hand away and there was his cock.

Fully erect, silken, shining lightly at the tip, wet. I watched as Tristan crossed his hands at his wrists over his head, pulling at the scarf around his neck as he did so. "Undress slowly," his voice purred. "I will be here. I can feel you. Do it…but slowly."

I tried to. My hands went to the zip on my dress. I tried to force myself to feel the fabric, the skin warm just beneath it. Slow. Another part of me wanted to tear off what I was wearing and throw myself on him. Beg him to take me. It would be so easy.

I looked over and a smile was playing on his face. "I know. Don't you think I know? That's why I make you do it. Don't disappoint me now." And with a smirk he settled back on the pillows, his hands now grasping the very hard evidence of his own longing. I looked at him and I finally pulled the dress over my head. Then the bra, one strap after the other, dropping over my shoulders, wriggling out of the silky fabric stretched taut over my breasts. Everything felt stuck, as though something was keeping me from pulling off all my clothes as quickly as I wanted. I unhooked the bra and let it fall with a little flourish to the floor.

"Nice," he said. His eyes were blindfolded, but I felt he knew exactly what I was doing as though he were watching. His hearing super acute, every sound creating a picture in his mind. And he showed me, taught me, reminded me, the mind is the most powerful source of feeling of all. Once it's practiced. Once it's trained. I hooked my thumbs under the elastic of my panties and pulled them down, slowly, even more slowly, ridiculously slowly.

"That's right," he murmured. "Until you can't stand it."

It went on forever. I could hear his breathing, a loud, steady pressure in the air. A drip of sweat dropped from my forehead to my breast.

"You're wet...everywhere...your skin. Inside. Outside." Tristan whispered. How? It made no sense but he knew. He knew. He was a magician. I was sure of it. Something other. Just like the first glimpse I'd had of his eyes, the look that passed between us. There was more there, something mysteriously powerful.

I moaned. "Tristan." Unconsciously, I stared to wipe away the fine sweat on my forehead that was threatening to drip into my eyes.

"No, leave it," Tristan commanded. "I like you wet. Slippery. Sliding over me." I watched his mouth move beneath the strip of black silk covering his eyes. "Come to me now, love."

Deliberately, I moved over to the bed. Tristan spoke again. "You know what to do." I tore open the little packet with my teeth, and prepared him. Then I climbed on the bed, careful not to touch him again. His body was humming with electricity. I thought I could hear it, a low throbbing frequency. Pure energy. Under control. There was always an inch of separation, humming, the power between us, the way you can feel something when you put your hands together yet not quite touching. A force field. Total energy building up. I held myself over his taut body. It was difficult not to touch him, his smooth skin, the scars, that tattoo, the veins, pulsing, blue under the pale surface. I clenched my fists. He laughed, mocking me. "Do you want to hit me darling? Or something else?" And he smiled. So close, yet not. Not. All that force rising up. I moved forward. Soon. Soon we would touch. And there would be nothing else. Every inch became a lifetime, nothing but time. Everything was time and energy between us. Like recreating the world, an animal gift. Since the start of light.

My thigh grazed his side and we both let out a sound. Unrecognizable. Lower. Lower. All of me was tense above him. My legs burning with the pressure, not to touch, to go even more slowly. Down, lower. Almost. Then nearly there. I shifted my hips up slightly, trying to capture him without hands, leaning forward, hovering over his chest, my breasts finally meeting his, lightly grazing the skin, nipples touching. His breathing was more ragged now, a long distance runner, his heart beating so loudly, I felt I could see it, hear it, feel it just beneath me, release, want. I would have him. I stretched my body out as long as I could, guiding my hips over him. There, just the tip touching. He let out a long hiss. I came down a little lower there. I moved my hips down his body. There. And there. I pulled on the scarf around his neck. Tristan let out a low moan. A heat like fire lit under my skin everywhere. A drop of sweat dropped onto his chest. He twitched as though I'd burned him. Lower.

"Yes, love. Now." When I didn't move, his voice was a low pleading groan. "Lily. Please," Tristan murmured. I still didn't move. And then he tore himself from the bed, and with one swift motion, he was inside me. Then he pulled out again, nearly all the way. The sound that left his throat was a howl of sheer desire, restrained, tied down. I could feel just the tip of him moving, pulsing slightly, slowly, as I lowered my body down on his. His breathing was ragged now. It echoed in my head, again, in, out. I couldn't remember when I'd breathed. Slower. I could feel him bigger inside me, wider. A little bit further. Both of us taut with waiting. Another year of waiting. Another one. The emptiness. The hollow feeling inside. Begging to feel. Hollow like the universe. Burning. His skin was on fire. Further. Holding myself over him, not touching anywhere but there, another movement of skin a little bit further. Another drop of sweat. His breathing rougher, he let out a low moan when I sank my hips down, like another longing partially satisfied. I could feel him, hot inside me. It was almost hard to grip onto him, his skin and mine slippery with sweat. Wanting him, all the way, the last inch down, all of him, all he had. No, it was too slow. Someone cried out. That much. That little. Another galaxy. All that waiting. Another mile. Hot, his beating hot heart. I had the sheets gripped in my hands now, pulled up with the effort not to slam against him, his blood beating in mine. And then he couldn't hold on any longer and he thrust up inside me, a wail desperately crying out like the last final barrier crossed.

His hips were moving, again, again, steady. Then he stopped, his breathing harsh. I writhed around on him. This couldn't go much longer. Every moment going higher, listening to Tristan moan, a long low keening as he kept moving in tiny spirals, tiny. The almost invisible patterns he traced were breaking open worlds inside me. He was calling out to me now, his voice all small encouragements, we needed this to stay alive. He thrust again, his hands on my hips, over and over, little movements, moving me where he wanted. Then he almost imperceptibly started pulling out and back, slow, long, drawing me along then almost out. "That's it, my love," he breathed. "Hold on. Hold on to me." I clung to the muscles in his arms, as he raised them over his head, the end of the scarf wrapped around his fingers, pulling taut. And we had the perfect tension, rocking steady, a heartbeat, timing, timing like the music, matching. Then his hands dropped, to grip my arms hard, harder, not stopping, the rhythm between us beginning to break up on the crests of his voice moaning, breathing. I tried to hold on but he took over, and calling out for me to go with him, he arched up underneath, his head thrown back, as I pushed myself on to him as deep as I could, tightening around him, my skin on fire, gasping, his low voice, a wild cry, a final groan, and shaking, he grabbed me, clinging on, and we held on, beating pulse like flames, and everything went black as I fell against his chest.

chapter twenty-five

L.A.

And finally the big day arrived. We were staying for the night in the hotel, partially because it was more convenient, partially because the record company wanted to know where Tristan was at all times, even though they presented it as a perk of the event. A professional dresser and makeup artist came by in the early afternoon to make sure our outfits were correct, and to do our hair and makeup. "It costs a lot of money to look like I just screwed someone," Tristan said to the woman as she rubbed the ends of his hair with pomade, then sprayed the roots with hair spray. She laughed but ignored him. I got a similar treatment, but mine took even longer. I did look good though, I thought, even if it was alarming to think this was probably as good as it was ever going to get. For a moment, I understood the pressure of having to be on camera all the time. Everything had to be right. Or the moment was gone. Except it'd be gone anyway.

Tristan poked his head in, and approved the proceedings. "I like your hair like that. You look fantastic, Lily." He winked at me. "The glories of Hollywood. Maybe we should do this more often?" He gave me a little smile, and went out to the living room, while the makeup artist gave me a small container of powder and a brush with strict instructions on how and when to apply it, especially if I was going to be on camera. I had a feeling I'd forget, or not realize that I was shining, and not in a good way, just before my big moments. Hopefully my Tristan-approved hair and the general aura that Tristan gave off would be enough of a distraction.

Then came the waiting. It was only an hour, but ten minutes in, I wished the makeup artist had stuck around to give us something else to think about. Tristan looked edgy. I tried to distract him with a question about L.A., how it had changed since he'd started coming here. I knew Tristan wished that they still held the awards at what was now the Gibson Amphitheatre. "It's a shame,' he said. "Another historic piece of L.A. going—torn down in favor of the Harry Potter Experience, or some such shit. I've nothing against Harry Potter, mind…it's just a shame." Then he started pacing around the vintage two bed villa, as usual making everything seem small in comparison. If he had started shoving furniture out of the way, it wouldn't have been surprising. He walked back and forth a few times, finally heading to the kitchen, where he flung open the silver fridge, and pulled out a tiny bottle of Stoli, and downed it before I could say a word.

"Tristan?" I ventured. "Are you ok?"

He pulled out half a bottle of champagne, and reaching for two glasses from the stocked cabinets, he came over and sat down heavily on the sofa. "Shit, Lily, touring, promotion, the whole business. Here we are in the lap of luxury, and all I can think about is the end of things. Not to be pessimistic, but how to go with the flow, ride the tides, stay afloat—all these fucking metaphors, and yet all I see around me are things going down, and I'm not sure the new ones are a decent replacement. They're thinking of tearing down Madison Square Garden. It's not like it is the greatest place acoustically, but it's got history. Everything goes. Even us." He poured out the champagne. He jumped up again. "Let me get you a straw. That's what they use to stop the lipstick smearing." He came back with the straw, and seeing the look on my face, finally smiled. "You pick up some interesting tips of the trade in this business." We sipped at the champagne. It did take the edge off, just a little. Then Tristan started speaking again. "This is why people go crazy, Lily. You're at the top, the fans are screaming, the limousines are waiting. Anything I want from girls to guys to drugs to anything you can think of is a phone call away. A phone call away, Lily. If that. That's it. I can tell Adrian to get me something, and he'll get it. That's his job. He may try to talk me out of it—that's his job too, but he can't stop me." He refilled his glass, and I sipped at mine through the straw, slowly, wondering where all this was going to end. "Trevor—Trevor could stop me. But where is he? He should have been here by now, but got held up." He stood up abruptly with his glass and pulled back the blinds to look out on the grounds and the path that led up to the pool.

"Five hours. Then it will be done. One way or another," I ventured.

Tristan paced. "I know. And the after parties. Don't forget them." He came over and sat back down next to me. "I feel desperate, Lily. Desperate. I don't know why. I want to enjoy this, and the more I want to, the more I realize I can't. Stupid, really. Millions of people dreaming of doing this, and here on the inside, what is it? Tension, anxiety. Competition, whether you want it or not."

I took his hand. "I used to think people put up with the games. Then I finally realized they start them. It's the only thing that gets them up in the morning, figuring out the rules, using them, hurting people."

Tristan took a deep breath. "I don't like all the games, Lily. I don't care how well I look like I'm playing them."

I looked at his hands, and then up at his eyes. They were dark, hurt. Watching him, I had that feeling again, of a very long tunnel, the spaciousness of his thoughts, this moment, his soul. Fragile. No one should see that, I thought. It's like an invitation to demons.

"We won't play. We will just turn up. And Tristan?" I squeezed his hand and glanced away, suddenly embarrassed.

"Lily?"

I gave a small laugh. "Nothing. Just something like I'll stand between you and the gates of Hell to keep you safe." I sipped some champagne through the straw, feeling foolish.

Then my glass was on the table, and his arms were around me, pulling me on to his lap, holding me to his chest. I could feel his strength returning, and I closed my eyes and felt the warmth of his body, so much larger than mine, all around me.

The bell rang and we both jumped. We stood up and Tristan brushed at my dress with his hand. "I've creased you. Shit."

My smile couldn't have been bigger. "Fuck it. Let's go give them something to remember."

"Lily." His face said everything.

"Tristan."

* * *

The red carpet was stretching out over the stairs, and a collection of women, most of whom seemed to be blond, and who were all wearing some of the highest heels I had ever seen in my life, stood precariously at intervals to help celebrities and actual musicians. All of them seemed almost as incapable of navigation over the carpeted path as each other, trying to get through the phalanx of photographers and TV journalists with microphones awaiting them, while the lines of fans hovered dangerously close to the action. It was a like a gauntlet, some kind of trial by fire that each person had to pass through before they would be permitted inside, where more cameras would attempt to catch their every expression, praying for some particularly newsworthy gaffe or outburst. If they were really lucky, there'd be a nipple slip.

I watched as a woman with long dark hair tottered over to Steven Tyler, trying to keep his attention on where she wanted him to stand for the banks of flashing cameras. He looked pretty good, all things considered. The high heeled helper finally managed to neatly extricate his companion and guide her over to a waiting area, out of range of the cameras. Her dress barely covered her boobs, each standing up individually, separate in a way that made me think of a wax mannequin. There was a certain dead look to her, as magnificent as her outline was, and the amount of skin she was showing. I still had the feeling that she needed to be kept away from any open flame. The helper had guided him over to the area, and was talking at him, when Tyler finally looked up at the cameras. It was though a switch had been hit. He exuded energy, keeping up a constant series of little movements, turning towards the banks of photographers. It was impressive, his posing, that he could even keep his eyes open wide and smile, the constant repeating bursts of light bouncing off him as he turned one way then another. One of the photographers called out, "Over here Steven!" and the cry was picked up by another, then another, until it looked and sounded like nothing more than a frontal assault. Finally it was over, and the woman in heels came over and guided him further down the brand-named alley of logos on white backdrops and the unreality of outdoor red carpets, up to the next group, who would actually ask questions.

There were a few people ahead of us, and Tristan looked uncomfortable. I reached out and squeezed his hand, even though we had mostly agreed not to give any of the paps a shot of us acting as a couple, if we could avoid it. But he looked down at me, and nodded his head, smiling. "It's a fucking zoo," he murmured, low enough that no one could hear, although the name of the latest celebrity to be in front of the cameras was ringing out clearly, drowning out most human interaction. "But it's all worth it," he said, his mouth curled in a half smile. "We get to the end of our lives, and everyone can say at least I tried hard." He laughed. "15 minutes more of our non-fame…" but he trailed off, as he noticed another woman made wondrously tall with her skyscraper heels headed our way. Defiantly, Tristan raised my hand to his lips, let his tongue follow the delicate bones to the fingertips, then released it. I looked around. No one had noticed. It was too blatant, yet it wasn't blatant enough. Only a hand.

The woman in high heels was now approaching Tristan, reaching out her hand, ostensibly to guide him. He flinched, then seemed to realize that she needed support, her left ankle slightly turned to one side in an uneven step that looked painful. He extended his arm, and she took it, gratefully, and he let her lean on him, while appearing to be guided over to the photographers. I followed a couple of steps behind, and when she released him, he held out his hand to me. I looked at him for a moment, and his mouth went up again in that half smile, as he tilted his head. So—it was up to me. How much of it did I want? If anything made sense, all this did not. It would be a very definite statement, but perhaps that was a good idea. Or not. But the blinding smile Tristan gave as I gave in and headed in his direction wasn't just noticed by me. The paps went crazy—and why not? He looked beautiful, in his element, and was playing the game the way he wanted to play it. His hand reached for mine, and he pulled me to his side as he ran his other hand through his hair, and posed us for the cameras. The light of the flash was almost painful. "Look out and up and raise your eyebrows," he whispered. "Find something, a point to gaze at." We turned and posed from another angle, the paps yelling out. "Tristan! Tristan! Congratulations! Over here. Look over here. Tristan. Oi Hunter! Her name? Name? Tristan!"

Finally our high-heeled minder came over, and moved us away from the shouting, along to the interviews. I stood back this time, but still close enough to hear the interviewer.

"Tristan Hunter. Well. Congratulations on your first nomination. How does it feel to have this solo success come now?"

"Well, it feels good. Of course. Thank you. Yeah, I've got a great team of people, Trevor Sears—I'd like to thank him particularly for keeping the faith. He's been with me since the start."

The interviewer waited for Tristan to finish his quick thanks, then went back to her questions. "You've been away from L.A. for a while now. How does it feel to be back?" That was tactful enough, I supposed. They couldn't really say what they wanted if this was going to go out to teenage suburbia. But still. We weren't through the interview yet.

"It feels good. A lot of fans out here, and of course I lived here for a while, you remember, so I had to do some of the old things…" The interviewer looked as though she were about to pass out, whether from fear or excitement over what Tristan was possibly going to say. Something that would get this segment repeated and her face seen over and over again.

"The old things…like the parties…?" She prompted.

"Oh man, there are so many parties. But you can ask the driver. The first thing we did when we landed was go out… and get a burger. Driving with the top down, it's like a classic song. You just can't find it anywhere else."

She looked a little disappointed, then saw me, and her face lit up. "And you are here tonight with…"

Tristan turned around, and nodded to me, and I came over. He slid his arm around me, and the solid warmth of it was good, even though I suddenly felt cold. I was about to have my big TV moment, and I wasn't sure I was ready. "This is Lily, Lily Taylor, the writer and journalist." He turned and his smile was so warm, so real, I could have kissed him right there, and I didn't care if a thousand interviewers were waiting. He winked at me, before turning back to the interviewer, and with another slightly amused look at both her and the camera, announcing very precisely who designed my dress. A perk of the party had been the offer of the dress to wear. The presenter said, "It's beautiful," just as Tristan interrupted her.

"It's a great story—I'll give you the short version—we went to his party and I was admiring his tattoos. So he told me where to go to get this one," as he began unbuttoning the top half of his shirt on camera, dropping his beautifully tailored suit jacket down off his shoulders, and pulling his shirt to the side to reveal the gorgeous delicate traced image of a bird, something between a phoenix and a hawk, carrying a rose in its mouth, a staff and sword in each clawed foot. The interviewer gasped, and looked half as though she wished someone would stop him because he was taking off his clothes on camera, and half as though she wished someone would help him take off more. "And we found this lovely dress with his help for Lily to wear tonight. And the suit. So wish us luck." And he expertly bent down, showing still more skin and the muscled lines of his torso before kissing her two times on each cheek, dangerously close to her perfectly outlined mouth, a nod to Hollywood with a European twist. She waved, a bit breathless, before returning to the camera to sum up which award Tristan was nominated for and segue on to the next interview.

We turned away and started walking towards the entrance, and he pulled me closer to him, as he headed us in the direction of the auditorium. "Fuck that's enough of that. When do we get drinks? Food? Anything."

"Nice move with the tattoo there," I said, squeezing his hand.

"Yeah, my naked chest broadcast into homes everywhere. Bloody hell, did I show a nipple? Who knows. Don't try this at home kids." Tristan laughed. "The whole thing is so ridiculous, but I know what they thrive on. That should keep them talking, for a few minutes, anyway." We passed through the doors, watched by some of the largest security guards I'd ever seen. No one was getting in there.

I looked around, at the guests and the industry people, at the celebs, and at the whole spectacle. It was fascinating, but strange, gilded, as though what was underneath was cold and grey and unfinished and needed embellishment. We found a bar, and even though we'd said we wouldn't, we both asked for a glass of champagne, then moved on to collect our swag bags, filled with whatever nonsense that needed promoting. I peeked inside. A book on successful juice dieting and some foldable ballet flats, in case during the limo ride back to the hotel, you started regretting all the choices you'd made earlier in the night, from drugs to overly high heels. There were some other odds and ends, but I didn't really care. Tristan had pulled me over to an out of the way bit of wall, and was stabbing at the numbers on his cell phone, while I held his glass. I looked at him quizzically—and he mouthed "Trevor," before holding the phone to his ear. He moved his head up and down, to some internal beat, before smiling and tucking the phone between his neck and his ear. "Trevor. Mate." He listened for a bit. "Yeah, my tattoo. Skin sells, or so I've been told. Yeah." He laughed. "Look, you need to find us so we can sit down. Yes, of course you're sitting with us. Suppose I win, you bastard?

Looks a bit wrong me gesturing out to the bleachers when I say my thank yous." He listened again. "Ah she's here? Of course she is. Where's Paul? Here too. Naturally. Looking for their photo op. Well. Not in the mood. We're near the swag and the bar. Where else? Get here." And he neatly dropped the phone into his hand from under his ear, and stabbed at it again, before injecting it into the front pocket of his trousers, the fabric so thin and smooth you could practically see the apps on the screen. He downed his champagne, and placed the empty glass on a passing waiter's tray. "He better get here soon. I suddenly feel a bit like walking out of this whole thing."

"Tristan. It's ok. I mean it's ridiculous. But. A few hours from now it will be done. You'll get through it. We'll get through it. And by the way," I added, swallowing another mouthful of champagne, "before I get caught up in this sugar icing world—thank you—thanks for saying writer before journalist back there."

"Well." Tristan grinned. "Well, you are. And they are not. And a distinction should be made. Although I think my parade of flesh may trump anything else I said."

"That's why you did it." I didn't mind. It just needed to be said.

"Yes. But no. Sex sells. And while their mouths are hanging open, they aren't asking me inane questions. Much better that way. Besides I love that hungry look." He winked at me, and I blushed. But he kissed my forehead, and had that strange look around his eyes again when he said it. I wondered what he was thinking. I'd finally learned mystery was to wonder, not know, or even ask, and we stood there, side by side, watching the glittery crowd and looking out for Trevor.

Tristan saw him first, another tall head in the crowd, and murmured "thank god" under his breath. I finally saw him, on his own, in an elegant dark three piece suit, and looking more like a gangster than a record boss. He passed through the crowd, as though they were invisible, neither looking to the left or right, and sliding in between the barely dressed and the overly dressed with complete indifference, his face a mask. When he caught sight of Tristan, he permitted himself a rather self-satisfied smirk, but the big hug they exchanged when they were in arm's reach of each other was tight and real. Then he bent down and kissed me on the lips, while squeezing Tristan's hand. I was almost too startled to laugh.

"At last," I said. "I've been waiting for you to do that since the first interview."

He studied me for a moment, before putting his arms around both of us. "I know. Tart." And Tristan giggled, and we went off, the three of us, to find our pretty good seats at this delusional homeroom fair, where the kids got to show the world what they'd been up to and maybe take home a certificate. I put my arm around Trevor, and found Tristan's hand and held that, and when I looked around, it was pretty obvious we were making the impression Trevor had hoped for. I laughed. Maybe this wouldn't be so bad after all.

* * *

We finally found our seats, the big paper signs stuck to the back whisked away by the ushers. Tristan was saying hello to some people, and Trevor and I sat down, leaving a space on the aisle. There were only seats for the three of us. I suddenly wondered if I had taken AC's place. "No AC?" I murmured to Trevor.

He leaned to whisper in my ear. "Too much like a reunion then, we all thought. Then Paul would definitely be wanting in. AC didn't want to steal Tristan's thunder."

"Probably better to have me as a plus-one in front of the cameras."

Trevor gave me a sharp look. "That's not it. Don't disappoint me, Lily."

I looked back at him, embarrassed. It had been a petty thing to say. "Sorry. Really. Sorry. Don't know what came over me."

Trevor put his hand on my shoulder. "That's better. Besides, he'll be at the after-party. Plenty of opportunity for photographers to make a year's salary." He smirked. I laughed. You couldn't take any of it seriously. It was like trying to build with water. Tristan came up beside us, and slid in to his seat. "What are you two plotting?"

Trevor gazed at him. "Your demise, naturally. Now act like a rock star, and for god's sake don't make any faces when some mainstream pop group wins for best alternative band. Those pictures have a half-life longer than californium."

Tristan started laughing. People looked around. "Pinch me, both of you. No, not now. At the time. This is why Botox is so handy. I need my Joker smile ready at all times out here."

We settled in. The stage hands were running around frantically. Nothing artificial there, I thought. The intro music was stopping and starting. The cameras were in place, beginning their swiveling observation of the crowd and the marks on the stage where the spotlights would be. Then finally, the lights went down, the red lights on the cameras were bright, and the cheesy over-dramatic voice of the announcer echoed out in the auditorium. "Welcome to the 22nd MUT Music Awards. And now your host…"

I stopped listening. Trevor was nudging me. He whispered in my ear, "Where do they find these people?" And a bit louder, "Being at the awards ceremony is a sure sign that you no longer scare anyone, or are even relevant." He glanced over at Tristan. "Present company excluded, of course." Tristan laughed. "But really? Who thought it would be a good idea to choose him? You can just imagine the conversation. 'He was cutting edge twenty years ago, but if we have him then we can avoid all those other frightening people who might not say what we tell them. This one thinks it might be a comeback. Funny.'"

Tristan leaned over me. "Hush, Trevor. Next you'll be telling me there's no Santa Claus…wait." They both sniggered. The host was waxing lyrical about the great musical guests we had coming up. Then we went to a commercial, and everyone visibly sagged. The host went to the side of the stage for a powder touch-up.

Trevor made a small noise. "And it's only the beginning. Not even the possible thrill of a streaker, now rendered totally unnecessary by the fact that everyone is already naked. Maybe the auto-tune will break. One can hope."

The announcer came back on, and it all burst into life again. The first of the musical guests flounced on to the stage, wearing a body suit and feathers, accompanied by 10 dancers.

It was all very slick, choreographed. The dancers did splits and spun on their backsides as the singer promised she would deliver real love, not fake. Tristan smiled, conscious that the camera was headed our way. "You can pinch me constantly," he whispered, trying not to move his mouth. We applauded.

"This is just fantastic," Trevor said, clapping enthusiastically. "Three hours of manufactured excitement." He looked over to Tristan. "What evil deed did you do to get nominated to this?" We all smiled broadly as the cameras swept the audience.

A couple of nominations followed. The same person won for both. They did their best to look surprised, and grateful. "At least he is talented," said Trevor. "Risk-taker, no, but he has mentioned his influences. It's something, isn't it? If you're going to steal, at least get them a few record sales with it."

Tristan nodded. "He's a superstar. Not as polished in private, but he knows how and when to shut up. And that's not a bad thing."

"He mentions a lot of people. I hope you have your list. They live for these moments, quite rightly."

Tristan smiled, then we went to a commercial. His expression changed immediately. "Trevor. You know that won't happen. It's great to be nominated. It opened some doors— and wallets. But I'm here to lend it all credibility. Not to actually win." He lowered his voice. "Besides, you would have heard by now."

Trevor shook his head. "True, true, and true, I'm afraid. But your smile is dazzling."

Tristan laughed. "When in Rome. It was recommended I have a little paint and polish. My teeth hurt."

Trevor rolled his eyes. "Dear god."

It went on like this for another hour, a blasting musical interlude with dancers followed by nominations. The usual people were winning as usual. Then it suddenly was our turn. The announcer began his intro, reading off the autocue, adding pauses to make it seem more spontaneous, a trick that he had clearly been taught how to do. But he was good at it. Or maybe it was just that I suddenly felt nervous. I wanted Tristan to win. Despite everything wrong with the whole exercise. I just wanted him to win. The presenters came out, an attractive actress from a show about angels, and a guitarist who had won a couple of years ago with his band. The names were read out, one at a time. Tristan watched what each person did, if they waved, if they stood up. I could almost hear him mentally calculating. What would make him stand out? What would be noticed? How far was too much? Finally his name was called out. The announcer intoned. "And Tristan Hunter for *Some of Us Remember the Future*." And Tristan half-stood, bowing slightly, waving to the announcer, then turning to the crowd, and making sure to wave to the audience. A small section in the balcony burst into screams and cheers. He really smiled then, and blew a kiss with both hands in their direction. Then he sat down.

Trevor leaned over, pinched him, and grabbed his hand. "Good luck, mate," he said. We all sat up a little straighter, and watched them open the elaborately printed envelope. The actress read it, and looked a little confused, then looked out at the audience. For a moment, I thought maybe Tristan had won. Coming from behind. Then she beamed. "And the award goes to N37!" We applauded. Tristan had a smile on his face. Once the applause died down, the presenters accepted the award on their behalf, and a short video of the band, who were on tour, came up. They waved their awards around, and thanked everyone. More applause, and we cut to a commercial.

Tristan turned to Trevor. "At least I like their music. It could have been so much worse. But tell me you didn't know."

Trevor shrugged. "Whenever they have to do that video link, and the awards get sent out, there's always a leak. But rumors are rumors. I hadn't heard anything definitive from anyone I trust." He smiled a tight smile. "Besides, who doesn't love excitement and a party." I laughed. He looked at his watch. "45 minutes more of this bollocks, and we can head to the af-ter-party and mingle with the cream of the planet." He low-ered his voice. "Seriously mate, if these things were real, you would be winning it all. Fuck knows you deserve it. Best fuck-ing thing out there." He looked around and smiled. "You have your name out there now, again. And people know you aren't just a memory. Play the game a little longer, then go back to what matters. Leave the nonsense to the people who are still playing their adolescent games."

Tristan looked around. "At least I've got a little core group of fans out there."

Trevor nodded. "Bigger than that, mate. Fuck, I know. Brilliant idea. Hang on." And he pulled out his phone, and began typing a message. I glanced over. Twitter. I tried not to stare, and held Tristan's hand.

He grinned at me. "Still love the loser?"

I looked back at him. "So it does matter to you."

"I'm only human, Lily. Believe it or not."

I squeezed his hand. "Oh, I believe it. And yes." I gave him a quick kiss, suddenly careless of all the cameras and industry people. "Fuck them."

Tristan smiled, but it didn't quite reach his eyes. "It's ok. I'll be all right in a minute." He leaned over to Trevor. "What are you up to?"

"Brilliant idea. This is why you control your own Twitter instead of leaving it to some self-proclaimed community manager. Just dropped a hint on one of the sub accounts that tries to pretend it's on the inside, that a certain someone may be doing some publicity shots outside the auditorium briefly after the ceremony."

Tristan looked curious. "How did you do that?"

Trevor had his evil expression on. "Made it seem like a DM went astray. Asking for extra lighting to meet us at the side door."

Tristan laughed. "It's a good thing your evil genius only plays in the fields of the music industry. God help us if you'd gone into politics."

Trevor regarded him. "How do you know I haven't? I could run an entire small country by Twitter and text." He pulled out his phone. "Damn. A coup. Well. It was fun while it lasted."

I watched the two of them exchange insults and snark about the people on stage. I said nothing, just listened. Trevor's cruel banter was raising Tristan's mood more than any of my earnest protestations of love could. As it should be, I thought. Not everything ran on love. Or that kind of love.

At the final thank you and goodnight, followed by the voice-over thanking the individual sponsors and going through the brief legal explanations of the voting procedure, the audience began to twitch. Release was in sight. As soon as the cameras were off, the entire energy changed. First it sagged, then it was like a horse leaving the gate in a race. There were people to talk to, after-parties to go to and be seen at, all the amusements that the industry had to offer. And after over three hours of being on their best behavior, the audience was starving for any actual entertainment. The bloodier, the better. Trevor checked his phone. "Excellent. Limo will be there to save us from too many fans and photographers. Let's go pretend you're surprised, Tristan. And Lily. We're going to fade into the crowd and let Tristan have his moment in the spotlight, like Venus rising from the sea. We don't want to interrupt the flow of love and lust coming his way. And underwear. Though it's hard to say one has truly lived until they've had a pair of damp knickers thrown at their face." Trevor twisted his face into an expression of astonishment. "Isn't this fun? Say yes, and let's escort our star to his loyal and possibly deranged fans."

chapter twenty-six

L.A.

The after-parties had gone on late, but it was still not full dawn when our limo dropped us back at the hotel. The man on front desk noted our arrival, handed Tristan and AC their keys, and went back to reading something.

"He was entirely too calm," Tristan muttered as we tottered along the path by the pool leading to the villa. "Well, nothing to see here. Move along, move along." AC giggled.

I wrapped my arms around myself. "I thought it didn't get cold in L.A. I'm chilly."

Suddenly both men had their arms around me, their hands smacking into each other as they circled my waist. We all cracked up. "That's better, isn't it Lily?" AC purred.

Tristan smirked. "Very subtle. I won't look around, but I'm sure front desk guy is filming your ass, right now."

AC shrugged. "He's welcome to the view. May it entertain him for the rest of his shift. Here's my villa, anyway. I will wish you two good night." He started to pull his arm from my waist but I could feel that Tristan had grabbed him by the wrist.

"Don't play that way. I haven't even raided my minibar yet…wait, yes I did. But it will be replenished!" Tristan flourished the key. "You're coming with us. I need another witness if I have to complain they didn't give me enough."

AC grinned. "You're an idiot. Besides, the record company sent over a basket of goodies and champagne. It'll be in the room."

Tristan looked at him, unfocused. "How do you know? Maybe yours is different."

AC giggled again. "I know, big rock star, let's compare."

Tristan shouted, "A challenge! I love a challenge."

"Shhhh," we both whispered, and we all started laughing again. Tristan managed to open the door with the key, and we stumbled in.

"Look," Tristan said delightedly, "there is a basket."

"But it's not cold," AC sniffed. "What's in the minibar?"

"What's in your pocket?" Tristan grinned. "I'll get the bottle if you get it out."

"So demanding." AC sat down on the sofa, and I sat next to him. Tristan came over with the bottle, and unwrapped and carefully popped the cork.

"Glasses. I forgot." Tristan muttered.

AC put his hand on his shoulder. "Forget it. Like race car drivers, right Lily? From the bottle."

"I don't mind," I said.

"Good," AC answered, and passed me the bottle. I took a long swig, and when I went to put it down, looked at what AC's hands were doing, then back up at Tristan.

AC saw the look on Tristan's face, and followed it back to me. "You're not going to tell on us, are you Lily?"

I shrugged. "No. Not tonight. But…"

AC stopped what he was doing and took my hand. "Just tonight. Really. Mostly. Promise." Then he glanced at me. "Do you want some?"

I looked at Tristan. It seemed he was waiting. "You'll do it anyway, just in the bathroom without me watching."

"Probably," they both said.

"Then yes. Better here than there." I grabbed the bottle. "I'm not perfect, I never said I was."

"Lily! Stop it. You are. It's just a bit of fun." AC looked at me. "You are pretty perfect, actually."

Tristan waved the bottle towards us. "She is. She really fucking is. Come here, darling." And he managed to take the little spoon and gesture towards me at the same time.

AC laughed. "No, rock star. You come here, and cuddle on the sofa. Lily, you're going to spoil your dress. Take it off. I hear all 5 a.m. parties happen in underwear." And he screwed the cap back on the vial, and stood up. Once he was sure that he had our attention, he started to take off his jacket. Draping it carefully over a chair, he began on the buttons of his shirt. Tristan and I watched.

"Come on Lily," AC called, "come up here. Next to me. Look, there's another chair for your dress. See? Tristan's watching."

I stood up, and looked over at Tristan. "Only if you want to," he mouthed to me. But the look on his face was something else again.

I went and stood next to AC, who stopped what he was doing to undo the zipper on my dress. "Oh, little hooks at the top. Fine craftsmanship, this. Soft." He undid the zipper, and ran a finger down my spine, snapping the back of the bra gently against my skin, and then continuing downwards. "Very fine craftsmanship here." He left the dress on my shoulders. "Let's do it together," he smiled. Then he lowered his voice to a whisper. "He'll like that. A lot."

Tristan's voice startled us. "Are you actually wearing underwear, AC?"

AC pretended to be shocked. "I'm offended. I wouldn't scare Lily like that."

"I've seen one before, I think," I smiled at him.

He bent his head down and leant it on my shoulder. "I know. And you've seen his too. The standard bearer." He whispered again, turning his head to my ear. "But mine's quite nice, really." He stroked the line of my back that the open zipper revealed. "Loves attention. And your elegant underwear."

Tristan coughed. AC grinned at him. "Excuse me. Where were we? Wait Lily, let me unzip. A little adjustment. Can we finish at the same time? Ready?" And I almost forgot what I was doing, as he slowly unzipped his trousers, and shaking his hips very slowly, let them fall to the ground. He was wearing short boxer briefs, with a wide black elastic band at the top. The silky fabric didn't leave anything to the imagination. He hadn't been lying about liking the underwear. Or any of it.

AC picked up his trousers with a flourish and laid them on the chair. "Lily. You waited. That's all right, now you've got both of us watching you. That's better, isn't it?" He grinned.

Before either of them could say anything, or I could think, I dipped my shoulders forward. The dress cascaded off my breasts, and slid to the floor. I stood there for a moment, before I bent forward from the waist, being careful not to step on it with my high heels, and picked it up with one finger, letting it trail over the arm of the chair. Then I looked up at them. A wave of hair half covered my eyes. I could still see them. They were watching. Very intently.

AC cleared his throat. "Nice. Very nice. I think that deserves a present. Come sit by me." He lifted up the bottle again.

Tristan groaned. "Bloody hell, AC. It's not subtle, is it?"

"No one has to do anything with it, Tristan. Do they, Lily?" I shook my head. I felt slightly dazed. AC took my hand and I sat next to him, one of his beautifully shaped thighs touching mine. He really did have a nice body, compact, curved, but strong. It was an intriguing combination. "Now come sit next to us. We won't even make you undress."

Tristan got up from the chair, and sat next to me on the sofa. The fabric of his suit tickled one leg, and AC's soft skin was warm against the other. Without any enhancements, I was already a lot more awake. AC seemed relaxed, but in that watchful way he had. I knew he was assessing the mood. He was a lot like Tristan in that way. I just wondered what he would decide.

Then Tristan jumped up. "I feel overdressed. And hot." He winked at AC.

"I knew you would. Come on Lily, let's sit back and watch the master at work. No one does it quite like he does."

"Take off his clothes, you mean."

"That too. Come on, Tris. Make us suffer."

Tristan was standing where we were, his hands holding open the suit jacket, like he was opening a curtain. He had already started, but when AC said that, he stopped, and shrugged off the jacket, and tossed it across the room. "Stiffer," he murmured. Facing us, he undid each button, until the shirt was hanging loose, a rectangle of skin between, that line of hair dipping down below the waistband of his trousers. Then slowly turning around, he dropped the shirt so that his arms were tensed and straight, the muscles in his back framing his spine, his whole body taut, while the shirt remained drawn across his hips, his clenched hands cuffed by the fabric. His head was slightly turned away from us, and he stood there, every muscle flexed.

"Holy fucking hell," murmured AC.

Tristan released his fists, and still with his hands behind him, pulled off each cuff, slowly, and let the shirt fall to the floor. Still with his back to us, he then bent forward, his head nearly to the floor, and pulled the shirt between his legs. Coming up slowly, every muscle in his back and legs straining, his ass a perfect curve, he finally stood up and stretched his arms over his head. The shirt followed the jacket, thrown roughly to a corner of the room. Then he turned to face us, his hands touching himself to find the zipper, quickly undone. The button came next, and swaying his hips from side to side, the trousers slipped along his hips, his thighs, his calves, to the floor. He threw them on the chair. He'd already taken off his shoes at the door, as he usually did, so he was now barefoot and completely naked except for a pair of black briefs. He then pulled them out, away from his body, and looking down, snapped them back into place, one hand sliding slowly over what was covered, while making sure that nothing escaped. They were just small enough that it was a possibility.

"I thought these were bigger," he said. "I might as well not have them on." He had an evil expression on his face.

AC drank some more champagne, then coughed, offering

me the bottle. "No," and his voice came out a little strangely, "I like to suffer. Lily? Did he pass the test?"

It felt like I had to speak over my beating heart. "Yes, I think so." Everything hurt, just a little bit.

"Tristan, that means you can come and sit with us." Deliberately, Tristan walked in front of us, his hips at eye level, his tight briefs molded to his body, inches away. AC's hand gripped my leg. I shivered. "He's good," AC murmured. "Here Tristan, drink some champagne, you deserve it."

Tristan took the bottle, drank, then looked down at AC's hand. He placed one of his own on my other leg, and stroked it gently. "Nice legs." He leaned over and kissed me. I had the distinct impression he was enjoying the distress he was pretending to ignore. He leaned back, his stomach fluttering with his breathing. AC shut his eyes. Tristan sat up, every muscle flexing, and picking up the bottle, stretched back again. "That actually was a fun party. Much better than I thought it would be."

AC didn't answer. His hand was making a little circle on the inside of my knee with his left hand, his body turned towards us. He put his other arm around me and met Tristan's hand coming from the other side. I could feel them lock their fingers together, hands warm on my skin. And we sat there, saying nothing, feeling the line we weren't going to cross coming a little bit closer.

* * *

The room was filled with bright sunshine when a loud knocking came from the front door. We'd all finally crawled into bed last night, this morning, at the point when the tension of keeping everything at bay and the excitement of the day and night had finally hit all of us. I barely remembered lying down. Tristan looked around blearily, saw me on one side and AC on the other, and crawled out the end of the bed to get a bathrobe, and see who wanted something. I looked at the iPhone dock the hotel so thoughtfully provided. 12:30 p.m. Not too bad then. I sat up, and felt the beginnings of a headache.

I could hear Tristan talking to someone, and the sound of a tray being put down. Two trays. China clinking together. Then the door closed, but there was still talking, which grew louder. Tristan opened the door, and there, standing behind him, an amused smile on his face, was Trevor. "Good morning Lily. AC. Here you are. There's breakfast out there—when you're ready, of course."

I glanced over at AC. He was sitting up in bed. "Hello Trevor. Did you bring us coffee? Bless you."

"Full-service. However, it's my breakfast as well. I haven't been awake that long myself. I hope you didn't think I was out running, or something equally ridiculous. Lily, there are some berries out here for you."

"Thank you, Trevor. I'll be out in a minute."

"Take your time, my dear."

He left, leaving the door slightly ajar. But a moment later, he was back, his eyes gazing at us through the half open door. A thin smile animated his face.

"And we should probably check out at some point. Not to mention all of us leaving together, slightly more discreet, n'est-ce-pas? See you in a minute."

AC laughed, as he climbed out of bed, stretching first one

arm then the other. "And I thought I was unsubtle." He walked to the bathroom, and gave me a little wave before shutting the door. My eyes followed him. I couldn't help it. Whether it was the memory of the night before, or curiosity, I couldn't tell.

But we had just woken up together. Again.

* * *

When I came out in my bathrobe, Tristan and Trevor were sitting at the table, coffee in front of them. When I came in, Trevor picked up the paper. "A nice picture of the three of you this morning. 'Tristan Hunter and AC Clark, formerly of Devised, with Lily Taylor. Hunter was nominated for best alternative album last night.' A good picture of the three of you. Although there is another one in this paper. 'Hunter and Clark, the bromance continues.'" Trevor coughed, and drank a sip of coffee. "Bromance? Is that what they're calling it these days? I thought it was fucking..." He trailed off. "Lily. Come sit down. I'm back off to London today. Leave these jokers, and come with me."

I smiled at him. "Trevor. For you, anything. But I thought we were going to an island, or a small country somewhere. Aren't I your Evita?"

"This is why you must never underestimate this one, Tristan. A long memory. Even longer than...my trip back. But I will see the three of you in London. One week? Two weeks? More rehearsing." He went back to his paper. "Music."

Tristan laughed. "Yeah, we'll be there. Don't worry."

Trevor grimaced. "I'm counting on it. And don't bring the comestibles. You're getting careless." He pulled the vial out of his pocket. "Found this on your table when I came in."

Tristan looked away. "Fuck." A big smile spread across his face. "I guess we were distracted."

I tried to contain a laugh.

Trevor looked at me, then back at Tristan. "If it makes you forget this, then I'm all for it." He took my hand. "Lily. You have the patience of a saint. Don't forget to give Dave my regards." He raised both our hands to look at his very expensive watch. "Time for you to get ready. If AC ever relinquishes the shower. Let's say our goodbyes here, kiss kiss, yes, both of you. And try to behave. Try."

An hour later we were all walking through the bright sunlight to our cars. I waved to Trevor as he got in. He wagged his finger at me, but the look of concern on his face was real. I nodded to him, acknowledgment, understanding. He inclined his head, then gave me a sharp look. I mouthed back, "I will." His thin smile reappeared. Then the door shut. I waved at the tinted glass as the car pulled out.

I was standing there, thinking what it meant for a man like Trevor to trust you, when Tristan and AC's voices broke through. "Lily! Come on sweetheart." They were both standing there, a poster shot, sunglasses, leather, holding the car door open, dark and light so close together, one taller, almost menacing, the other, more slight, his crooked smile more of an invitation.

I got in.

chapter twenty-seven

L.A. to New York

The flight back seemed longer than usual. Tristan slept mostly. AC was reading. I kept dozing off then waking up with a start. I'd look down at the land below, when there was a break in the clouds, and you could see the earth, alarmingly vast, yet almost touchable, like a map come to life. So much had happened down there. Restless, I walked around the plane a bit, just to get my legs moving. It all appeared normal. Just another flight. Rows of heads. The haphazard collection of people coming or going.

When I came back to my seat, AC touched my arm. "All right?" he said. That same way he had, a little like Tristan, of seeing into you.

"Yeah, I'm ok. Just taking a tour of the plane," I answered. He reached for my hand, and glanced over at the sleeping Tristan. He looked so tired, yet softer, calmer in sleep.

"Thank you for letting me come back with you." AC looked at me. "You didn't...you don't have to do this."

"What?" I stared back, surprised. "No, I'm glad you're

here. Really." I nodded towards Tristan. "He wants you here. I don't think I could have stopped him, even if I'd tried. Or wanted to," I added, seeing the expression on his face.

AC took my hand. "Oh, you could have, Lily. You really could have. I don't think you realize..." He trailed off. "Anyway, I hope you're glad I'm here." He smiled, a little too brightly.

"I am. For real." I leant down and kissed his cheek. "Stop worrying, ok?"

Tristan moved, and half opened his eyes. "Are you two all right?" He peered at us, sleepily.

"We're good, Tristan. All good. Go back to sleep. Well, let me get past you first," I said. And he watched us both for a moment, something like a child's contented smile appearing on his face, then he closed his eyes again.

AC and I looked at each other. I thought I recognized the emotion that seemed written clearly on his features, that sort of fierce pride and that other thing, the one that made people do crazy things, and change their lives. We both smiled. We had a lot in common, after all. After a minute, he started to say something, but what came out was, "I think New York City will be fun," and he went back to his book. He squeezed my hand though, as I climbed over them to get back to my seat by the window.

* * *

But now, getting out of the cab from the airport, AC seemed a little agitated. Going up in the elevator. I wondered what he was thinking. It reminded me a little of the very first time I'd been here with Tristan, a buzzing under the skin, all anticipation. But when the door finally opened, he calmly stepped in and took a moment looking around.

"It looks good, Tris. I like what you've done with it. New sofa. Very eclectic." He winked at me. "Now to order lots of takeout and leave the containers under the chairs."

Tristan gave us both a hug. "Come on, I'm beat. Let's go find menus. You can both order something for us while I shower." His broad grin set the mood, as he dropped his bag and guitar case and kissed me happily. I could hear him humming as he headed for the bedroom.

AC's presence seemed to settle Tristan, and he wasn't as tense as he had been right after the tour. We spent a few days going to galleries, museums, finding new restaurants for dinner. It was like being a tourist, and we each had a list of things we wanted to see. And we had opinions on every painting, every spring roll, every cab ride. Talking about everything. Arguing into the night, pulling out records. Then we stopped going out, and ordered dinner in, watching old movies. And every night, AC would come with us as far as the kitchen, say goodnight, then he would head back to the living room, to the made-up bed on the sofa. And Tristan would grab his hand, and pull him into the bedroom. Nothing happened. But we were all tangled up in one way or another, the sheets pulled at angles from the pressure of our bodies. I could feel AC's hand on my back and Tristan's long legs against mine, one light touch, one heavy, reassuring one. Tristan seemed to be sleeping very well. But I would lie there awake in the big bed, eyes open, staring, then finally go and make some tea. Back in bed,

I'd plug in my headphones in an attempt to lull myself to sleep. One night I came back from the kitchen to find AC watching me. "Are you all right, Lils?"

I brushed aside all the things I wanted to say, and looked down at the sleeping Tristan, wrapped up in the sheet. "I'm good. Really. Just insomnia. It happens."

AC grinned at me in the darkness. "There's a cure for that, you know."

"Yes, I know." There was nothing else to say.

I climbed into bed. His hand didn't reappear on my back. I pulled the duvet up, and stared at the stairs to the bathroom. It was going to be a long night.

* * *

A few nights later, we headed off in a town car after dinner to a club Tristan had heard about. It was supposed to be hard to find, and edgy, but when the car pulled up after a 25 minute drive, it just looked like just another steel door hiding another industrial space filled with dim light bulbs and makeshift stages. AC looked at him. "How do you find these places, Tris?"

Tristan shrugged. "Come on, it will be fun. At least no one here will have heard of us, or care. I wouldn't mind that."

AC pushed him towards the door. "Bemoan the trappings of fame. 'Why can't I have a normal night out?' If there is beer in cans in one of those silver steel tubs, you owe me 50 bucks and a night in a nice place."

Tristan shoved him back. "Shut it. Look around. I might as well give you the cash now. Besides, you might pull. I hear the women around here go for that sad, lost look you do so well."

"Works for you, bitch." They both giggled as they fought over who would open the door, then who would go up the narrow stairwell first. When we got to the top, no one even looked twice. We passed over money, our hands were stamped, and we went into the darkened room. One whole side was glass windows looking out over the skyline, broken with the uneven brick walls and water towers of the warehouses and tenements. The other side was a long brick wall, half covered with what looked like an old theatre curtain. There were some rescued sofas, strategically placed in corners. Some of them already contained their complement of couples getting to know each other better. I turned around when AC squawked with laughter. "A fucking tin bucket! Cans! PBR. Bud Light." He shoved Tristan again, then wrapped his arm around him. "Buy me a Bud Light so I can keep my girlish figure."

"Cheap date," Tristan snorted.

AC grinned. "No, just cheap." And he messed up Tristan's hair affectionately.

"Make that two," I added, coming up behind them. "Then let's go outside. I want to see the view."

AC put his arm around me. "A woman who knows her own mind, I like that. And you know what? I think you're right." He tapped Tristan on the shoulder. "Get a six. Let's go hide outside."

Beers in hand, we opened the sliding glass door at one end of the wall of windows, pushing aside the draft curtain, and stepped over the ledge. There were a number of people out-side, smoking, talking. A couple was leaving their spot at the corner edge, and AC quickly claimed it for us.

"This isn't so bad," he said. "Fresh air. Nice view of the Empire State." He looked over the edge. "Hey, there's another club across the way. We can check that one out too." Tristan shot him a look. "Kidding, kidding. This is fine."

We stood there, looking out over the low rooftops, to the glittering skyscrapers only a few miles away. A dog started to bark.

"It feels like a movie set," I said. Tristan and AC agreed, then started talking about the videos they had done with Devised and the places just like this where they'd been filmed. I listened to them reminiscing. With the article pretty much wrapped up, it felt good to be able to enjoy their stories with-out keeping a tally of what might work in the writing. Still, I listened for the details. I couldn't help it. They were arguing about which one was the best, when I interrupted.

"I finally saw the one AC starred in. Not sure how I missed that one. AC demonstrating his prowess as a lover on screen. Actually it was interesting. Not your usual boy meets girl story. And all the kissing." I clinked my second beer with AC. "Nice."

"Oh, really?" AC moved closer to me. "Tell me more."

"Here we go," I laughed. "Nothing to tell really. You just looked like you knew your way around a kiss." AC was study-ing me, and I was glad he couldn't see me blush in the dark. I looked out towards the skyline, suddenly wishing I was still smoking. I couldn't look at Tristan. "No, it was an interesting concept. That's all." I swallowed some more beer.

AC laughed. "You hear that, Tristan? She thought I looked like I was a good kisser on that video we did." He smiled. "Back in the day, wasn't it? One of the most enjoyable shoots we ever did."

Tristan smirked. "That's because the director decided you should be the one kissing the girl."

AC poked at Tristan's chest. "Oh you poor love. You were usually the love interest—while the rest of us watched."

"There's a reason for that, AC." Tristan winked.

"Is that so? I thought I was doing all right the other night." He punched Tristan in the arm playfully and turned to me. "Watched the video a couple of times, did you Lils?" He didn't wait for my answer. "What do you think? One reason why you thought I was a good kisser."

Tristan was staring at me, his eyes steady and deep. I turned from him to AC, trying for a joking tone. "You know, the usual." I thought about the video, but different images kept appearing in my head. AC at the end of the bed. AC in the limo, teasing Tristan. AC, taking his clothes off, standing there... I tried to think of the video. "You looked like you were enjoying it. And—your face..." I faltered. I wasn't sure how to put it. I suddenly felt the weight of every word, like a key in a cylinder lock. Every variation mattered. I felt like I'd been stripped bare. I looked away.

AC's voice brought me back, gentle but insistent. "Go on, Lily. I'm curious, really. What did you see?"

I closed my eyes. What had I seen when I watched the video? Something that had made me curious about him, made me watch his moves, look at his eyes when he played. Something there that I hadn't noticed before, and now I saw every time I looked. I tried to remember the scene, his arms around the woman, who seemed very willing but very normal. In fact, unlike most videos, she wasn't the half-dressed writhing focus. It was all him. The camera closed in on him, watching him rearrange his body for a better angle, watching him make her more comfortable, bending in, her slight movement, the crease between his eyes, as his mouth moved with hers... How to say all this? I shook my head, and gazed up at him, forcing myself to look into his eyes. That look. That strange sadness and quiet observation under the jokes. Waiting. Knowing how to wait.

"You didn't take, you gave. You looked so intense, your expression. But you were so gentle with her, you never overpowered her, never pushed her. You let her come to you. Your body was there. For the taking." I couldn't help the small nervous laugh that I tried to quash before I said anything else. "Like you were really enjoying yourself. Not a power trip."

AC smiled, a slow sweet smile that reached his eyes like watercolor paint filling a wet sheet. I shifted. I felt like I'd forgotten how to stand. "Power can be fun too, though." He turned towards Tristan and the look that passed between them was warm, grateful, secret.

Tristan smiled. "Glad to hear it."

AC's expression didn't change. "I know." He reached out and placed his elegant guitarist's hand on Tristan's shoulder, and gave him a quick squeeze. But then he turned back to me. "So Lils. Want to take it for a drive?"

My eyes widened. His light eyes had turned dark, full of an emotion I wasn't sure I recognized.

AC now reached out his hand for me. I expected him to

touch my shoulder, but he held my hand, softly, like we were on some teenage first date. It was reassuring. Yet. Oddly frustrating. Like it wasn't enough. "One kiss. See if we can replicate the video. No harm there, right?" He gazed up at Tristan. "Tristan here will watch, make sure we do it right." He paused, and this time the pressure on my hand increased slightly. I looked at him, surprised. He just smiled, that same slow sweet smile, like he had all the time in the world, and everyone else would eventually catch up. "What do you think, Lily?" Here his arm was curling around me and then we were standing side by side. "Time, that thief. But you have all the time you need now."

I felt frozen, even with the energy of his body thrumming through me, warm, tempting. Too tempting, too much to process. I tried to stand still, pretend I didn't feel him, so alive next to me, insinuating his arm further around me, slowly, so slowly. Another band started playing inside, louder than the last one. The bass was rattling the windows. He leaned over.

"Whisper something to me. Something you like. Follow it with a kiss. We can start there." And he tilted his head, ever so slightly. I could see the contours of his ear, the slight slope of his neck, his skin, all clean, all perfectly shaped. It struck me that with my heels, we were almost the same height. It would be so easy, too easy, to press my lips against his ear, slip down to his neck. Would he shudder? Would he like it gentle, or wet? I shut my eyes. My mouth seemed even closer than before to his skin. I could just say something. A conversation. In a club. That's all it was. How close did mouths get to ears when they whispered? It had to be obvious, everyone could see us, couldn't they? I felt completely exposed, yet it seemed as though a curtain had settled down between us and the rest. They could all be staring, I had no idea. I just kept looking at his neck. Did he just bend it slightly further? He was under me now, and he was offering himself up, I could feel it. A game, a tease. Just for a moment. My eyes were fixed on the smooth line of skin behind his ear. A desperate desire to trace the ridges of his ear with my tongue came to mind. It was though one little cord was holding me back. One connection to sanity.

His voice broke through. "It's loud out here. I'm a bit deaf in that ear from the amps. Come on, Lily, talk to me. I think you've got something to say." Like a silver scissor, the words cut through my last hold on restraint. I found myself up against his ear, but there were still a few millimeters separating us, all propriety intact.

I could think of nothing to say except everything I was thinking of. And I couldn't say that. So I repeated his words, brain already disconnected from conscious thought. The tunnel vision of desire. Sensory overload. My voice came out. My eyes seemed to be shut. Too much, too much. "It is loud. Like clubs always are." Like a low whisper, I almost thought I could hear his thoughts. Desire entering into the game, sly as it always was, elusive, suddenly present.

"Yes." His voice was slow, dissolving my thinking. His neck was still curved beautifully, like a dancer. I could see one vein, beating below his ear. I hadn't realized I was still staring. "Your mouth, Lily. Use it."

Resolve broke, and I crossed the wide river of space separating us, broke through that barrier. Then my mouth was on his ear, softly feeling it under my lips, my fingers on his neck, my nose tickling at his soft skin. I heard him sigh, from very far away. Then my tongue finally darted out to taste him, his small sculptured ear, all nerve endings. I traced the curve and bent down to his neck. The way he tilted his head, it was like total surrender. I had the impression I could do anything I liked, anything I wanted, and he would just smile that slow smile and watch. I pressed my mouth against his neck and pressed my breasts against his arm. Just a little, to try and relieve some of the pressure. It was the way he reacted, it had to be. The way he moved.

AC's voice was firm. "Stop thinking, Lily. You've always been curious, haven't you? It's the way you are." His hands came up and touched my face, so lightly. My eyes were closed, all sensation. Somewhere around us, I could feel Tristan, his watchful, edgy energy. It was too late to wonder or worry. His voice broke through again. "Can we kiss now?"

I moved my mouth blindly towards the sound of his voice. If I opened my eyes it would all be over. This way it was a like a dream, a pleasant, painful dream. Then his lips were just touching mine, soft, with barely any pressure, silken, a flowing circle. It made me want more, and there was no more. Just the gentle heat of his mouth on mine, promising, nothing else. Then his tongue slipped in between my lips, the same way his arm had snaked around my body, slow, waiting, exploring, like he had nothing else to do but this, forever. When his tongue pressed more resolutely against mine it was like he had entered me, the soft wet firmness of his tongue. Everywhere. I wanted him everywhere, and it scared me. I was breathing heavily, and my hands went up to his shoulders, about to push him away.

And then he pulled away first, his mouth instantly by my

ear. "Imagine, Lily. The two of us. All my slowness, all his power. You could go from one to the other. Me to him. Him back to me."

I looked at him, unable to say anything, my breath still ragged. He ran his hand, warm like honey, slowly down my neck and over my breasts, stopping finally to rest at my waist. "I could corrupt you. Tristan wouldn't mind, he's already there. Remember all those games we played together, Tristan. Back in the day. I think this one would be better though."

I looked up at Tristan, unsure what I would see in his face. He was looking straight ahead, his eyes black. I knew that look, he was making his mind up about something. But his eyes. I'd never seen them like that, like he was ill, dark circles around his eyes, his long lashes standing out against his skin, barely any color left at all. Then his jaw tightened, and he nodded to the air. Tristan watched us, and then glanced quickly around the room. He took one of each of our hands.

His voice, when it finally came, was a low steady beat. The tone alone decided everything. He spoke very slowly. "You two are probably my best friends in the world. Well, Trevor. Bloody hell, if he were here I'd probably say yes to him too." He pulled us over to an even darker corner of the terrace. Quickly, while gazing around to make sure no one was watching, he pressed both of our hands against his hardness. Even through his jeans, the heat was rolling off him in waves. His eyes fluttered shut and his muted groan tore through my skin like a knife.

"This is a terrible idea. Or a great one. But let me direct." He pressed us to him once more, letting out a long sigh. "Fuck," he lowered his voice another octave, "I could come right now." AC pulled me closer to him and dragged both our hands down Tristan's considerable length, ducking between his legs and pressing up between them. "Fuck, Lil. AC. If this were one of the old clubs…"

AC pressed again. I was shocked how hard he pushed our hands against the darkest places, almost hard enough to bruise. Tristan took a deep breath in. "Remember that one, Tristan? You know which one I mean. That one." It was all he said, but he turned to me, pulling our hands away from Tristan, and placing them on me, on the same spot they had been on Tristan, but with such lightness I almost wanted to feel what the other touch was like. His fingers explored briefly and I rocked against him, almost involuntarily. I let out a long sigh I didn't know I'd been holding and it came out as a sob, almost.

My hand flew to his cock and I traced it, finding the wetness starting to come through the jeans at the top, the softness at the bottom, gradually tightening under my fingers. I had to touch him, see if this was real.

AC hissed. "Slowly, love. So you're more like our friend Tristan here. Hot. Impatient. Once we reach you."

I squeezed him again and leaned over and he murmured very low in my ear. "Careful, darling. Do that again, and I'll come. I want you wetter, much wetter before that happens." And then his mouth was on mine and his tongue pushed against me, then our bodies were finally close, touching, his hands on my hips. I was weak, my heart beating insanely fast, a fine sheen of sweat forming between my breasts. Then he pushed me away. "Tristan, kiss her. She's worried." And I saw his wink in my haze of lust.

Tristan's strong arms wrapped around me and like a heroine in an old movie, I was picked up, my toes just balanced on the ground, my shoulders back against his arm as he held me to him. His mouth was so different, insisting, demanding. He took me and his long body curved over mine, as AC stood and watched, approving, his smile saying everything words didn't need to speak. Then his whisper broke through. "We're finally getting an audience. As much as I'd like to oblige, I think we better go. Now."

Tristan held me close to him, and AC took the other side, and with the practiced expertise of many quick get-aways, they found the back door to the street, while Tristan called the driver to come get us. We stood there, dazed, sep-arated, breathing in the cool 3 a.m. air, not saying a word. It had been raining earlier, and the streets were still wet, slick with oil from delivery trucks. The orange light of the halogen streetlamps cast a strange glow on the tan bricks and netted windows of the warehouses and merged the green and black of the garbage skips into almost the same color. When the car came, Tristan pulled open the door, and slid quickly to the far side, pulling me with him, as AC maneuvered himself in, one hand on the seat and one on my hip. He yanked the door shut, and said "Go, watch for paparazzi, there's going to be some."

Tristan lay back against the seat, his long legs stretched out in front of him. He reached over and took AC's hand and placed it in my lap, so that all our hands became intertwined. "Now we've done it," was all he said, and he threw his head back, and closed his eyes. AC took his other hand and traced the veins in Tristan's neck. "Careful, AC."

"Fuck careful." And I found myself pressed back against Tristan, as AC turned my face to his. "Kiss me, Lily. Like you want." He laughed, quietly. "Tristan will watch, make sure we're doing it right. Like you want, Tristan." His hands slid to my hips. "Tristan. Tris." His voice dropped to a low murmur. "Tell me what to do. Tell me."

Tristan's eyes were shining in the dark, piercing. "Kiss her, AC. Kiss her the same way you're going to fuck her later."

chapter twenty-eight

New York to London

A week later, the house seemed strangely quiet. We'd just seen AC off in the taxi that was to take him to the airport for his flight back to L.A. His face as he waved at us, as the cab pulled away, revealed his familiar mix of humor and understanding, his eyes very green in the early morning light. But some of the sadness that had always clung to him, even when he smiled, was gone. He seemed a little lighter, a little further away from some edge of disaster. We stood and watched until the cab was out of sight, then walked for a couple of hours, stopping for coffee and special handmade donuts from the place on the Lower East Side, the Doughnut Plant. Crème Brulée donuts. Tristan said we needed it—sugar to make up for lack of sleep. A treat to make it all a little easier. Then we headed home, talking about the future. The plan AC had was to really move out of L.A. and ship his stuff to New York, to Tristan's storage facility. Then he would head over to London, where we'd all be together again. Trevor wanted everyone over there to rehearse and organize. "I'm done with America—for now. You can all come to me," Trevor had pronounced. We thought we would go over in another week or so.

Tristan picked up his mail, and flipped through it as we went up in the elevator. "Here, this is for you." And he handed me a little manila envelope with UK stamps. I didn't open it until we were sitting in the kitchen, and Tristan was getting some water out of the fridge. "So another official invite from Sarah?" Tristan held out his hand and I passed it over for inspection. "Oh good, she's invited me by name—not just a plus one." He read the note that came with it. Apparently she had wanted to remind us, firmly but politely. So she had resent the invitation, along with a request on her notepaper that we stay in the house for a couple of days before the wedding. "Look, she says she sent one to Trevor as well." Tristan stopped reading. "I was a little worried when he was flirting with her, to be honest. He seemed really smitten there for a minute. But Trevor has hidden depths. All seems to be fine."

I didn't mention that I'd wondered that as well. "Yes, he does."

"He's very likeable, really, once he lets you in. He's careful. The type to learn too well from his own mistakes. And very good at reminding others never to repeat them." Tristan laughed.

"He is good at that."

Tristan glanced at me. "Yes." He finished writing up the notes he was working on. "We are going, right?"

"I suppose. Yes." I held out my hand for the invitation, and re-read it. The paper was very heavy, and the card was beautifully embossed. "It's good timing actually."

"It is. We deserve a little holiday. And I've been thinking about what to do." Tristan flexed his hands and stretched out his long arms towards me. I came over and sat in his lap, making him groan, and he started to tickle me.

"Whatever you want to do," I said, draping my arms around his neck and softly breathing in the sweet smell of his skin. I sighed happily against him.

"I'm not certain. I think…well, that is—it's easy for me to say." Tristan stopped, and kissed my nose.

"What's easy for you to say?" He seemed very serious underneath the playful exterior. It was obvious he had something on his mind.

"The tour. You. I want you settled. Unless you're coming for the whole thing."

I'd been thinking about it too, thinking of the time on the road. Everything that had happened. The moments that had been harder than I ever could have imagined.

Tristan nodded, watching my face. "Exactly."

"I didn't dislike it. So not exactly. It was definitely interesting." I thought back to the 4 a.m. wake ups I had, sitting in peaceable silence with the bus driver, watching the long stretches of highway disappear under the wheels. Threatening James over the DVDs. AC standing at the end of the bed in the hotel room. "A lot happened."

Tristan smirked. "Very true. But it was hard work."

I tried to laugh. "But I like minibars. Limousines too, generally, depending on the ride."

"At any rate, rides aside," Tristan winked at me, "The tour. Asia—Japan mostly. Then briefly in South America. And on to Europe. You don't have to come. Or you could come for the parts you wanted. But I was thinking it might be nice if you were based somewhere." Tristan stopped.

I looked at him. "Based...where? What about New York?"

Tristan had an awkward grin that he was trying hard to hide. "Change is good? Seriously, now. What would you say to London? I know you used to live there. Have you ever thought of going back?"

"A lot happened there. But a lot's happened since. I don't know. Yes? But what about everything here?"

"You're going to be angry, but I spoke to Dave." He still looked pleased though.

"You spoke to Dave?" I couldn't believe what I was hearing. I could only manage to repeat him, parrot-like.

Tristan bowed his head. "I understand. I overstepped. But I don't feel like lying about it, and I didn't want to make any plans until I knew what it would mean—for you. For me, it doesn't matter. I can be anywhere. I'll be on tour, in a hotel. But you. I'm not going to take your life away from you."

I started to say something, but Tristan interrupted me.

"No, don't say anything. Not yet. I know you. I know you don't trust things. I don't want you to feel like you owe me something, or that you can't make a move unless I approve it." He kissed the top of my head. "I'm sorry if you're angry, but I needed to know what the situation was."

I kissed a finger and put it to his lips. "I'm not angry."

Tristan looked surprised, then he put on a face of mock shock. "You're not? Even though I compromised your...something. Sovereignty over yourself. Whatever that means."

I smiled. "I haven't agreed to anything yet, so not necessarily. But that's not why you did it. You have to know things, that's just you. I don't think it was controlling."

He laughed. "Maybe a little?"

I pretended to weigh it up. "Maybe a little. At least you're sharing it with me. You're not keeping it a big secret. But what did Dave say?"

Tristan looked serious again. "He said as long as you could come back for consults, he already considered you more of a free agent now. Not a jobber."

"Really? So I can go?" Somehow, in the back of my mind, I figured I'd be staying in NYC, writing up articles, while Tristan circled the globe. Maybe flying out to see him. Waiting.

Tristan picked me up and stood up with me, wrapping his arms around me. He dipped his head very close to mine, his lips warm and soft against my ear. "I love you, you know."

The words came out of nowhere. "You're not leaving me behind then."

Tristan shook his head. "No. No." He kissed my head. "Oddly enough, I seem to like you. Better still. I want you around, close by."

"So, London? Globetrotting? What else?"

Tristan looked sheepish, if such a look was even possible on a man six foot two wearing skin tight black jeans and a ripped white t-shirt. "You really do know me too well. Now you are going to hate me. I confess. It's bad."

"What the fuck have you done then?" I was smiling. This had to be good.

"Sarah, your friend? She of buxom figure and impending nuptials?"

"Oh god, what. Please don't tell me you've rented a house near them—I will kill you. Having her drop around every morning for tea would probably sap whatever strength I have left."

Tristan looked startled. "It's not near them. But she did find us a house. Well. With Trevor. He suggested it." Tristan looked pleased. "Remember what he said about wanting me back on the other side of the pond."

"Yes. But I could have done that." I shook away the image of Tristan chatting on the phone to Sarah.

"Yes, you could have. But she's there. And she happened to have a friend with a house. Although apparently she and Trevor had a grand time driving around looking at houses."

I interrupted him. "Where is this house, and can you afford it?"

Tristan started to laugh then, until I had to join in. "Yes, love, I can, and it's outside of London, and it has a garden, and a sweet little kitchen, and the little living room has a fireplace."

"Really?"

"Really."

"But…"

Tristan stopped me. "But you told me yourself every flat you ever found had building works and an annoying room-mate. Maybe this will break the curse. Though I am certainly annoying. I can be very demanding." Then Tristan pulled me to him and nipped at my neck, a few times for good measure.

"That's true. To be fair, I was always desperate when I was looking. Though a few times the curse caught me on the hop."

"Doesn't matter. Listen. I have some photos. It looks

cute. Sarah said she'd go over there and film a tour for you. Apparently it belongs to a friend of a friend, and she is thinking of selling. Which is wonderful, because I hate estate agents. I've been meaning to invest. Honestly, I didn't think the solo album would do as well as it has. Might as well do something smart with it."

I was speechless. "You'd do this for me? Really?"

"It's not just for you. It's for us. We seem to be, no scratch that. We are an us." He smiled, a dangerous half-smile. "And larger. More than I'd ever hoped."

"But…"

"Lily. Listen. Now you're with me." Tristan pulled out his phone. "Look. One picture. You hate it, it's history. History. But have a look. You decide. I'm saying nothing,"

I stood up to go over to him, and then sat back down, suddenly filled with panic.

Tristan pulled his chair over to mine. "Come on, look at it."

My eyes were tightly closed. Suppose it was good. Tristan's voice interrupted my thoughts.

"Suppose it is?"

"That's just strange. You responding to my thoughts like that."

"Usually you like it." He held up the screen. "Look. There's a trellis and wisteria and a little garden with peonies. See the kitchen? It's small. Perfect."

I peeked through my hands.

"It's got a blue Aga stove. You like those."

"How the hell do you know?"

Tristan snorted. "Please. Stop reminding me how many idiots with memory issues used to inhabit your life. The doors lead to the garden. There's a bench and some neglected rose bushes. If you need a barbeque, I'm sure there's room. In case you miss America."

I smacked his arm. "Shut up."

Tristan laughed. "Good, your eyes are open. You needed to see where you were punching. Excellent. Now look. There's a little living room. Room for a decent sofa. Wood floors. Oh, is that a fireplace?"

I punched him again. "Seriously, you're in the wrong business."

Tristan smiled. "That means I'm getting to you. I'll take it under advisement. But I'd have to stop the leather. Or it could be part of the full service." He winked.

"Not going to happen."

He swung a long arm around my shoulders and kissed me on the cheek with a loud smack. "Ah, Lily. You know me so well."

I leaned my head against his shoulder and breathed in the scent of him. Clean t-shirt laundry smell, the faint lingering of the German designer cologne he liked at the minute, leather from the jacket, something else that was him alone, hair, sweat, passion. I looked up at him, and his eyes bore into mine. There was this great silence for a moment, then he pulled back slightly and said, "Now look at the upstairs."

I laughed. "You know how to get what you want."

A smile spread across his face. "Usually. Now look. Sash windows. Tree hitting panes in rainstorms. There's some work that needs to be done, but it's a house. Ongoing project. It's not a manor house. Besides, it's a rental—for now. So, what do you think?" He looked excited. There was a trace of the boy in his face, the lingering bit of energy that clings to every man.

I looked at the screen, and scrolled through it with a fingertip. Passing through like this, it seemed almost doable. Changing the picture when it seemed like enough.

Tristan took the screen from me. "Lily. Listen to me. It's very easy to forget that the future doesn't have to be the past."

I nodded, lips tight. There was nothing to say.

He put the phone in his pocket. "If we feel like it, we can rent a car and have a look. When we're there. But that's next week." He stood up. "Come on, let's go outside. Fresh air. Glass of wine? Maybe we can evict someone from their table again." The expression on his face was like a kid inviting another to go get into trouble.

"Heartless, you are." But I reached for my jacket.

"It's our little secret."

* * *

We hadn't mentioned the house again. Not even while packing, not even on the plane to London. But I knew it would come up again. We had left a few days early. Tristan couldn't seem to stay still. And while it had something to do with that fact that Trevor had already assembled the band in London for more rehearsals, there was something restless in his eyes. Something that had been there since the tour and that hadn't completely disappeared. Once AC had left, we had taken to walking every night from 9 to midnight. Hidden under a variety of hats, Tristan had managed to avoid being recognized—

too often. Even then the topic of the house didn't come up. And when Trevor called and said they should meet up, when could that happen, you're coming over for this wedding anyway, we should have a chat with Adrian, do you want to look at rehearsal space or leave it to me, that was it. Tristan was booking our reservations for the next morning.

So here we were staying in a small hotel, avoiding the spotlight for a couple of days before we went on to Sarah's. London still smelled the same, I thought. We had been walking through Primrose Hill, looking over the city sprawled out over the river valley. Between us and Crystal Palace, the distances seemed to lengthen and shrink as the light changed with the clouds moving by in the breeze. That familiar golden light through the patches of dark cloud. It was an ancient view, and I thought Tristan was more clever than he knew, bringing me here early. To think about everything.

The idea of the house remained in the background. And sitting in the small living area of the hotel room, a pot of tea brought up by room service, cricket on the TV, I could feel it coming. And when Tristan turned down the volume on the commentators, I knew that moment was here.

He sat down at the table, and poured out more tea for both of us. "Lily."

"Tristan."

"I haven't brought this up again, but we…" He set his cup down. "Hell, Lily. We need to talk about this. It's not that bad is it, the idea of living with me? Having a house? It's been good, I thought."

I shook my head. "That's not it. You know that's not it. I'm sorry. Yes. Maybe it's the wedding. No. I don't know."

Tristan looked at me, lips in a thin line. "You're a terrible liar. But maybe you really don't know."

I sighed. "Tristan. I'm doing my best. Show me the house."

He smiled. He couldn't help himself. And it struck me, that maybe this was something he really wanted. Something I should say yes to regardless of anything else. I focused, and he had his phone out, going through the pictures.

Tristan swiped his finger across the screen. "And here—there's an extra bedroom. For guests."

I smiled at him. "For Trevor. And AC. Except he won't need it."

Tristan frowned. "Don't be so sure, Lily. What we do, the three of us—that's a choice. Nothing says anything needs to happen just because it did. We're friends, lovers, not cell mates."

I nodded. I didn't know what to say.

Tristan put his arm around me. "It's a spark. It's creative energy. It needs space."

I buried my head in his chest. "But…" I wasn't sure how to go on. I could feel Tristan smiling into my hair.

"But what? Don't hide what you're thinking. Not now. Please." Tristan sighed. "Lily."

"But, then why are we together? Why the little house? Why every day for us? What about AC?"

Tristan held me tighter. "Because. Because we work to-gether. Remember? 'Better together than apart?'"

I nodded. "But you care for AC."

Tristan shrugged. "Yes. I do. So do you. And it's not doing him a disservice to let him do what he wants. When he wants to be here, with us…" He looked at his hands. "We want what we want. It's a question of respect. And," he paused to scroll to a picture of the kitchen, "look. Love is care. Not control." He winked at me. "Sometimes."

"As long as you're not doing," I poked at the stove on the screen, "all this because you think you should, or because it's easier." I looked up at him. "I couldn't bear that."

"Easier? You?" Tristan spluttered. "Hardly. Lily. Listen. Love isn't just one story. This is ours. Let it be. Stop asking why it's different."

"Ok. Yes. But. Everything we've been taught to think…"

He interrupted me. "Is nothing compared to what's possible." He bent down and kissed me. "Since when did you care what you've been told?" He rolled his eyes. "Easy. You. What an idea."

He kissed me again. And then pulled away, and looked at me. He carefully put together a thick strand of my hair, and started twisting it around his finger. He gave a little smile, then pulled on it, hard, so that I lost my balance and fell against his chest. He tugged again, and then his mouth was on mine. Not for the first time, I wondered where the hell Tristan had learned to kiss. Maybe it was just because he so obviously liked doing it. Kissing for him was something to be appreciated on its own, not a stop on the way. He always took his time. I had forgotten to wonder where his skills had been acquired when he broke away, and began pulling me across the room by the lock of hair as he backed towards the door. "We don't have anywhere to go right now, do we? We're seeing the house in a few hours, I've got a driver, it should take just over an hour to get there, if we're lucky…"

I interrupted him, astonished. "We are? You must have been very certain I'd agree."

He tugged on my hair again, and gave me that crooked smile. "You can always say no." He smiled at me. "Want to say no?"

I couldn't resist him. That impish, slightly dangerous smile. "No," I answered, and he laughed.

"Come on then. I hate to be rushed." And Tristan dropped the lock of hair and picked up my hand, bringing it to his lips. Then holding my hand, he made me follow him into the bedroom.

* * *

Afterwards, lying there on the white hotel sheets, surrounded by pillows, and very naked, everything felt right. Tristan let out a long sigh.

"Better? Less tense?" He laughed. "No, seriously. Are you all right? This is good, isn't it?" He shifted so he could wrap his arm around me. "Be even better in our own place. No more front desks."

I laughed. "They're not all so bad."

"You say that now. Tell me how you feel in five years."

"Tristan?"

"Hmm?"

"You don't really believe all that crap you were talking before, do you?"

Tristan burst out laughing. "Lily. You're too smart for me."

"Hardly. Do you?"

He pulled me close to him. "Some of it. Depends on the

day. But really, I don't like being told what to do. Simple. People strangle themselves with their own made-up rules. I'd rather not do that to myself. Or anyone else. You. AC."

I took a deep breath. "So. You're really here because you want to be?"

Tristan rolled on his back and pulled me on top of him. His face was lit up. "At last! She gets it. Better late than never, though." He smacked my backside. "Come on, my love. We've got a home to inspect."

chapter twenty-nine

London

We had finally checked out of the hotel, and decided to get a cab to go up to Sarah's house. Tristan thought there was a certain risk in booking a car and driver to take us up there, especially after he'd noticed the driver who had taken us out to see the house taking a cell phone picture of us. "Not that I mind," he'd said, "but ask first. Especially if I'm doing something on my own time." So we found ourselves in the roomy back seat of a black cab, heading through London, our suitcases with us to save time getting in. My dress was already there. Tristan had brought along the suit the designer had given him for the awards show. And holding hands, flung together slightly at turns and traffic lights, we watched the streets go by.

The visit to the house was been more fun than either of us had expected, except for the snap-happy driver. I wanted to talk about it on the way back, but Tristan had put a finger to my lips, nodding up at the driver. Afterwards, at dinner, he had said something that made me realize again how important this was to him. "I'll be fucked if we get this place, and then a little army of photographers starts camping out by the road. Fans I can just about handle, as long as they don't come to the door wanting a cup of tea. But I'd like this to be under wraps." He laughed, a little bitterly. "At least for a while." He looked thoughtful. "It was a little far away though, wasn't it? I wonder if we could find the same sort of thing in London. Almost easier to disappear in a city."

The cab stopped in front of the house, and there was Nick at the door, waving, then running over to help us with our bags, like he'd just remembered we would have suitcases. Then he greeted us warmly, a kiss for me, and a solid handshake for Tristan, and ushered us into the cozy house. I suddenly felt I was looking at everything with new eyes, comparing, weighing the possibilities. The rooms were small but the overall effect was welcoming. The sound of the door shutting seemed protective, instead of claustrophobic. After we dropped our bags in the living room, Nick ushered us into the kitchen, where he had a bottle of wine and a selection of antipasti laid out on the wooden table. The olives were huge and green. Everything seemed brilliantly colored and fresh. We all started speaking at once, and Tristan laughed.

Nick grinned. "I guess I'm lonely. Sarah's been at her mum's for three days now. Thought I'd demonstrate my domestic talents. So I went to the Italian deli." He suddenly looked shocked. "Oh my god. Aren't you macrobiotic or vegan or something? I can get something else." He started to get up.

Tristan waved an arm. "Not this week. Even if I were, this looks fantastic. I'd never turn down a meal like this. Thank you."

Nick looked really pleased, like he had done something particularly good. Then he seemed a little nervous, like he'd just remembered everything. Having a famous person in the house was not a normal everyday thing. For him.

"Hey, Nick, let's open the wine. Tell us about all the preparations. I think you look remarkably calm," I said, pulling out a chair. Tristan followed me, and we sat down, while Nick fished around for a corkscrew.

He laughed. "It's a wonder what wine will do. Explains the Greeks and Romans, without a doubt."

"Not Californians, though," Tristan said slowly.

Nick laughed, and pulled open the cork with a flourish. "In all fairness though, it's been a boon to this bridegroom. Settles the nerves beautifully." And he did seem to relax, just a little, which made Tristan less on edge as well. I watched them talk, helping themselves to food, wondering how I had let such different people into my life, wondering what I had that they had in common. Nick poured me some more wine. "So quiet, Lily. Not like you. Here, eat something."

And we sat there, doors to the garden open, the sound of the builders a few gardens down breaking the quiet. Nick was describing all the hurdles, the caterers, the vicar breaking his ankle, Sarah's mother thinking it was a bad omen and nearly insisting they change the church. But he seemed to take it all in stride. Even though the wedding was tomorrow, and Sarah was out staying with her mother in the country, near Oxford, where the wedding was to take place. They had found an old stone parish church, about 10 miles from where Sarah's mother lived, in a small village. With the church came a charming vicar who was willing to let them add to their wedding vows at the last minute, as they kept making little changes to what they wanted to say.

The second bottle open, Nick clapped his hand on Tristan's shoulder. "You should try it. This nuptial bliss." His face changed as he realized what he had said. "You know what I mean. You understand. We're very happy." He paused and looked around. "Well, except of course for our house being turned upside down and becoming a repository for stray bits of tulle and lace. I can't say I understand all of it, not particularly. But it seems to make the ladies happy, so who am I to argue. And I get on quite well with her mother. Her father likes me as well, thinks I'm solid. That's important…" He trailed off. "I'm getting off topic here. Anyway, yes, it's a good thing. You should take it up." Tristan said nothing, but nodded calmly, and carried on drinking his wine.

We all sat there in silence, listening to the planes fly overhead, and the radio on at the house next door. I excused myself to go up to the loo, and left them there. Tristan had mentioned the cricket, and Nick was describing the last time he'd been to Lord's to see the cricket and how different it was from when he was a boy. Tristan was nodding and looking calm, if a little out of place, bracelets and long hair, and a t-shirt, his leather jacket hanging over the back of the chair, while Nick was trim as usual in his button down shirt and cargo shorts, which all the men of London seemed to have affected during this very warm summer. Still, it suited him. He looked as though he could be at an expensive office picnic. Tristan, as usual, looked like he had just rolled out of bed, or climbed out of a dungeon of a studio at 5 a.m. I walked through the house. It was true—Sarah had even taken to tying ribbons and tulle around the bannister. It did have the air of a slightly mad tea party or dress-up party gone wild. I splashed water on my face in the small bathroom and glanced at myself in the mirror. I looked satisfied. There was no reason to want more. I already have more than I ever anticipated, I thought. Or dreamed of. I spent a moment trying to sift through the tangle of my feelings. Was I a bit jealous? Maybe. But it felt childish. Petty. Sarah was happy and that's what counted. And so was I. I didn't have much faith in man-made institutions anyway. Life had brought us together. That was more than enough. I pulled on the cord to turn off the fan, and shut the unpainted old pine door behind me.

When I came back downstairs, Nick and Tristan had both left their chairs and were walking around the edges of the small lawn in the garden, seemingly examining the roses while Nick pruned them indifferently with a small set of clippers, but actually deep in conversation. I turned and made my way back into the kitchen. It looked like one of those moments, when men finally ask each other questions. Nick was definitely nervous. I couldn't blame him. As lovely and mad as Sarah was, it was a big step after all. And I was glad to see that Nick and Tristan seemed to get on, as improbable as it was. It would have been completely impossible for me to believe it only several months ago, and here we all were.

I turned on the kettle to boil water for tea, and stood looking at the cupboards. Compulsively, I opened them, one by one. The neat arrangement of cups in one, glasses and wine glasses in another, dishes in the next was at once reassuring and unnerving. I'd never really put down roots, whatever that meant. I didn't put up pictures. Hell, I didn't even own a wine glass. I always thought I'd be moving on. Unpacking always felt dangerous. You couldn't run if your stuff was scattered around. But ironically enough, most of my belongings were scattered around. Things I'd given away, stuck in someone's garage, sold for peanuts—I could see them all like a parade marching past—each thing representing a different time in my life. But that's all they were, I thought, things. Except I missed them, sometimes. And looking out at Tristan and Nick, who was now evidently showing him how to prune roses, I wondered what it was I did want.

I shut each cabinet carefully, feeling a little like I was in a museum, and went to throw a tea bag in my mug and pour out the water and some milk. I took a deep breath, and blinked a few times. This was as stable as it got. And I loved him, I loved Tristan more than I thought it was possible to care about anyone. He was loyal, he worked hard, he was crazy, he wanted more from people than most of them were capable of giving. I sat down with a thud at the wooden table. That was it. There was one of the traits, one of the many, that we had in common. Wanting more than most people were willing to sign up for. I stirred my tea, and stared off into space. Everything suddenly felt a little too real, a little too close to the bone. It all was a weird dream, and then it would end, and here we were, whirling in space, thinking all our little problems really mattered. I put my elbows on the table and closed my eyes, leaning my head on my hands. Love. What we needed, what kept us going, and so scary, so uncertain, so dangerous.

I heard footsteps coming in, and I quickly wiped my eyes and brushed back my hair with my hands and put on the best imitation of a smile I could muster. When Tristan's head appeared from the other side of the red partition wall dividing the hall from the kitchen, I did smile. He was so lovely. Not just beautiful and talented, but someone who did what he believed in, or tried. He had suffered, but most people didn't know that and he didn't tell them. But I knew. He came over to me and tugged at my hand to pull me off the chair. I walked the two steps into his arms and he kissed the top of my head as he held me. "Lily, love, what's wrong? You disappeared."

I tried to give a half laugh. "I needed tea. Just a moment by myself."

He pushed me back slightly, so he could examine my face. "That's not all of it. Is it the wedding? Nick?" He frowned.

I shook my head quickly. "No, it's not Nick. Or the wedding. Not really. Just me."

Tristan waited, still and patient.

"It's ok." I stepped out of his arms. Then I pointed to the cabinets. "Look." I opened one, then another. "She...they... have wine glasses." I opened another one. "Look. Plates, all neatly stacked." I waved my arm to indicate the room. "Cookbooks. Prints. Paint colors chosen. Do you know how long I've lived with bare white walls?"

Tristan watched me, carefully. I suddenly felt like I'd made a fool of myself, harping on about things that didn't matter, not really. There were people living in trees. They were happy. I didn't need colored walls. Or matching china. I cleared my throat. "It's ok, forget it. Having a moment."

Tristan's face changed. "You don't need to front it out, Lily. That's not what I'm here for." He opened a cabinet and peeked in. I smiled watching him, his long fingered hands holding the pine door carefully, as though it might break. "It is incredibly neat. Some people are just like that." He shut the door. "Where are your things, Lily? Do you have any? Things from childhood?" His eyes were very blue it seemed, through the hazel and grey. I felt a bit like I was being x-rayed. I closed my eyes.

"Some. Not much. Some things in storage at an old friend of my mother's house. I gave a lot away. When I moved. Some stuff got lost in transit. That sort of thing."

"And childhood possessions?" Tristan took my hands in his.

"Gone, really." I leaned on him. He smelled green, like cut stems and earthy heat. "I don't know what happened to everything. Well, that's not true. The furniture was auctioned off." I broke off. "I guess…other things just went with it."

Tristan had his arms around me, his head leaning against mine. "You're a good friend, you know. To come here."

He was warm. I moved closer. "I am? But it's her wedding. That's normal. I am her friend."

Tristan was stroking my hair. "It's salt in an old wound."

I shook my head, furiously, but I didn't say anything.

He held me tighter. "We can make this better. Lily." And he lifted my head away from his shoulder and rubbed a thumb along my cheekbones, before licking off the tears from his finger. Then he leant down, placing his mouth on mine, so perfectly, his lips soft. I felt another tear roll down and he caught it on his tongue. I choked out a little laugh. He was so silly, doing this. I'd be fine.

I hugged him tighter, and whispered against his mouth. "I'm just emotional. Isn't that right? Weddings. All that."

Tristan didn't say anything, but he kissed me again, his mouth soft, his body solid against mine. Then he pulled away, and fixed his eyes on mine. "I will make this better."

I had to smile back at him. His face was so serious. The sound of Nick coming up the steps from the garden broke through my thoughts. Standing almost on tiptoe, I kissed him quickly on the mouth. "You already do."

* * *

The wedding day dawned fresh and bright. It looked as though we were going to avoid the rain, and Sarah would have her wedding pictures outdoors after all. We had come downstairs early, to get some breakfast before all the craziness began. But we hadn't been sitting there long before the doorbell rang. Nick got up from the table to answer it, and came back in the room with a tallish blond man with a vaguely athletic air. It was one of his friends from work who had offered to come over and help him get ready. His large gold band seemed to be part of his somewhat fleshy hand, set there in the skin. He came in the room and caught sight of Tristan, who was sitting at the kitchen table with a cup of tea, reading the papers. He blinked. "I'm sure, aren't you..." rose and died on his lips, as Nick made the introductions.

Tristan, as ever, was unflappable. "Andrew. Nice to meet you. Any friend of Nick's is a friend of mine," he laughed. "Nick and Sarah are nice enough to let us stay here for the big event."

I shook his hand too, and Andrew leaned down for a quick peck on the cheek, friendly. "Happy to meet you." I didn't realize I was examining him until Andrew looked quizzically at me. "Or again. You look so familiar. Did we meet on that dreadful Thames boat cruise for Nick's work do? The one where they ran out of drink, and there was a staged mutiny to make them end it early?"

Andrew laughed. "Oh god, that nightmare. What a laugh that was. We threatened the captain with everything we could think of, including all jumping off into the Thames at once. On only one side of the boat." He let out a loud laugh and peered at me again. "Ah right, Lily. That Lily. Of course."

I could feel Tristan tensing up, even at a distance. I looked over to him, but he was already getting up. "That Lily. Yes, absolutely. The one and only. Well, nice to meet you. We've got to go get ready ourselves." I said some pleasantries to Andrew about the weather, then went over to Tristan. He was now standing by the sink, with his tea mug in his hand, asking Nick if he needed any help. Nick glanced up at me, then away, then back to Tristan. "No, no, you two go on. The cars will be here in two hours. That's enough time, isn't it?" He gave a wave to Andrew who was unzipping his suit bag. He turned to me and gave me a big hug. "Lily, I'm terrified. She loves me, right?"

I hugged him back. He really was nervous if he was actually touching people. It struck me that it was the first time we'd really made contact since the breakup, so many years ago. I patted him on the back. "You're finally making an honest woman of her. She'll only love you more. Once you get through this and don't tread on her dress, that is." He looked stricken. "It's just nerves. You'll both be fine. It's a big day." He looked pale. "You're doing the best thing. You're the right kind of nervous." I took Tristan's hand. "Now we've got to get ready. Thank god Sarah picked a simple dress, otherwise I'd make you late." Now Nick looked somewhat sick to his stomach. "Kidding! You'll be fine. It's all good. If you need us, we will be upstairs."

Nick managed to recover enough to wink at me. "I wouldn't want to catch you...I mean disturb you."

"Nick! On your wedding day? Aren't there laws against that kind of thing?"

And just like that, Nick was back to his old self, all hint of emotion banished. "All the more likely you'll be breaking them, my darling Lily. Now shoo. Andrew here is an old hand at this and has promised me between his sartorial skills and his flask, he'll get me through this."

Behind me, Andrew laughed. "Got it right here. Never too early. Dutch courage, isn't that right?"

I gave Nick a kiss on the cheek. "She's a lucky woman. Good luck today, Nick. I mean it. I'm glad the two of you found each other...for real."

"Thanks Lily." He shook hands with Tristan, who was a looming presence at my side. "Tristan. Thanks for being here."

"Good luck mate." He put his arm around me, and we headed to the narrow staircase leading to the upstairs.

I stopped at the bathroom again. "I'm just going to splash water on my face. I'll be there in a minute."

"I'll come get you if you take too long." Tristan grinned. "It's showtime."

A few minutes later, I was going up the stairs to the very top of the house. "I'm washed and pressed, ready to get dressed," I sang out as I opened the door to the little attic room that Tristan and I were in. Tristan was resting on the bed, completely naked except for a pair of black briefs that just grazed the tops of his hip bones. The rest left little to the imagination. It wasn't only the inky black color of the soft fabric clinging to every turn, each shape, every line, until you weren't sure if it all was responding under your gaze, or if it was pulsing ever so slightly with each breath he took, every vein in his body swelling and rising on every heartbeat, it was the way he inhabited his body, so casually, as if he were unaware of the effect he could have. I pulled my gaze away and followed the graceful sweep of his long legs, crossed at the ankle. His wrists were crossed just above his head, and his eyes were closed. It looked as though he were declaring himself, and his wants, simply waiting for someone to make what he wished for come true. Tristan breathed in deeply, and the smooth expanse of his torso rose and fell, the muscles stretching over his ribs, all flexing under his silken and pale skin.

I didn't want to break the moment. I wanted to stand there and look at him, a living portrait, one that told me all I wanted to know about what I needed and where my boundaries were on this earth. I watched his stomach rise and fall, his breathing steady. I needed to disturb him though if we were to be on time. I was tempted to blow the whole thing off. We would just stay here all morning, watch the sun move across the wall if we weren't watching each other, until evening came. We couldn't.

"Tristan," I whispered. "We should get dressed now." I watched as a slight smile spread across his perfect mouth, making me wonder if he had been asleep at all, or if he had known the whole time that I was there watching him. My bet was on his constant watchfulness. His eyes slowly opened, and he looked at me.

"No."

I stared back at him. Were we going to stay here, miss the wedding? I wondered for a moment what I would do if he wanted to. Would I miss my friend's wedding? "No?" I asked.

"I don't want to see you dressed. Yet. Or you me. It should be a surprise. An unveiling. Something special." Tristan's voice was low and deep, halfway between a command and plea.

"All right," I said hesitantly, "but I thought that was just for the bride and groom."

He laughed. "And why not us?" He rose from the bed slowly, and finally came and stood next to me. I wondered if I would ever stop being slightly breathless from finding him at my side, tall and solid, an undeniable presence. I watched him adjust his underwear slightly, then he playfully cupped himself in front and gave himself a slight squeeze. "Like what you see?" He winked at me. "Don't worry. I'll bring my suit and all that to the living room." He bent down and his lips touched mine, gentle but the weight of the restraint behind it was apparent. I shut my eyes. "Ah, no. Good friends go to each other's weddings." He winked again. "See you down there in a bit."

Tristan shut the door carefully behind him, and I sat down on the bed heavily. It was still warm from his body, and I wished that he were back here, his arms around me, telling me it would all be fine. It was all going to be fine. The dress was hanging in its bag, on a hook on the wall, my shoes under it. We were going to go to Sarah's wedding, it would be nice, and no matter what, in several hours, it would all be over anyway. The supposedly biggest day of her life, and for us, a nice party and a way of sharing her happiness, or at least being part of the experience. I took off my t-shirt and yoga pants, and began the slow transformation from normal me to special party me. Special wedding me. Tristan hadn't wanted us to see each other until we were ready. Everything about the day felt weighty and symbolic, from his crossed wrists and exposed flesh, to the dress, to just being here. I put on my bra and panties, La Perla, a gift from Tristan that he had sworn faithfully not to rip, cream champagne lace, delicate and silken against my skin. I walked over to the window for a last look at the garden before I put on the dress. I knew I'd feel anxious the minute I had it on. The garden was deserted now, the green leaves still bright in the lengthening late summer sunlight, gentler now, though still carrying the remnants of bright blue sky clarity.

I unzipped the bag carefully and extracted the dress. It was beautiful—a simple cream-colored dress in a floating crinkle chiffon. The hem was uneven, shorter in front then dropping delicately to nearly floor length at the back. The waist was lightly cinched. It looked like something a Greek goddess might wear. I hoped I could pull it off. It had looked nice in the fitting room, and I was very grateful that Sarah hadn't insisted on matching satin bridesmaids' dresses. I lifted it over my head and it slunk down my body like water, the silk lining sliding over my skin, as the heavier chiffon followed. It still smelled of store, and tissue paper and boxes, and reminded me of the happier moments of my childhood, when new clothes appeared, and I could barely dare to wear them, they were so perfect and beautiful. It fell to the ground, weighted slightly to give the dress drift and body. I looked at myself in the mirror. It was beautiful. I hoped he thought so. I shut my eyes. I really wanted him to.

* * *

Tristan disappeared into the kitchen when I came downstairs. He had decided to ride to the church with Nick and Andrew. "Your car is here, Lily. You'll go first." Nick said, pretending to cover his eyes, while Andrew snickered at us.

Then Nick was smiling. "You look beautiful, Lily. Really."

"Thank you." I waved at them. "Don't get lost."

The two of them shook their heads, chuckling. I thought I heard a distant laugh from the kitchen. "Promise," said Nick. "Enjoy your time of solitude. Off you go."

And I went out to the car, getting in carefully, trying not to catch the long hem of my dress of the door. The driver shut the door behind me, and got in behind the wheel. "Congratulations miss. You look fine."

I started to say, no, it wasn't me, but I decided it was too complicated. "Thank you, you're very kind," was all I said. We pulled out, leaving me with my thoughts, and a vague worry about the car behind us. I tried to watch the scenery going by. Everything was so familiar. Once again, I wondered if I could imagine the entire trip to the edges of London in my head. I felt like I even knew where the traffic cameras were. We were heading out on the A40, and had passed the old Hoover building, before I finally closed my eyes. It was just a car trip. I opened the window. I felt a bit dizzy, but resisted the urge to ask the driver to either stop or turn around. It would all be fine. A song went through my head, and I let it play out, then wriggled, thinking suddenly I was creasing the dress. "Vain," I said to myself. Then I went back to the song, and tried to watch the road go by.

We finally arrived at the church. There hadn't been too much traffic. Even so, it had taken nearly two hours, but we weren't late. Sarah had timed and arranged everything, and knew exactly how long the journey could be, and budgeted for that. So when I emerged from the car, the song still playing in my head, I felt calmer at least, knowing I had time to catch my breath. And it was a lovely place. The leaves not as green as in the height of the summer, but still hanging on, maybe even more beautiful, rich and lush, all too aware of the autumn nudging at them from around the corner. The air out here was cleaner too. I breathed it in, listening to the birdsong. I felt slightly detached from the small crowd that was gathering now in front of the church, heading in by twos, very neatly. I stood there and watched them.

I jumped when a hand rested gently on my shoulder. I spun around, movements naturally slowed down by the dress. You couldn't move very fast in a Greek goddess ensemble, I discovered.

The very tall man in front of me was smiling at me, almost gently. "Lily. You look absolutely magnificent. Ravishing. No. You look simply beautiful, which you are." Then as if he couldn't resist, "Well done you."

His suit fit him perfectly, just cut differently enough to make it clear that he wasn't quite like the rest. "Trevor. Thank you. You look fairly spectacular yourself. Nice suit," I nodded.

He leaned down to hug and kiss me carefully. "That designer," he said, moving back to appraise me again. "Your L.A. party was a huge success. He might even outfit the tour. But let's not talk shop. Where's Tristan?"

"He decided to ride with the bridegroom. Something about not wanting to see me yet."

Trevor's small smile creased a bit more of his angular face. "He is a romantic, under it all." He waved his hand as though to take away the words. "But here we are. Shall we wait together for him? I don't believe we are sitting together in the church, so we can chat." He raised my hand and did a small dance step away from me. "Or we can just run off together. You do look stunning, Lily. That style suits you perfectly. Come over here, on this little rise." He took my hand and started to lead me a few paces over to a slight rise in the terrain, capped with a tree and some purple salvia. "Unless your shoes won't do grass?"

"No, it's fine," I said, stepping carefully next to him, my dress in my hand.

We stood there, chatting idly about London, the nice weather, and wondering what Sarah's dress would look like, when another car pulled up. I could hear doors shutting, then a slight gasp. Someone squealed and I knew it was him.

"Fangirling at someone's wedding. Imagine." I laughed. "Should I hide behind you?" I asked Trevor, playfully.

"Lily. No. But turn away. Here, let's move over here." And we walked a few yards further into the grounds surrounding the church. "I'll keep an eye out."

I saw Trevor raise his hand and wave. I stared at the stitching on his suit jacket, feeling my heart beat. My stomach felt hollow. I shook my head. Silly.

Trevor leant down to me. "You can turn around now."

And I did as I was instructed, turning very slowly. And there he was. Tristan looked magnificent, a halo of light behind his head from the afternoon sun, his dark suit making his tall figure seem like a dark slash against the green and gold background of the churchyard. But his face was caught in a smile, a look of delight that contrasted with his intense stare. He walked the five steps to me, never taking his eyes from mine. "Lily." He took my hands in his and raised them to his mouth. "Lily. Beautiful woman." He kissed them, then held them out to admire the dress. His eyes went back to mine, and he pressed my hands to his heart. "I'm…" he trailed off. He grinned. "I seem to be speechless."

He finally looked up over my head. "Trevor. How are you?" Then he turned back to me. "Lily. I just need to handle something here with Trevor. I'll see you inside, all right?" And he and Trevor exchanged a look which seemed significant, but unreadable.

Trevor took my arm, gently but firmly. "I'll be right back, Tristan. Let me just escort Lily back over the grass." He was silent, and I began to feel uneasy.

"Is everything ok?"

Trevor nodded. "Not to worry. Just need to sort something out." He kissed my hand quickly, and covered the ground back to Tristan in a quarter of the time. I watched him go. Then he turned and saw me watching, and waved me on.

My stomach felt even more hollow now, and I entered the church alone. I took an order of service from one of the ushers, and was guided to a seat in the third row. I surveyed the empty place next to me. Then I followed the light from the stained glass and examined the altar. The mysteries of life. The power of ritual. I wasn't immune. I looked up at the large window looming over the sanctuary. And I said a prayer, silently asking for the support to guide me through whatever was going to happen next. I shut my eyes and swallowed, and took a deep breath. I needed to calm down. Now.

Shaking my head, and fixing a smile to my face, I began inspecting the crowd. Sarah had a large family, but I'd really only met her mother a few times. I didn't see her anywhere yet. She was probably arriving with Sarah, fussing over the dress. There was Nick, standing next to his father, waiting at the back. Everyone was nearly seated, and the doors began to close, to give the bride privacy for her entrance. Trevor and Tristan hurried through them just before they shut. Trevor had his hand on Tristan's shoulder, a serious look on his face. Then he nodded, and they separated, Trevor to his seat. Tristan was guided by a slightly star-struck usher to his place next to me.

"All right?" I asked.

He nodded. "All sorted. Not to worry."

Then the service started. Nick and his father walked up the aisle, and stood at the altar, both looking very serious and dignified. Then the doors opened, the wedding march began, and Sarah entered. Everyone murmured their appreciation. Her dress was very full, the skirt billowing out with each step, her tiny waist cinched in, lace and satin, delicate, molded to her body. She looked stunning. I glanced over at Nick. He had that smile on his face, halfway between admiration and panic. But Sarah made it to the front, and Nick gazed down at her, a genuine warmth suffusing his usually distant features. I was glad. This was how it was supposed to be. If you were going to do this sort of thing. Love. There it was.

The vicar led us all in a hymn. Tristan's warm voice going over the old words and notes. I didn't know why I was surprised, almost shocked, that he seemed to know it. I glanced up at him. He fit everywhere, he fit nowhere, special, transcending boundaries. It struck me that that's what he did—he pulled the spiritual out of moments and made it real, so you could see it, touch it. His special skill, his calling.

He saw me looking at him, and smiled. "Piano lessons at church school, singing in the choir." He closed the hymnal and put it back on the shelf under the seats of the polished wooden pew.

We sat and listened to the vicar's sermon, stood for another hymn, and finally the vows began. They were just reading the two stanzas from the poems they had chosen to represent their promise to each other, when I felt a hand reach for mine. I tried to grasp back, but I felt his fingers move mine apart, and grasp them at the base. Then I felt a cool, smooth band of metal slip on to my finger, and slide down. Before I could do anything, another one was placed between my thumb and forefinger, and I held on, almost about to drop it. I looked up at Tristan. He was facing the ceremony, as though nothing was happening. I looked down. His hand was across his body, resting on his other arm, waiting. I picked up his finger.

"That's it," he whispered.

I slipped the ring on to his finger until it was seated. And stared at the band of silver colored metal for a moment. Platinum. Then I looked up and around. Everyone's eyes were on the bride and groom at the front.

"Will you?" Tristan whispered, just after the vicar had asked the same question of the bride at the altar. "Say yes, Lily."

"Yes." I gazed up at him.

Tristan watched me, his eyes full of expression. "Ask me."

"Will you?" My voice trembled.

He leaned down to kiss me, gently. "Yes," he whispered into my mouth, as the crowd cheered the pronouncement of husband and wife.

I felt the tears start, hot and unexpected. He grasped my hand tightly. Skin. And then his eyes were wet. "I know."

A voice came from behind us. "Shh. There's a wedding going on."

* * *

The rest of the ceremony went by in a blur. The only thing I could focus on was Tristan's warm hand, wrapped tightly around mine, as if I were a balloon that might get snatched away by a sudden breeze. Then it was over, and we were outside, in the grey cool air of a British late summer's day, waiting for rain, and the emergence of the wedding party. Tristan was still holding my hand. I couldn't look at him. Not yet. I just held on.

Sarah and Nick finally came out, to great cheers and handfuls of bird seed and confetti. She looked beautiful and slightly stunned, and Nick seemed to embody all the qualities of settled masculinity, with a quiet, happy look around his eyes that spoke of the gladness of a house finally complete, a chase successfully concluded, a desire fulfilled. They waved to the small crowd, and they did look apart from everyone else, the trappings of the ritual hanging heavy on them, and giving them both the weighted presence of royalty. They moved through the crowd, carefully, one of the flower girls holding on to the small train as though she had been entrusted with the movement of the planets. When it was finally time for her to relinquish it, she turned to her mother, shaking with overwrought tears. The car pulled away over the small gravel forecourt and out on to the road, honking, tin cans crashing merrily on the pavement. The guests started filing towards their own cars, in order to head to the reception.

Tristan turned to me, and pulled me by the hand around the corner of the church, and stopped under one of the yew trees. "You followed your dream, Lily. You didn't know where it would lead you, but you listened—and you didn't give up. Somewhere along the road, you found me. I wouldn't presume to think that I'm your entire dream—but will you share with me?" He fell with a graceful swoop on one knee, extending an arm to the skies and out, to encompass everything.

I sank to my knees, careless of my dress, of anything else but Tristan. He wrapped his arms around me, as I rested my head in the crook of his neck. "Yes."

The End

www.ingramcontent.com/pod-product-compliance
Lightning Source LLC
Chambersburg PA
CBHW030619250626
47154CB00006B/1853